PENGUIN BOOKS

Love, Iris

Love, Iris

ELIZABETH NOBLE

PENGUIN BOOKS

PENGUIN BOOKS

UK | USA | Canada | Ireland | Australia
India | New Zealand | South Africa

Penguin Books is part of the Penguin Random House group of companies
whose addresses can be found at global.penguinrandomhouse.com

First published by Michael Joseph as *Letters to Iris* 2018
Published in Penguin Books 2018
001

The publisher is grateful for permission to reproduce an extract from
The Life That I Have by Leo Marks (copyright © Souvenir Press Ltd, 1999),
reprinted on page 444 by permission of Souvenir Press Ltd.

Set in 12.55/14.9 pt Garamond MT Std
Typeset by Jouve (UK), Milton Keynes
Printed and bound in Great Britain by Clays Ltd, Elcograf S.p.A.

A CIP catalogue record for this book is available from the British Library

ISBN: 978–0–718–15540–7

www.greenpenguin.co.uk

For David, for everything

Prologue

Then

Mornings like this morning were Iris's favourite kind. Tom always preferred springtime, when the sun was high, and everything was burgeoning and bursting. Of the two of them, he was the lay-a-bed, groaning with reluctance at the early starts the farm required, and had done since they were small children. But he hated it just a bit less in the spring and summer, as it was light, and there was no chill in the air when you threw back the blanket. Autumn days were Iris's. It made no difference to her that the tip of her nose was often cold when she woke up, and it was still dark outside. She liked the mists and the nip in the air, the colours of the leaves and the crunch of them under her boots once they'd fallen.

Tom said she was contrary and melancholy in her choice. But he still sat on the fence in the yard with her, in the few minutes before work started, both clasping a cup of hot tea with their whole hands, warming their fingers, not talking much as they came round.

Most of their friends in the village came from much larger families, often with six or seven other siblings. But it had always been just her and Tom. Irish twins, people called them, Tom just ten months older than her. There had been two more, born when Iris was barely old enough to remember her mother's round belly and tired face, but both those boys had been born already dead. After the births, her mother had been pale and tearful and quiet for what felt like forever, and Iris remembered her and Tom climbing up into the bed she shared with their father and, each on one side of her, trying to cuddle her into a smile or a tender touch, tears streaming down her face. Iris didn't know why there had been no more babies after that last loss. It was just the four of them, and it was just her and Tom.

Everything was about to change. She knew it. It was all anyone talked about these days. Everyone huddled around the radio and pored over the newspapers and talked about war. Her parents and the other older people – they all remembered the last time, and seemed full of dread, gaunt-looking and anxious. They saw it differently from some of her and Tom's friends, gung-ho to stop Mr Hitler. Ignorant bravado, their father called it, willing Mr Chamberlain on last autumn when he'd promised peace for our time. No one seemed to doubt, though, that there would soon be war. Mothers were red-eyed in the grocer's, especially now they were talking about conscription in the spring. And everything would change once it started. She didn't want it to, but, at the same time, there was an inexplicable excitement, a horribly guilty feeling you daren't say out loud because you couldn't even explain it to yourself. Sometimes, before the war had started to loom large, Iris thought she loved that nothing ever changed – that the landscape of her childhood was the vista of her almost-adulthood – and, sometimes, that thought had been unbearable. As she looked out this September morning, on the land she knew so well, her brother hunching his shoulders against the early chill, she only wondered how their lives would be . . .

Now

She's called Iris.

She's Gran to me. Mum to my mother. Mrs Garroway to the doctors and the administrators, and to these burly, kind men in green uniforms lifting her out of the back of the ambulance now, in a way that was far gentler than their size suggested. A patient. A bed blocker.

But she's Iris. Iris Mary Rose Garroway. She was born in the spring of 1921, on 3 April. She doesn't know for sure, because she never asked, but she was almost certainly born at home, because people were, then. At home on a farm.

She's ninety-five years old.

She weighs just a pound or two over eight stone. Far, far less than she should. She was bigger once – curvy even, with broader hips than she ever liked, although she was always just a bit proud of her waist, trim even after my mother was born, she said, and photographs showed it. She doesn't eat enough now. She has no appetite to speak of, and in hospital the nurses haven't had the time, or the inclination perhaps, to sit with her and feed her. Even when I've gone in, with morsels of things I know she loves, she hasn't been very interested, nibbling to be polite, because she still remembers politeness, even if she doesn't know to whom she is showing it. She was taller too. Five foot six. It's amazing how old people shrink. She's barely five foot now, but seems much, much shorter, because osteoporosis has bent her spine into a cruel curl that directs her face towards the floor and hunches her shoulders. Her cardigan hangs off her, and her feet look too narrow for the sheepskin slippers they wear. Her eyes were very blue, before the yellowy film of age covered them over. She must have been born with them that blue: her mother chose the name because of them. She was supposed to be called Rose, but her mother changed her mind. It wasn't just the colour of them that was pretty. They'd shone and twinkled when she laughed, crinkling at the edges, always upwards, so she looked perpetually optimistic and cheerful. She's been old all of my life: she was sixty when I was born, and even in my earliest memories the hair that had once been thick and chestnut-brown – you could see it in photographs – was salt-and-pepper-grey. But I do remember the sparkling eyes.

She wasn't always this desiccated old lady, hunched, fragile, frightened, you know. Of course not. None of them ever were. None of the people in this new place where she's come to live – the last place, most likely, where she will ever live. She was all of the things we are, and have been. She was a girl, a young woman, a bride, a mother, a friend. She ran, and swam, and rode a bicycle. She laughed, and she loved. She lived.

But she can't remember that now, not most of the time, anyway. There are moments of lucidity, but they are fleeting, and they happen less and less often. They torture us less and less often. When she's lucid, you wonder if she knows where she is, and what she's become, and it's an unbearable thought. It's easier when she's absent. She remembers her mother, a crochet shawl around her shoulders, rocking a stillborn baby she can't yet accept has no need of rocking. She remembers tastes and smells from her childhood on the farm – she'd still know how to milk a cow, although she hasn't done it for decades, or make a daisy chain on a lazy summer afternoon. She knows all

4

the words to her favourite hymn – 'I Vow to Thee, My Country' – but she doesn't know who the Prime Minister is, or how she got to this place, or at whose behest she is here.

And now she can't even remember me. It's been weeks since she used my name, except to repeat it when I've said it, quizzically, rolling the syllables as if she's hearing them for the first time. Sometimes I think she's forgotten me entirely, although I still hope – hope for the little, occasional miracles of her knowing me without being distressed about who and where and how she is now.

And I don't think she will ever know this baby – her great-grandchild – I have growing inside me. I want to whisper it to her. I haven't told anyone, and I haven't wanted to, not yet, but, standing here now, I want to lean in and whisper it to her. But I don't. Because I don't think I can bear it if she doesn't react. I have so needed her, all my life, and now, when I think I may need her more than ever before, I don't want to face the truth that I can't have her.

Tess

London was suddenly Christmassy. The season of mists and mellow fruitfulness gave way almost overnight to the season of spending on credit and hot chocolate with whipped cream. Bonfire Night was over, and the city apparently couldn't wait to wrap itself in fairy lights, knowing how much prettier it looked when it twinkled. It lent the damp, chilly weather – nights drawing in fast – and the grey buildings the magical veneer of cheer and the promise of festivities to come. The windows of the West End were dressed for the season in jewel-bright colours and sparkle. Tourists were meandering through Carnaby Street, taking it all in through a selfie lens. Nobody seemed to be in a hurry.

Except for Tess, who *was* in a crashing hurry. She'd been in back-to-back meetings staring at a flipchart since lunchtime – which had been, for her, a rather hurried warm lettuce and dried-out falafel affair at her desk – and now, released at last, she was weaving her way impatiently through the lackadaisical crowds. It had felt like a day without end – more problems than solutions, and hardly a moment to sit at her desk and actually think. It wasn't that she hated her job – part of a Human Resources team in a City firm – she was good at it, and most of the time she enjoyed what she did. Right now, though, the company was restructuring after a large merger, and it seemed like major, and often painful, decisions were being taken on a daily basis. It was hard to keep up with the schedule being imposed from above. And at the moment it was simply interfering just a bit too much with her actual life. Taking up space in her brain she very badly needed for thinking about other things. Those being, in no particular order: the precise whereabouts of her difficult mother, her very poorly grandmother, her boyfriend and, oh yes, who'd leave it until last on the list? Her new, very, very new pregnancy. Confirmed as of just a few hours ago, between the falafel at lunch and a Kit Kat at tea break. The pregnancy test she'd bought had been burning a hole in her desk drawer, until she'd peed on it in the bathroom, telling herself it would almost certainly be a negative and she could get back to worrying about all the other stuff she was worrying about. A plan that had not gone terribly well when it came out positive, and she'd had to punch both her knees in the stall to stop her legs from shaking. And go back to the meeting. And talk about cost per square foot, and bodies per floor. At that point taking the test at home had seemed like a much better idea, hindsight as beneficial as ever. Bloody hell. She realized as she walked that she was muttering her list. And swearing gently.

It almost made her laugh out loud, that listing of preoccupations. She'd read somewhere that creative people did it more than other types, because processing out loud made things clearer or something. Not true. Not true at all. None of it was clear. She was too old to let a difficult relationship with her mother distract her from her everyday adult life: that was the stuff of teenage years, when shared domesticity made it impossible to ignore. She hadn't lived with Donna for – God – fifteen years or something. She was too old to be so invested in, and vulnerable about, the health of her beloved, but undeniably elderly, grandmother. It wasn't like it hadn't been coming. She was ninety-five, for Christ's sake. Tess was afraid she was too sad. Was it right that it hurt her this much? Right that she should be so very terrified of the only ending that was possible now? Even in this new age of living longer, that was a hell of an innings, as the crass saying went. The boyfriend thing was odd too. She should feel wonderful about him, not anxious. He was a great guy (didn't everyone say so? Okay, nearly everyone . . .), they were happy enough, it was all how it was meant to be . . . The pregnancy – okay – so that was a curveball of elephantine proportions. But she was thirty-five. She was sexually active. Not exactly an immaculate conception. But still, bloody hell.

Tess realized that she was breathless, and sweating, despite the damp chill in the air. Neither was a good look. Or a classy way to arrive. And she wasn't quite as late as she thought she might be. Bugger it. There was an empty park bench with her name on it (actually, it had someone else's name on it, but they weren't using it, so for now it was hers), and she sat down gratefully. Just for a minute. She closed her eyes, and willed the swirling thoughts in her brain to settle and still. She concentrated on breathing in and out. She'd read about it in some article on Mindfulness in the hairdresser's a couple of months ago. Be present, Tess. And other aphorisms for 'calm the hell down'. It worked, though. She felt her heart rate slow, and the breathing steadied. She felt marginally, and no doubt temporarily, less crushed by the weight of everything.

One thing at a time. Get tonight over with. The rest

would have to wait a while longer. Tonight was enough to be going on with. She could juggle only so many balls at one time. She could be only one persona at a time. She had to push everything else to one side for now, or she'd cry, and crying wasn't an option. Her mascara was definitely not waterproof. Tonight, she was playing corporate wife. Not an actual wife, in fact. But 'partner' was too professional and girlfriend was too Upper Sixth. Corporate wife was the persona required this evening. It was one of Sean's fairly interminable work dos. Drinks (but never more than two since that embarrassing incident a while back) and dinner (always chicken, for some reason. Always.), speeches (invariably self-congratulatory) and an Uber home at eleven, if you were lucky.

The two of them had met at exactly such an event. An old university friend of hers had begged her to be his plus one, and since she'd had nothing better to do and a drop-dead gorgeous new dress she'd been waiting for an occasion to debut, she'd said yes. She'd been the age (early thirties) and stage (three or four boyfriends of more than six months duration in the last six or seven years. Approximately three fifths of peers married or engaged. Not quite panicking, and espousing the theory that a man was strictly an add-on optional extra to an independent, fulfilling life, but yet aware that Mr Right was unlikely to appear in her front room uninvited on a Monday night during *Silent Witness*) to say yes to all sorts of things. Casting her net. Putting her secretly girlish dreams out in the universe, Deepak Chopra style. She hadn't known about the chicken, or the speeches, then, or she'd have said no, and then she might never have met him.

He was the tallest man in the room, which was always a

good start. At six foot five he was the tallest man in most rooms, unless his father and brothers were there too. They were a family of lanky giants. Impossible to lose in a crowd. It turned out her mate Stuart had known him, and when he'd come over to say hello, she'd had to crane her neck back to look him in the face, and that's when she'd noticed the eyes, which were lovely. They'd been sat on different tables for the dinner, and they had kept catching each other's eye during the speeches, which was fun, and even exciting. When she'd excused herself to go to the loo, she was pretty sure he'd followed her: he was lurking in the hallway when she came out, feigning surprise that she was there too. Numbers were exchanged. He'd called the next day. Drinks. Dinner. A concert at the O2 . . . It had been textbook, really.

And before she knew it, they'd been a 'couple'. They were almost exactly the same age, but it always felt weirdly to Tess like he was several years older. He seemed so much more sorted than she was. He was ambitious, and successful, and . . . just grown up. She'd been thirty-two then, but in some ways she'd still felt like a twenty-year-old, playing at being an adult and waiting to get caught out. It was quite a trick, she realized, seeming like you understood everything even if you didn't. Sean was self-assured, and confident (mostly, if not always, without that confidence tipping over into arrogance), and it was very attractive.

Their lives had meshed so easily, and so fast. It was a bit like being on an emotional Travolator. Sometimes she forgot they'd been together for only two and a half years. A dot-to-dot relationship, with everything done when and how it should be. Three dates before the first time they had sex (good, if not spectacular, sex, but improving with time, familiarity and some drunkenly brave instructions). Six months before their first holiday (beach, Turkey), and the meeting of the parents (could have gone better, on both sides, but they were grown-ups, not kids, so it didn't bother either of them unduly). A year before they moved in together (his place – bigger, better and nearer the Tube were his three arguments, only two of which were irrefutable). Symbiosis had happened almost before she'd realized it. Which sounded irresponsible. And possibly was. Sean's healthy salary paid exactly sixty-five per cent of their mortgage, as well as their utilities. Tess's home had been a rental, and she'd given it up without too many pangs. Sean had already bought his place: it made sense. It wasn't necessarily her type of thing – it was a modern two-bed apartment with no character, but the building had a gym and a lap pool. Sean used both most evenings. She'd had a paddle in the first week and gone nowhere near it since. And gyms were her Room 101. She'd 'girlified' the space by stealth, as her best friend Holly called it, and it was certainly comfortable enough, although she sometimes missed her rather scruffier rented ground-floor flat in Battersea, with its high ceilings and Victorian tiled fireplace. His corporate insurance paid for their medicals – his idea, not Tess's. It felt terribly middle aged to have a medical when there was nothing apparently wrong with you. His Avios points sometimes flew them on their holidays. And they drove his car. Tess also had her grandmother Iris's Renault Clio, which was knackered, in truth. Tess had railed against it at first, this imbalance in their wages and thus in their shared life, at least over a bottle of wine with Holly. They were the gender pay gap, in coupled form. They both had good degrees from good universities. She was better at Sudoku than him. And multitasking. And crosswords. Sean had laughed and told her he didn't care, and eventually she'd accepted it. And if it was a betrayal of her feminist principles to appreciate having a bit more disposable income at the end of each month as a result of this arrangement (new Jigsaw outfit just because . . . oh, go on, then), she kept the betrayal to herself.

And this was the price she had to pay – three or four times a year she played his 'trailing spouse' (this, apparently, being a real expression) at these ghastly events, held regularly, no one quite knew why, in the banqueting rooms and Freemasons' halls of the City. Tess dressed up, lipstick and everything, and tried hard not to mind when whichever man she was seated beside glazed over when she answered the inevitable question about 'what she did'. Thank God, she had always consoled herself, that at least she didn't have to say 'homemaker' or 'stay-at-home mother'. Now her stomach lurched. It couldn't possibly be the tiny foetus lurking in there, protesting, but it felt like it might be.

So, today, she had a statement necklace and four-inch heels in her tote bag, posher hair and actual lipstick. The tools with which to transform herself from real working woman into an adornment who'd had nothing else to do all day but prettify herself. Christ, it was such a ridiculous anachronism. All she wanted to do was to crawl home, change into her pyjamas and eat a pint of ice cream in front of Netflix. Call and check on Iris. Text a bit with Holly. And fall into bed.

She needed to digest this. She had never wanted to talk to Iris as much as she did now. The ache of knowing she couldn't – or, at least, that she could, but that Iris wouldn't respond, not properly – sat painfully in her sternum. She pulled her phone out of her bag and scrolled through the contacts, her thumb hovering over Holly's number. But that wasn't fair. It was Sean she needed to tell. It was Sean's baby.

She tried to imagine the conversation, realized she couldn't. She didn't know how he'd feel. Hell, she wasn't entirely sure how she felt. It wasn't real yet. Saying it out loud might make it real, but she was lost for words. Something odd was gnawing at the edges of her mind. Something off note. It was frightening. It wasn't as it should be, even if you accepted that life was not like movies and television.

She needed a plan of action. And the brain space to come up with a plan. Not tonight. So that was the plan so far . . .

Tess shook herself out of the reverie. She was calmer now, but she was getting cold too, and she was officially almost late. Sean didn't like late. Cinderella: you and your as yet secret unborn child shall go to the bloody ball. Like it or not. The rest will have to wait.

She had her game face on by the time she walked into the hall ten minutes later. And her Tom Ford power lipstick. She picked up a glass of champagne from a tray held by a waiter. Put it down again. Picked up a glass of orange juice. And scanned the room for Sean. He was right at the back – she spotted him immediately, towering over his companions, and waved to get his attention.

He was at her elbow a moment later. 'Hello, darling. You made it.' He kissed her cheek. She wondered randomly when he'd started calling her 'darling'. Possibly just this evening. Possibly just on these evenings.

'Am I late?' He didn't appear to notice the orange juice. Although after the embarrassing incident (that was what they both called it: she'd groped someone's bum, back in the early days when lust was liable just to come on with the speed of an anaphylactic shock, and the bum turned out to belong to a senior partner, not Sean), it was probably what he expected.

'Barely . . . Come and meet Guy . . . I've told you about him.'

Tess fixed her smile and fluffed her hair. She'd never heard of Guy. And they were off . . .

December

Okay. Deep breaths. You're okay. I mean, I'm okay. You're probably okay too. I've no idea, actually. It's Week 4. I think. I googled, and tried to work it out. Work out exactly how old you were in there. Not pinpoint the actual moment of conception, you understand. My sex life isn't exactly E. L. James-worthy but it isn't so tragic that I could do that . . . It's very early, anyway. If I wasn't so ridiculously set-your-watch regular, I probably wouldn't have a clue yet. If pregnancy tests weren't so incredibly scientifically advanced and accurate, I'd still only be wondering. I took three tests on three different days, two more after that one in the office, and they all said the same thing. It's about four weeks. The website I found (I read these things avidly, and then delete my search history more often than a teenage porn addict) tells me the embryo – who up until now I have thought of as a sort of nebulous and shapeless fizzing and sparkling collection of cells, performing magic on itself like in The Sorcerer's Apprentice, *but it's you – splits in two this week. One half will become your placenta. That's the bit that is going to connect you to me absolutely, albeit all grossly and bloodily: some women eat it afterwards, apparently,* or wrap it in a muslin cloth with herbs and carry it around until it falls off of its own accord. Ew. Ew. Ew. I'm the 'please, never show me that' type of mother, baby mine. Hope that's not a disappointment. This way what I eat can nourish you. (Note to self: must replace Pret à Manger almond-croissant-and-large-latte breakfast with yoghurt with fruit and seeds and healthy tea if can find one that doesn't smell funny.) What I breathe will be what you breathe too. (Next note to self: no more following smokers down the street like a nicotine Bisto-kid, you filthy, regretful ex-smoker who still loves the smell so long as it's fresh and not stuck in curtains.) The other half of the embryo — that's actual, real you. Everything that will ever be you is you already. It's hard to get my head around. We did this at school — never had a notion of what an extraordinary, mind-blowing thing it is that my body can do this. I'm Boudicca, Joan of Arc and Xena, Warrior Princess, all in one. And your body is doing this. YOU ARE SO CLEVER. Growing and developing at a faster rate than you ever will again.

You're not a lump of cells. You're the miraculous start of a tiny human. In Week 4 you become an actual baby, though to be honest, in the image on my laptop, you don't look like much of one. And so, I become your mum, ready or not. Willing or not. Able or not. It's rather extraordinary that all this action can be going on deep in my belly with absolutely no outward signs or feelings. Turns out my body makes me more aware of itself and its workings when I've eaten too much white bread than it does when I'm splitting an embryo. And the truth is, baby mine, I'm not sure how I feel about you yet. You weren't planned. Sorry, but you weren't. You weren't even — what do people say — a twinkle in your father's eye. Five days ago, you were a vague, long-time-off, 'we will because that's what people do' kind of a notion. Like everything else about my life, I realize. I'm not sure I'm ready. I'm definitely not sure Sean

is. Oh God. Sean. But look . . . I'm thinking about what I need
to eat, about not inhaling smoke from passers-by. That tells you
something, and it tells me too. I just need a minute.

It certainly wasn't unusual for Sean to be up before her,
but this level of – well, chirpiness – was as unusual as it
was unacceptable so early in the day. They'd been home
late, from an interminable dinner. He'd been in a very
good mood, expansive, chatty and affectionate. He'd told
her he'd been proud of her, that she'd looked gorgeous. He
had wanted to make love, and she'd put him off by feigning
exhaustion, realizing only as his hand strayed across her
backside in a very familiar opening gambit that she
couldn't, yet. That something was very different now.
Admittedly, he'd gone straight to sleep, not noticeably frustrated by her refusal, leaving her staring at the ceiling for
ages. Par for the course. She'd always thought of the two of
them as broadly compatible in most areas, except this
one. Sean was the proverbial lark, she the proverbial owl.
No, that wasn't true. Owls came to life at night. Tess
peaked for a couple of hours around 6 to 8 p.m., and was
pretty much comatose (in bed or upright) by 11 p.m., always
had been. She wasn't sure what kind of animal that made
her. But since it was appreciably more true in the winter,
perhaps she was the proverbial tortoise or brown bear. She
had new thoughts to keep her awake now. Thoughts Sean
had no notion of.

Tess had never been 'a baby person', as she thought of
them. Not, at least, a person who felt sure and certain
babies must be in her future in order for her future to look
rosy. And complete. She wasn't even sure she liked babies.
They seemed to be a lot of work and worry, and to offer

relatively little reward for both. Women at work had babies. Tess handled their maternity leave. Mopped their hormonal tears, allaying their professional fears as best she could. Bought cakes and balloons for their leaving parties and took their phone calls when they were anxious about coming back to work. When the tiny people who had caused so much disruption appeared in the office in their car-seat thrones several weeks later, and everyone crowded around to coo and marvel, Tess felt fairly ambiguous. They weren't all beautiful. Some she struggled to find a compliment for, sure at least that one ought to be forthcoming. 'Adorable outfit' was a safe standby if all else failed. And some of them were far too noisy. Which invariably led their nervous, fluttery mothers to proclaim that they were hardly ever this unsettled, which Tess invariably did not entirely believe. Their arrival did not make her uterus contract with envy or anticipation, and their departure was usually a relief.

She had felt differently about Dulcie, her god-daughter, the first baby she'd been very involved with. Dulcie had been beautiful, and placid, and Tess had loved her from the first moment she saw her, as she loved Dulcie's mother, Holly. Her little cries had seemed like communication and not like complaint. Her every sneeze and shrug and wriggle had been miraculous, and not boring at all. Tess had fallen in love, but didn't remember even a tinge of envy. She'd been the first non-'bloody relative' to visit the hospital. Holly had sent her husband, Ben, away, and the two of them had sat on the bed with Dulcie sleeping between them, and gazed at her while Holly graphically recounted the horrors and indignities of labour. The gentle sing-songy tone of her voice, and the way she couldn't take her eyes off the baby, convinced Tess that she didn't mean a word of it. Tess had picked up Dulcie and deeply inhaled the scent of her, and listened to the tiny snuffling sounds of her, and wondered at her delicate fingers and the dark sweep of her long eyelashes, and she'd loved her straight-away. There'd been no deep ache in her womb for one of her own, or even a frisson of excitement at the notion that one day it would be her turn. Holly doing this was like all the other things they had done differently from each other. Right for her friend, she was sure, but not for Tess. And now that the peaches and cream baby was fourteen years old, she loved her still. Tess was definitely heading Holly's way at last. She put her hand on her flat belly, dipping as it still did between her hipbones as she lay on her back, and wondered . . .

Sean's iPhone sprang to life with the egregious sound of a clanging church-bell tower at 6 a.m. Monday through Friday, a full hour before Tess needed to be roused. Her phone was altogether gentler with her – it made the sort of sounds they play in posh spas – but Tess always felt slightly like she should stand to attention and be wearing some sort of uniform that included spurs when Sean's went off. On the average day, by the time hers – located on the chest of drawers across the room so that it forced her out of bed – did its thing, Sean would have cycled at least five miles on the racing bike he kept anchored in some sort of contraption in the sitting room, facing the television. He'd have wiped down the bike (which always made Tess laugh – gym etiquette at home, where she never went anywhere near the bike unless they had people over for dinner and she wanted to hang their coats on the handlebars). He'd

18

have eaten his healthy breakfast, showered, dressed . . . and left. It was how it had always been. Even when they'd first been together, and everything had been a novelty, she'd seldom been able to tempt him to stay in bed, instead of jumping up to check the markets in Tokyo, even with her best tricks.

This morning, though, the spa chimes had rung, Radio 4 had delivered the seven o'clock news, and Tess was considering what she might wear, focusing on the minutiae of her day to avoid the enormous subject of the busily splitting embryo within, as she had been doing for almost a week now. She knew – it had registered from day one – that it wasn't quite right, wanting to keep it all to herself. She ought to be bubbling with the news, fizzing with it. Maybe that would take a while. Maybe it was shock . . . She'd wake up one morning brimming like she was supposed to, and she badly wanted to wait for that morning, project everything as it was meant to be. So she planned her outfit, her hands resting on her still very flat tummy under the duvet, and listened to the news.

And yet Sean was still here.

And he was humming loudly. That almost never happened. Frank Sinatra. *That* never happened. He was more of a Drake kind of a guy.

Tess rolled out of bed and, wrapping herself in her dressing gown, padded into the kitchen where the humming was coming from. Sean was apparently scrambling eggs. He smiled cheerfully at her over his shoulder.

'Morning. Want some?'

Tess shook her head and groaned. 'Too early . . .'

'I've made you tea.' He gestured towards a mug on the table. 'I was going to bring it in.'

'Have I slept right through the rest of the week, and it's actually Saturday?'

Sean laughed. 'No. It's definitely Thursday.'

'You never cook breakfast in the week.'

'God. I'm that much of a creature of habit?'

'You're really asking me that?' He was the actual living definition of a creature of habit. He knew it and she knew it and everyone who knew him knew it.

'Fair enough.'

She liked this Sean, though. He was . . . light somehow. Almost frivolous. This Sean would probably take baby news very well. She wondered how long he was hanging around for.

'So what's it all about, then?' She looked at her watch. 'It's . . . 7.15, and you're still here. You're eating' – she went over to the stove – 'eggs *and* bacon. It's a Thursday.'

He couldn't have guessed, could he? As the thought suddenly flooded her brain, she wondered whether it would be a relief, and decided that if it made him smile and scramble eggs on a Thursday and be like this, perhaps it might be. Perhaps. Perhaps. Perhaps. Now she wanted to hum.

'All right, Inspector Clouseau, there is something.' Her heart pounded. Sean's back was to her, as he spooned egg on to toast beside the stove. She wondered if her chest was flushing pink, like it always did when she was nervous, and pulled the dressing gown tighter around herself. 'Sit down. Drink your tea.'

'I need to be sitting down and drinking something hot and sugary?' She tried to laugh at her own vague attempt at humour, but even to her the sound was just a little brittle. She sat down, and cupped the mug in her hands to stop from fidgeting.

He joined her there, with his plate and cutlery, and didn't speak while he ground salt and pepper on to his food. Tess realized she was holding her breath, while he carefully and precisely, as was his way, cut off a square of the toast with his knife and fork.

'How do you feel about New York?'

Tess blinked and swallowed as the conversation veered off the track she had imagined for it.

'New York *City*?'

'Yep.' His voice was patient and slow, like a teacher talking to a kindergartener. 'New York City. How d'you feel about it?'

She shrugged. 'I . . . I like it.'

'You loved it, didn't you?' Objection. Leading the witness.

'Loved it? I mean . . . I had a good time.'

'We had a *great* time. Didn't we?'

They'd been Christmas shopping there. Two years ago. Their first Christmas. A long weekend in a nice hotel in Midtown, facilitated by air miles and financed by the anticipation of a nice work bonus. Sean's work bonus. She hadn't thought about it in ages. But they *had* had a great time. She remembered that now she'd had a few seconds to readjust to the fact that he did not want to talk about her pregnancy, the pregnancy she'd been keeping from him for, oh, five days now. A great, clichéd, skating-in-Central-Park, ram-raiding-Macy's, too-much-bacon, cinnamon-on-your-hot-chocolate, sex-in-the-morning-as-well-as-at-night-because-we're-on-holiday time.

He was watching her face, smiling broadly. She mirrored the smile, conscious that it didn't quite reach her eyes.

'Why are we talking about New York?'

Sean took a deep breath, his eyes never leaving her face. 'Because they've offered me the New York job.'

He said 'the New York job'. Not 'a New York job'. *The* job. It felt like the completion of a conversation she hadn't been present at the beginning of.

'What New York job?'

'*The* New York job.' There was an almost imperceptible note of irritation in Sean's voice. They both heard it, and Sean corrected it when he spoke again. He put his hand across hers, back to being the kindergarten teacher.

'They want me to *run* the New York office.'

It certainly and instantaneously explained the Frank Sinatra. *New York*.

Tess bought herself some time by taking a big gulp of tea. 'Wow. Congratulations. That's . . . that's amazing . . .'

'It's bloody fantastic. I mean, I wanted it, I've wanted it for ages. I thought maybe another year or two . . . but it's come up now.'

'Did somebody die?'

'No! Andy's leaving.' Again, the feeling of having missed something. Who the hell was Andy with no surname? Then the vague recollection of drinks and dinner a few months ago with a broad and tall American with that uniquely thick hair only American men seem to have, and those very straight, very white teeth, and his monogram embroidered above his heart on a cotton shirt.

'You know Andy.'

Not exactly. A Martini, two courses and an espresso with a bloke who liked to talk about himself a lot. She sure as hell knew Andy better than Andy knew her.

But Sean was allowing only very brief pauses in which she could catch up. 'So it's Andy's job. And they want me to start relatively soon. I mean no pressure, obviously. We're talking months, not weeks.'

That's a relief, then, Tess thought ruefully. Although of course these days she was all about the weeks *and* the months. Thirty-six weeks to go. Eight months. If they were going through with it. If it was real, and really happening. When the company said no pressure, she didn't imagine they meant that they'd wait thirty-six weeks.

'I mean, of course they understand we've got things to sort out (there it was, the first *we*) – renting this place out, finding somewhere there, that kind of stuff. Visas, obviously – a mile of red tape, for sure, but they have people to help with that – a whole department of people. But start as soon as that's sorted . . .'

Tess watched him while he spoke, replies or interjections clearly not required at this point – his familiar face in what she recognized were unfamiliar raptures. She stopped listening, but he didn't stop talking, and so she was tuned out of the exuberant diatribe. And she felt like she was at the top of a black run on her skis and they'd made the decision to set off down the mountain without her permission – as so often happened when she was at the top of a mountain on skis, and she'd got her angle all wrong, and pointed downwards before she was ready. Exhilaration, excitement, panic and sheer terror, swirling in a nauseating maelstrom in her stomach.

'Please say something.' As if there'd been a space. Or even a pause. 'What do you think?'

'I . . . I . . .'

'I've sprung it on you. I'm an idiot. I'm sorry. I know it has implications for you, and it's not straightforward. I know that. You need some time. I'm just so *bloody* excited. I should have chosen a better moment. But this all happened yesterday, and we were late last night, and so sleepy when we came in, and I have barely slept, and I just couldn't hold it in.'

The comparison was so obvious a child could have drawn it. New York was Sean's baby. And *he* hadn't been able to hold it in. *He'd* been fizzing and brimming and desperate to share it with her. *He* hadn't been hugging this new information to himself for five days.

She knew this was the optimum moment, now, to tell him. It should have just burst from her. Not a yes, or a no. Not a weird revelation one-upmanship, even though she'd so win that contest.

'It's just a bit of a shock.'

'But we've talked about it before.' His tone had become imploring.

He was right. They had. Of course they had. But it had formed part of those daft couple conversations over their time together. Mostly at the very beginning, when you still had sex in places other than the bedroom, and could get sort of drunk without drinking, just from being together. The kind that happened on long walks and in dark corners of restaurants and on lazy Sunday mornings. Full of what ifs and dreams and future plans. The trouble was, she couldn't remember the last time they'd had one of those. And she knew that for her two things had changed dramatically since the last time. Iris. How could he not understand, after all the time they'd been together, how central Iris was to all her thinking? And this baby. Was it Sean's fault those things hadn't the chance to be uppermost in his mind, or was it hers?

So this was the moment. To make it their news, not hers. To start. So why couldn't she form the words?

'I thought you'd be excited too.' The first tiny note of something in his voice that she didn't have a name for. A casual bystander would miss it; you had to be one of the two people in the relationship to hear it, the infinitesimal inference that she was spoiling it for him. A mere hint of resentment which, once she heard it, was her cue to make it all okay. To smooth it over, compensate for her disappointing reaction. This time, though, there was something else, as she opened her mouth to speak. Rising in her throat.

She lurched forward, her hands cupped at her mouth.

'I think I'm going to be sick . . .'

He'd been kind. Because he was kind. He'd tucked her back into bed, blaming last night's dinner, or a bug circulating at the office. He'd even called her assistant and said she wouldn't be coming in. If his care had been slightly mechanical, his interest distracted, his kiss on the top of her head perfunctory, she could only be glad. It clearly hadn't entered his busy, preoccupied head that it could be anything other than a transient illness. And then he couldn't get out of the flat fast enough, already racing towards his shiny future . . .

Tess missed Holly. If she'd been here, that's who she'd have called. That's who she would have told. That's who she would have listened to, whose advice she'd have taken. But Holly was away – on the holiday of a lifetime. Three and a half weeks in Australia with her family. The Barrier Reef, Uluru, Sydney, Perth . . . She'd been planning it for more than a year, and dreaming of it for far longer than that. She'd left the minute the autumn term at the private school where she worked had ended, sending a breezy and excited voicemail from the airport departure lounge. She'd be seeing the New Year in from Sydney Harbour, and she wouldn't be back until a few days after that. She'd uploaded a few pictures so far on Instagram — the three of them shiny, happy people, with a variety of exotic-looking backgrounds — and Tess, of course, had done no more than 'heart' them. It wasn't fair to land this on Holly when she was so far away. She didn't want to say it over the phone, and she didn't want to write it down, blunt and factual, in an email or a text. But she was counting down the days. Of course Sean should hear it first, but she knew it would be much easier to say it to Holly. A dress rehearsal: get all the nerves out before the real thing . . .

Tess gladly put her head under the duvet and closed her eyes, gratefully asleep again, her body and its overwhelming need for rest winning over her brain and its endless machinations. It was two hours before she woke again, and that was only because her mobile phone, on the bedside table and horribly close to her left ear, jolted her from sleep.

'Is that Tess?' She knew the voice, but in her fog, she couldn't immediately place it.

'Yes. This is Tess.'

'This is Carol Thomas. Your grandmother's neighbour . . .'

Tess sat up, wide awake at once. Another tremor of nausea at the sudden movement, overlaid with a shiver of dread. She hadn't called last night. She called most nights. Every night, probably. But she hadn't last night. It had been late, by the time they'd got home. She hadn't called.

'Hello, Mrs Thomas. Is everything all right?' She knew it. This was it. And she hadn't called.

'Carol. Call me Carol. Please. I hope it's okay to call.'

'Of course . . .'

'It's your grandmother.'

Obviously. Tess wished she'd get to the point, kind and careful though she was. She was frightened.

'She's very poorly.'

Relief flooded warmly over Tess. Poorly wasn't dead.

'She's had this cold. I know you know. She's been in bed for a few days. The carers have been coming in, of course, as usual. But this morning, I popped in, and she . . . well, she wasn't right, Tess. She was . . . it seemed like . . . she was having trouble breathing. I didn't want to wait for the carer. So I called an ambulance.'

'Oh, Mrs Thomas. Carol. Thank you.'

'That was about half an hour, perhaps an hour ago.'

'And they took her –'

'Yes. She's at the hospital. I told them I'd call you. It is right, yes, to call you, and not your mother?'

'Yes. I'll call my mum. Let her know. You did exactly the right thing, Carol.'

'Okay. Good. I can go in, if you need me to . . . The boys won't be back from school for a few hours.'

'No. No. That's very, very kind of you. I'll come. I'm coming now.'

There was no need to call the office, who weren't expecting her. Thank God the nausea seemed to have passed. In truth, it had probably just been superseded. Twenty minutes after she'd hung up on Carol, Tess was in the car, damp-haired from a hasty shower, and afraid. She could feel her blood pounding in her temples and wrists and in her chest. She pulled out too quickly at a junction, causing a driver to brake sharply, and a surge of adrenalin to course unpleasantly through her. The man in the other car honked angrily at her, flipped the bird as he drove past her, his mouth forming a silent, angry slur. Tess gripped the wheel hard, and forced herself to slow both the car and her breathing down.

She'd known Iris wasn't well, dammit. She'd last seen her a week, maybe ten days ago. It felt like longer with everything that had happened since. Her grandmother had had a hacking cough that shook her narrow shoulders, and a wheeze on every breath, in and out. She'd lost some weight too, and she had no weight to lose. She'd been particularly absent, as if she'd needed all her energy to breathe, and had none left for memory. She'd looked at Tess but not really seen her, and given short, vague answers to her questions. Their relationship veered this way and that now. Sometimes Iris was still parental, and sometimes it was completely reversed and Tess felt like the adult. Mostly it was both at the same time, within the same visit. But, poorly, Iris had never seemed quite so small, and helpless. There was never so little evidence of the woman she had always been for Tess. She had left profoundly sad. Tears had swum in her eyes and she'd stopped to fill the tank with petrol, even though it was half full already and she normally drove it on fumes, because she had needed a moment. One of the carers who came in twice a day had been with Iris. She'd been particularly kind and calm and reassuring and, besides, Tess had had no choice, with work in the morning and the rest of her life ninety miles up the A303.

Her grandmother's dementia had crept in so slowly and so gradually that it had been okay to ignore it for a long time. Iris was an old lady – it was easier, at first, to put things down to that. That wasn't terrifying. In the beginning, Tess was too busy processing the fact that the upright, vital woman she had known was shrinking in every way. Well into her eighties, Iris had been very much like the Iris she'd always known. She'd seemed like a considerably younger woman. Tess knew Iris had known for some time before she did that what was happening to her wasn't just 'wear and tear'. Known before the doctor had confirmed it. It hurt to remember some of the ways Iris herself had tried to cover it up. She'd put notes in her purse, and by the telephone. She'd learnt to cover up what she'd forgotten. Always happy to share her opinion in the past, she'd held back, listening for facts, and framing her responses with the information you'd just given her. It all made sense, in the end, when you looked back.

One of the carers had told her once that making a cup of tea took twenty-seven different, separate thoughts and actions. That was why it was so hard for a person with a loss of short-term memory. Your brain had to do twenty-seven different stages, just to make a cup of tea. How colossally terrifying it must have been for Iris . . . as one by one the twenty-seven dwindled away. To multiply that fear – the fear that you don't know how to make a cup of tea any more – by a hundred, by a thousand everyday functions. Tess came to see the escalation as something close to a blessing. Not for her, but for Iris. When the function of remembering that you weren't remembering started to fade, the fear must too. She hoped that was so. She needed to believe that was so. It was unbearable to think of Iris being frightened.

The disease crept along slowly. She'd googled, read up. It wasn't always slow. It could progress at breakneck speed. Or it could creep. With Iris, it crept. For the first year, it hardly progressed at all. But then, oh so gradually, Iris had declined. Like a full-colour photograph left to fade in the bright sunshine. Less and less of her seemed to remain. Like dementia was nibbling at the edges of her . . .

Iris had been adamant about staying at home for as long as she could, and Tess knew how hard she had worked at convincing the roster of carers whom the council sent in that she was coping. Tess had helped when she could, complicit in the subterfuge. She did her grandmother's food shopping on the internet, so all Iris had to do was to let the man in with his bags. Whenever she visited, Tess spent time reorganizing the cupboards. Iris put beans with washing powder, and toilet rolls behind the biscuits, but she'd sit with a cup of tea and chat while Tess made sense of the chaos. She paid all Iris's bills. Iris kept notes by the oven, reminding her to switch it off, though, increasingly, Tess bought microwaveable things. She ate less and less heartily anyway, often preferring a bowl of soup to a full meal. Sometimes Tess found a microwave meal cold and congealed still in the machine. She'd remembered to put it in and switch it on, but not to take it out, the ping ignored and the meal uneaten.

Iris had always been immaculate: that changed. Tess would find her in dirty, unironed clothes – tea stains on a blouse, food marks on a skirt. Sometimes, she smelt less than fresh, and her hair had that sebum odour which meant it hadn't been washed. She remembered bottles of perfume on a dressing table, a scent she could almost conjure up. Iris ironing in front of *Coronation Street*, saying she felt less guilty about watching a soap opera if she was doing a task at the same time. Teaching Tess to thread a needle and sew on a button. A wicker basket with pins and spools of cotton thread.

But Iris's life had become a delicate balance between holding on and letting go, and Tess knew that she fought to find this balance on her own. Sometimes, often, Tess felt like she'd let her grandmother down. Sean said it wasn't true but the feeling persisted.

Over time, 'Don't let me go into a home. Never. Promise' had become 'Don't let me ruin your life, love. Promise.' There was no answer. And now there were no pleas. Iris was past the point of advocating for herself or for anyone else. The passivity of it was deeply sad for Tess. It was the opposite of the Iris she'd known.

Now physical ill health may be forcing their hands, or removing the decision from them entirely. Sitting in traffic, feeling the panic rise as she went in and out of first gear, Tess didn't know which would be worse.

She called her mother's mobile phone from the car, on her hands-free.

Donna didn't pick up: the call went to voicemail. They mostly did.

'Mum. It's me. They've taken Gran to hospital . . . that cold she had seems to have got worse – Mrs Thomas – Carol – the lady next door – she called an ambulance . . .'

Tess paused. If her mother was screening calls, she'd see her name, maybe pick up. She waited for a long moment. Nothing.

'So I was off today anyway. I'm on my way there now. I don't know what you're up to. I don't even know where you are, actually, I realize. But I'll call again once I've seen what's going on. Okay? I'm in the car for another hour or so. Call me if you get this message . . . I've got the hands-free on, so I can talk. If you call . . .' She pushed the button to end the call, cross at the tone of her own voice. Why had she sounded like a little girl? Desperate for her mother's help? She'd taught herself years ago not to need it, and God knows she hadn't had it in a long while. And yet there it was, the wheedling tone. The lonely-little-girl plea for help.

Gigi

Gigi would never *actually* throw the 4.5kg free-range bronze turkey she was holding, hands wide apart clutching the heavy platter, hard and fast at the wall of the dining room.

Of course she wouldn't. She wasn't that kind of woman. Was she?

Besides, they'd only had it redecorated last year.

But that was exactly what she was imagining as she stood on the threshold. And thinking about it, just for a few seconds, was strangely fun. Bernard (weren't all turkeys called Bernard? She'd had to name him – they'd spent so much damn time together) would hit the wall, halfway between the oak sideboard and the coving, making an unwipeable Bernard-shaped grease mark on the striped wallpaper, before sliding down to slump between the decanter and Richard's father's ugly clock. Butter trails would slowly follow him. The Royal Doulton platter from their wedding dinner service would shatter with a satisfying crack, sending its hateful burgundy and gold border all across the carpet. She'd been trying to wash off that gold she'd so adored when she first married for years now, but it clung. Bacon strips might be left dangling on the lampshade, Daliesque.

And their faces. That was the best part of the imagining. Their shocked and horrified faces.

Did every happy homemaker feel this way just before Christmas lunch, Gigi wondered. Or was it just her?

Clearly she was simply delirious with exhaustion. And should have eaten something before that first glass of Prosecco Richard had poured. And the second one she'd poured for herself in the kitchen when no one else was in there, swigging it down in two great gulps. Damn bubbles sent it straight to your toes. Delicious feeling most of the time – slightly debilitating when we you were doing a Christmas dinner. It wasn't Bernard's fault, any more than it was anyone else's. She'd ordered him five weeks ago, from that good butcher in the parade. She'd collected him on the 23rd, queuing up early under the red-and-white-striped awning of the shop with the other smug organized women, ticking things off their endless lists while they waited, and telling each other who they were feeding on the 25th, as if this was in any way interesting. Between then and 5.45 this morning, when she had staggered downstairs, bleary-eyed in her dressing gown, he had commandeered a whole shelf in the refrigerator, relegating the vegetables to a covered bucket in the back garden. Then he had come out, coming closer to room temperature while the oven heated up and she peeled potatoes and parsnips, wondering for the umpteenth time why you had to carve that cross thing in the bottom of every Brussels sprout. Then he had a studded onion shoved up his arse along with some fancy herbs tied with kitchen twine, had been anointed with a coronary-inducing amount of butter, and at last had taken pride of place in the oven. Since then he had been tended more attentively than the average ICU patient – looked at, basted, had his thighs skewered to monitor juice flow, and, eventually, as his moment approached, he'd been dressed up smartly in a streaky bacon waistcoat with tin-foil epaulettes on his wings.

It would be fair, at this point, to describe her relationship with Bernard as a love/hate one. She felt sure the feeling would be mutual, if Bernard didn't currently have an onion in the cavity where his heart had once been. She'd certainly had more physical contact with Bernard than with anyone or anything else in the last twenty-four hours.

Seven hours to prepare (well, a lifetime for Bernard, to be honest), twenty minutes to eat. If she was lucky.

She wasn't even hungry now. Of course, she had just shoved a chipolata wrapped in yet more streaky bacon into her mouth in the kitchen. But that was only because it didn't fit on the edge of the platter and it was tidier to eat it. Richard would have placed it on a saucer, wrapped it in cling film and put it in the fridge to take up valuable real estate. And that would have made her want to kill Richard, which was not festive. Better all round to eat it.

It was fair to say that Gigi was hot and bothered. More, even, than Bernard. She too was trussed up for the day. It was Christmas, and that was what you did. That was what they had always done, particularly her darling, compliant boys. Her daughter, Megan – sometimes, it seemed to Gigi, more like a different species than simply a different gender – had rebelled, aged around fourteen or fifteen, and started to come down on Christmas morning in fleecy pyjamas with what Gigi called Hedge Backwards hair, but that hadn't been one of the many, many battles Gigi *had* actually picked with her, and eventually, by the time she was seventeen or eighteen, she'd gone back to actual clothes. The hair was a work in progress, and it was still one of the battles Gigi didn't pick. She drew comfort from the fact that every other girl Megan's age looked similarly dishevelled, albeit, mystifyingly, after long minutes of attention in their bedroom mirrors. Perhaps it was the music they listened to while they primped that made it stand up on its ends that way. Gigi was dressed up. She had a new dress, as she had done every Christmas forever. Fashion editors in magazines, and people who came on *This Morning* to tell you what to do, always said big girls should wear things that hugged their curves, which in turn would make said curves appear smaller. Gigi was reasonably certain this wasn't true, because when you wore one of those dresses that hugged your curves and walked past a mirror or shop window and wondered who the pig in Lycra was, dying of shame did seem a palatable option. What was wrong with skimming, draping, disguising? And yet, she was wearing one. It had a tight inner lining like a sausage casing that promised you'd look a size smaller once you'd shoehorned yourself into it. It screamed so on its big, bright label, so that everyone in the queue behind you in the shop knew how dissatisfied you were with your size. You thought it meant you'd look a size smaller than you had been before. What it actually meant was that you'd look a size smaller than Demis Roussos. And Gigi was wearing tights, which she hated. Mostly for their tendency to roll down at inopportune moments. Although this dress was so damn tight, rolling of any kind seemed unlikely.

Enough, Gigi, she told herself. Get a bloody grip and get on with it. You know perfectly well you're not going to throw Bernard at the wall. You're going to put him down in front of Richard, who will carve him slowly and painstakingly, while everything else you've put on the table hot goes cold, thus earning himself half the credit for the meal, which you will not begrudge him. And you're going to eat Christmas lunch with your growing, beloved family. The tights will roll, the zipper will strain, too much wine will be drunk. It's as traditional as taking all the strawberry creams out of the Quality Street as soon as you get the metal tin (never the plastic) home from Sainsbury's.

And here they were, around her table. Her people. Her life. Richard, her husband of thirty-seven years. Much more than half her life. Her handsome firstborn, Christopher. Next to his wife, Emily. Her younger son, Oliver. And his very new – to them at least – girlfriend, Caitlin. And the bonus baby of the family, born ten years after Olly, wild-haired Megan.

There were two firsts this year amongst all the rituals and traditions, and the soundtrack of the King's College choirboys and the Jackson Five. This was the first year there was no one with them from the older generation. Richard's father, James, the last grandparent still living, wasn't here. He was ninety, quite confused and entirely infirm. And he was twenty-five minutes up the road in the nursing home they'd put him in five years ago, when caring for him at home became too difficult. They'd decided it wasn't worth moving him to the house for Christmas this year, certain James was too far gone now even to understand what was happening. At least, Richard had decided, and Gigi had acquiesced, although she'd felt slightly ashamed of the decision ever since. Richard had framed it as being 'too much for her', with 'everything else going on'. It wasn't. It was too much for him. They'd go tomorrow, Richard had decreed, when there was less going on, and spend the afternoon with him.

And it was the first year when there was a Moses basket in the corner. It seemed symbolic, somehow. One out, one in. Megan's old Moses basket, in fact, empty for years in a bin bag in the loft, and now, marvellously, full of Christopher's new baby girl, Ava. A perfectly small and smooth and beautiful and miraculous baby, sleeping to order at the moment, arranged in something pink and cashmere that some friend who had never had to do a baby's laundry had bought her, looking for all the world like an Anne Geddes photograph.

Barring the odd fantasy of domestic Armageddon, and who could blame her for those, these were the good days. She felt a familiar flood of love for the people in this room. These *were* the days. The days when all was well. When she could tell herself all the days would be well, and believe herself.

It was the presence of the fruit of her union with Richard which reminded her that union hadn't always been as difficult as it was now. As predictable, and as unfulfilling, and as lonely. She and Richard were partners in this family firm, more, it sometimes seemed, than they were lovers or even friends. These occasions provided the proof that the business of being them had been successful, a profitable one. She clung to them, and tried to bank the joy they brought her.

So, there in the doorway, Gigi did *not* throw the turkey. She held it aloft like Mufasa in *The Lion King* and called attention to herself and to it with a loud and typically theatrical 'Ta da'.

'Wow, Gigi!' This was Emily, Christopher's entirely adorable wife. She always knew the right thing to say. And, right now, 'Wow, Gigi' was definitely the right thing to say. Christopher himself was peering anxiously in the direction of Ava's basket, making sure his mother's 'ta da' hadn't woken her, but she'd forgive his new-parent neurosis, as she'd forgive him almost anything.

'Smells fantastic, Mum.' Now Oliver spoke, her second son. So sensitive and kind she'd always somehow imagined he'd grow up gay – a notion undiscussed with Richard but one she was so beyond okay with by the time he was eighteen that she'd felt slightly affronted at the parade of very lucky girls he'd been bringing home ever since, in a flamboyant and blatant display of his heterosexuality.

And then, never one to disappoint, completely self-absorbed Megan's 'Thank God for that. I'm absolutely starving. Can we eat now? Please?'

Gigi almost simultaneously play-glared at Megan, beamed at Em and Olly, grimaced apologetically in Ava's direction and avoided Richard's eye, as he hadn't spoken. He was standing in front of his place setting, sharpening the carving knife on the steel. Very slowly. She put Bernard down in front of him, trying not to wonder why he hadn't done that earlier, or to mind that he hadn't poured the wine yet either.

'Here you go.'

'Well done, G.'

'Come on everyone. Tuck in while your dad carves.' She bit her tongue on the rest of the sentence – 'or everything else will be cold', brandishing a serving spoon with a determined smile on her face.

'Ava out for the count?'

'Fingers crossed.' This was Christopher, who was still wearing an expression of slight post-traumatic stress disorder, though his daughter was almost three months old now. He liked order, Christopher. He'd been the neatest little boy Gigi had ever known. His Enid Blyton books had always been arranged alphabetically on his bookshelves, and he always knew if you'd put one of his model airplanes back in the wrong place after you'd dusted. Knew and minded, badly. Although he clearly adored Ava, he had struggled, she knew, to accept the disruption to his routine she had wrought with her tiny ineffectual fists and her loud cries. Thank God for Emily, who had taken to motherhood like the proverbial duck to water, facing down the chaos and the newness with an almost bovine tranquillity. She was so very, very good for her son. Oh, the relief of your child finding someone they not only loved and fancied, but someone who was good for them.

'She's completely milk drunk, Gigi. I knew what I was doing when I accepted that sherry this morning . . .' Emily giggled. 'She'll be out cold well past the Queen's speech, I'm guessing.'

'Is that okay?' Christopher hadn't known about the sherry, and now he looked more worried than before. Emily rolled her eyes fondly.

'Didn't hurt you lot much. I certainly drank through all three pregnancies, and all three breast feeds.' Gigi didn't mention the two cigarettes she'd also smoked, one with each of the boys. It seemed unnecessary.

Megan sniggered. 'You did?'

'Absolutely. And you turned out all right. Mostly. I wasn't chucking back vodka Red Bulls – the odd glass of wine or sherry. A pint or two of Guinness . . .'

'Have we got any Red Bull?' Megan asked, as if hearing the drink's name had planted a marvellous thought. She'd been down the pub last night with her schoolmates, all excited to be reunited after their first term at uni, and keen to escape the Christmas rituals of home. She hadn't come back until well after closing time – Gigi had heard the door close carefully at around 1 a.m. She'd thought that once Megan had been away for a few months, she'd be able to sleep properly when her daughter was home and out, but the cruel trick of motherhood was apparently that she still couldn't. 1 a.m. And it still showed on her at 1 p.m. The hair was at its most Caitlin Moran this afternoon, and Megan's skin was pale and, Gigi, thought, just a little on the clammy side. She'd only emerged from her room about an hour before everyone had been called to the table.

'No, we have not.' Gigi was unsympathetic. She'd been tending to Bernard while Megan swanned off to the pub without so much as an 'Anything I can do?' and if her daughter was paying the price today, she felt only a tiny shiver of distinctly unmaternal *Schadenfreude*.

'Olly? Would you pour the wine?' She ignored Richard's slightly reproachful glance. After so many years of marriage, they both caught the subtext and tone.

Olly, who evidently didn't, jumped up and grabbed the bottle from the sideboard. 'Sure.'

'Now, Caitlin. Dig in. Every man for himself here . . .'

Caitlin was not the first girlfriend Oliver had ever brought home for Christmas. She was just the first one none of them had ever met *before* she appeared on Christmas Eve, unannounced and unheralded. A secret girlfriend, no less.

Gigi knew it was unfair to be suspicious of very slim people, but she couldn't help it, any more than some very slim people, she knew, could help deciding at first sight that she was lazy and undisciplined, which was equally unfair. But still, Caitlin was a very slim person. And she *was* forcing herself to say 'slim' and not 'skinny'. Very slim, very pretty, very quiet. Either shy or aloof. Gigi hadn't decided which yet.

Oliver had been the final one to arrive last night. Megan had already been home a few days, since term ended. Christopher and Emily had arrived in the early afternoon, fresh from a couple of days at Emily's parents, with a pantechnicon of baby stuff that had taken the best part of an hour to unload and install in Christopher's old room. Olly, in true Olly style, had rung late afternoon to say he'd missed the train he'd planned to catch, and he'd be on the next one. Missing trains was practically a hobby of his – you never really reckoned on his catching the one he said he would. Richard had gone to collect him at the station at six-ish and texted at a quarter past to say he was on his way back and that Olly wasn't alone, but travelling with a girl. Richard was tantalizingly light on details. Like father like son.

From a practical point of view, Gigi – in full-on hostess mode – hoped it was a girlfriend type of girl. It was a bit late to worry about Olly's moral compass, and, besides, there were just no more beds. Chris and Emily were in the guest room, since Ava and her clobber had annexed his old single. Megan was in hers, and that just left Olly's four foot six double. Her mind whirled with the possibilities, if she had to find another room. Megan would have to move, and share with Ava, and she'd have to strip her bed. And she'd be seriously irritated and no one needed that. The mystery girl would need clean sheets . . . and towels . . . Better that it be a 'girlfriend' girlfriend.

Gigi sort of despised this preoccupation with domestic detail. Other people made stuff like this seem effortless and easy. Bohemians. Did they all sleep in other people's sheets, though, and dry themselves on towels that had been in other people's armpits? And not mind? She hadn't always been obsessed with her washing machine. She wished she wasn't now but she didn't know how not to be. So her brain whirled and whirled with domestic detail and she couldn't stop it. She'd gone to the linen cupboard for a clean bath sheet and hand towel, and put them on Ollie's bed. She was bound to be a 'girlfriend' girlfriend, wasn't she? But, then again, how *could* he? Just spring it on her . . .

Truthfully, though, she knew exactly how. Olly didn't think like the rest of them. He was the polar opposite of his brother. Disorganized, laid back to the point of horizontality, nonconformist to a fault. A free spirit. This was *exactly* like him. It was Caitlin who'd been nothing like she'd expected.

Olly's girlfriends up until now were usually, if not exclusively, much like him. Light-hearted, giggly, game. The bungee-jumping type. This girl, this new girl, didn't seem to be any of those things. She looked serious. And she was quiet.

Richard had gone to The Swan for a pint with his sons this morning, as was their habit. He'd poured drinks for the girls before he left, and they'd congregated in the warm kitchen, apart from Megan, who could not, of course, be roused. Ava held court in her bouncy chair, gurgling and flailing happily so long as someone cooed over her every couple of minutes, while Emily made bread sauce and chattered easily. Caitlin had been really hard to draw in, giving short answers to their questions, and eventually excusing herself, ostensibly to make telephone calls to her own family. Emily had raised an eyebrow and smirked. 'Not Olly's usual!' Gigi had raised a finger – ssh – to her lips. But she'd been thinking the same.

Under the bright spotlight of Gigi's spoon-wielding

attention now, Caitlin helped herself to a few vegetables, no potatoes, roast or mashed, and a ladle of gravy Thumbelina couldn't have had a strip wash in.

'Are you sure you've got enough, love? There's plenty . . .' Gigi couldn't help herself.

'Leave her be, Mum.' Oliver's tone was gentle, and he smiled at her, but Gigi caught the soft and subtle realignment of loyalties in his words.

Eventually, Richard finished carving and, with the platter passed around and crackers pulled (this felt odd and slightly awkward, ever since the youngest child stopped being enchanted by the pungent bang, or interested enough in the 'gift' within to clamber on the carpet to find it), the family ate.

Richard seemed suddenly to remember the required public vote of thanks owed to his wife, and clinked his glass formally with his knife, though there was scarcely enough noise to merit it.

'To the ever competent Gigi. Thanks, darling. For the delicious lunch.'

For some reason Gigi's imagination conjured up the highly charged table scene in *Moonstruck*, where Olympia Dukakis toasts her husband in dramatic Italian. '*Ti amo*.' 'Ever competent' was hardly '*Ti amo*', even if it came with a 'darling'. Hey ho.

Gigi saw Caitlin and Olly exchange a glance she couldn't immediately interpret, and then, as he held his glass aloft and took a deep breath, she knew at once.

'Before we all get stuck in again, I had one more little thing . . .'

And Gigi found, to her surprise, that she wanted to shout *NO*. Almost as much as she had wanted to throw the turkey. She didn't even know why. It came from somewhere deep within her. From the uterus, she thought.

And it wasn't your run of the mill 'no one's good enough for my boy' stuff. She couldn't get Christopher married to Emily quickly enough. She'd adored the girl since the first time she'd met her, in the second summer of their university years. She'd loved her ready laugh, and her earthy frankness, and her transformative effect on Gigi's frankly uptight son. She'd practically cheered when she'd changed Christopher's sheets after their first stay, when Emily had been meant to be sleeping down the hall in the guest bed, and found a balled-up pair of pink lacy knickers.

Gigi wasn't *that* mother. But she wanted, now, to make this moment stop, and change how it was going to go.

'I know you've all only just met Caitlin. I've sprung her on you, a bit. I know. So I may as well spring something else on you, while I'm at it . . .'

Gigi looked desperately at Richard, but he was staring at Olly. His fork was halfway to his mouth. Dark meat, with gravy dripping.

'We're planning on getting married. So I suppose . . . we're engaged . . .' He reached down to the table and picked up Caitlin's hand, bringing his mouth down to kiss it. She couldn't see his eyes.

Gigi's heart pounded. Maybe she *should* have thrown Bernard.

Tess

Week 8. Maybe. You're three times as big as when you got going. You're the size of a pomegranate seed. That put a new spin on my couscous, butternut squash and hummus salad, I can tell you, baby mine. You even have early brainwaves, although I don't know much about that stuff and I'm not clear what that means. I don't think you're having deep existential thoughts at this point. It's taking all your energy to grow. You'll never do so much, so fast, in the rest of your life as you're doing now. And a heartbeat, you have a heartbeat. You're pretty prehistoric-looking, in truth, like a kind of angry, determined, kidney-bean thing with tiny fists. You're all heart — it's big — like a third of the size of the whole of you — and vivid red. You're a bit freaky, no offence. I keep wondering if I love you, but it's such a wonderfully weird thought; mostly I think I'm fascinated by you. I hope that's not the wrong thing to say. The site says your heart beats three times as fast as an adult heart, so now I take a moment and listen to my own heartbeat, my palm on my chest, and try to count the two extra beats between mine and yours, but it's too fast and I can't really do it. My boobs hurt like hell, and I dislike getting up when the alarm goes off marginally more than I have done before. I'd like to curl up and sleep more. I haven't been that sick. There was that first time, and three or four more, but just in the morning, and mostly I was queasy, not full-on nauseous. Like when I went on a ferry when I was a kid. And I'm glad about that. I hate being sick. One girl I worked with was sick in her handbag on the Tube. Maybe I won't get that. Not everyone does, I know. I wonder whether my mum did but I can't ask her. Might as well rent an advertising hoarding opposite her house and hang a poster. Nope — I'm not ready, although the website says it's okay to tell loved ones now, and start thinking about your birthing team (what's wrong with doctors, midwives and the people who bring you the good drugs? That sounds like a winning team to me). Nope. You're still my secret . . .

I keep thinking about Donna. My mother. Trying to remember what she was like when I was little. Searching out my earliest memory of her. But my earliest memories are of Iris. The recollections of bedtime storybooks read in bear-hugs, and cool hands on my hot forehead, and breaking eggs into bowls to mix cakes, are all Iris. It frightens me a bit that I can't remember the Donna of my childhood nearly so well. That a lot of those fragments are of Donna tired, or cross, or just absent. It frightens me a bit that I call her Donna, think of her as Donna, more than as Mum. Iris doesn't seem to have passed on all those nurturing, calm and capable mothering traits to Donna. What if I don't have them either?

It's Christmas. I thought I'd do it now. Like maybe I'd put a big red bow around my pregnancy test — the one I've kept, stuck at the back of my knicker drawer — and lay it under the tree for Sean. Maybe we'll be like a Hallmark made-for-TV movie.

You keep going, baby mine. Whatever is happening out here, what's happening in there is under way. Out here I don't look any different. No one is treating me any differently because no one knows. A woman got on my bus the other day with a BABY ON BOARD *badge. No bump. Perhaps she thought she might chuck up in her handbag and didn't want everyone else to think she was a lush or a junkie. But already happy for even strangers to know. I bet she's told her loved ones and is even now assembling her birthing team. I'm the freak.*

Apparently, it's understandable for my hormones to be all over the shop right now. So that's why part of me wants to be told not to lift heavy objects and to be given seats on the train and to buy tiny white clothes, and feels irrationally, tearfully angry about the people who aren't telling me and standing up for me and selling me tiny white clothes. Iris, Sean, and the strangers on public transport and in shops. Even though I know they can't because they don't know. Pretty bloody crazy, huh? I bought some folic acid because the website said it was good — I think I'm a bit late, but I'm taking it now. I was mad at the assistant in the chemist's for not saying something. And they're never supposed to say something. When you buy condoms, or tampons, or thrush treatments. That's their job — not saying something.

I bought you a Christmas present. How ridiculous is that? It was this stupidly soft and strokable grey rabbit, about six inches tall. I was in the M&S Food Hall and it was by the gift cards, and I just put it in my basket. When I got home and unpacked the food, I didn't know what to do with it. It's in the knicker drawer with the pregnancy test. But it's yours, baby mine. Merry Christmas.

The hospital ward had done its best to make itself festive. They were doing pretty well, considering the patients either didn't know they were there or didn't want to be, and the visitors were mostly passing through between present unwrapping, the Queen's broadcast, and falling asleep with a box of Roses and a Baileys Chocolat Luxe in front of an Agatha Christie film. The nurses were resolutely cheerful, although she was sure most of them were missing something better by being here. There were paper chains and tinsel hung across curtain rods, and a small tree at one end by the double doors was strung with fairy lights. An open tin of Celebrations sat on the counter of the Nurses' Station. There was a quiet soundtrack of Christmas songs playing.

Tess's mum had promised to meet her at 11 a.m., but she wasn't here. Iris was asleep, flat on her back like a corpse, sheets and blankets neatly tucked in on either side, her arms laid at her sides. The mask of last week was gone, as was a lot of the paraphernalia – the tubes and the monitor – that had been there while the infection rampaged, and her breathing was even and peaceful, although she was still very pale and fragile-looking. Tess realized she missed the machines – they'd been proof of her being alive, and now, with everything gone, lying this way, she actually looked dead, apart from the shallow rise and fall of her chest. She looked smaller, and older, and frailer. Her hair needed combing, and Tess itched to do it, but she didn't want to wake her. She sat watching her, a thin plastic cup of thin plastic-tasting tea in her hand, feeling what Christmas spirit she might have had earlier wane, and her irritation towards her mother rising.

She'd left Sean to get here at the agreed time. They'd opened their stockings in bed. She'd asked him, and he'd agreed, to let the subject of New York rest while she dealt with Iris. She felt bad about using her grandmother as an excuse. That wasn't really it. If she'd wanted to go, if she'd been free to go, she'd have said yes, and that would have been that. At least it seemed possible it might have been that way. Now there wasn't so much an elephant in the room as a Big Apple. And a tiny baby.

She'd kissed Iris's cheek when she'd arrived, and now she held her hand. She wanted to talk to her, that was what she normally did, but she felt self-conscious in a ward un-usually full of visitors and forced gaiety, so she stroked her hand, and sat.

Sean hadn't come with her. He patently hadn't wanted

to, and the only other time he'd come, earlier in the week, he'd stressed her out, so she hadn't pushed. Today she'd come down on a coach and taken a taxi from the station. Sean had said he'd pick her up at midday; they were due at his parents' at one. It didn't occur to him that the last thing she might feel like after this was sherry and charades with his family. It was what had been arranged. She knew he planned to tell them about New York and that the question of her own future would hang in the air. She dreaded the inevitable questions.

She'd determined that she'd speak to Donna today, and now she wasn't here. It was far from the first time she'd felt let down by her mum. This would be the fourth Christmas in a row she hadn't spent the day with Donna, although it had been sporadic even in her teens and throughout her twenties. Donna didn't really 'do' Christmas. She was a rabid atheist, and a declared non-materialist. And clearly not a big fan of family. A Goan yoga retreat was more her bag. For several years now, she'd gone to India for at least three weeks, always, and quite deliberately, across Christmas. 'You don't mind, darling . . .' she'd always said, passive aggression and resignation dripping from every word, 'you've got my mum . . . the gang of two . . .' And the truth was, she was right. They were happier without her. If it wasn't all Downward Dog poses and cocktails at sunset, Donna's Christmas Day invariably began with a Christmas Eve hangover and an epic lie-in. Tess and Iris liked the morning service at church, neither a staunch believer, but both keen on belting out carols and being dressed before midday. She'd continued to spend the day itself with Iris over Sean since he'd been on the scene, usually meeting up with him on Boxing Day. Christmas Eve and Christmas

Day were for her grandmother, and if either missed Donna amidst their festivities, they didn't mention it. Donna had a knack of calling from overseas just as they were about to sit down to eat or watch the Queen. Last year, she'd Face-Timed halfway through the Bond film neither of them were particularly watching, and Iris had peered curiously at her bronzed daughter, a palm-fringed beach behind her, repeatedly saying only that modern gadgets were amazing, weren't they? Tess had been relieved when they'd hung up.

Ritual and routine had only grown more important as Tess had been forced to acknowledge Iris's illness, and now Donna's bohemian lifestyle stood in even starker contrast. It sometimes – no, often – felt like Tess was the mother and Donna the child. The last two Christmases had been especially poignant. Sean had wanted her to be with him, but she'd refused his mother's invitations. They'd been sad, those days. She'd tried to remember everything she and Iris usually did. But it was like doing those things with a stranger who'd never done them before. This, ironic-ally, was easier.

Even knowing what was happening with Iris hadn't persuaded Donna to alter her plans. Not that Tess had expected it to. She hadn't asked, and Donna hadn't offered. Tess didn't know where her mother's aversion to family and convention came from. She felt like her own affinity had skipped a generation over Donna and come directly to her. Her mother was jealous, she knew, of Tess's relation-ship with Iris. But they were just more alike.

She had come to see that her mother was not an unkind or a malevolent person, but a careless one, raising selfish-ness to an art form. As an adult, Tess recognized it. And forgave it, to a degree, because she knew she was more or less okay. She had been almost enough as a mother – close enough. Tess had always been fed, and cared for, and, she knew, loved in Donna's own fashion. She'd had a sense, always, of her mother's unhappiness. As a child, it had been bewildering. But if it hadn't been for Iris, the ballast in Donna's storm, she knew she would have been damaged by it. Perhaps she had been anyway. Perhaps this weirdness about the pregnancy was less about Sean and more to do with Donna than she wanted to admit. She had constantly prided herself on emerging relatively unscathed from the comparative emotional wreckage of her childhood.

Donna had divorced Tess's father, Harry, when Tess was two: she had no memory of living with both her parents, and precious few of Harry himself, who had absented himself from his daughter's life seemingly easily enough.

When Tess was five, her mother had remarried Martin, Tess serving as flower girl, and she'd stayed with him for seven years. Tess remembered three or four years of shouting and door slamming, and then three or four more years of quiet, seething resentment before he'd packed and left. She saw more of him than of her biological father, but these days that had boiled down to two or three lunches a year where Tess looked at photographs of Martin's new family and Martin apologized for making such a mess of his marriage to her mother, seeking perpetual absolution for something neither of them really held him responsible for.

There'd been no more husbands, but for the rest of the time Tess lived at home, and, in the years since, there had been a rolling cast of 'uncles' and friends who'd come and gone. None cruel or inappropriate, but some kinder and more interested than others.

While Tess was a child, Iris had papered over all the cracks. Her husband, Wilfred, had died the year before Tess was born, and Donna had no siblings. So there was only Tess, and Iris had lavished all her love and attention on her granddaughter. There had been long holidays at her house, and long letters during term time, when Tess couldn't escape to Wiltshire, where Iris lived. Once Tess had grown up, Iris had talked about it more. 'It's my fault,' she'd said. 'I spoilt her. Your grandfather used to tell me so, but I wouldn't listen.'

Tess had never believed that was it. There was something restless in Donna. She'd never been unkind, never neglectful in the crueller ways. She'd been inconsistent, and that was probably far worse. Unkindness would have chipped away at a child's unconditional, dependent love. Inconsistency meant Tess had lived on the shifting sands of her mother's life, and sometimes it had been hard.

Tess remembered other girls, in the first term at university, crying for their mothers, heading home eagerly for reading weeks. For her, aside from the time she'd spent with Iris, university represented the first real freedom, and she'd loved it. She'd never gone home for more than a few nights since. And their relationship gradually became easier for it. The less Tess needed from Donna, the less Donna's failure to provide it mattered. If Tess had shut her out, now, of her adult life, she hadn't done so to be cruel or to hurt. It was a habit.

But, with Iris's increasing illness, it had become harder between them again. Tess felt unsupported. She felt protective of Iris, and hurt on her grandmother's behalf. She couldn't understand why her mother wasn't sadder: when had she made the transition from truly caring to seeing her own mother as something akin to a burden? Maybe there'd been no transition. Perhaps Iris was now what Tess had always been: a duty, an unwanted responsibility. It was hard to co-exist with Donna, in this experience of Iris's deterioration. If Tess wasn't so tired, and so worried, she suspected she'd be angry, and then angrier still at the waste of energy.

And she didn't feel the slightest desire, yet, to tell Donna she was pregnant.

Several people arrived to see the lady in the next bed, with a poinsettia in a pot. A small child climbed up on to her lap to show a prized new toy, one arm flung around her neck. The stocky solidity of the toddler made the old lady seem even more frail.

And then Donna was there, breathless and mumbling an apology of sorts for her lateness. She kissed Tess briefly, but not Iris. Tess thought she barely looked at her as she sat down.

For ten minutes they kept a superficial, quietly singsongy conversation going across the bed.

And the proper conversation was yet to be had. Tess kept her voice low and soft. It seemed unlikely Iris would hear or could understand, but still she almost whispered.

'Can we go downstairs, to the cafeteria? We need to have a talk . . .'

Donna grimaced. 'Sounds ominous.'

'Mum . . .'

Her mother put her hands up in a gesture of surrender. 'Okay. Okay. Now?'

'Yes. Now.'

She kissed Iris's cheek, and squeezed her hand. Across the bed, Donna bent over her mother, and planted the lightest and quickest of kisses, almost as if she didn't want to touch her.

In the canteen, Tess asked for two pots of English Breakfast tea. Choosing a table near the window, the two of them studiously stirred and poured their drinks, not speaking.

'You know she can't go home from here, don't you, Mum?' Tess tried to keep her voice gentle.

But the edge of irritation and defensiveness was immediate in Donna's reply. 'Who has said so?'

'It's obvious.'

'Not to me. She's so much better. You said so.'

'The chest infection is better. That's true. But the chest infection isn't why she can't go home.'

Donna shifted uncomfortably. Tess had tried to talk to her about this before – before this bout of infection, and long before – when Iris had been diagnosed. She was always met with this response. Her mother couldn't bear to think about it, let alone talk about it. She had never really adjusted to the new reality of her own mother's illness, Tess realized. It seemed extraordinary that there should still be an element of denial, but she knew part of her mother wanted to believe Iris was absent-minded, forgetful . . . that she was just old.

'Mum. We've got to talk about this.'

Donna's tone was wheedling. 'Today? It's Christmas, for Christ's sake, Tess . . .' She gave a hollow laugh, hearing the irony for herself.

Her mother had taken a piece of foil from the tray left on their table. She was smoothing out the wrinkles, methodically, with her fingernails. It meant she didn't have to look at Tess.

'I know. But you've . . . not been around a lot.'

'Don't have a go.' Donna was belligerent now. So quickly. Tess considered leaving it, and realized she couldn't. Donna would be on a plane tomorrow, and she might be gone for weeks. She didn't have weeks.

'I'm not, Mum. I promise. I know it's Christmas. I know this is hard. But I honestly think we need to start thinking about a plan –'

'We've had a plan. It's been working well enough, hasn't it? You make it sound like we've just left her to it.'

Tess refused to rise. 'I know that's not true. But as she changes, obviously the plan has to change too.'

Donna didn't respond. She folded the damn foil over and over into a tiny, smooth square. Tess tried to quell the resentment and frustration rising in her. She was opting out.

Donna hadn't been there when Iris had woken. She hadn't seen Iris's distress when she realized she was hooked up to drips. She hadn't seen the fear in Iris's face when she didn't have a clue where she was. She'd scanned the room with frantic eyes, and visibly relaxed when they'd alighted on Tess. She still knew her. But for how much longer?

'I've been speaking to the doctors. Not just the ones treating her. The dementia specialists. They've spent some time with her. They've recommended a change in care.'

'Well, I can't have her.' The sentence hung, selfish and clumsy, in the air between them. She crumpled the tin foil again, threw it into her empty cup.

Tess took a deep breath. 'I know.' As if I'd let you, she thought. As if I'd trust you for one bloody minute to take proper care of her. Not a chance.

'I'm not asking you to, Mum. And I can't either. I've got work . . . and . . .' she let her voice trail off. 'Neither of us can meet her needs now. She needs proper care. Around the clock. From trained people.'

Best to ignore the fact that Donna wouldn't want to try.

'She needs specialist care.'

'A home?' She said it like it was a dirty word.

Tess nodded. 'Somewhere that specializes in dementia.'

'She's not that bad.'

And how in the hell would you know, Tess thought.

'Is she?'

'She's getting worse, Mum. I don't think she's properly able to take care of herself at home. Not physically. Although you can see that she's getting frailer, it's mentally that's the problem.'

'It's that bad?'

'You know it is, Mum. Look, I know it's hard. It's hard for me too. But we can't ignore it. We're all she has.'

Donna sniffed. 'Poor old Mum.' It was the softest thing she'd said in ages. Tess realized she'd rather her mum maintained the hard carapace. It made all of this easier. It was easier to be angry at her inadequacy. She couldn't carry her too.

'And anyway, she can't stay here. Once she's well, they'll need her bed. That's how it goes now. She's been assessed. The doctors agree . . .'

'When did all this happen?'

It's been happening, damn you. For months and months. Before this happened. And after . . . I've been here every damn day. They think I'm her bloody next of kin. You've left it all to me.

Tess was determined not to fight.

'They've been coming to see her. They agree that residential care is what she needs now. I've been looking into it. I've got some suggestions –'

'Got it all planned out?'

'Someone had to, Mum.' She couldn't help herself.

Donna looked at her hard, for a long moment. Then

smiled, gentle for once. 'I'm sorry, love. I haven't been much use, have I? I just hate all this.' She raised both arms at the room. 'Hospitals. Sickness. Death . . .' She drew out the syllables on the last word. 'I hate it. I hate seeing her lying there.' Her voice broke.

'I know.' Tess heard the resignation in her own voice.

'Forgive me?'

'Nothing to forgive.' Tess wasn't sure either of them believed it. It was something Donna said. She'd always said. *Forgive me?* Tess had been answering that way since she was quite young. The list of things for which Donna may or may not need forgiveness was pretty long by now.

Donna's tone had become conciliatory. Something had clicked. She reached into her bag, fumbling around until she found what she'd been looking for – her vape. Tess hated the vape. Ridiculous thing. Like a cross between a ballpoint pen and a dummy. 'Is there somewhere you like, love?' She'd also extracted a refill. It usefully meant she needn't meet Tess's gaze as she fiddled with it, gearing up for a fix.

Tess nodded. 'I have a brochure . . . there's a place that's much nearer to me.'

Donna nodded her head vigorously. 'That'd make your life easier, wouldn't it? I know you're busy . . . If you think it's right . . . you know her better than I do.'

She was right. She was also ready to go, Tess knew. She was acquiescing to make good her escape.

Donna shrugged her arms into her coat and folded and refolded her scarf, combing at its fringe with her fingers. Fidgeting.

'Will we need to sell the house? Those places are bloody expensive, aren't they?'

Tess took a deep breath. 'She's got quite a lot in savings.'

Not that they'd go far. The places she was looking at were eye-wateringly expensive. They all seemed to be. 'But, yes, probably . . . if . . .'

'If she lives with this for long?'

'Yes.'

'And she might?'

'There's no way of knowing.'

Tess wished there was.

'Will there be a lot of legal stuff to sort out?'

'I've got power of attorney.' This was the part Tess had most dreaded.

Iris had asked her, not long after her official diagnosis, if she would agree to her signing a power of attorney authorizing Tess to make decisions about her property and financial affairs, and her health and welfare. They'd been to her solicitor and signed the papers. Iris had asked her not to tell Donna. And Donna hadn't asked. Tess remembered Iris's words on the subject of bypassing her own daughter now: 'She wouldn't want it. I know she'd rather you had it.' Tess wondered now what Iris had meant — exactly — and why she hadn't asked.

There was a very long pause. Tess could see that Donna was deciding how to react.

She sniffed hard. 'Well, that's that, then. I figured she'd have done that. So it's all up to you . . .' She couldn't read her mother's tone, although the slight shrug of Donna's shoulders made her sad. There was resignation. But there was resentment too.

'I'd like your blessing.'

'But you don't need it?'

'I don't, no.' No sense sugar-coating it.

Donna smiled. 'You'll do what's best, I know. My mum

did the right thing, choosing you. You're a good girl. Tess, look. I've got to go. Didn't you say you did too?'

Tess looked at her watch. Sean would be waiting for her in the car park.

Donna gave her a quick hug. 'I'm sorry, love. Love you and leave you. I'll give you a ring . . . Sorry.'

She always was . . .

Tess wanted to say goodbye to Iris. She might even be awake. In the lift back up to the ward, she pulled her phone out of her bag. Sean had texted. 'There in 5.' Eight minutes ago. She quickly texted back that she'd be out in a couple of minutes.

Iris wasn't awake. There was a young nurse checking her vital signs. Tess had seen her before, but not much. She couldn't remember her name. Cherry, or Cheryl. Chantelle maybe. It was too late to ask. 'I'll just be a minute.'

'No worries. I've only come to say goodbye. My boy-friend's waiting downstairs.'

The nurse smiled. 'Plans?'

'His family.'

'Do you get on with them?'

Tess shrugged and grinned. 'They're okay.'

'I can't stand my boyfriend's mum. She's a right moody cow.' She rolled her eyes, hand on hip. Tess didn't know how to respond to that.

'That was your mum, before, right?'

'Yeah.'

'She's really nice.'

Tess looked at her. She was looking at her watch now, two fingers on the inside of Iris's translucent wrist. 'You're not often here at the same time.'

'No . . .'

'She takes the morning shift, right, mostly? You do the evenings?'

'I –'

'You've got work, and things, she says. She's dead proud of you.'

'My mum?'

She nodded vigorously. 'I can see the resemblance, now, when I see the two of you together. Different styles, but you can tell you're family.'

Donna hadn't said she'd been visiting. Tess knew that she'd come, that first day, responding to the message she'd left on her phone, and again today. She hadn't known there had been other times. The doctors hadn't said. The nurses hadn't mentioned it, until now.

'She reads to your gran. You know she's asleep most of the time, but you can still hear, can't you? Says it's her favourite. What was it . . . She told me. Stella someone . . .'

'Stella Gibbons?'

'That's it. Said it was your gran's favourite. Cold something . . .'

'*Cold Comfort Farm.*'

'Yep.'

It *was* her favourite. She'd read it to Tess the summer she was ten. She said she'd read it to her mother when Donna was about that age. Tess had forgotten.

'That's the one. A chapter or two every day. She's got a nice voice, too.'

All Tess wanted was to go home. She felt exhausted – every part of her was heavy and sluggish. Christmas was of no interest whatsoever. Christmas with Sean's family simply felt like an ordeal to be got through in the hours between now and when she could crawl back into her bed. It wasn't just her mother, or the hospital and Iris. It was very physical. The sickness of the first few weeks had mostly passed, but the exhaustion was worse. She'd been nauseous only in the mornings, but the feeling lasted all day. She put her head back against the headrest in the car while Sean drove, and dozed, grateful for the Christmas radio.

She couldn't process what she'd learnt about her mother visiting Iris. She wanted to ask her, but she knew Donna was on her way to the airport, and then someplace far away.

Sean's parents lived in a mock-Tudor house in a cul-de-sac in a Southampton suburb. His father, Clive, was a retired surveyor and obsessive sailor. His mother, June, had been a primary-school teacher. His two elder brothers, Jack and Luke, were also in property – one a developer and one an estate agent – and when the conversation wasn't about tides or boats, it was about new estates springing up in the area and what they were worth per square foot. None of the wives appeared to be remotely interested in what interested their husbands, so gatherings at Sean's house were always very gender divided – boats and square feet in the lounge, school-gate politics and fashion in the kitchen. The secret bump would grant instant admission to the club that had previously kept Tess subtly but definitely on the periphery. They were friendly enough, Susan and Jayne, but it was always apparent that they thought they had nothing in common with her. She joined in, agreeing enthusiastically with their bombastic pronouncements about other women she'd never met. But they often started sentences with 'You wouldn't understand but . . .' or 'I know it's probably not your kind of thing . . .' and very early on she'd given up trying to prove it was other-wise. Mostly because they were right: she didn't understand and it wasn't her kind of thing, most of it. The only other young mother she knew really well was Holly, and Holly never seemed to be this preoccupied with nonsense or . . . to be so catty, frankly.

They had five ever-so-slightly interchangeable children between them – three feral boys and two highly sequinned girls. She hadn't completely got a handle on names or par-entage in the early days and it was far too late to ask again. They took very little notice of her anyway, so it didn't seem to matter.

This baby, the secret bump, would be their cousin. It was a very bizarre thought. Sean wasn't really a family guy (his words), so this was only her third or fourth time being with them all. She felt absolutely no familial connection at all. They were not bad people. But they were not her tribe. Holly was her tribe. Iris was her tribe. They probably thought she was stuck up. Or just boring.

She watched him now, with his nephews and nieces. The girls seemed shy around him. Shy or disinterested. He threw a boy she thought was called Jake, about five years old, blond and whippet-thin, up and over his shoulder, leaving him hanging down his back, ineffectual fists beat-ing in delighted protest, while he continued talking to his brother as if nothing was happening, and drinking from a bottle of beer. Rough-housing, Iris would have called it. Was that how he'd be, with one of his own? Would he be the sort of dad who took the kids to the park on his own on a Sunday morning so their mum could have a lie-in? Or who'd sit on the floor and build endless brick towers to be pushed over? She wasn't sure he would be. Sean's life was so . . . neat. Sean's time was so carefully apportioned. People changed, didn't they? When the tiny humans came and destroyed everything in their path, you didn't mind, because of all the amazing love . . . the love you could read about and have described to you but couldn't possibly understand until you felt it. Wasn't that right?

New York didn't come up until after lunch, when the children's sugar high had worn off a little, and they were slumped in front of whatever Disney film it was. The men had done the dishes to a chorus of amazement from their wives, and then brought a tray of tea into the dining room.

Sean cleared his throat. 'So, I have news.' He looked at her, almost for a permission she didn't grant. Continued anyway. '*We* have news . . .'

June sat forward excitedly, her red-paper hat rakishly across one eyebrow, her hand brought up to her mouth.

'I have been offered a job in New York. A really good job, one that I really want to do, and I have said yes!'

June sat back and pulled her hat off. That wasn't what she'd expected.

For the next five minutes, everyone spoke at once, with a hundred exclamations and questions. The odd dreadful ham American accent. Sean's dad came around the table to shake his hand, and his nearest brother slapped his back appreciatively. June, on her left, squeezed Tess's hand and she wasn't sure as she looked into her face whether it was excitement or sympathy, but decided it was a mix of both.

She was grateful when Sean put a hand up to stop them all. 'Hey, hey – too many questions. We haven't worked it all out yet. Give us a minute . . . You'll be in the loop, when there is a loop. I just wanted to tell you since we were all together. The detail is to follow, okay?'

'As long as you get an apartment we can all fit in, Sean. There'll be a steady stream of us heading over to visit . . .' She realized no one had addressed a specific query to her – they had all just assumed she'd be going too.

But she hadn't decided. It was four weeks since he'd told her. Four weeks and five days since she'd found out she was pregnant. He'd moved things right along on his end . . . She hadn't done a thing. She'd told herself Iris was the reason. But Iris was the excuse. She was probably about eight weeks pregnant. This was ridiculous.

The traffic was mercifully light on the drive home. It was Sean's turn to sleep. He'd drunk his fair share of red wine with his turkey. He'd offered to tune in the radio to whatever she wanted to listen to, but all Tess wanted was the blessed sound of silence. It had been an endless day.

At home she called the ward at the hospital, to be told that Iris had been asleep most of the day, as she was now, and comfortable. Then Tess stripped off, letting her clothes stay where they landed, slid into her dressing gown and curled up on the bed while Sean changed. Her head was throbbing.

'It was a good day, right?'

She found she barely had the energy to answer. 'Hmmm.'

'Did you see my mum's face, before I said about New York! I swear she thought I was going to announce our engagement.'

He looked over at her but she didn't meet his stare.

'Or propose . . .'

Tess picked up the remote control from the bedside table. An hour of vacuous television suddenly appealed. And switching it on might shut Sean up.

'Ew. There's nothing cringier than a public engagement.'

'I knew you'd think that . . .'

And then, while she flicked between channels, he was suddenly on his knees by her side of the bed, taking the remote control gently out of her hand, and by the time her fuddled, exhausted brain realized why he was down there it was too late to stop him doing it.

'So I've waited.'

'Sean.' Her tone did not deter him.

'Tess. I love you. I want you with me in New York. And always. Marry me.'

'Wait . . .'

'Why? Why wait?' He looked crestfallen, and she knew she'd given the wrong response. She could kick herself. She'd been too slow to head him off. Kick him, for having such an extraordinarily lousy sense of timing.

'Because I have to tell you something.'

'What?'

'I'm pregnant . . .'

Gigi

It was clearly called Boxing Day because you woke up feeling as if you'd gone ten rounds with Tyson the day before and lost on a technical knockout. It was still dark. The LED display projecting on to the ceiling showed 6 a.m. when Gigi opened her eyes. Ridiculous. Unnecessary. Cruel. Richard was clearly having no such inner monologue with his body clock. The rounded lump of him, back to her as always, was completely still, and he was doing that combination snore and raspberry blowing that had heralded his fifties – so much more annoying than the straightforward snore. Gigi groaned and rolled over for the extra hour she knew she needed and deserved, but, before she could go back to sleep, she heard Emily and Ava out on the landing and simultaneously realized she needed the loo. She gave up and followed her daughter-in-law and her irresistible granddaughter downstairs, in search of a cup of tea and a cuddle.

Emily was nestled into the corner of the deepest sofa in the sitting room, gazing at Ava, who was peacefully latched on to her left breast. She smiled sleepily up at Gigi when she went in with a mug of tea in each hand.

'I've woken you up, haven't I? I'm so sorry. I crept down so Chris could sleep a bit longer . . .'

Gigi waved away the apology and stooped over the pair of them, smoothing Ava's visible cheek with the back of her finger.

'Ssh. Don't be daft. I was already awake.'

'Liar. You must be knackered, after yesterday.'

'Rubbish. It's just a roast with some fancy bits.'

'Rubbish yourself. It's a Herculean labour. Can't imagine I'll ever be able to pull it off . . .'

'Course you will. When you have to.' Gigi curled up in the opposite corner. 'You've got your hands full, anyhow, just feeding this one right now.'

Emily's fingers played in the morning quiff of Ava's baby hair. 'One very greedy one.'

'What about the expressing?' There'd been some talk, the last time she'd seen Emily, of what Emily had called 'the milking machine'. Evidently Emily's mum was of the opinion that Emily should be expressing milk now, so that Christopher could do his fair share of night and early-morning feeds.

Emily turned her nose up disdainfully. 'Hated that machine. Never felt more of an Ermintrude. You should see what it does to a nipple, G.' She held her thumb and forefinger wide apart.

Gigi grimaced and folded her arms protectively over her own chest.

'Besides, truthfully, I don't mind this bit. The night feeds. And the early ones. Actually, it's rather lovely. Peaceful. Just me and her.'

'And me.'

Emily blew her a kiss. 'And Granny.'

'I shouldn't bother with the bottles, then. If it's easy and you don't mind . . .'

'I suppose I'm being a bit selfish. Chris might like it just as much as me.'

Gigi didn't suppose so. 'Who has the stitches and the dodgy pelvic floor, though?'

Emily laughed. 'Quite right. Screw Daddy, hey, Ava?!'

It had been that way from the first time Christopher had brought her home, when she'd bounced into the kitchen, sat down at the table with a mug of tea and made them all feel like she'd been there forever. She'd never made Gigi feel like the mother-in-law. She'd never staged the silent war the wives and girlfriends of her friends' sons had – those first couple of years where the younger woman had to make it clear to the older woman that they'd been usurped and replaced. Very Animal Kingdom. Gigi was profoundly grateful for that: she'd never wanted the war. In some ways it had been a relief to hand Christopher over. Emily could never have what she had had of Chris, and the same was true of what Emily had of her son now, and it was all absolutely as it should be.

If she was completely honest, though, it wasn't true in the same way about Oliver. You loved your children equal amounts in vastly different ways. Christopher, Oliver, Megan – they were all so very distinct, and so was the way she felt about them.

Emily's voice was low and conspiratorial now. 'So . . . what do you make of Caitlin and the very big announcement?'

Gigi shuffled a little closer, although she thought it was unlikely that either Olly or Caitlin were the 6 a.m. sort, earwigging in the hall.

'Bloody hell . . .'

It was the most cogent thought she could offer this early and this soon.

'I know, right?' Emily was delighted. 'Chris and I couldn't stop talking about it when we went to bed.'

Gigi felt a stab of envy. Richard had barely said a word

about it or anything else when they went to bed. Their bedroom had become something of a Trappist Monk's affair of late. He'd mumbled something about a good day, and Olly being a piece of work, patted her hand by silent way of thanks for it all, and been asleep before she'd taken off her mascara.

'What did Chris say?'

'He said it was bloody typical Olly.'

'I suppose he's half right. Though even for Olly it was a bit of a –'

'But what about her?'

'Letting him?' Gigi could hear the incredulity in her own voice.

'Exactly. I mean, wouldn't you want to get to know us a bit first?'

'She didn't really seem that interested in getting to know us.'

Emily nodded in furious agreement. 'What do you reckon? Shy or aloof?'

'Aloof.' That was the truth.

'Oh dear. I think you might be right . . .'

Gigi realized she'd hoped Emily might say 'shy' and make her feel bad for her own answer.

'I mean shy might explain being quiet and not eating properly and all that Princess Di fringe-gazing, but it doesn't really explain not doing the dishes or even offering to do them, or choosing to go for a walk when we're all about to play Balderdash, or going to bed from a position of wakefulness. Everyone knows the Christmas rule is that you fall asleep sprawled on the sofa during the Bond film under a blanket of sweet wrappers, and *then* you go to bed when you wake yourself up with your own snoring . . .'

'Prosecution rests, milord.' Gigi winked.

'Oh God, I'm being a bitch, aren't I?' Emily gazed down at Ava's downy head. 'I'll turn my milk sour and give Ava the squits.'

Gigi laughed. 'You've just said all the things I thought.'

Emily sat Ava up on her lap, leant forward into an open hand in a position so utterly familiar and dear to Gigi that she thought she might just spontaneously lactate, and began to rub and pat her back to elicit the magical burp.

'We'll have to drag her out of her shell, though, won't we? If she's a Gilbert-in-waiting? I want a sister-in-law I can hang out with –'

Ava burped, far more loudly than someone so small ought to be able to.

'Clever girl!' both women said simultaneously, in their baby voices, as though the involuntary digestive response was Mensa-worthy.

Emily handed the lollopy bundle that was milk-drunk Ava to Gigi while she refastened her nightclothes. Gigi put the baby high on one shoulder and inhaled deeply from the crease in her neck.

The long driveway of Clearview House was flanked by trees, like one of those long avenues in France – the trees Napoleon planted to give his troops shade, many years before they'd needed it. Now that was what you called planning ahead . . . So named because of its position on top of a hill, the building possessed a view that was indeed clear and rather lovely. You could see for miles on a good day, which this was not. The house was big, and beautiful. Palladian? Was that the word? Gigi wasn't up on her architecture, but it was grand. First pages of *Country Life* grand. You could almost imagine you were a house guest at a glamorous shooting party or something, where Anthony Hopkins was the butler, as you drove up. If you ignored the ambulance and the municipal-style signage to the visitors' car park tucked around at the side. And, once inside, the faint and universal institution smell was hardly *Downton Abbey*. Faint but omnipresent.

The reception area was optimistically dressed with a lit Christmas tree and a pile of obviously fake presents. Someone had evidently brought in homemade mince pies – an unlidded tin sat on the coffee table with last year's magazines. The receptionist greeted them warmly, relentlessly cheerful as always.

'Merry Christmas, Mr and Mrs Gilbert. Did you have a good one?'

'Great thanks,' Richard answered. 'You?'

She smiled. 'I was here. I'm not off until tomorrow. We'll have our dinner then. Me and the kids.'

He nodded. Gigi smiled back. 'Someone else cooking, I hope, if it's your day off?'

'Ha, ha. I wish!' She pushed the buzzer that admitted them to the inner hall. 'Mr Gilbert Senior is in the day room, I think.'

The dreaded day room. Richard called it God's waiting room. To its face, working on the principle that no one sitting in it really heard you. His father had been in the nursing home for five years. Richard still wasn't comfortable here; it was painfully obvious. Gigi didn't feel that way. It always took her aback, just for a moment, to see her beloved father-in-law as he was now – he loomed so large in her memories as a different person. But she liked it here. They were kind, and it was calm and peaceful most of the time. Easily the nicest of all the places they'd visited.

Progressively managed, with compassionate and committed staff.

She had a very definite memory of how James had been. Tall and upright. Proud and strong. Funny and warm. Twinkly. That was a good word. And now he was here, and, most of the time, he was the exact opposite of all those words, and most of the others you might have used to describe him thirty years ago.

Richard's mother, Mary, had died not long after Richard and Gigi had met, and after thirty-five years of marriage. Gigi never met her. She and Richard weren't serious, not at first, and Mary was already ill, so there'd never been a good time to introduce them. Richard hadn't taken her to the funeral either, although she would have gone if he had asked. She hadn't even met James until a couple of months after that. Theirs had been an almost immediate connection. The first time they'd met – over a Cheddar ploughman's in the pub – they'd found acres of common ground – left-of-centre politics, a deep and abiding loathing of Paul McCartney's Wings, the ability to perform the Dead Parrot sketch with one hundred per cent accuracy, and a vague daydream of driving around New Zealand in a campervan one day. They laughed at the same daft things. Often things Richard didn't find funny – although, of course, she'd been so in love with him at that point that she hadn't noticed, or maybe she had noticed and just hadn't minded. She'd wished she'd known James earlier – while he was losing Mary, and afterwards. She always knew she would have helped.

For the first ten years after his wife's death, James, proud, sad and determined not to be a burden (his word, not theirs), had rattled around in the large Arts and Crafts house the two of them had shared, surrounded by the memories he'd held so dear, and which had, in fact, imprisoned him in his grief and in the past. James lived more than three hours by car from where Richard and Gigi had set up home, so elaborate plans and arrangements had to be made to see him. Her own parents were much closer, and it showed in the relationship. Retirement hit James at the same time as bereavement, in a perfect storm of the unfamiliar and frightening, and it took him out at the knees. He'd commuted to work in London all their married life, leaving before seven in the morning and returning in darkness. His friends had been the husbands of her friends, and, without the glue of his wife, his life simply and quietly came apart. There was no shape to it. The garden, given over almost entirely to grass when Richard had been a boy and trained into something altogether lovelier by Mary over the years, became painfully immaculate because it was essentially all he had to do. The precisely trimmed hedges and perfectly pruned rose bushes made Gigi profoundly sad.

In the early 1990s, after a health scare – an angina attack in the garden, not serious but tremendously helpful at the time – he'd finally been persuaded to sell that house and move into a smaller home much nearer to Richard and Gigi, in a village with a proper sense of community. It was where Gigi's own mother and father lived. The new home, along with the will and the connections of his in-laws, had given him something of a second wind, and he'd had probably fifteen good years there – playing bowls with Gigi's father, Harry, pottering in his small garden, and being genuinely helpful and useful to Gigi, who had come to adore him. She was back at her work as a midwife, and the boys were like puppies, and there was suddenly, magically, a job for him to do. Chris and Olly had worshipped him. When Richard was time-poor, focused on work and paying the mortgage, and not, anyway, a father of the wrestling and building variety, their grandad had all the time in the world for them. He picked them up from school and walked them home the long way, through the woods, taught them how to fish and tie knots, and read everything Tolkien ever wrote to them. He'd been wary of Megan at first – unsure of how to be with a little girl – but she'd enchanted him, and he'd done serious time at her fairy tea parties at the end of his garden, sipping water from a miniature cup and making small talk with dollies. The garden was pleasingly haphazard, and even a little overgrown, and Gigi loved each weed that sprouted while he was busy being Grandad.

Gigi's dad had died in 1998, the same year Megan was born – and after that her mother, Violet, and James had become a bit of a double act, tackling the supermarket together and going to matinee shows at the cinema in the afternoon, 'when the stench of nachos isn't so strong'. There was no romance – neither of them had had the remotest interest in that sort of connection, both treasuring memories of a beloved spouse – but they had been wonderful companions for each other.

And then, around the time Megan turned four, something had started to eat away at the edges of James's brain, even as his age made him frailer and weaker – almost suddenly. Gigi had made excuses and allowances for his memory lapses and conspired with Violet and the kids to hide his forgetfulness from Richard, for all their sakes, but when he brought Megan home from a walk in the park and left her outside in the buggy in the driving rain because he'd forgotten that she was in there, even she had been forced to confront the reality of the situation. Once she'd accepted it, it seemed to speed up. The man she'd known was disintegrating, from the outside in, and from the inside out. For another few years, they'd struggled on, maintaining a patchwork of care between themselves and the NHS, and then, eventually, private home nurses. But it wasn't fair, on any of them. Violet said it was almost like being widowed twice.

And so he'd come here five years ago. It was what he'd needed – the right thing. Richard had power of attorney by then, and he had insisted, and James was his father, after all. He'd argued that the toll on Gigi was too great. But she'd always felt like that was an excuse – and she'd always resented him just a little bit for it, even though she grudgingly admitted how hard it had become. He needed pretty constant care, proper medical attention – a holistic approach to looking after him. It was the right thing to do. Gigi knew it. But she'd hated it. More even than Richard, she thought. They'd found the very best place they could. The nurses were committed and kind, and they treated the residents as people, not inmates. But she still hated it. His lucidity came and went, but he'd been particularly with it the day they'd first left him there, and his face as they'd gone – betrayed and frightened – had haunted Gigi ever since.

Clearview was ferociously expensive – almost the dearest place they'd looked at. James had insured against his need for social care and released capital from the sale of the home he'd shared with Richard's mother, when he'd downsized. So his bills were covered. Gigi had friends facing far harder decisions. She knew people who'd had to make heart-breaking choices and compromises because they simply couldn't afford places like this. She never stopped being grateful that she and Richard didn't have to, and it made her cross that Richard still pulled a face about coming here to visit his dad. She wondered what would happen by the time they needed the same type of care. Generations like James's had wanted to leave something behind for their children. Generations like hers probably stood no chance. It was often the thought of that, and not this place itself, that made her sad. James was safe and cared for, and he would be until he died. And that made him lucky, even in the misfortune of his illness.

And now he was the last man standing, after Violet died in her bed, of an unheralded and catastrophic stroke, two years earlier. Gigi's sense that he was the last link with their pasts made him seem even more precious. Placing a new-born Ava on his lap a few months ago – the first great-grandchild – had been so very poignant for her. He hadn't a clue who the baby was, but he'd held her carefully and stroked her smooth pink cheek with his gnarled finger, murmuring gently that she was beautiful, exactly the way he had done with Megan years before.

Gigi had spent her working life in hospitals. But she worked at the other end. The good end – the happiest moment. Midwifery was ninety-nine per cent of the time about the beginning of life, full of promise and excitement and the future. This half-alive, half-dead state sometimes freaked her out. It was just so damn sad, the idea that, after everything, at the end, this was what there was . . .

'How are you, Dad?' Richard had a special tone he used for James now. Like a vicar, Gigi always thought. A vicar talking to Sunday school. It jarred with her, and, she suspected, with his father, even if through the fog.

James looked up from the television, where the cast of *EastEnders* appeared to be celebrating Christmas with their customary *joie de vivre* and love for all mankind. A younger, healthier James would have left the room, shaking his head in disdain, if such a programme had been on. His head sat pushed forward on his neck now, his shoulders hunched like a vulture. He was thinner these days, so his older sweaters – like the navy zipped cardigan he was wearing today – hung shapelessly off him. He'd always been so tanned from the gardening, stark lines on his muscled upper arms and thick thighs from shorts and t-shirts. Now his skin had the thin, parchment quality of elderly people who spent most of their time inside. His eyes were watery and red. And today, she realized, completely empty.

Upstairs, in his room, there was a large corkboard, on which were pinned photographs: pictures of James and Mary, one from their wedding, and through their decades together. Of Richard and Gigi, and the children – all labelled with their names. There was a new, arty, black-and-white shot of Ava, taken the day she came home from hospital, the camera up very close to her precious face, all bush-baby eyes and flattened new-born nose. YOUR FIRST GREAT-GRANDCHILD, AVA MARY! Gigi had written beside it.

Some days, James did a passable impression of the man he'd once been. You could have a conversation with him, do a few clues in the crossword. Some days, much rarer ones, thank God, he was visibly distressed, stuck in a period of time you might not understand, asking for his own mother or begging to go home. He would cry. He was never in the day room on those days. Distress could be contagious.

Some days, he was just vacant, like he'd been emptied out. Today was clearly one of those days.

'Who are you?' he asked, politely curious.

Gigi pulled a footstool nearer to James and sat down on it, taking his hands in her own. 'It's us, James. Richard and Grace.' Everyone in the world but him called her Gigi, and they had for as long as she could remember. He never once had. Grace was such a beautiful name, he had said, right from the start. The name her parents had chosen for her. And the name he would use. And he always had. She was better at the voice, she knew. Years of practice, pitching her tone right with labouring women. That bit, at least, was not so very different. James nodded ponderously, as if he knew, but that was just a reflex. Three minutes later, he might well ask again.

For a long time, too long, Richard had persisted in painstaking explanation. Who he was, why his father was here, how long his mother had been dead. James might grasp the news for just a moment, his face crumpling in tears and shock. Then forget. Then ask again. Maybe it was easier for Gigi to give up on that lucidity because James wasn't her father. Maybe it was just how the two of them were. Eventually she'd persuaded Richard to stop endlessly going through it. It broke James's heart each time, she told him. Why would you do that? They would visit and sometimes he would know them and sometimes he wouldn't, and, either way, he would most often accept the visit happily enough, and sometimes make small talk and let them sit with him while he watched television. When they left, he never once turned his head to watch them go.

Richard read the newspaper now. He might point out the odd story, fish for an opinion on something – but really he was hiding behind the broadsheet because it was too hard. It wasn't as hard for Gigi. She'd never needed much of a reply in order to keep chatting. Hell, she quite often talked to herself while she did housework. This wasn't so different.

And she'd noticed, this last while, that Richard was more affectionate with her after they'd visited James. 'You're brilliant with him,' he'd say, admiringly. Sometimes, he'd just hug her, or spontaneously take her hand as they walked back to the car. It definitely wasn't why Gigi kept on coming. She came because she loved James and she wanted to see him and because it was the right thing to do. But it was a nice perk. She never told anyone. How to say that visiting the dementia ward of the old people's home was a kind of romantic foreplay? Something got lost in translation.

They went to the pub on the way home. Em and Chris had taken Ava visiting, and Megan was in a different pub, so there was nothing to rush home for, except a fridge full of leftovers to conjure into something for supper later. She'd suggested it. He never would have done. But he acquiesced easily enough.

'Is he getting worse, do you think?'

Gigi shrugged. Richard was obsessed with gauging his father's state. He said this every time. 'I think he's getting worse.' He confirmed his own suspicions, without Gigi having to offer an opinion.

'Poor bugger.' He shook his head. But this conversation was depressingly familiar, and Gigi wanted to talk about the fully living. She swept imaginary dust off the round oak table, then tapped the surface gently once to bring the meeting to order.

'So . . . are we going to talk about Olly and his bomb-shell?'

'Bombshell? Was she *that* good-looking?'

'Hilarious. You know what I mean. Be serious, will you? The m-bombshell. Marriage. What d'you think?'

Richard took a long swallow from his pint, and then shrugged. 'I don't think it'll happen.'

'They seemed pretty sure.'

'Olly was pretty sure he was going to be an architect.'

'Oh, come on. That's different, And that was years ago. Not the same thing at all . . .'

'But I think it *is* the same thing. Olly's all about the great idea. Not the follow-through.' Richard was always a bit hard on their middle child. Gigi always compensated. That was the muscle memory of their parenting.

'What about Caitlin? They're a couple. It isn't all Olly . . .'

Richard shrugged. 'I didn't really talk to her much, one to one.'

'She didn't really talk to any of us.' That was her point. This conversation was like playing tennis with someone whose returns always hit the net.

'True.' Gigi waited for him to say more, getting quietly infuriated when he didn't.

'That's kind of the whole point. Do you remember when Emily first came home with Christopher?'

'Not really.' Richard looked sheepish.

'You do. She was warm and friendly and she fitted in immediately. I knew, straightaway, that she was right for Chris.'

'They were very young . . .'

'I still knew.'

'And you're saying you don't know about this girl?'

'That's exactly what I'm saying . . . I mean, I didn't expect to right away. We were lucky with Chris. I know that. But something. Something.'

'They seemed happy together.'

'Did they?'

Richard smiled indulgently, which was irritating. 'You don't think, my darling, that this is a bit more about you?'

Richard always looked pleased with himself when he said things like this – like he'd figured out something clever. Clever, insightful, emotionally continent Richard. She'd like to punch him in the face. The frustration of being misunderstood washed over her.

'What do you mean?' She knew her tone had changed. It was too subtle for him to hear, because for that he'd have to have been properly listening. But she heard it.

'You've always been different about Olly.'

She didn't want to admit that he was right. She sighed and picked up her drink, letting her eye wander to the dancing flames of the fire in the grate.

Sometimes, these days, Gigi felt like she and Richard were two complete strangers on a blind date in the Tower of Babel.

Tess

Tess felt like she and Sean were playing themselves through the rest of Christmas. As if an invisible director with a script – not one written by her – was whispering instructions in their ears. Something had shifted, when he'd proposed and she'd blurted out her counter offer of parenthood – she couldn't define exactly what, except that it made everything feel pretend. He'd pulled her into an instant embrace, but she'd had the very odd feeling that it was like a soap opera hug, where the camera settled on the hidden face of the hugger, which conveyed their full spectrum of emotions, and the hug-ee saw none of it. He hadn't repeated his proposal, and the offer, not repeated or retracted, hung like smog in the flat. He'd said it was amazing – shaking his head – but he hadn't said it was wonderful. He hadn't said any of the things he'd have said if she *had* written the script – there was no stroking of her still-flat stomach, no singing 'My Boy Bill' in the shower. When he'd popped round to Sainsbury's, he hadn't come back with flowers. He hadn't even told her not to lift anything heavy.

But he hadn't rejected her either. He hadn't said he didn't want a baby.

She willed herself not to push. It was a lot. She'd had the time to get used to it, and she knew even she wouldn't have been able to articulate, at first, everything she felt. It wasn't like this baby had been planned and longed for. Babies had been at the very edge of her imagining of her life. Something vague and abstract for the future. Falling pregnant had been what made her want to be a mother – the ambition was very wrapped up with this particular child for her. It hadn't done that for him. That much was clear. She forced herself to wait for him to speak first. He'd given her that chance for New York: she owed it to him.

It was strangely easy to avoid the subject between Christmas and New Year. She knew that that in itself was very wrong. There were drinks parties and dinners with friends, where by mutual agreement neither marriage nor children were discussed, and where gaiety – albeit other people's – just carried them along. Everything was fairy lights and bonhomie, and you could hide yourself in it. And there were her quiet, sad visits to Iris. Donna sent a quick text or two – she'd arrived safely . . . a picture of the beach . . . Sean worked on the 28th, 29th and 30th, staying late at the office on the pretext of catching up on paperwork. When he got home, he feigned tiredness, claiming exhaustion every evening as a preamble to an early night, or, worse, letting himself fall asleep on the sofa in front of television shows he wasn't watching, so that she was in bed asleep before he got there. Once there, he didn't try to kiss her deeply, offering instead a peck on the cheek and turning his back to read or endlessly check his phone.

By New Year's Eve, Tess was ready to explode. Five days. Five long days when they hadn't properly talked about any of it. They were supposed to be meeting some old university mates of Sean's in a West End hotel for New Year's Eve. It was a big black-tie do, with a three-course meal, a band and dancing. Normally, she'd have been excited, but she couldn't summon up any enthusiasm. Sean

84

spent the afternoon with his friend Tim, over from Dublin for the party. Tess went to visit Iris.

She told her about the baby. She had to tell someone.

Iris was awake, sitting up in bed. She looked much better. When Tess approached the bed, she smiled vaguely at her. No recognition, but no distress either. Tess had taken flowers – some vibrant orange ranunculi.

'Aren't they beautiful,' Iris had exclaimed. 'Ranunculi. I always loved those. How did you know, dear?'

I know because I've always known, Tess thought sadly. They're my favourites too, because they remind me of you. You always said they were one of the only flowers that got more beautiful as they got older in the vase, not fading or dropping their petals. You joked that was how you wanted to age. You used to buy them pretty much whenever you saw them, and they always made you disproportionately happy. I know like I know you like Garibaldi biscuits, not Rich Tea, and Earl Grey, not English Breakfast. And like you used to know I preferred strawberry sherbets to lemon ones, and would eat a bagful, even though I'd get those slightly sore ridges on the roof of my mouth from eating too many at once.

'I've got some exciting news,' she offered, leaning over, speaking in a whisper, close to Iris's ear.

Iris didn't react.

Tess sat on the chair next to the bed.

'I'm pregnant, Gran. I'm going to have a baby.'

'Baby?' She said the word vaguely, as though it was foreign, and unfamiliar.

'Yes. A baby. I'm pregnant, Gran. The baby is coming in the summer.'

Iris stared at her. And it would be hard to describe to anyone else, but it was as though the clouds parted, and the

85

sun suddenly shone through on her grandmother's face. For the first time in ages, she said her name. 'Tess! My goodness. A baby? You?' Her voice was full of emotion. 'My darling girl. That is so wonderful.' She reached her arms out and Tess stood and bent into her embrace. There was normally no strength in Iris's arms but now she clung to Tess's neck. When Tess straightened up and pulled back to watch her grandmother's face, Iris dropped one of her arms to touch Tess's stomach. 'It'll be a beauty, Tess. Boy or girl. You were the most astonishing child. Those enormous eyes. And so much hair. We had to brush it off your forehead, right from the start.' She lifted her hand and pushed Tess's fringe back from her eyes, staring straight into them. She was completely lucid. As if the import of Tess's news had dragged her back. Tess wanted to stay that way forever, with Iris's hands on her.

The moment passed. Clouds blew back across the sun. 'That's nice, dear. Babies are very happy news.' She patted Tess's hand gently, but anonymously, as though she was someone she was sitting next to on the Number 9 bus. 'That's nice.'

Tess's eyes filled with grateful tears. 'It is nice. It's very, very nice.' But the sun had gone down. Tess stopped being Tess. Iris stopped being Iris. But Tess had had the moment, and it mattered more than anything else.

At home, later, Tess stood for ages in front of her dressing-table mirror, sideways, staring at herself. Thinking. Sean wasn't back until 6 p.m. – they were due to leave at 7 p.m. Tess was in the bedroom when she heard his key in the lock.

'Sorry. We went to the driving range to hit a few balls. Traffic was monstrous on the way back. I had to drop Tim at his hotel – he didn't have his gear with him . . . Better jump in the shower . . .'

He came into the bedroom. Tess was sitting, dressed in jeans and a sweater, in the armchair in the corner.

'You're not dressed.'

'I'm not going.'

'What's wrong?'

'How can you ask me that, Sean?'

He sat on the edge of the bed nearest to her.

'Come on. I thought we'd agreed we'd sit with this a while . . .'

'Do you have any idea how strange that sounds?' Her voice sounded flat and dull to her. She was exhausted by the charade.

'To whom?'

'To me. It's ridiculous. You have to talk to me –'

'Everyone's expecting us.'

'I don't give a fuck.' Now she was finding some energy, some fight. She hardly ever swore. Iris hated it when women swore. She hated that word almost worst of all. But it fitted the mood. 'I can't sit there for another night and not know what you feel, Sean. I won't do it.'

He rubbed his face, exasperated.

'You want to know what I feel?'

'Yes. Yes. Of course I do.'

Sean took a deep breath, and ran both hands through his hair, rubbing his head too hard.

'Okay. I feel like the timing is all wrong for us.'

Tess felt like he'd winded her. 'The timing?'

'Yes.' Another deep breath. 'I don't think it's the right time for us to have a baby.'

She could barely breathe.

'I love you. I want to make a life with you. Right now I want that life to be in New York. I want to enjoy you, enjoy us.'

'And you don't want a baby.'

Sean shook his head, sat back, deflated, against the bed. 'Not this baby. Not now. I'm sorry. That's how I feel.'

For a long moment she didn't look at him, and neither of them spoke. She could hear her own breathing, weirdly loud in the room.

She turned to him: he was looking at her intently, wild-eyed. He knelt up, came close to the chair.

'Say something, Tess.'

She held her hands up, incredulous, feeling herself shrinking from him into the back of the chair. 'I don't know what to say. You've shocked me. You've completely and utterly shocked me.'

But he hadn't. Not really. His silence across the last week had been almost as eloquent, almost as blunt, as what he'd just said. What was shocking was hearing it out loud. What was shocking was realizing he was prepared to say it.

'See? That's why I didn't want to talk about it. It's not an easy thing to say to you. To explain.'

'Seemed easy enough, in the end.' She was trying to keep her voice moderate.

'That's not fair.'

She threw him a warning glance. 'We're talking about fair now?'

'That's not what I mean, and you know it.'

'So that's how you've felt from the very beginning?'

'No.'

'You've just been trying to figure out how to break it to me?'

'No. Not like that.'

'Trying to time it right.' She could hear the heavy sarcasm in her voice over the word *time*.

'No. I don't know. I didn't mean that. It was a shock. We were taking precautions . . .' The phrase was awkwardly formal.

'They don't always work.'

'I know. I'm not accusing you of anything.'

She gave a hollow laugh. 'That's something.'

'Tess, don't be like that. Listen to me. We have years and years. We can have a ton of babies. As many as you like.'

'But not this baby?

'Can you just take a moment, and think about what I'm saying? Would it be so terrible, to wait?'

'Do you know what you're saying?'

'Yes. Of course I do. I'm not an idiot.' He looked at the carpet.

'What you're asking me to do?'

'How pregnant are you? It's a few weeks, isn't it?' He'd put his hand on her knee. The inference was obvious, and monstrous.

'You bastard.' She shoved it roughly away and stood up.

'Tess . . .'

She'd never slapped a person before, but she slapped Sean now, with the full force of her rage.

'Do you know, Sean, I wasn't sure how I felt about it either. Not at first. I was just as shocked as you. Just as scared. But I never' – she put her face close to his – 'I never once thought of getting rid of it. Never.'

Sean rubbed his cheek, swinging his jaw from side to side. She'd hit him hard.

'It's a baby. It's our baby.' She corrected herself. 'It's my baby.'

He reached for her again, but she couldn't let him touch her.

'You can't possibly love me and ask me to do this.'

'So how come I do, then?' His voice was almost surprised, wistful.

'And how can I possibly love you?'

'Don't you?' And now wheedling. The whiff of manipulation prompted another surge of rage in Tess.

He touched her arm. 'Get off me. I can't be near you. Just go.'

Sean took two, three steps back from her.

'Don't do this to us.' Sean's eyes were full of frightened tears now. 'Please, Tess.'

She sank on to the bed. He stood in front of her.

'Who's doing it, Sean?'

'I'm sorry.' He sounded like a boy. Imploring.

'Me too.'

He left her there after a minute of silence. Through the open door she could hear him in the kitchen. The kettle boiled; cupboards were opened and closed. She couldn't move from the edge of the bed. Eventually he reappeared and gently put down a mug of tea by the side of the bed where she was sitting. She couldn't look at him. Something had changed, and she knew it couldn't be changed back. Whatever happened now. Whether she understood, whether she forgave, whatever he did or said.

'Can we get past this?'

'I don't see how.'

'I can try . . .' She raised her hand to stop him from speaking. They were both crying now.

'It won't work. It's too late. This . . . this will always have happened. You will always have said that. If we go ahead, if we have this baby, how am I supposed to forget that you once said you didn't want it? How would it work?'

'I'd get used to it?'

'It doesn't work that way, Sean, I don't think.' She sniffed. 'And if I don't have this baby, how am I supposed to ever, ever forgive you?'

Week 9. I will never tell you why, baby mine – never. What he said, what he wanted. But now I know and now I am sure. He triggered something in me, something I wasn't sure was there. I'm a bear. A mother bear. And I will tell you right now: I will love you more than anything in the entire world. I already love you with a love that is stronger, and fiercer, than I believed myself capable of, or than I have ever come close to feeling before. And it will be enough.

Gigi

It was odd to realize the lengths to which you could go to disguise or deny or ignore your unhappiness, and odder still the moments which stripped that away and forced you to confront it. Mostly it was other people who held up a mirror you had to stare at. Or tiny moments.

Most of the time Gigi was fine. 'Fine.' The answer she always gave to the question of how she was. And most of the time it was true. She went to work, and helped people, and ate biscuits and joked with her colleagues, who were friends too after all these years, and moaned about management, and she came home again. She checked in with her kids by email or text, more rarely by phone. She flicked through the Sunday papers and wondered if she was a cruising type of person, and, if she was, would she choose Norwegian fjords or the exotic East. She watched television, and listened to the radio, and formed opinions about the news, and read her book-club selection religiously before the monthly meeting at The White Horse with her colleagues from the maternity ward. She kept house and baked and took the car to the car wash. Weighed herself periodically and made promises to eat less and move more, and bought things on sale that were just a bit too small, because she intended to slim into them. Held dinner parties, and from time to time went to the posh makeup counter in the department store and asked them to update her look with a new lipstick or attempt to preserve her youth with an expensive eye cream. Gave money to good causes. Visited her father-in-law and sat with him, trying to get the *Pointless* answer on tea-time television. Tried to see the films nominated for Oscars so she could say, when the time came, whether she agreed that the winners were deserving. She was funny, and warm, more a listener than a talker, and far, far too proud to let anyone see that anything was wrong.

Most of the time, she looked at Richard and willed herself to remember all the good things about him. Not to resent washing his socks, or his falling asleep in front of any television programme that started after 9 p.m. Or that he didn't talk to her any more – always the crossword at breakfast, the news at supper. She flicked through her memories of better times. He was a good man. A kind man. He didn't shout, he hadn't a violent bone in his body, he never had a go at her if she bought a new dress, he didn't go on at her to lose weight. He'd fathered her children, and the two of them had provided for their family.

She tried. And still . . .

Watching a mother answer a dozen questions her son asked her in the supermarket, helpless against the irresistible pester power of the toddler in the trolley – the absolute fondness with which she talked to the child, the tenderness . . . could make Gigi cry in the aisle, where five minutes earlier she'd been busy with a list, trying to remember whether she needed washing powder or icing sugar.

A husband in front of her in a queue could put his hand on the small of his wife's back, and stroke her, lean in to whisper something in her ear, and the possessive, intimate gesture could make Gigi ache.

And sometimes, at 3 a.m., as Richard slept soundly beside her, she could feel complete despair and utter loneliness, even as she tried to count her blessings instead of sheep, and be gripped by the terrible fear that her life might always be just like this – like the best bits of it were all far behind her, and what was left was a slow decline to a state like James's with only moments of joy, and all of those vicarious.

She had tried, really tried, to talk to Richard. Much more than once. But he wouldn't meet her in the middle. He waved away her concerns with rhetorical questions – we're okay, aren't we – we're so lucky, aren't we? He had a way of making her doubt the seriousness of her issues, blame tiredness or menopause or empty-nest syndrome, and by the time she realized it was a confidence trick, the moment had passed, blown away by Richard's bluster. And she went back to ignoring it.

But somewhere in the back of her soul, she knew that whatever Richard said, and however often he said it, this feeling was relentless and, eventually, it would not be ignored. It was like watching the tide go out on a beach. Gradually, bit by bit, and oh so slowly, the waves receded. Whether you wanted them to or not.

Tess

January

By mid-January, Iris was physically well enough to be discharged and Tess couldn't procrastinate any longer about deciding where she should go. There was a space at Clearview. There wasn't always. Someone had had to die to free up that place. The woman who phoned was gentle but firm. She needed an answer about Iris. Tess said yes, please, she'd take it, pending a visit, which was hastily arranged. She'd burst into tears when she put the phone down. She felt utterly overwhelmed. Nothing in her life was as she thought it would be. She needed to move out of Sean's flat. He'd left, that night, eventually – that dreadful New Year's Eve, when it had become clear to him that no amount of tea or apology or explanation was going to lead to resolution. He stayed with friends, she presumed, although she hadn't asked.

She'd gone to bed, fully clothed, and cried herself through to midnight.

In the days that followed, they'd avoided seeing each other. She knew he'd been to the flat – presumably to pick up clothes and his post – but he'd done it while she was at work, where she'd been going through the motions, preoccupied horribly by what was happening. After a week of this weird, unnatural way of living, he'd come to see her,

95

texting to ask if he could and ringing the doorbell of his own flat.

Sean had looked drained and tired when she'd opened the door: there were dark circles under his eyes that hadn't been there before. She felt a rush of pity for him. He'd made the storm that had engulfed them, but now he looked so pathetic, shivering in the rain.

'What's happening?' His arms were out, his palms upturned. He looked vulnerable, pleading.

She made her voice sound stronger than she felt.

'Well, it's over. I'll move out. As soon as I can get myself sorted.'

'I don't mean . . . I don't need . . . I don't want you to go.'

'But I have to. We can't carry on living together. We're clearly going in very different directions.'

'This is madness. How did we get here?'

Tess felt herself harden against him. 'You know how.'

Sean shook his head in an almost violent gesture, and raised his hand like a stop signal.

'I want you to forget what I said. I'm sorry. I was wrong. I can't lose you, Tess.'

As she answered, she knew she meant what she said. 'You already have.'

'I don't believe that.' Still the head shake. Denial.

Now she resented having to explain it to him.

'You can't just put it all away, Sean. It doesn't work like that. You did say it. I can't forget it. This has to be it. It has to be over. You'll end up hating me in the end. Or I'll hate you.'

'I couldn't hate you.'

'You'd be surprised.'

'I'm sorry. I'm so, so sorry.'

She didn't doubt it. He looked close to tears.

Perhaps he interpreted her silence as weakening. He reached out to touch her hand. 'I can make you forgive me.'

It was a bad choice of words, although he wasn't to know it. It was Donna's phrase. *Forgive me.* She pulled her hand out of his and folded her arms protectively across herself. It was Tess's turn to shake her head.

'Maybe I could. But I couldn't forget.' She looked at the floor.

For a moment they both stood in silence. Then Sean sniffed hard, rubbing his hand under his nose. His voice was quieter when he spoke again.

'They've asked me to go to New York, for two or three weeks.'

'When?'

'I'm leaving the day after tomorrow.'

She nodded. 'It's what you wanted.'

'I wanted it with you.'

But just with me, she thought.

'You wanted it for you, Sean.'

'You make me sound like such a prick.'

She didn't mean to. She was trying to be honest. But she daren't back-track on anything now.

'I'll be gone by the time you come back.'

'Where will you go?'

'I'm going to ask my mother if I can stay at hers for a while.'

'Christ, Tess. You and your mum?'

'She'll probably be away. She most often is.'

'Still . . .' Sean knew what her relationship with Donna was like. But she couldn't let him in.

She put her hand up to stop him. 'It's only temporary.

I'll find something else. Besides, it's not really your problem. Not any more.'

She knew she sounded brittle, and harsh. It was the only way she could do it. She was holding it all together, hanging on by a thread. If she let him be kind, if she leant on him in any way at all, she might shatter.

'It'll be my baby too.'

'Don't you dare.'

But she knew he was right. He turned and walked away.

Tess made herself focus on Iris. With Sean in New York for a few weeks, she needn't ask Donna right away. That would take a bit of working up to. She'd need to tell her about the baby: nothing else but that truth would make sense to Donna. She'd sent her an email asking when she was home, but she hadn't heard yet. That wasn't unusual. Donna usually checked emails only when she was near an internet café.

What mattered first was getting Iris settled. Tess, and the baby – they could wait. She booked an appointment with her GP, which was in ten days' time. She wouldn't think too much about it until then. She had the appointment at Clearview to get through first. One thing at a time. If she could just take things one thing at a time.

It was a particularly horrid day, grey and cold and drizzly, but that seemed appropriate. If Clearview looked okay on a day like this, it would look more than okay when the sun shone. And the brochure hadn't lied. The long driveway swept around towards the house, perched high. Tess parked up around the back, and walked to the front entrance. The manager, Claire, gave her the tour. She was a large, smiley woman, with a calm and reassuring way about her. As they walked, she talked enthusiastically about the facilities, and respectfully about the residents. She'd had a grandfather with Alzheimer's, she told Tess, who'd died long before this kind of place was available. Her voice broke very briefly when she spoke about him, and she took a deep breath before she carried on speaking. That was why she was so evangelical about matching the right care with the person. Tess completely believed her. If it was a sales pitch, she was buying. But it didn't feel like it was.

Tess knew it was a nice place, as places like this went. As places like this went, it was actually pretty wonderful. It had been described as 'cutting-edge' in an article Tess had read when she was trying to decide where Iris should go, designed after the Dutch model. It specialized in Alzheimer's and dementia patients, so it was custom-built for their needs, rather than adapted to try to meet them. It was avowedly non-medical in feel, the brochure claimed. It was set up more like a village, designed to be familiar and comforting for its residents. As well as en suite rooms for all its residents, set on corridors that had street names like King Street and the Green, rather than numbers and letters, it had a small pub, with a darts board and a wooden bar, a hairdresser's and even a tiny sweet shop, with old-fashioned sweets in big jars. A vast noticeboard in the entrance lobby advertised a huge array of activities – sing-along sessions, games afternoons, movie nights – *Arsenic and Old Lace* was on tonight – next week it was *The Sound of Music*. She wondered if her grandmother would ever be well enough to make the most of any of it.

Iris was ill enough but not too ill to be here. Tess was quickly growing used to the intricate processes and exacting criteria of healthcare for the elderly, the paperwork and the administrative hoops. The bronchitis that had seen her admitted to the geriatric ward of the local hospital had responded well to the antibiotics and that part of Iris was better. Tess had wondered long and hard in the dead of night whether she was glad about this, whether it would've been better for Iris to have died. Whether Iris would want to die, if she really knew what was happening to her. Part of her knew Iris would hate this half-life she was living, but not as much as she hated the burden her living it placed on Tess, the fixer. The larger part of her responded like a child to the illness, became tearful and anxious, and wanted to pray she would recover. In recent times, the scales had tipped slightly, but she had still felt more relief than anything else when the young doctor with the shy smile had said Iris was doing well enough to be moved.

She'd seen several places she couldn't have borne to leave her. But at this place, she thought maybe she could. It was much nearer than the hospital, thank God. She could come and go much more easily, and see more of Iris than she had done when she was in Salisbury. It had a good feel and a warmth – an optimism, almost – that had been missing in other places.

It was terrifyingly expensive, but Tess had been surprised at how much Iris had saved between her husband Wilf's pension and the money they'd invested when he was alive. They'd lived, she realized, more simply than they had ever needed to. Iris's house had to be worth somewhere near half a million, she guessed. It seemed like an enormous amount of money. But this place would cost an enormous amount of money too. It was a hateful sum. But it had to be done. She tried not to think about how families of younger sufferers felt. People who couldn't possibly afford this kind of facility. Imagine having to leave someone you loved somewhere you hated? This was bad enough. They were impossible decisions. At ninety-five, Iris's life really was finite. Ten years seemed impossible – two or three more likely. Possible that she wouldn't live the rest of this one. But if Iris lived to be a hundred, it would cost almost half a million pounds for her to spend those years here. It was an astronomical amount. There'd be nothing left to show for her life, or Wilf's.

Tess knew what Iris would have to say about it. She'd hate it both politically – she was fiercely proud of the NHS and instinctively mistrustful of anything she perceived as threatening it – and she'd hate it personally. 'Christ, darling. That's a lot of holidays . . . Bugger that. I'll take the long walk. Pass me the paracetamol and the whisky. Ice flow here I come . . .'

She'd hate it more if she knew about the baby. Iris had that generation's interest in leaving something behind. She'd worry less about Donna, but she'd want to do something for the baby. Tess could hear her on the subject, almost as if she was actually speaking.

But she didn't know about the baby. She didn't know about any of it. She'd forgotten what Tess had told her. She'd probably never really taken it in. And she never would, now. Knowing what Iris would want to happen didn't help Tess.

This was her decision and hers alone, and she was making it in this place. Whatever it cost, Tess was going to pay it. Even if Iris never went to one damn fitness class or listened to one sing-along. She was coming. It was the best that Tess could give her.

Someone appeared in the corridor and told Claire there was a phone call she needed to take. Claire put her hand on Tess's arm and asked if she minded.

'We had to send one of our residents to hospital last night. I've been trying to speak to her son – he's away on holiday.'

'Of course. Please do.'

'Please feel free to have a look in here, rather than coming back to sit in the office. By all means chat to some of the carers. Have a cup of tea . . . I'll be right back.'

Tess helped herself to a cup of tea from the heated jugs on a table by the door. She was pouring milk and stirring the mug when a woman came and stood beside her. She wasn't wearing the pink tunic the staff all seemed to be wearing.

'Hiya.'

'Hi.'

'Are you okay?'

'I'm just . . . I'm waiting for Claire. I'm on a tour.'

The woman looked at her curiously. But the curiosity felt strangely uninvasive, just kind.

So Tess explained. 'My grandmother . . . she might be coming here.'

The stranger nodded understanding, and for a moment busied herself making a coffee.

'Do you have someone here?'

'My father-in-law. He's that one, over there, in the red jumper.' She gestured towards the fireplace, to an old man in a winged-back armchair.

'Do you mind if I ask you, if he's . . . is he happy here?'

'Bless you. There's a question . . .' She smiled ruefully. 'He'd hate knowing that this was how he'd ended up.'

'So would my grandmother.'

'He'd be foaming at the mouth at how much it costs, and I'm pretty sure he'd have topped himself if he'd known.'

Tess laughed with relief. 'I was just thinking the exact same thing about my gran.'

'But that is the only silver lining in the whole bloody awful cloud, isn't it? They don't know . . .'

This was the first conversation Tess had ever had with someone in the same position, she realized.

The other woman was still watching her face intently. 'It's brilliant here, by the way. Do you want to sit down a minute?'

She pointed to a table by the window, and Tess nodded. 'If you've got time.'

The woman looked over at her father-in-law. 'He's nodded off. I like to think it's not my conversation.' She laughed. 'I'm Gigi, by the way.'

'Tess.'

'Nice to meet you, Tess. Are you here on your own?'

'Yeah. My mother couldn't make it today.' She didn't know why she felt she needed to add that – convention, she supposed.

Gigi took a sip of her tea, and a bite of the shortbread biscuit she'd put on her saucer. 'Well . . . the truth is, Tess, I have no clue whether he's happy or not.'

'Is he . . . does he have Alzheimer's?'

Gigi shook her head. 'Dementia. Same difference, really. I'm guessing your grandmother does too?'

'Yes.'

'But *we're* happy with him here. It's an excellent place. Truly. The staff are brilliant. His care is exemplary.'

'How long has he been here?'

'Five years.'

Half a million. Tess couldn't help the thought. It was like Gigi read her mind.

'Yes. National debt of a small Third World country. I know . . .'

'My grandmother's ninety-five.'

Gigi avoided the obvious response – that she was highly unlikely to stay so long.

'I know it's only any good if you have it, I know.'

She doesn't know if I have it or not, Tess realized.

'There are other places . . . are you local?'

It's okay, Tess wanted to tell her. 'She has . . . I mean, we can afford . . .'

Her eyes were suddenly full of tears, and she bit down hard on her lip to stop them. It was something about the way Gigi was looking at her.

'Oh, you poor girl.' Gigi squeezed her arm. Tess had an absurd thought that she wanted Gigi to put her arms around her. That she wanted to tell her about all of it – about her mother, about the baby, about Sean, and his impossible request. This complete stranger who was being kind. But of course she didn't.

'Then do it. You won't have to worry about her. When you can't get here. I mean, you'll always worry, you always do. But you're young. You must have a life . . . You can't spend all your time here. It's worth it to know that when you're not here, your grandmother is being properly cared for. Treated with kindness and respect. Like a person. With dignity. That's priceless . . .'

'You're right.' It was exactly and all she had needed to hear.

'What's her name, your grandmother?'

'Iris. Iris Garroway.'

'What a lovely name. One of my favourite flowers, the iris. Does she have blue eyes?'

Tess nodded. 'Very blue. They were.'

'And where is she now, love?'

'She's been in hospital with a chest infection. She was home before that, in Salisbury, with carers.'

'We tried that. It worked for a while. There just comes a point when it isn't enough, doesn't there?'

Tess nodded. 'And we're there now, I think . . .'

'Then you're doing the right thing. For both of you.'

And from this woman, this complete stranger, with the kind face, Tess took the permission she needed. There was no one else to give it.

Week 10. You're the size of a kumquat, if you please. If I can make it all about me for just a moment, I'm supposed to have skin that is suddenly clearer, and more supple. My hair – which has apparently stopped falling out – is meant to be thicker and more lustrous than before . . . in short, I am meant to be glowing at this point. Perhaps I am a late bloomer, because I don't think any of this stuff is happening.

You, on the other hand, are busy with much more important things. Your angry little fist stumps have emerging fingers and your feet are getting some toes. Five on each foot, I hope. In the pictures online you look all thoughtful, like someone in prayer, your new digits forming a triangle as you put your hands together. Your head is still weird – the back of it runs into your neck like a seal or how John Irving describes the back of Garp's head in a book I read once and never forgot.

The GP was amazed it had taken me so long to come and see her. She said first-time mothers were always in a hurry to get confirmation, get their next appointments booked. I think she was a bit suspicious of me, truthfully. She looked at me hard from behind her glasses like a stern headmistress. Not that any headmistress ever really had to look at me sternly. I was a bit of a goody-two-shoes. Is it wrong that I hope you are just a little bit naughty? Just William-type naughtiness – nothing hardcore. I wonder if I will ever be able to tell you off. Whether I am capable of strictness. Anyhow . . . the doctor certainly was. She had to send off straightaway for the first scan appointment. That's in a fortnight, baby mine. I will get to see you – real, actual you, instead of the pictures of other people's babies I pore over on the internet.

She glossed over the subject of your father. (If only it were that easy.) I swear she glanced at my ring hand. It was all very PC. She referred to my taking a partner or companion for the scan. Emphasis on not going alone. I've watched enough films and TV shows to know that sometimes there's no heartbeat. Or something else has gone wrong. Or there are two heartbeats and it's twins. You need a person. I feel like I know there's only one of you, and I feel very certain that you're fine. I feel it. Apparently, though, we're higher risk, you and me. Good to know. I have leaflets for terrifying risky-sounding tests I have to decide whether I want. Nuchal fold. Amniocentesis. I haven't read them yet. I may never read them.

I'm an elderly primigravida, by the way. That's what she called me, and what it said on my notes. It means old for a first-time mother. Nice.

Your great-grandmother is coming out of hospital. And going straight into a care home. I'm making myself say it to prove it's

true. You know how I feel about it, about her. You must do.
You're wrapped close to my heart, so you have to know.

   And your grandmother isn't here.

   Sometimes, apart from you, I feel quite alone. You're not much
company, to be brutally honest . . .

   Now, your godmother is back. Holly. She's the best company in
the world. And she's going to be so bloody excited about you . . .

Gigi

Gigi thought about the anxious-looking young woman at Clearview House as she sat on the train into Central London. She'd been very pretty – huge bush-baby eyes, and a warm smile – but she'd had such a sadness in her lovely face. Gigi had wanted to scoop her up and bring her home – a wounded bird to be cared for. She was too young to be shouldering all the responsibility, bless her. She wondered why her mother hadn't been with her: she couldn't imagine any circumstances under which she'd leave that kind of decision about James or Violet to one of her own children. She hoped the girl would bring her grandmother to Clearview. Although Gigi had a feeling it wasn't the only thing making her sad.

She knew she was intuitive about people – instinctive. It was one of the things that made her a good midwife. She almost always knew how a woman wanted to be treated in labour – and how to deal with their birthing partners. Anxious about-to-be-new parents trusted her, which helped so much. This tendency to read people, whether she was trying to or not, spilt over into her life outside of work. She was the kind of person people told things to. Or wanted to. The girl had wanted to, she'd known. There was more to her story, Gigi guessed. If she saw her again, if she brought her grandmother to Clearview, maybe she'd tell her.

Gigi watched the houses speed by. She was on her way

to meet Olly for lunch, a treat they both tried to make happen a few times a year — just the two of them. Of her children, he was the one she'd had the least one-to-one time with. Christopher had had the exclusivity of being the firstborn, and Megan long days when her brothers were at school, and then years when they'd been absent altogether. Olly was the sandwich child. Maybe she'd been making up for it ever since. She knew everyone thought he was her favourite. He wasn't. But if he had been, who'd have blamed her? His joy-versus-worry ratio was streets ahead of the other two, even if his siblings' joy was just as joyous.

These trips were amongst her favourite days. She'd choose a restaurant near his office, and book herself a ticket to an exhibition at the V&A or Tate Modern for the afternoon, after Olly had gone back to work. She'd been a big shopper, once upon a time, but stuff had lost a lot of its allure in recent years. She'd accumulated more than enough. It was experiences and memories she wanted now. That let you know you were officially middle aged, almost before anything else. That and a new fondness for big knickers and flat shoes.

There'd been a heavy frost last night, but now the sky was that unlikely and rare cobalt-blue you always hoped for on cold winter days, and almost never got. Gigi seldom read on trains — she liked the thinking time of journeys. She looked out of the windows at the back gardens and playing fields of the suburbs, and then at the cranes and scaffolds of new builds as the train swept in through Wandsworth and Vauxhall and then Waterloo. She walked across one of the Golden Jubilee footbridges, stopping, as she always did, as near to the exact middle as she could figure, taking a moment to look at St Paul's, its domed roof glinting in the bright sunshine, and the Millennium Wheel, and the Art Deco clock just along from Charing Cross. It was her very favourite view of the city.

She'd booked a tapas restaurant in Covent Garden, arriving first, as was usually the case. Gigi settled herself into the leather banquette and perused the menu with a glass of Fino sherry while she waited for her son. Olly's office was a few minutes away, on Great Queen Street, but he was habitually at least five minutes late for everything – a habit which drove Richard to distraction – so she didn't look for him at once.

When he did come in, pink-cheeked from the cold and open-jacketed as usual, she felt the familiar flush of pride that he was hers. He was tall and slim, blond and doe-eyed, but it was his smile that people remembered. His grin, as the saying goes, went from ear to ear. Like a kid's. His ready laugh was loud and unselfconscious. He had old-fashioned manners, and she loved that about him too. She heard him before she saw him, thanking the waitress for her offer to hang up his coat. She had Richard to thank for that, at least; Christopher also had them. Slim was Richard's gene pool, but the rest – from the unruly curls he only partly tamed with male-grooming products, to the sense of humour, to the sheer love of people – that was her.

You weren't supposed to love one of your children more than the other, and she hand-on-heart didn't. In a *Sophie's Choice*, who'd-she-hand-over, deep-in-her-uterus way, of course she couldn't choose between them. She lived for all of them, she'd die for any one of them. She knew them all. And adored them unconditionally. But you could definitely enjoy one more than the other, even if you never admitted it to anyone else, and, for her, that child was Oliver. Christopher was her first, her pride and joy, but the anxious child had grown into a careful and watchful man and he'd caused her the most worry along the way. There was a wonderment in Meg's being a girl, after two boys, and a connection between them. She cherished their bond. But it was different with Olly. He had always – simply – just made her happy.

He'd been a fat Buddha of a baby, smiley and placid. Happy to be plonked down on the rug where he could see what was going on. Then a boisterous and adventurous toddler, and an inquisitive and bright child. He'd been good at lots of things, brilliant at very few, and unworried about whatever he found difficult, which had struck Gigi, even at the time, as a good balance. It meant he kept up in class easily enough and played on most sports teams at school. He never fell out with people – had no time for it. He didn't worry about much. He ate her out of house and home, and went to far too many parties through his teens, because everyone invited him, but was better than most of her friends' sons at reporting on his whereabouts and knowing his limits with alcohol. He had, once, been spectacularly sick in the back of her car after a party. But he'd got up unprompted at seven the next morning and cleaned it all up before he went to school, instinctively understanding the route to forgiveness.

He'd taken a gap year after school, which Richard had been afraid would turn into a gap life when he announced, from New Zealand, that he was extending his trip to work as a tour guide on one of the bus companies that specialized in ferrying young people around. That's when he'd worried her the most, probably, delighting in posting video clips online of him sky diving in Queenstown, white-water rafting in Rotorua and canyoning in Auckland. She'd slept lightly that year, and checked her phone much more often than was healthy. My God, how she'd missed him. It was like a dull ache – omnipresent and sore. Richard joked that he'd meet a Kiwi and never return, but Gigi couldn't share the joke. She couldn't describe how much she'd hate that. But he'd deferred his place at university only one more year, and he'd come back eventually. Gigi knew he'd found it quite hard to settle, but he had. Richard was relieved his life was on a more even, conventional footing, but Gigi sometimes wondered if he'd really got it all out of his system. And when he'd graduated, she'd been proven right when he took another year and worked his way around the US.

Thus he was almost twenty-five years old before he even began to think about what his father called a 'proper job', and, seemingly unconcerned with material possessions or security, he'd fallen on his feet with a job at a small digital start-up run by a mate of his from uni days. The mate had the technological know-how, and the good idea. And, it turned out, Olly could sell it, in his snow-to-Eskimos way. They'd made a successful team. Though Olly was just joking when he did his best Del Boy and declared 'Next year we'll be millionaires', rubbing his hands and showing his dimples, Gigi understood enough to know that it was entirely possible – maybe likely – that at some point they would indeed be. She knew it bugged the hell out of Christopher, earnestly and worthily working his way up a corporate ladder. It even rankled slightly with Richard. And gave Meg an entirely unrealistic impression of the job market for young graduates. But she couldn't begrudge Olly his good fortune. Something about getting back from the universe what you put out into it . . .

'Darling.'

'Hiya, Mum. I'm late. Sorry.'

She looked at her watch. 'You're actually early. On Olly time . . . Not to worry. Lovely to see you, sweetheart.'

He leant over and kissed her, his cheek cold against hers, and squeezed her shoulder, then sat down opposite and put his napkin on to his lap.

'You look gorgeous.'

'You too, sweet boy. Cold.'

'I know.' He rubbed his hands together, blew between his fingers to warm them. 'No scarf.' He grinned.

'I'm starving. The food is so good here. Let's order first, shall we, and then we can talk?'

Gigi was used to waitresses being somewhat taken with her son. She let him charm this one for a moment while he ordered for them both – braised Ibérico pig's cheeks with squash purée, roasted salt cod, stuffed courgette flowers, burrata with smoked aubergine salad and *patatas fritas*. Two glasses of white wine.

'Sounds delicious.'

'How are things?'

Gigi gave a small shrug. 'All fine. Nothing much to report. Not here to talk about me!'

'Oh, is that right? What are you here to talk about, Mummy dearest?' His eyes were dancing, his tone teasing.

'I think you know, my boy.'

'Caitlin.'

'Caitlin.' She laid her palms on the table and leant forward slightly. 'Discuss . . .'

'What would you like to know?'

'Everything.'

'Shall I cancel my meetings for this afternoon?'

'Do you need to?'

He laughed his booming laugh. 'Okay. Okay. I'm an open book.'

'You didn't tell us. Not so much as a heads-up.' She made a mock stern face at him.

'And I should have done. It was all meant to be a bit of a surprise . . .'

'Well, it certainly was that, darling.'

'Good surprise?'

'Surprising surprise.'

'That's a non-answer.'

'I'm your mother. I want you to be happy. That's all.'

'I know . . . and you want to know how many you're catering for.'

'That too!' He winked at her. 'So?' she asked.

'So?'

'So . . . are you happy?'

'I am.' There was something about his reply that didn't entirely ring true. Perhaps it was the way his smile failed to reach his eyes, and his eyes didn't quite meet her gaze when he spoke.

The waitress arrived with the wine and some olives, and they both smiled up at her as she put the glasses down on the table, although she only really noticed Oliver.

Gigi impaled a black olive with a cocktail stick and wagged it at him. 'Start at the very beginning . . .'

'Okay. Okay. The very beginning . . . We met five months or so ago. In the office. She was with an ad agency we had a meeting with. You can see she's a beautiful girl.

We didn't go with the agency, in the end, but I had her number, and I liked the look of her, and she'd seemed nice, so I rang her, chatted a bit, and then I took her out.' He put his hands up. 'That's about it. Bit of a non-story, I'm afraid. No meet-cute, as they say in films. The rest is history . . .'

'You've been seeing her for five months. And you never mentioned it.'

'Nope.'

'And we never met her.'

'No.'

'What's that about? We're not the Spanish Inquisition.'

'It wasn't deliberate. It's just . . . well, she's not all that into family.'

Gigi thought of gorgeous Emily, and Ava, and the joy she felt when all her chicks were in the nest, followed immediately by the unwelcome thought of how empty her nest felt without them all, and a small hard lump formed at the base of her throat. Caitlin wasn't 'all that into family'. Family was everything. Everything.

The waitress starting coming with plates of tapas. For a moment, as she pushed things around on the table to make space for them, and then refilled their water glasses, they didn't talk. Olly served them both, and they tasted their food, and murmured appreciative noises for a minute. Gigi tried to ignore the lump still in her throat. She realized she'd been hoping to hear about a thunderbolt – an encounter that had swept him off his feet, knocked him sideways, rocked his world. That's what she'd always imagined for him – for this golden, glorious boy. That when she appeared, it would be spectacular. Ridiculous. This seemed . . . this seemed too ordinary.

'So what's Caitlin's background? Where did she grow up?'

'All right, Inspector Morse. I'm getting to it . . . She's an only child. Horrible divorce. When she was quite young, I think. Her dad buggered off with a friend of her mum's – something like that. She still sees them both, but she was sent off to boarding school when she was eleven and got shunted between the two of them in the holidays. Not entirely happy in either place. They both remarried, she doesn't especially get on with either step-parent. Her dad actually lives in Scotland, these days. That's where he was originally from. He's got a couple more kids, much younger than Caitlin.'

'How old is she?'

'Twenty-six. I think the kids are really young – ten – that sort of thing . . .'

'Okay.'

'It's not like she refused to come and meet you or anything like that. Five months isn't that long. We've both been busy. Not avoiding you, I promise. I just think she doesn't, you know, *get* the whole family thing particularly.'

Gigi didn't know how to respond to that. It wasn't true. She spoke to him at least once a week, even if he didn't come home for a few months at a time. He could have told her, and he'd chosen not to. She wasn't sure why. But 'the whole family thing' was pretty much her life, and the thought of her son married to someone who didn't quite 'get' it was just awful. She looked down at the tines of her fork.

'I'm sure she'll warm up a bit, once she gets to know you all . . .'

How will that ever happen, Gigi wondered.

It seemed so strange. That this girl was *the* girl. There'd been lots, over the years. Blonde, brunette, red-headed, thin as a rake, plump, bright, daft as a brushed head. All sorts of girls – some had made fleeting appearances and never been seen again; some had been around for a few months, come on summer holidays and weekend breaks to the Lakes. Once, not long after Olly had got back from the States, there was one – Angie – that Gigi had thought might be a keeper. He'd been with her for a year or so, and they'd practically been living together in a flat in Clerkenwell. He'd been with Angie when Gigi was ill, and she'd been great. Come home for the weekend and just cooked dinner for everyone, like it was no problem. Gigi remembered hearing the two of them laughing in the kitchen, washing up together, and wondering if she was the one. They'd broken up and Olly had never really talked about why, but he'd been dating again within a couple of months, so Gigi didn't worry too much for the state of his heart. But there had been no one like this one.

'She's not your usual type, Olly.'

'I have a type?'

'You know you do.'

He smiled. 'I know she's not.'

Gigi let her unspoken question hang in the air.

'You want to know why?'

'I want to know that *you* know why. I'm not marrying her. You are, apparently.'

Olly shifted uncomfortably in his seat. 'It's time to grow up. Isn't it?'

'You're almost twenty-nine, Olly.'

'But I've been flying by the seat of my pants for years. It's time to get serious.'

Caitlin was serious all right.

'I've changed, Mum. At least, I'm trying to . . .'

You don't need to change, Gigi thought. You don't need to change a thing.

'What came first, Caitlin or this change?'

He thought for a moment. 'She asked me, you know?'

This was new and seismic information. Gigi tried and failed to remember how Olly had phrased his big announcement on Christmas Day.

'How modern.'

Olly's laugh boomed. 'Don't play the old-fashioned little woman. You're with it. You're a cool mum.'

'I'm so not.'

'You want that last courgette flower? I can always order some more . . .'

'You have it.' Gigi wasn't as hungry as she'd thought.

Olly speared it and put the whole thing in his mouth at once. He looked seven years old.

She wouldn't lose him. She wouldn't say boo to a goose. If Caitlin was what he wanted, she might not understand it but she didn't need to. It was his life. And she knew she'd do anything in her power to remain in it. She had given him the opportunity to make her understand, and he hadn't managed to do so. But that was her problem, not his. It was what it was . . .

'So . . . a new daughter-in-law. Do you have any idea when?'

Olly shook his head. If he was surprised that the interrogation was over, he didn't let it show. 'We haven't got that far. We still have to get a ring. Haven't even done that . . . No hurry, I don't think?'

None whatsoever, Gigi thought.

'And will it be quiet? You going to slope away and do it in secret somewhere?'

'I wouldn't do that to you.'

'Promise.'

Olly squeezed her hand. 'Absolutely. Not sure we'll go for the full monty, like Chris did, but I promise you that you and Dad'll be there. Of course.'

'And am I allowed to get to know Caitlin?' Or at least try, she thought.

'I'm sure . . .' It wasn't the most emphatic of answers. Gigi let it go.

By mutual, unspoken agreement then, they drew an invisible line under that part of the conversation. They covered his work over ice cream, and Richard, James and Meg over coffee, with politics and film in between. Out on the pavement she showed him the latest pictures Emily had sent of Ava on her phone. He hugged her tight and kissed both cheeks.

'Love you, Mum.' He'd always said it, even when he was a teenager.

'I love you, darling.' He turned and walked away.

'Olly?'

He turned back. Gigi took the three steps necessary to be close to him again. She put her hands on the lapels of his coat.

'It's the rest of your life, you know, sweetheart.'

'Mum . . .'

'You be sure. You be sure you're going to get what you need . . .' Her voice broke, and hot tears sprang to her eyes.

'Mum?'

She sniffed sharply, patted him and stood back.

'Go on. Off you go.' And he was gone.

She watched his back until he turned left at the top of Catherine Street. Turning reluctantly away from him, she started back towards the tube. In her handbag, her mobile rang.

It was Olly.

'Were we still talking about me, Mum, just then?'

She hesitated.

'Because if we weren't. You know, if we were talking about you, it's okay. You can, you know. Talk about you. To me. I just wanted to say that . . .'

And then he hung up, which was just as well: Gigi realized she wouldn't have been able to answer him.

Gigi didn't bother to express her doubts to Richard when she got home. Time was, he'd have understood the nuance of what she was saying, but they'd been closer then. Too often now she found it frustrating trying to explain her thoughts to him. He'd brush off her concerns, full of platitudes about its being Olly's life, Olly's decision. He might even mock her – tease her that she had different rules for her favourite child. So she held her tongue and told him how delicious the burrata was, and talked about the V&A exhibition, although she'd barely noticed what she'd been looking at as she wandered around, distracted by her conversation with Olly.

She talked to her friend Kate about it, at work – confessed that she was confused by her son's choice. Kate, who knew Olly, leant against the desk with her arms folded, nodding sagely.

'It'll be the sex. I bet she's a wow in the sack. Men'll do anything for amazing, mind-blowing sex. You said she was gorgeous. She'll have cast her sexy sex spell, mark my words.'

'Ew. This is my son we're talking about.'

'Don't be all Victorian with me. You know what I'm talking about, I know you do . . .'

'Sex doesn't last.'

Kate laughed. 'That's a profoundly depressing statement, if ever I heard one, from a still-married woman. I mean, I've been in the desert for years, but don't tell me you are too . . .'

Gigi thought, but didn't say, that just maybe not having sex with the man you are married to, who's in the same bed as you, might be infinitely more depressing than lying there alone. She was too proud, too private, to admit it, even to Kate. It was such a failure. Out loud, she managed, 'I just mean the novelty wears off. It's not enough, is it?'

Kate shrugged. 'I wouldn't mind.' She circled her hips suggestively. Gigi hit her gently with her clipboard and walked away, shaking her head, glad to bring the conversation to an end.

Emily was slightly more helpful. She drove down with Ava on Gigi's day off, and they took her, bundled up against the cold so that just her eyes were visible, for a long walk. Emily put her in a sling on her chest, and Gigi tightened the straps. 'She looks like a mummy.'

'I'm paranoid about her being too hot, too cold . . .'

'She's fine. Snug as a bug.'

Ava fell immediately, obligingly, to sleep. The first part of the walk was steep, and they didn't talk much.

'Blimey. I'm out of shape.' Emily stopped and arched her back, hands on her hips. 'This is the bit where I pretend to admire the view so I can catch my breath.'

Gigi couldn't have loved her more. They stood panting for a moment. When she could speak again, she said, 'You've got twelve pounds extra strapped to your front. I've got thirty, all over. And they're not detachable.'

'True. Great lump.' Emily kissed the top of Ava's sleeping head. 'This one, not you.'

Once they got to a flatter section, Gigi related her conversation with Olly. At least, the part about Caitlin. The part about her she would keep to herself. Emily just listened while she spoke.

'So what do you think?'

'You don't think . . . maybe . . . no. Never mind.'

'No. What were you going to say?'

'Well, it sounded ridiculous, even just in my head, so I stopped.'

'What, Em?'

'You don't think she's interested in him because he's . . . because he might be worth something . . . worth quite a lot?'

'A gold digger?'

'See. I told you it sounded stupid.'

'I hadn't thought of it.'

'You said they met at work, that's all . . .'

Gigi pondered this. Emily had nudged her into a new thought – not that Caitlin was a gold digger, per se. That seemed so old-fashioned, and so cynical. But maybe it wasn't mad to think that she might be seeking some . . . some security. Safety. With the background Olly had described, it didn't seem beyond the realms of possibility.

She didn't express the thought to Emily. It wasn't fully formed enough.

'Let's you and me take her out for lunch or something, shall we? I'll leave Ava with my mum. Or – crazy thought, ha, ha – her father could have her . . . We'll all go together. That'll ease the pressure, right? Make it more like lunch and less like a job interview.'

'Is that how it felt when you first met me?'

'No. Course not.' Emily put an arm around Gigi's shoulder. 'Love at first sight. She's not much like me, though, is she?'

'Not prima facie, no.'

'Sounds like she had a bit of a rubbish childhood, from what Olly told you. That's bound to make you wary, isn't it? Of a close family . . .'

'I'd have thought it might make you want to be a part of it.'

'And it might, Pollyanna. Eventually. My guess is that the worst thing you can do is push. It's early days.'

'And isn't that Olly's fault? We've only just met her, and they're planning their wedding already.'

'Are they?'

'Well, no. I don't think they are just yet. But they're engaged . . . Not that there's a ring or anything. You know Olly. Never knowingly organized.'

'You're hurt.'

Gigi smiled ruefully. 'I am, a bit.'

'I get that.' Emily rubbed her arm. 'I do. Even I had a twinge. And I'm just the sister-in-law.'

Gigi leant her head on Emily's arm, immensely grateful for the understanding.

'You want to make everyone happy, G. You're a classic pleaser. You want to love everyone. Just give it time. How could we not win her over in the end? We. Are. Delightful.'

On cue, Ava opened her eyes and gurgled contentedly.

Gigi nuzzled into what seemed likely, beneath all the wrapping, to be her granddaughter's neck, full of love for this baby, and her wonderful mother.

Tess

Tess pulled off her cross-body bag, disentangling it from her long scarf, and slid heavily into the booth.

'Sodding Northern Line. Sorry. Have you been waiting ages?' She blew a kiss theatrically across the table.

'Hours.' Tess was ten minutes late at the most. Holly smiled broadly at her, totally forgiving, and lifted an almost empty glass of white wine. 'You know I like to make the most of a rare night out . . . Want one?'

Tess had been ready for this. Thinking it through last night had made her realize that every single social interaction she had, had ever had, or could ever have with her oldest and best friend, would inevitably involve alcohol, with the brief exception of the first trimester with Holly's own baby. After which she'd drunk pints of Guinness with righteousness. It had never struck her before. At any kind of meal, definitely. Maybe breakfast would have been safe, but Holly never had time for breakfast, and sliding it until 10 a.m. on a weekend totally legitimized a Bucks Fizz or a Bloody Mary. Even if they went to the cinema, Holly would wait until the lights went down and then produce mini-bottles of wine with plastic straws from the Mary Poppins-esque handbag that went everywhere with her. Holly didn't have a drink problem, Tess knew. But there was always wine. She could have suggested a bracing walk, but that would have been so out of character Holly's antennae would have been immediately alerted.

So she'd been ready. She was definitely going to tell her tonight. But this would be the first time she'd said it out loud to another human being apart from Sean, and Iris, and she realized now she didn't have the words ready at all. This had to go better than either of those times. She nodded, and watched Holly pour a glass she knew she couldn't drink, picked it up, clinked and sort of fake-sipped from it. She wouldn't get away with that for long, but it bought her a few minutes at least.

'How are you?'

'Knackered. Jet lag was a bitch. Took us all out at the knees. They say it's a day for every hour of time difference, which I can't even quite work out, but going straight back to school and work . . . I reckon it's still going on, to be honest.' They'd talked for ages on the phone when Holly got back. Mostly about the trip. Tess hadn't wanted to tell her other than face to face. She wanted to see her expression. There was so much to tell. It had been easy enough to distract her with a series of leading questions about the holiday. Holly had been brimming with it. Now she was here . . . 'It's been crazy this week. We're deep in rehearsals for the play and I've got parents' evening next week, and you know the damn parents are infinitely more trying than their kids.'

Tess did know, because it had been one of Holly's recurring themes for years – almost as long as she'd been a teacher.

'What's the play?' She wasn't desperately interested, but it seemed a good diversionary tactic while the right words sorted themselves out in her head. Might have been better to blurt it out the second she'd walked in . . .

Holly grimaced. *Much Ado About Nothing.*

'Christ.'

'Christ indeed. Not my decision, obviously. Head of Drama's been desperate to do it for ages. He's got his Benedick and Beatrice in the Fifth Form now, so there was no reasoning with him. Twenty-five-odd cast members. Twenty-three of whom can't seem to learn their lines, and, even when they have done, don't seem to be able to deliver them with the vaguest sense that they understand them.'

Tess laughed. 'It can't be that bad.'

'It's *always* that bad at this stage. More wooden than the stage upon which they tread. About as much humour as a cervical smear.'

'Sounds awesome. You must get me tickets. I'll bring friends!'

'Oh, it'll be all right. It'll be better than all right, in the end. It'll all come together after an appalling dress rehearsal and a bollocking from the Head of Department. Happens every sodding year. It'll be all right on the night. I'll need a month in a sanatorium, but the parents will love it. Well, some of the parents will love it. Some will complain about that too.'

'More anecdotes for *Surrey: A Novel*.' Holly rolled her eyes and gurned.

Surrey: A Novel was Holly's imaginary magnum opus. A revenge work she'd been planning as long as she'd been teaching children, and raising one of her own, in the county: a collection of all the absurd, competitive, pushy-parent, passive-aggressive stories she'd gathered from her own, and her friends', and colleagues' experiences. It was their shorthand for ludicrous, laughable, heart-breaking stories from the frontline of Home Counties parenting (which was a good subtitle, in fact). After years of listening, open-mouthed, Tess had begun to doubt that it would ever find a publisher, even if Holly committed it to paper, on the grounds of utter implausibility, and also being totally litigious, probably. But since she'd met Sean's sisters, she'd doubted that far less, and even wondered if *Hampshire: A Novel* might make a suitable sequel. There was probably enough for a whole series . . .

'I'm channelling Joyce Grenfell for all I'm worth.'

'You cannot choose to blow at Edgar . . .' They could do the whole monologue between them. That, and most of Victoria Wood's sketches.

Holly laughed. 'Not another word. I'm having a night off.'

'And how is my fabulous god-daughter?'

'A night off, I said!' She paused, and considered. 'Monosyllabic. Messy. Selfish.' Holly shrugged, then softened. Her voice was quieter. 'I think she's okay, Tess. There's a lot of work, this year. Lots of pressure. Way more than there was for us. But I think she's okay.'

'You think?'

Holly shook her head. 'She's having some trouble with the girls in her year.'

'Girls can be horrid.'

'You don't know the half of it. Worse than our day. Definitely foul. It's unbelievable.'

'What's going on?'

'I can't quite get to the bottom of it yet. I just know she's getting left out of stuff she used to be included in – she's home more, the house isn't full of giggling Gerties like normal, she seems a bit sad . . . She doesn't want to tell me. She's embarrassed, I think. It won't help to push. You just have to make yourself available, you know. And hope they tell you what's going on in the end.'

She drained her glass and poured herself some more, noticing Tess's glass was still full. She put the bottle down deliberately and narrowed her eyes at Tess.

'Okay. So that's us. You now. I'm available. And I hope you'll tell me what's going on . . . You've been crying. For days, it looks like. Your eyes! You look like an adorable, stylish bloodhound. And then there's the huge boobs. I clocked those when you sat down, but until you sat wetting your lips with a Chenin blanc, which I know full well to be your favourite, I just assumed you were experimenting – quite successfully, I'd have to say – with new lingerie . . .'

Tess smiled. Relief. She should have known she couldn't fool Holly for long. Holly's guessing was doing the hardest part for her.

'But . . .' Holly leant forward.

Tess nodded.

'Tess? You're pregnant!'

Tess took a deep breath. 'I am. I should have known you'd guess.'

Her friend's eyes filled with instant tears. She proffered her hands, and, when Tess gave her hers, she squeezed them tightly.

'Bloody hell, Tess.'

'Bloody hell, Holly.'

For a moment they sat, staring at each other, caught in the spell and the enormity of the fact.

'What, when, where, how?' Holly was laughing and crying.

'I'll gloss over the how, unless you need specifics.'

'No. No, of course not. Ew. I just mean . . . I mean . . .

wow. Wow. You're pregnant, Tess.' She shrugged her shoulders with a shiver of delight.

'What do you think?'

'I think it's bloody fantastic.' Holly watched her friend's face. 'Isn't it?'

Tess was horrified to realize that her eyes had filled with instant hot tears, and she didn't immediately know what kind they were.

Holly just sat for a moment, holding her hands, and Tess thought how much she loved her friend. Remembered a conversation fifteen years ago – same basic facts, very, very different tone – when Holly had told her she was pregnant with Dulcie, her god-daughter. On paper, there'd been far more reasons to be guarded in happiness about that baby: Holly had only been twenty years old, still studying, barely solvent, not sure where she stood with Joe, Dulcie's dad – but Tess remembered Holly's joy vividly. It had shone out of her, a glow of certain, sure delight. That should have been more complicated – on paper it was – but somehow it had been simple. So simple, to be happy for her.

'How long?'

'Ten weeks or so.'

'Bloody hell! That's two and a half months.'

'No flies on you.'

'Shut up! Two and a half months. And I'm just hearing about this now?' Her voice was full of mock indignation.

'Is it any consolation to know that you're only the third person I've told? And one of those was Iris and I'm not sure that really counts.'

'I'm just teasing. You know that. I'd have hated it if you'd told me over the phone.'

Holly pursed her lips, almost spoke, then changed her mind and said something else.

'How are you feeling?'

'Tired. Sick-ish. Only some of the time. Actually sick – only a few times. But I think that's mostly in my head, you know? Boobs are sore.'

'And huge, by the way. Very Gina Lollobrigida. God, I remember that . . .' Holly smiled sympathetically. 'Happy?' Her voice was gentle.

'I think so.'

'Surprised?'

'Utterly. I was on the pill, for God's sake.'

'Ah . . . a pill baby. I know a few of those.'

'Really?'

Holly nodded, assuming the clipped vowels of a public service announcement. 'Even the most reliable forms of modern contraception are not one hundred per cent reliable.'

'Yep. Well. I'm one of the one per cent.'

'Or the baby's the Second Coming.'

'Don't laugh at me –'

'I am so not laughing, hon. Course not. So, we've established it was a surprise. Good surprise?'

Tess nodded gently. 'I think so, Hols. I think so.' But then the tears came again, and this time would not be checked, rolling down her cheeks as she was racked by sobs.

'Honey . . .' Holly slipped adroitly out of her side of the booth and in beside Tess, putting an arm around her shoulder, stroking her hair. 'Ssh . . . ssh . . .'

'It's not just that. Not just the baby.'

'What, then? Tell me?'

'Oh, it's everything. It's Iris. She's going into that home – the one I told you about . . . It's Mum . . . It's work. It's Sean.'

'What about Sean?'

'He doesn't want the baby.'

'What?' Holly's eyes widened, her glass stopping half-way to her mouth.

'He doesn't want it. At least not at the moment.'

'Well, you can't put a baby on hold.'

'I know. He's been offered this job in New York. He wanted us to go together.'

'And a baby is inconvenient?'

'Something like that.'

'What a schmuck.' Holly had never been unbridled in her enthusiasm for Sean. They were oil and water.

Holly had tried, tried hard, when Tess and Sean had first got together – there'd been a series of forced, not-quite-jovial drinks and dinners and days out. Holly had never exactly said she didn't like him, but they knew each other so well that Tess had guessed. Saddened by the reality of a world where her boyfriend (and possible life partner) and her very best friend in the world didn't get on, she'd pressed. Holly was uncharacteristically unforthcoming until Tess got exasperated and Holly got tipsy one night, and even then all she would offer up was that she thought he had a bit of a stick up his arse, but that she was sure, over time, Tess would be able to extract it. Tess hadn't asked her again, and, by mutual agreement, these days they mostly met up on their own, or on girly days out with Dulcie. There hadn't even been many of those lately.

'So, it seems we've broken up.'

'Christ. Why haven't you told me any of this, you daft

mare? I knew you'd gone off the air a bit since Christmas, but I assumed it was more to do with Iris.'

'And it partly is. It's all happened at bloody once.'

'And I haven't been asking the right questions.'

'That's not your job, Hols. I'm not saying that at all —'

'I am. I've been preoccupied. Work. Dulcie. I'm sorry.'

'Don't be stupid. Besides, I'm telling you now. I've been curled up in a ball most of the time since it happened.'

'You poor thing.'

'It's all such a bloody mess.'

'You're still living there?'

'He's in New York for a few weeks. I've told him I'll be gone by the time he gets back.'

'Where will you go? You know there's always a room with me, don't you?'

'You're lovely.'

'I'm serious. Any time.'

'I'm going to ask Donna. Until I can sort something else out. She's got the room.'

'I've got the room. And we actually get on.' Tess thought of telling Holly about Donna reading to Iris. But Holly was still talking. 'It'd be fun. We'd love it. You so should.'

'Less of the "we". Are you forgetting you've got a husband, and a daughter, and a full-time job?'

'And a best friend I love to pieces. We ALL love you to pieces.'

Tess shook her head. 'I need to sort myself out. And I will. I will . . .' She couldn't stop crying. People in the bar were looking at her. Holly threw them daggers and pulled a tissue out of her bag. Tess blew her nose.

'God, I'm pathetic. Pathetic. Embarrassing. Look at me.'

'You're not pathetic at all.' Holly's tone was fiercely protective, and Tess loved her for it, but she didn't believe her.

'I'm thirty-five years old, Holly, and I'm a total mess. I thought . . . I thought at least I'd be a bloody grown-up by now.'

'Whatever the hell that means.'

Tess laughed through her tears.

'We're all just winging it, Tess, you know.'

'Not you.'

'Yes, me. All of us. No one knows what the hell they're doing, least of all me.'

'I don't see that.'

'And when I look at you I see someone completely in control too.'

Tess sniffed loudly.

'Okay, not at this precise moment. Right now I see someone with panda eyes and a snot trail who has probably never needed a glass of wine more than she does at this precise moment, even though she can't have one.'

She took a swig from her own glass. 'I'll do it for you.'

'Someone with too many balls up in the air just now.' Holly patted the back of Tess's hand. 'Over-juggling. That's it. It's all going to be fine.' She drew out that last sentence and emphasized each word. It's. All. Going. To. Be. Fine. As if she simply wouldn't tolerate anything else.

Tess remembered the first time she'd laid eyes on Holly, all those many years ago. As first meetings go, it had been memorable for several reasons. Mostly because Holly had been almost completely naked and swearing her head off. And then because Holly had rescued her from the worst holiday of her life. Love almost at first sight. And pretty much love ever since. Like Iris, Holly was one of the great constants in Tess's life – more like family to her than friend.

It had been total happenstance. One tweak of either of their plans, and they'd never have met. Even now, maybe especially now, that thought was unbearable. They'd both been travelling in Europe – Holly with a boyfriend, Tess with two schoolfriends she'd vaguely stayed in touch with while she'd been away at university. It was supposed to be a three-week trip by train. And it was supposed to be fun. It had turned out to be a bit of a disaster. She'd gone with Mary and Alice almost by accident, without thinking much about it. She'd wanted a holiday – they were going – they'd hatched the plan in a pub and not really thought it through.

By Gare du Nord in Paris, she'd realized she didn't have as much in common with them as she'd thought she did, and a growing sense of foreboding had settled on her before they crossed the Swiss border. She'd kept her head down and acquiesced, even though it was abundantly clear that, at almost every decision point, she wanted to see different things, eat different food, head in entirely different directions. By Berlin Hauptbahnhof (when she'd have much rather been pulling in to Vienna, longing as she was to see the Spanish Riding School), they'd realized it too and formed one of those near-imperceptible alliances as girls can, still ostensibly including her in everything but not really, with that subtle cruelty that can be breathtaking. The Berlin Wall, although it had been brought down more than a decade earlier, felt like an allegory. By Centraal Station in Amsterdam, Tess was feeling about as welcome as Typhoid Mary and considering a moonlight flit. Scandinavia was next, and she honestly didn't think she could face it. They'd trudged single file to the hostel Alice and Mary had chosen, in the Overhoeks district, and at reception they'd persuaded her that their best bet was to take the two private rooms available – one twin and one single – because they were en suite, and weren't they all tired and dirty, and wasn't it worth the few extra euros for a really comfortable night? All of which was ill-disguised code for them excluding her, and she knew it, of course. She'd have minded more if a night away from the two of them and their inane chattering, a hot, private shower, and the opportunity to dress and undress without trying to keep herself semi-covered with a towel the size of a large pocket handkerchief weren't so very appealing.

The rooms were on different floors – Alice and Mary smiled insincerely at her as they exited the lift on the second floor – and it was on the third that she saw Holly. Naked except for a pair of leopard-skin bikini knickers, holding the door of her room open with one leg whilst hoiking a rucksack and its contents into the corridor.

'We are done. This is so over.' Tess registered brief surprise that the girl was English. It was such un-English behaviour.

'What am I supposed to do?' The whiny voice belonged to a tall, skinny boy – good-looking, but too slight, and far too posh for Tess – who followed his belongings into the corridor and began trying to gather them together.

'You, Ben Forester, are supposed to fuck the fuck off, in whichever direction you fucking well want. You are confusing me with someone who gives a toss. Just leave, and leave me the fuck alone.'

She put special emphasis on the last *fuck*, threw Tess a

look that might have been apologetic, or deliciously conspiratorial, and slammed the door.

Tess skirted gingerly around the worldly goods of the guy, who had coloured bright red and was refusing to look at her as he shoved lurid floral boxer shorts into the top of his bag, and let herself into her room as quickly as possible to spare him further humiliation. She took off her own rucksack and threw herself gratefully on to the single bed, for once unencumbered by a top bunk. It wasn't the deepest mattress in the world but the sheets smelt clean, and to her left she could see into the small shower room and – a chorus of celestial angels sang – her own toilet. She smiled broadly to herself. Just for now all was well with the world.

God, how she wished she'd done that to Alice and Mary about three capital cities ago.

She must have fallen asleep despite the allure of the bathroom. When she woke up it was dark outside and there was a note pushed under her door, a hastily written scrawl from Alice and Mary explaining (gleefully, no doubt) that they'd got no answer when they knocked (she bet they hadn't), and so, assuming she was asleep or out already, they'd gone to find some dinner without her – that they'd see her in the morning, they hoped (they didn't), for the tour of Anne Frank's house.

She might well have stayed there – revelling in the solitude, and possibly planning her escape – if she hadn't realized she was ravenous. She stepped out into the corridor just as, four rooms along, the girl in the leopard-skin knickers, hidden now beneath low-slung camouflage trousers worn with a crop top and a denim jacket, was locking her door. She looked closely at Tess.

'It was you before, right?'

Tess nodded.

'I'm really sorry about that. That was really awkward, I bet. Not a spectator sport.'

'Don't worry . . .'

'I'd just totally completely had enough of him, you know?'

Oh, yes, Tess knew.

The girl seemed intent on explaining herself. 'It's been *three long weeks.*' She drew out the syllables for dramatic effect. 'I had *no* idea what a complete and utter drip he was. I just got tired of making all the decisions and doing all the planning. I was more like his bloody mum than his girl-friend.

'Then I find out the bastard slept with someone else just before we left.' The girl was wide-eyed in her indignity. 'I mean, part of me is impressed.' She chuckled. 'At least it showed . . . gumption. Which is more than I've seen in him for the last three weeks. But he had to go.'

'And has he? Gone, I mean?'

'Expect so. Train straight home, I reckon. I think his adventure is over.'

'And what will you do?'

She shrugged nonchalantly. 'I'm not sure.' Tess detected no hurt or even uncertainty, and she envied this girl her composure. 'Right now? I'm going to find one of those famous coffee shops . . . wanna come?'

Tess was surprised to find that she did want to. She nod-ded. 'All right.'

'Good. So . . . I'm Holly, by the way.'

'I'm Tess.'

Holly put out her hand and shook hers in an unexpect-edly formal gesture. They looked at each other properly.

Holly had blue eyes, and a full, sensuous mouth. Her nose was dusted with freckles under a light golden tan. She was lovely.

'And I don't normally say fuck that much.' Which was the first, and pretty much only, lie Holly ever told her.

It was the first great night of Tess's trip. By the time they'd smoked the obligatory spliff, which neither of them particularly enjoyed, eaten a delicious dinner, which they both did, in a small café by a bridge, and sunk a few beers, their alliance was cemented. Holly had conflated Mary's and Alice's names into the entirely suitable 'Malice' and advocated the treatment she had doled out to Ben as a fitting one for them.

They had little in common apart from their ages and the happenstance of their geography. Holly was, Tess quickly realized, quite posh. She'd been to boarding school, travelled a great deal in comparison to her and, unfortunately, called her mum and dad 'Mummy and Daddy'. It was easy enough for Tess to forgive her, though, because she was just so much fun. Unlike Tess, she knew exactly what she wanted to do – she was going to be a teacher, she said. Starting in September. Tess envied her that certainty – she had a history degree and no idea of what to do with it, bar a certainty that banking and accountancy and all things numbers were not for her.

Before they'd parted that night, back at the hostel, they'd agreed that Tess would abandon Malice and travel on with Holly. They'd spread the map out on Tess's bed and made a plan which – finally – included Vienna and the Lipizzaner horses.

Holly was hilarious and warm and brave and cool. Being

with her could still bestow the exact same feeling of borrowing those qualities, and being safe from the rest of the world, as it had that wonderful Dutch night. Even now, it still could. And they'd never looked back.

Now, here in the wine bar, Holly ordered her an orange juice and soda, and sat holding her hand until she stopped crying and could form words again.

'What did he say? Tell me exactly.'

'He said the timing was off.'

'Charming. What the fuck did he mean by that?'

'I think it just came out. I mucked it all up . . .'

'What do you mean, you mucked it up?'

Tess took a deep breath.

'He told me about New York. I already knew about the baby then but for some reason I just couldn't tell him. He wanted an answer about New York right away . . . I stalled him . . . He was busy with work, I was busy with Iris . . . I think he was giving me space. Anyway . . . we got to Christmas without really having talked about it properly. Then we went to his mum and dad's and told them about New York, and everyone just assumed, like he had, that I'd be going. And when we got home, he proposed . . .'

'Jesus.'

'And *that's* when I told him.'

'Before or after you answered him?'

'Instead of answering him.'

'Right.' There was a sharp intake of breath from Holly. 'I told you it was a mess.'

Holly leant in close. 'Hang on a minute. Just a minute.'

'What?'

'You're going to have a baby, Tess. You're going to be

a mum. Don't let you and me, at least, lose sight of that . . . I mean, I know things are a bit screwed up. I can't promise you anything or that everything will work out where Sean's concerned. But you've got to remember what's important. What's most important. And what's most important is also being happy. So happy. So incredibly wonderfully happy. You are going to have a baby! That is fanbloodytastic.'

Tess felt her heart race. She put her hands down to her stomach, still relatively flat under her sweater. 'Yes, I am!'

Holly put one of her hands on top of Tess's two. Tess pulled one out and placed it on top of that, so Holly put her other hand on that one, and the two friends looked at each other, eyes bright and shiny, smiles conspiratorial. Tess lay her head on Holly's shoulder.

'Hols?'

'Tess?'

'Don't go back to Australia.'

'I'm not going anywhere.'

Dear baby mine,

I am going to have to wait until you are much, much older before I explain to you about your dad. I will need to make you understand that I didn't mean to get all of this – get you – started in this messy sort of a way. I didn't ever expect to be doing this on my own. Well, I'm not entirely on my own now. I have people. You'll have people. Not many, maybe, but they are very, very good ones. We'll be all right. I hope you will understand that I didn't want to stay with your dad just because of the biology part, or because that's what I'm supposed to do. That just wasn't possible. I'm not going to cut him out of your life: that would not be fair. I'll make something work so that it doesn't hurt him and doesn't hurt me too much. So that it is best for you. I don't want there to be fighting. Not too many lawyers. No wrangling about money or visitation, or where you'll spend Christmas. I'd hate that for you. You're the only victim. We're both volunteers, me and him. And I promise to remember that. I promise.

Mum

Gigi

Caitlin was every bit as glossy and glamorous at lunch as she had been at Christmas. More so, actually, in her smart navy work clothes and power heels, with a good handbag. Everything about her was neat and buttoned-up. Gigi felt a bit plump and country-bumpkinish by comparison. And then a bit cross with herself for letting this kid make her feel that way. Caitlin was just as quiet and equally as disinterested in food, ordering a salad of goat's cheese and beetroot and really eating only the beetroot. And, if anything, slightly more brittle than she had been before.

Richard had counselled against this. It was too soon, he said. It was confrontational, he said. She should meet up with her a few more times with Oliver, before she tried to do it on her own. Which was easier said than done. She'd issued a couple of invitations, but there'd been reasons why they couldn't. Reasons that sounded legitimate, but left her feeling they weren't, quite. She'd told Richard she only wanted to get to know her a bit more – to share some time when she wasn't overwhelmed by Christmas catering, and Caitlin wasn't overwhelmed by people. Richard harrumphed, raised an eyebrow, and repeated that he didn't think it was a good idea.

Within five minutes she had the distinctly uncomfortable feeling that about this one thing, at least, he'd actually been right.

Olly had been surprisingly positive (or pragmatic) about it, by contrast, when she'd rung him to ask for his approval and Caitlin's email address. He was his usual easy self. 'I'd like it if you three were friends. As long as you don't go OTT, and quiz the poor girl to death, then why not?' She'd promised they wouldn't.

She'd sent her an email, to avoid a telephone kneejerk reaction. Deliberately casual. Fabricated a reason why she and Emily would be in the vicinity of where Caitlin worked, asked if she might have time to meet them. Suggested a little lunch place she knew – not too posh, but quieter than a lot of the eateries in the West End, so they'd be able to have a proper conversation. She'd half expected her to say no, and wondered whether Olly had had a hand in her saying yes, although he'd said he'd stay out of it.

Caitlin had responded promptly, and said that would be lovely, thank you, emphasizing, though, that she had afternoon meetings that day, and would need to be back at the office by 2 p.m. at the latest. So the parameters had been set, and her escape route mapped out.

On the morning in question, Ava had woken early with a fever – nothing too dramatic, but enough to make Emily feel she needed to stay at home with her (or at least to make Christopher think that Emily should stay at home with her instead of him, as she explained ruefully to Gigi on the phone). So she had to go alone.

She had the distinct feeling Caitlin didn't believe Emily's excuse, as she explained it straight off.

They busied themselves with reading the menus and making food small talk. Gigi looked at her while she ordered. She was a pretty thing. Her eyes were anxious, but lovely – wide and dark and long lashed. Her skin was clear

143

and fresh-looking – completely unlined – and her hair, up today in a neat chignon, was thick and shiny. She was lovely to look at. But Oliver wasn't a shallow man. That would not be enough. She knew it.

Gigi had begun by ordering sparkling mineral water like Caitlin. By halfway through she'd beckoned the waiter over and ordered a glass of white wine.

She'd promised Olly she wouldn't ask too many questions, but it was difficult to keep the conversation on the right side of an interview. Mostly because Caitlin's answers were clipped and not expansive. And because she didn't have many questions to ask in return. There were clearly things she didn't want to talk about – the wedding, for one – and where they might live. Gigi tried to steer her to talking about how she and Olly had met, hopeful that the opportunity to gush about someone they both loved would warm her up, but she hadn't taken that bait either, confirming the facts Olly had already given her and not spicing them up with a dash of girlish excitement.

They talked more than you should about the food in front of them. Gigi found herself feeling uncomfortable. They were almost finished eating, and Caitlin hadn't directed one really interesting question at her.

Once the waiter had cleared their plates, Caitlin's still a third full, and they'd ordered mint tea, she decided to brush away the small talk and try to be real.

'I invited you to lunch today so I could get to know you a bit better. It was so sudden . . .'

'I know. It must have seemed that way to you.'

'Well, even to you, it's been quite a quick thing.'

Caitlin nodded, which wasn't exactly agreement.

'But I suppose when you know, you know?'

A tight smile.

'And I do so hope we can be ... well, friends.' She daren't push it any further than that. For a second, before she replied, Gigi swore that Caitlin blanched.

It made no sense. Caitlin was acting as though she'd already pushed too hard – like she'd shown up with wedding magazines and a lie-detector test – like she had given her a reason to be suspicious. Someone or something had done a right number on this girl – she was going to be a much tougher nut to crack than Gigi had imagined. If you'd ever be able to crack her.

She tried again, less careful now – careful wasn't getting her anywhere. She needed to leave lunch with something that made her feel she'd moved the dial, even if it was only a fraction. 'Listen, it's him you're marrying. Not the rest of us. Not me. Olly. All I need to know is that you love my boy.' It wasn't a question, and it didn't get an answer. The bill had come by then, and it was easy enough for Gigi's remark to hang in the air while the credit card was processed and the waiter asked if they'd enjoyed their meal.

It was a lie – it wasn't all she needed to know from her. She needed to know that Caitlin was going to make him happy, that she wasn't going to take him too far away from her. That her motives were pure – not motives, even. Feelings. That she had a softer, gentler side, even if she only ever showed it to him.

'I wouldn't be marrying him if I didn't love him.'

'Of course not ... I didn't mean ...'

And then it was ten to two, and Caitlin could legitimately give her thanks, and run away to her possibly fictitious meeting, after an air kiss and no eye contact.

*

Gigi left lunch with more questions than answers. And more unsettled by the thought of this woman becoming a part of her family than she'd been before.

Emily, knowing where she'd been, texted her when she was on the train home, playful. 'So? Did you thaw Elsa?'

'Nope. Still frozen.'

She typed 'Let it go . . .' She put musical note emoticons next to it. And a yellow face crying blue tears of laughter.

But Gigi wasn't really laughing.

Tess

In the end, Tess had to email Donna to ask about the house. Holly had persisted in her offer to have Tess at hers. It was tempting, but she knew she couldn't. An old phrase of Iris's kept rolling around her head – something about visitors being like fish . . . she couldn't remember it properly. She'd been hiding out at Sean's, but now he had emailed her, a strange, formal email, to let her know he'd be back in a week. He didn't say anything about the baby. He didn't ask her to be gone, but he didn't ask her to stay.

She knew she couldn't face him, whatever he might be feeling. It was frightening, being homeless and uncertain of everything. Exhausting too, this dismantling of her life, facing rebuilding. Alone in the flat – surrounded by things they'd bought together, remembering conversations and moments, she wondered if what she was feeling was regret. She played out scenarios in her head. Sean, contrite and grey with the fear of losing her, on bended knee with a Tiffany blue box and an impassioned plea. Or a tiny white velour Babygro. Was that what she wanted? A Hallmark happy ending? Maybe she wanted him to want it more than she wanted it herself. It was just fantasy. She knew it wouldn't happen, anyway. None of that – the grand gesture, the intense self-reflection – was Sean's style.

She'd heard little from Donna while she'd been gone. She'd replied briefly to Tess's long note about Clearview. Not unfriendly or unkind, but detached somehow. She had been due back sooner, but she'd extended her trip, and wrote that she might even stay a few more weeks. She was living in a beach hut, paying peanuts for it, she said, somewhere way off the tourist track (this made Tess smile. Was her mother *not* a tourist, then?) and feeling really connected. Those were her words. Really connected.

So she took a deep breath, wrote and asked.

Dear Mum,

Sean and I have broken up. I'm also pregnant. I intend to find somewhere else before the baby comes, but I was wondering if I could stay at your place for a few weeks while I do that. I'm still at his flat, and he's been away for a while, but he's due back soon and I'd rather not be there when he gets home. I clearly have to figure some stuff out. I have the key. Would it be okay?

Tess

PS Iris is doing well.

She read and reread the message before she pushed 'send'. It was stark, and, she supposed, shocking, but what else could she do? Donna wasn't here. Holly's life was busy enough. She'd looked half-heartedly at some rentals, but in truth she was overwhelmed by it all. She had to figure out what her maternity deal would be, what she could afford, where she wanted to be. She'd need room for the baby. She'd need childcare for the baby. She'd need stuff for the baby. There was so much to think about, and she'd buried her foolish head in the sand for so long that now it almost engulfed her. How could Donna mind? She was her mother. The house was empty. It hurt her pride to ask, but she told herself she'd sorted Iris out – the papers had been signed and the deposit paid to Clearview, a date set for transferring Iris there from the hospital – so she was free to work on herself. Just a few weeks. She'd be up and standing on her own feet in just a few weeks.

Donna didn't reply for two days. She'd said internet was sketchy where she was. When she did, her mother surprised Tess more than she had done in a long time, more even than *Cold Comfort Farm* had done.

Oh my love. Of course. Go at once, and stay as long as you like.
I so want to come home and see you, but I don't want to crowd you. Please say if you'd like me to.

Mum

Tess's eyes filled with tears when she read the message, and a lump rose in her throat.

Thank you for the house. I appreciate it. Please don't cut your trip short for me. I'm fine. Or I will be. I'll see you when you get home.

Tess wasn't surprised at the sound of the tiny little girl's voice inside her that wanted to say *Yes, please, Mum, please come home. I need you. I need someone . . .* She'd heard it a lot lately.

She moved herself and her stuff in that weekend. It didn't amount to all that much, packed up in Sean's hallway. Three suitcases, a couple of holdalls, and a few boxes, none so heavy she couldn't take it down in the lift to the car park herself. It all fitted in her car. She'd left everything she'd bought while she lived there where it was. It didn't seem much of a pile for a woman her age. It spoke eloquently and didactically to a life subjugated by stealth.

She'd brought one case into Donna's. The rest could stay in the car for now. It took a moment to figure out the keys – Donna had given her a set years ago, but she'd never used them. Eventually, the door opened, and she kicked a small pile of post out of her way as she walked in. She'd spent very little time in this house. She'd certainly never slept there. Her mother had bought it a few years ago, when she'd sold the house she'd lived in with Martin, when Tess was a girl. She'd downsized then, saying she'd rather have the money for travel than for a mortgage that tied her to one place. Her work was freelance, but lucrative enough to fund the lifestyle she chose. Her habit was to act like a perpetual gap-year student – work, save, travel, repeat. She was a portrait photographer. A good one. She hadn't always been. Tess had a clear memory of Donna finding a camera of her father's at Iris's house, when Tess was just primary-school age. She'd picked it up and fiddled with it – started snapping when she'd realized there was a new film in there, ready for pictures Wilf would never now take. Iris had kept those first pictures – a series of Tess and Iris cooking and laughing in the kitchen in Salisbury – on the wall in her home all these years. Donna had taken a course at college, encouraged by Martin – desperate still, in those days, to help her find what might make her happy – and then slowly she started to build up a portfolio, offering to shoot the new-born siblings of Tess's classmates, and the odd wedding. She took the most beautiful photographs – even Tess could see that they were special – and people loved them. They looked at what Donna had shot and felt understood – properly seen – their loveliest, happiest selves. Most of her work now came from referrals and word of mouth, and people always seemed happy to wait for her to get back from Goa.

The house was a pretty Edwardian end-of-terrace on a slightly scruffy street where some of the houses were starting to be done up with extensions and loft conversions. The encroaching tide of gentrification had yet to reach Donna's end of the road, but it was only a matter of time: they were near a park and a nice-looking primary school and quite close to the station. Downstairs there was a double reception room with its original fixtures more or less intact, and at the back was a kitchen with French doors onto a pocket-handkerchief lawn dominated by a large tree hung with fairy lights and lanterns. A small study was full of the paraphernalia of photography – lenses and flashes and tripods and those big shiny silver circles the purpose of which Tess had never really understood. The walls were lined with examples of her work – brides and babies and nuclear families, none of whom Tess recognized. Elsewhere the hallmarks of Donna's DIY were everywhere: in the eclectic paint-colour choices and wonkily hung curtain rails. Tess remembered a bedroom ceiling with constellations painted on the dark-indigo background in silver hobby paint. She hadn't thought of it for years, and now she could see herself, small and wide awake, staring up at stars, knowing their names – Orion's Belt, the Plough, Ursa Major – she could almost trace them with her finger. Who had taught her their names?

Donna had vast numbers of books – worn paperbacks in haphazard piles and big coffee-table books about myriad subjects like Ngorongoro and Toulouse-Lautrec. *Cold*

Comfort Farm was on the arm of the sofa. Tess picked it up and recognized it was Iris's copy. She held it to her chest for a moment, and then put it back.

Her mother's shiftless relationship with spirituality was well represented too – Buddhas, Ganesh figurines and dream catchers sat alongside kitschy religious talismans on most surfaces, and the fridge was a wall of aphorisms on magnets.

Tess realized, as she climbed the stairs, that she'd never actually been up here. Or, if she had, she didn't remember. Her mother's room was at the front of the house, with big sash windows through which the weak sunshine nevertheless flooded. She headed for the second bedroom, beyond the family bathroom with its tropical-fish shower curtain and chipped claw-footed bath. It was bigger than she'd expected, with a clean, neat double bed, a pine chest of drawers, and a Lloyd Loom-style woven chair someone had half-heartedly spray-painted pink at some point. She put her suitcase down on the bed and went back to her mother's room.

This was much messier. It would have made Sean twitchy. And that thought made Tess smile. She remembered messy. As a child her room in her mother's house (and that was always how she had thought of it, never as 'our house') had always been different from everywhere else, with its neatly made bed and tidily stored things. She and Iris were alike in that way. But in the same way that Donna had made her tidier, Sean had made her a little bit messier. She'd told him he was like the creepy husband in that Julia Roberts movie – the one where she faked her own death to escape him – who needed everything exactly in its place or he went off the deep end. She used to skew cushions and leave newspapers folded back on themselves on purpose sometimes. She'd left it immaculate earlier today. Not a thing out of place. Not a trace of herself.

It looked like Donna had left in a hurry a few minutes ago, not like she'd been gone for weeks. The duvet was pulled up haphazardly, and the pillows were just thrown any old way. At her dressing table, necklaces hung from the mirror, odd earrings glittered, and tubes and bottles were left with their lids beside them. Tess picked one up and sniffed at its dried-out contents, which still held the faint scent of her mother – part spa, part hippy. On the mantelpiece above the tiny fireplace were three pictures of her. Tess as the archetypal chubby smiling baby; Tess as a more pensive schoolgirl, with slightly buck teeth and a scraped back ponytail; and Tess three or four years ago, laughing, with Iris. This one was much in the style of the pictures downstairs in the study. Black and white, unself-conscious. Understood. They were all of her. Tess was surprised and touched. She sat down on the edge of Donna's bed and pulled one of the pillows on to her lap, hugging it to her. In spite of everything, she felt the comfort of family, of the familiar, here. So many of the things surrounding her now had surrounded her when she was a child. As alien as Donna sometimes was, as distant from her as Tess sometimes felt, and always had, in some ways she was home too.

There were no pictures of Donna with Iris. None. For perhaps the first time, Tess thought she understood just a little of what Donna felt about her and Iris. Jealous, yes. Rejected, maybe. Inferior? Well, Tess had done and said little to suggest otherwise. For the first time in ages, she wanted to know what Donna thought and felt – really thought and felt – about what was happening. This was like a little puzzle of her mother. The book, the photographs, sat oddly with the half-conversations and the self-imposed exile. Donna felt complicated, suddenly, to Tess, who had compartmentalized her differently.

Tess spent the rest of the afternoon in a cathartic cleaning frenzy. She closed the door on her mother's bedroom and concentrated on the kitchen, which did not bear close inspection. For three or four hours, she listened to the radio, losing herself in a play and *Gardener's Question Time*, and scrubbed every surface once she'd cleared her way through to it. It was mindless, satisfying work. When she finally finished, she made herself coffee in a clean mug and sat at the clean table, flicking through a terribly worthy vegetarian cookbook she'd found on the shelf earlier, wrapped in a coating of greasy dust, and thinking she might pop out afterwards and buy steak for dinner.

Outside, it was getting dark now. She wandered back to the front room and closed the curtains against the evening, feeling almost cosy. In the street, the sound of a car stopping, a door opening and closing, attracted her attention briefly, reminding her that it was quiet here, much quieter than where she was used to living. She heard a key in the lock.

'Hello? Tess? Is that you?' It was Donna's voice.

Tess went to the doorway, heart pounding.

'Mum?'

'I know you said not to, but I couldn't stay away . . .'

She didn't know until she heard her voice just how much she wanted to see her. She rounded the corner and walked straight into her mother's suntanned, many-braceleted open arms.

Tess

February

*Week 13 and a few days. Hey, passion fruit. I saw you yesterday.
Actually saw you. It was the most extraordinary moment of my
life, and, yes, slightly Sigourney Weaver in Alien. They put some
jelly and then a probe on my stomach, and looked around for a
bit, and then turned the screen towards me, and there you were!
People claim you can't really tell what you're looking at, but I
could. I could, I swear. I saw your arms and your legs and your
head. And, most important of all, I saw your tiny heart,
pulsating away.*

*Now this one is exciting . . . it says you can feel me – when I
put my hands on my belly, it says you can feel it. I can't feel you, of
course, not yet, but you can feel me. That's enormous news, baby
mine. I feel like I want to read to you now – poems, not
newspapers. We'll start with my favourites: Philip Larkin and
Roger McGough and Mary Oliver – and play you music – Bach
and Elgar for culture and Oasis and Nina Simone for fun – and
just talk to you, and keep my hands on my stomach all the time so
you know I'm here. I have spent twenty years waking up to the
Today Show on Radio 4 – shouting at the politicians refusing to
answer questions while I get dressed – but I can't listen to it any
more, and I'm trying not to use my stern and fishwifey voice around
you. The world is a dark and dismal place, baby mine, and I don't
want you hearing about it if you're up and listening. I don't want
you ever to hear anything bad at all. And there hardly seems to be*

any good news. I'm just hypersensitive. I cried at an advert last night. For frozen food. Everything makes me cry. Refugee crises, muggings, depression in the housing market. It makes me scared and sad. I'm shutting it all out. I want an absurdly, impossibly wonderful world for you – rainbows and unicorns and perpetual sunshine. Cue Louis Armstrong's gravelly tones. I want to protect you from anything bad.

You're coming along in there, lovely. Cooking nicely. Your funny head has the start of ears in the ultrasound picture, but you've still got your eye patches on. There's a nose getting more obvious too. I hope you don't have mine. I never liked mine – it has a bump and the nostrils are too big. My granddad had a great nose. It might be even cuter on a girl. What's not cute on this girl right now is what is allegedly my bump. For something the size of a passion fruit, you are certainly demanding some room in there. I wouldn't mind, except that the reorganization of my vital organs that you've caused isn't giving me the kind of bump famous and lucky people get – all neat and limited to their tummy region. I've got boobs like zeppelins, a muffin top, thunder thighs and nothing you could in all honesty call a bump. It's more of a slurry heap, making me wider and not at all cuter. It all just popped out with no warning. I woke up one morning and looked like Jabba the Hutt in the bathroom mirror. No warning.

I am spending an unhealthy amount of time staring at my stomach, looking in dread for stretch marks . . . so far so good. It wouldn't be your fault, of course, but I'd rather not.

Holly – that's my best friend, and your godmother – she came with me. I was going to be big and brave and go alone but she got wind of it and went mad. She took the afternoon off to come. She cried too. She squeezed my hand so tightly while they were looking for you and then she cried when we saw you.

I think I need to tell your father. He needs to know, right? There's no guidebook on how to do this. I need to figure out how to make it work with him so it's best for you.

Your granny is back. God, it's weird to think of her as Granny. Iris is the granny. She'll be your great-grandmother. Blimey. Donna – she'll be Granny. She came back from Goa, to be with us. And it was wonderful that she did. We're so different in so many ways, me and her. It's still a bit strange, living with her, like halls at uni in the first term – a bit best behaviour and feeling our way. Careful of each other. But I'm so moved by her being here. I didn't know I needed her. I've spent years conspicuously not needing her, and now I do, and somehow she just knew. And I can't help linking that – me and her – to me and you . . . it's like I understand something now that I didn't – that I couldn't – before. So you've given me a gift, before you're even born.

Tess

Tess put off going to Iris's house until she couldn't avoid it any longer. Holly insisted on going with her. It was the first weekend of half-term, so there was no marking or planning to do, she said. Dulcie was on a school trip to the Berlin Wall. 'Nothing compared to the cold war she's fighting at school,' Holly had grumbled, but Dulcie had insisted on going.

'I'm coming. It's going to make you sad. So you're not going on your own. Besides, it'll take my mind off worrying whether she's miserable or not. All that no one to sit with on the coach bull. Anyway, you're not lifting boxes and climbing around on loft ladders without me. No argument.'

'God. Poor Dulcie. I probably won't do any of that this time. And I don't think there even is a loft. It's more so I can see what's what. Make an inventory.'

It was clear to her that the house would need to be sold. And emptied before that. There didn't seem any point in delaying the inevitable. It was like pretending Iris would be coming home. And she wouldn't.

So some stuff needed to be sold. God knows what it was worth – Tess was no expert. Some given away. And, the worst of all, Iris's personal possessions sifted through.

And there was only her to take responsibility for it. She'd told Donna she was going. There'd been a long pause. Donna hadn't looked at her, and so Tess couldn't read her expression. She'd blurted out into the silence that Holly was going too, and then Donna had turned her face towards her, and she still couldn't really read the expression, but she'd smiled her acceptance, and said something about catching up with her VAT returns, and needing to book up some appointments, and the moment had passed.

She was glad, of course, to have Holly with her.

The drive down was slow and wet. Holly's Toyota was about the same age as her daughter, with about a trillion miles on the clock and a tape deck, on which Holly played ancient tapes she kept in a black vinyl case under the back seat. She had pretty much the whole *Now That's What I Call Music* back catalogue (although she'd stopped buying them when they were only produced on CD. The noughties were both a mystery and an anathema to her, to Dulcie's despair) and a weakness for nineties hits, which she still liked to raucously sing along to, holding an imaginary hairbrush up to her mouth when she wasn't changing gear or indicating. It was impossible not to succumb. By the time they were halfway down the A303, Tess was singing a duet with her to All Saints' 'Never Ever'.

'God. I could do with a pair of baggy combats right about now . . .' Tess pulled her sweater up and undid the button of her jeans. Things were getting tight. These were her fat jeans.

'I hear you. Me too. Mine are actual buns, though, as opposed to buns in the oven.' Holly giggled. 'Not as acceptable at all.'

This was their first reference of the day to the baby. Tess loved Holly for not going on about it, for giving her the space and time she needed.

Holly's phone pinged with a WhatsApp message. 'Check that, will you? It'll be Dulcie.'

Tess rummaged around in Holly's capacious handbag for the phone and squinted to read the message.

All okay. Dreading today. Sachsenhausen. Feeling sad already.

'Oh God. Ask her who she's sharing with.'

Tess duly typed in the question, then held the phone in her hand to await a response.

'Is that a concentration camp?'

Holly nodded.

'God.'

Ping. 'What's she said?'

'Give me a minute . . .' Holly was wound tighter than usual.

'Ella. It's fine.'

'Who's Ella?'

'I have no idea. Not one of "the gang".' Holly made angry air quotes with her free hand.

'Well, that's just as well, maybe?'

'Maybe. You can't get much from an instant message, can you?'

'Don't worry. She'll be fine. It's just a couple of days.'

'I hope you're right.'

'She's made of stern stuff, my god-daughter.'

'I used to think so. I'm not so sure now. You get enough knocks, it gets harder to get up . . .'

'You think it's serious?'

Holly shrugged. 'I don't know.'

'Can't those things just blow over? I mean, you remember girls. Depressingly similar to women, now you come to think of it. We were them. Remember Malice?'

Holly grimaced. 'God. Yes. You had me, though.'

'That's true. Thank God for you.'

'Tell her I love her.'

Tess typed. 'I'll tell her *we* love her.' She pinged the message back. 'With emoticons.'

The house was cold; the thermostat was turned down low. Tess wondered if Iris had been keeping it like that. It was a horrible thought. Post was thick on the mat – they'd had to push hard to open the door. More had been picked up previously, and was piled on the hall table, unread.

Holly put the kettle on while Tess looked through the post for anything that needed answering, although it was mostly fliers and pizza menus. The doorbell rang. It was Carol, Iris's neighbour. Tess didn't know her well – she had only moved in several years ago – but Carol had been the one to call the ambulance when Iris had become so ill. She'd come now to check on Tess, when she'd heard the car, she said. She came in, and accepted Holly's offer of a cup of tea. The sitting room was neat and tidy – the cushions on the sofa all straight, the remote control next to an old copy of the *Radio Times*.

'I turned the heating down – I wasn't sure how long she'd be gone, you see, and I know the bills are monstrous at the best of times. Didn't seem to be any point heating an empty house. I didn't want you to think she sat in the cold – I made sure she didn't.'

'You've been so kind, Carol.' Tess wanted to cry. Hormones.

The woman shook her head, dismissing the thanks. 'She's a lovely woman. I was glad to look out for her.'

Holly came through with some tea on Iris's old tin tray.

Carol said she was very sorry to hear that Iris wouldn't be back, but Tess could hear the relief in her voice, and she understood it.

She knew that in the weeks – maybe months – before the chest infection, Iris had been getting worse – two or three times she'd locked herself out, and once Carol had found her in the front garden in her nightdress, looking for something, and talking about the lavender that hadn't grown there for years.

Carol had a husband and two teenage sons of her own. She must have viewed Iris's increasingly unpredictable behaviour with some fear. She barely knew Donna, and she understood that Tess was at least a couple of hours away, with a job and a life of her own. When she called, after each incident, there was apology in her voice. She always said, 'I'm not complaining, I just thought you ought to know . . .'

She hugged Tess when she left – a quick and shy embrace. 'Please give her my love. I know . . . I know she may not know me, but, like I said, she was a lovely lady.'

Tess hated being here without Iris. All the life the house once had seemed drained from it. She had more memories in this home than anywhere else – all vivid, happy, colourful. It had been her safe space and her happy place. Where she had felt most loved, and understood. That was all gone, with Iris. Without her warmth, it looked sad. She thought she might cry.

Holly put an arm around her shoulder. 'Get a grip,' she said gently. 'Let's get on with what we came for, hey? You list, I'll write.'

Gigi

Check-ups had become routine in the last three years, and Gigi had spent her life in a hospital, but there was just something about that word. Oncology. It was the worst word on the long list on the board in reception that told patients where to go. Because of the fear, she supposed. Fear of the unknown, or fear of what was bloody well perfectly known.

Whenever there was a telethon or an advert on the television or an article in a magazine that said that one in two or one in three people would be affected by cancer, Gigi said a silent prayer. Let her be the one for all of them, for Richard, and Christopher and Olly and Meg. And Ava. Let her brush with it be the only time for all of them.

Because she'd had it, but she'd survived it. She'd been the very luckiest of lucky ones. A breast-cancer survivor. She hadn't even found a lump herself. She'd just shown up for a routine mammogram, because she'd been called once she'd turned fifty. She'd shown up like she'd been showing up for years for her cervical smears. Because that's what you did. She'd gone alone to the screening clinic. Barely even thought about it. She'd made an appointment for after a shift, so she wouldn't have to drive to the hospital and pay parking on a day off. She was meeting Meg afterwards, to shop for a dress for Meg's GCSE prom. Another dress. There were two already at home, still tagged and hanging on the wardrobe, under consideration. She was going to make the same joke at the till in yet another shop – that there'd been less fuss about her own wedding than there was about her daughter's prom. Try to dissuade her from the sluttiest options without incurring her teenage wrath. Take her for a Nando's on the way home – keeping those vital lines of communication open – and let Richard fend for himself. The mammogram was supposed to take half an hour out of that ordinary day. That was all. She hadn't really thought about it, bar remembering to shave her armpits in the shower, and choosing the whitest bra in the drawer. Not until she was topless in a tiny room, with her left boob shoved into something that looked like a meat slicer and the radiographer had stopped making small talk.

She'd known what that meant. She'd seen obstetricians do it. Sonographers. Concentrating hard, not able to make small talk. Because they knew something was wrong.

No one ever knew how quickly complete panic and sheer terror could descend on a person, unless it had happened to them. It was true, what they said. The world of prom dresses and food and everything else literally emergency stopped. And your disobedient, frightened mind leapt way ahead. And it was all bad – a kaleidoscope of what you'd say, when you told them. How you'd look bald. Whether you were a brave person, or a cry baby. Your funeral. How they'd cope without you. The things you would miss. You simply could not stop your brain. No Mindfulness technique or meditation could help you, in those minutes while you stood, vulnerable, and waited for the radiographer to bring the doctor in. Maybe there'd be room for all the good thoughts – optimism, hope, positivity. But not at the very start. Not for Gigi at least. It had been all dark.

And after they'd said they'd seen something they didn't like the look of, and showed her a grey cloud on the picture, and offered to biopsy her there and then, and asked her if she wanted to call somebody, the thoughts kept coming, even as she said no, thank you, she was fine. Even as she texted Meg, and told her she was staying a while longer with a mother she didn't want to leave, knowing that Meg would accept it, albeit grudgingly, because Gigi was often with a mother she didn't want to leave . . . As they gave her the local anaesthetic, on her side, near her armpit, and it hurt more than she'd thought it would, and sudden hot tears had sprung into her eyes, and she'd apologized to the nurse for crying because she couldn't help it . . . As the doctor dug around inside her with a thick needle, because the lump was buried deep in an F-cup breast, and that was why she hadn't felt it yet . . . And as she sat in the waiting area drinking a sugary tea they made for her, not letting her leave for thirty minutes, with a small dressing taped to her incision. The thoughts kept coming, and they were all dark.

There'd been a full waiting room when she'd arrived. By the time she had finished her tea, everyone else had gone home, and there were just two of them. Her, and a much younger girl she hadn't noticed earlier. Reflecting her pale, worried face back at her, sipping tea from a plastic cup and smiling weakly. When she had a frightened mother, Gigi always told her it would be all right. She'd smile determinedly. And it was all right. She couldn't think of a single thing to say to the frightened girl opposite.

A week, she'd waited for the results. A long, long week. She hadn't told a soul. How could she? Meg was in the middle of her exams. When the thirty minutes were up, she'd gone to her car, sat there and cried for what felt like ages. Then she'd blown her nose, wiped the mascara from under her eyes, turned the radio up very loud and driven home to her family. For seven days she kept her secret, kept it by concentrating on them. The third prom dress was bought; the two rejects were returned. Appointments for hair and nails and tan and makeup were made. Meg's flashcards were read and tested and read out loud again. Meals were cooked and cleaned up; babies were delivered at work.

She might have told Richard if she'd thought he'd help her. But she knew he wouldn't. It was enough to carry herself for this week. She couldn't carry him too. He'd fall apart. Be sadder than her, more scared than her, see things more darkly. That wouldn't help. That would come if it was bad news, and she already dreaded the weight of him on her, but then there'd be no choice.

She was at home, doing the ironing and watching doubles tennis at Wimbledon on Day 7, when the doctor who'd taken the biopsy telephoned her herself and told her she was sorry, but the lump was a malignancy, and she needed to come back in and discuss her options. It was the day of Meg's last exam. French. They'd been laughing the night before – she'd instigated a ban on English at dinner, and they'd spoken French. Meg had done that laughter-that-turns-into-tears thing a stressed teenager can do so easily, and laughed and cried that they'd probably made it worse and she'd be lucky to get a C. But Gigi had waved her off with a *bonne chance* nonetheless, and Meg had smiled and stuck her tongue out. Richard had the afternoon off to play eighteen holes of golf with a friend. It was the hottest day of the year so far, so she was ironing with the French doors wide open, though there was precious little breeze.

A funny thing happened. Knowing was appreciably less bad than not knowing. Now there had to be a plan. Now there was something to do. There was peculiar relief in knowing. Now positivity and optimism flooded into the cracks.

And when she did have to tell them, it was okay. By then she'd gone back to the clinic. Understood everything for herself. And she was ready to help them deal with it.

In the end, it wasn't nearly as bad as it could have been. They'd caught it really early. Her prognosis was very good. The treatment plan was minimally invasive breast-sparing surgery – a lumpectomy that would leave her breast looking much the same (still too big, she'd joked with the surgeon – she'd been hoping a great new pair of knockers would be the reward). If the doctors were able to get clear margins on the tumour, and they believed they would be able to, no chemotherapy. No sickness. No baldness. No getting half poisoned to death. Six weeks of radiation treatment. With side effects that should be limited to fatigue, or skin irritations. It was okay. Not nearly as bad as it could have been. And that was what she told them. No fuss, she'd said. Carrying on as normally as possible.

Megan cried. She was exhausted herself, by ten GCSEs, and the pressure of her own future bearing down on her, overwrought already. She asked a dozen or so questions, wanted a long cuddle on the sofa, chose to listen to her mother and believe her when she told her it would be all right, and then moved on, relatively quickly. She was young, with all the self-absorption and short-sightedness that comes with youth, and a childlike faith in the truthfulness of her parent. There was a prom, and a week in a villa on the Algarve with a friend's family . . .

Her boys were appropriately concerned, each different in their approach. Christopher immediately read up on every aspect of her planned surgery, googled every doctor at the hospital who might possibly carry it out and made a recommendation based on their star ratings. Olly sent flowers – a ridiculously large and over-the-top, artfully artless bouquet of exactly the sort he knew she loved, which came with a box of champagne truffles – and joked with her on the phone about wigs. He'd shave her head for her, he said, when the time came, and his too for solidarity. He'd professed disappointment when she'd said she wasn't going to lose her hair. They had laughed raucously. There had never been a situation in her life when Olly hadn't been able to make her laugh, and this one had turned out, wonderfully, to be no exception.

Friends were faultless too, filling the freezer with lasagnes and planning small treats. At work, her shifts were unobtrusively covered and shortened and rearranged so that she could stay at work, where she wanted to be, but do a little less. She took a week off after the lumpectomy, and then needed odd days after the radiation treatments, when she felt more tired than she could ever have imagined, and needed to roll over and sleep. But they helped lend her life the illusion of carrying on as normal, and for that she was very grateful. None of the women she attended for the whole time she was getting treatment knew or even suspected there was anything different about her at all: that was a matter of huge pride to her.

She spent more time at the home with James. He knew

nothing about any of it, of course, and she told no one else there, and there was freedom in that. It was peaceful, sitting beside him. Sometimes he was up to a crossword, or a Sudoku. More often they just sat. It was a habit she'd never really broken. Some people had yoga. She had James.

It was just Richard who let her down. She had hoped he wouldn't, but somehow wasn't surprised when he did. He had always needed her to be the stronger one – the manager, the coper.

She remembered the moment she'd realized that her marriage was going to be this way. It had been different times – they didn't think to live together before they got married. You'd describe their courtship as whirlwind, but it was just how it was in those days. Across a two- or three-year period almost every girl in her class at the nursing school met and married someone. As if life was one big game of musical chairs, or marriage a sort of contagion. The advent of Facebook had reunited her with most of them in recent years, and you could hardly be surprised that more than half of them were divorced. She knew she didn't want to marry a doctor – though some of her classmates viewed them as the Holy Grail of husbands – so when the nice-looking junior accountant she met in the pub expressed an interest, she let him take her out on a date. And another. He'd proposed after nine months, and they married five months after that, on a bright May day. She longed for a home of her own, and a double bed rather than the cramped back seat of his beaten-up Morris Marina. They'd been married less than a year when she'd fallen quickly and easily pregnant with their first child. They'd been very happy – it was sooner than was sensible, probably, but they both wanted the baby very much. She'd miscarried at eleven weeks. She vividly recalled the sharp pain that doubled her over suddenly that afternoon, the crushing sadness and disappointment she'd felt, the sense of failure she knew was wrong but couldn't shake, the wretchedness of the D&C that followed. Things weren't as good then as they were now. People didn't talk about it so much. You weren't supposed to mourn as though you'd lost a baby, and that was hard, because you had. And she vividly recalled that Richard couldn't cope. Didn't help. It forced her to swallow her own grief to help him through his own, and she registered even through the fog of sadness that this was a failure in him she couldn't have seen before.

They got past it, because you did. You glossed over what was missing, and made yourself focus on what was there, what was good. And life was good, in so many ways. Doctors gave them no reason to suppose this would happen again, and it didn't. She fell pregnant again the same year, and, although she held herself taut with fear until she was well through the pregnancy, and didn't, couldn't, enjoy it the way she knew other mothers who hadn't miscarried were able to, when Christopher was born, healthy and straightforward, it was good, and she was profoundly grateful for a long time. Richard found it easier to cope, and she was too happy to find fault.

But the pattern was set. Several years later, when Christopher broke his leg – a nasty compound fracture – it was Gigi who coped. When Olly suffered from asthma in his early years, it was Gigi who coped . . .

The balance had inevitably tipped more over time, with habit. When she needed to lean, he suddenly needed it more, and he sometimes threatened to push her right over in the process. So, of course, she learnt not to lean, but, little by little, almost by stealth, it eroded something at the very core of how she felt about him.

When she was ill, he should have been the person she could talk to, late at night in the silent house, about her deepest fears. He should have held her when she was exhausted. He should have made everything okay. He should have carried her across that period. And he didn't. And afterwards, she found she could never completely forgive him for it.

Perhaps she should have left him then. But that was too enormous a thing to have done. She was too frightened. Too bloody hopeful. Too damned grateful. And the children? How could she have taken them to the edge and back of that dark abyss, and then flung them headlong into another? She told herself anything and everything she needed to. That it wasn't his fault. That she couldn't expect him to change. To live with it. Just live, in fact. Nonetheless, as her belief that she would survive had grown, her resentment had grown alongside it. An insidious, insistent Japanese knotweed of a feeling.

So check-ups were routine now. And, with each one, the wave of returning fear crashed on a beach further and further out to sea, never disappearing altogether, but becoming more distant, an echo of itself. They were six-monthly now, and there'd never been anything abnormal. After five years even those appointments would stop. She'd go back to being almost like everyone else, who'd never had to turn left at the desk and follow the sign to Oncology. Almost. It was an act of will not to imagine a brain tumour behind every headache, a melanoma in every mole, but she practised it hard.

It was true too that it gave you a gift, being a survivor.

A brush with your mortality – it made you bloody glad to be alive. It made wasting days seem criminal. It made you less prone to road rage and being impatient in long lines. Less likely to wait to book that holiday you read about in the magazine. Less bothered about the three stone you kept losing (Atkins, cabbage, Slimfast) that kept finding you (bread basket, cake, cherry brandy) through your forties. It made you want to change everything black and white about your life into colour. It woke you up.

What did catch up with her at every check-up was the memory of how let down she'd felt by Richard at that time. She couldn't think it away as easily as the other things. She made a point of never going straight home after an appointment. She always had a plan with a girlfriend. Dinner, a film, a show . . . She needed a moment, and probably a cocktail and a good giggle, before she went home to Richard. Otherwise she might just tell him.

Today's was clear. As with all the others, Gigi didn't know how much she'd been dreading hearing something else until she heard the good news. You told yourself it was routine, but you didn't believe it, not in your deepest self. You were always waiting for it to come back, and on those days – on check-up days – that fear crept very near the surface of you, and lurked malevolently. The oncologist beamed when she was called back into the room, and closed her file decisively for another six months. And relief broke over her like a warm bath, reaching to the edge of every muscle and sinew that had held itself clenched.

Today's buffer between the appointment with oncology and Richard was mojitos with Kate. Gigi opened her handbag and took out her lipstick.

Tess

'Right, then, I'll see about getting us some teas, shall I?'

Donna always did this the moment they arrived. It was as if she couldn't bear just to be in the room with Iris. She had to be busy. Once the tea had been drunk, she'd collect up the cups and saucers, chattering about helping out the staff, them being so busy and all, and be off again. She'd tidy the drawers, smooth the counterpane, rearrange the photographs. Fidget and fuss until it was time to go. Which was ironic, since at home those small tasks never occurred to her, and went entirely undone. Tess knew she couldn't help it, that it was her coping mechanism, but nonetheless she usually ended up wishing she'd come alone.

The nurse who'd brought them in stood with her hand on the handle of the open door. Tess hadn't met her before. Her badge said her name was Sandy. She looked kind. Iris's thin white hair had been combed recently: she looked fresh and sweet. Tess felt the rush of gratitude she always felt for the tenderness of these carers for people they didn't love.

Tess sat down in the armchair next to Iris's, taking her grandmother's cool, powdery hand in her own. Iris gave it willingly without acknowledging Tess. The hand felt tiny and ineffectual in her own, the skin almost translucent, the veins prominent. Iris's engagement ring was twisted so that the small stones were facing into her palm. Tess gently turned it on Iris's finger. Iris looked from the ring to her face, and then back at the ring.

'She's been chatty this afternoon, haven't you, Iris? We had a bath, a lovely clean-up. And she was chatting away the whole time.'

Despite her gratitude, Tess bridled slightly at Sandy's tone of voice – undoubtedly gentle but too childlike. The use of 'we'. It seemed as inevitable as the smell in places like this.

Iris ignored the question, still staring at the ring.

'Yes, very chatty. Been talking about a Tom.'

'Tom?'

'Is that your grandad?'

'No. My granddad was Wilf.'

'Is he . . .'

Tess shook her head quickly. 'I never knew him. He died the year before I was born.'

'Well, it's definitely Tom she's been talking about today. Do you know who that is?'

'I don't think so.'

'Not to worry. That happens.'

I know, Tess thought. I know that happens. Someone like Iris – their brain can alight on any moment of their entire lives, real or imaginary, true or false. Their minds are kaleidoscopes. Their histories are tessellated. 'What's she been saying about Tom?'

Iris, who had been sitting staring ahead, her expression vacant, broke into a broad smile at hearing the name again, not entirely kind somehow, and now looked directly at Tess. Her eyes were suddenly alive.

'He didn't mean it. He didn't. He was trying to explain. That's all. He loved me. He loved me so much. And I loved him . . .'

She knew she shouldn't, she knew there was no point,

but Tess gently corrected her. 'You mean, Wilf, Gran. You were married to Wilf. Not Tom. Remember?'

There was a crack in the door of Iris's memory, and she could see the light through it. She wanted to push the door further open.

'Not my husband, you silly goose. I know that. He was very handsome you know. He had that limp. But he was still so upright . . .'

'Yes, yes. He limped. That's right.' Iris had told her. An injury from his time in the army, during the war. She felt almost excited.

'And do you know, he could still dance. Foxtrot. Waltz. He was a beautiful dancer, before. But he still danced afterwards. He used to take me to the Roxy, before you were born.'

'Before my mum . . . before Donna.'

Iris's brow furrowed. 'Donna.' But there was no recognition.

Tess felt desperate to keep Iris in whatever memory it was. 'Were you a good dancer?'

Iris looked out of the window and moved her head as though she was listening to music. 'Only with him to lead me . . .'

For a moment, Iris danced in her imagination, young again. Tess watched the unfamiliar movements, enchanted, and smiled.

Then, when the silent music stopped, she looked into Iris's face and immediately felt her own enchantment turn to sadness. *Where are you, Gran? Where are you today, hey? And why can't you be here, with me?*

Sitting quietly in the late-afternoon sunshine, Iris's hand in her own, Tess's memory strayed to the holidays when she'd been a child, and staying with Iris at her home in Salisbury. She had spent at least a month each summer there since she was seven or eight, and odd weeks in other school holidays, and God how she'd loved those long holidays – looked forward to them through the long, slow winters and interminable school terms, counting down the days after May half-term. Donna always bought the train tickets a few weeks ahead of their departure date – to get the best deal – and once the tickets were displayed on the small mantelpiece in their sitting room, Tess could let her excitement build. They spoke on the telephone, of course, and Iris sent cards and letters in the post, but there was nothing like actually being with her.

Even as a small girl, she had understood that her mother needed time by herself. For as long as she could remember, she had carried the knowledge that she exhausted her mother. That of all the balls her mother juggled, and talked about juggling in wearied tones at home, she was the heaviest and most difficult. She was too young to understand guilt, but she recognized that she was lighter at Gran's, where she didn't feel it. They had different smiles, Mum and Gran. Mum's had no teeth in it – her lips were pressed tightly together and the quick smile often didn't have time to reach her eyes. Iris beamed broadly, especially at her.

She used to feel a fizz of joyfulness, deep in her tummy, on the train on the way down, counting off the stations en route – Basingstoke, Overton, Whitchurch, Andover – while her mum read *Rolling Stone* and dozed . . . After the train pulled out of Grately Station she would pack her comics and colouring book and pencils away in her bag and sit with her knees jiggling on the edge of her seat, staring out of the window at the fields and villages flashing by. The last quarter of an hour was the longest – endless.

Then she'd be on the platform, and Iris was always there waiting, her arms spread wide for Tess to run into. Sometimes her mother stayed for one night, but most often the three of them would walk into the town centre and have lunch at a café where the market was and then Donna would return to London. Tess never recalled missing her mother, but she did remember wanting her to get on that train and leave the two of them by themselves. When she was twelve, her mum declared that she was old enough to travel alone, and she'd put her on the train with a packed lunch and a piece of notepaper on which she had written all her details, and all of Iris's.

Iris was available to her for almost all of Tess's sentient childhood, and the sheer heady marvellousness of having an adult devoted only to her – with nothing else pulling at her time – was the most wonderful thing in Tess's life then. Not even domesticity took her away – they did those chores together, and thus they were really a part of the play.

Her grandmother's house was on a nice, tidy street about ten minutes from the centre of town. Tess remembered when the window boxes used to be planted with lavender that she liked to run her fingers through, to release a waft of their fragrance. She could still smell them now, and the scent always made her nostalgic, and sometimes melancholy.

She could clearly remember the waking-up feeling of every morning. She'd wake naturally – no alarms or time pressures – in the big bed in Iris's spare room, with its yellow sprigged wallpaper from Laura Ashley, experiencing the delicious feeling that today, like yesterday and tomorrow, would most definitely be fun. She'd run into Iris's room and climb into her grandmother's even bigger bed for a cuddle, until Tess was quite old. Iris was always awake before her, it seemed, sitting up in bed with a cup of tea from the Teasmade, her glasses on and a book or yesterday's newspaper in her hands. She said old people didn't need as much sleep as young people. She would look at Tess over the top of her glasses as she opened the door and beam at her: 'Good morning, my angel.' Over breakfast – always, always with hot chocolate and Terry Wogan on Radio 2 – they planned . . . It might be a bus to the seaside, a trip to the market, a picnic by the river. Most often, though, they stayed at home.

Iris had a whole room in her house devoted to crafts. It was technically the dining room, but since she and Tess only ate at the small square table in the kitchen, or sometimes on trays with cushiony bottoms in the front room, when they were watching a film on the television, Iris said it was a sad and wasted room if you just kept it for that once-in-a-blue-moon stuff. She said it just reminded her of all the people who had sat and eaten with her and no longer could. On what must have been her dining table, there was a sewing machine, and a big green mat that it was safe to cut on, and usually some newspapers were spread out to contain mess, on the table, and on the floor underneath. On the dark-wood sideboard opposite the fireplace, alongside a photograph in a gold frame of her granddad, there were loads of boxes of amazing things: embroidery threads and small plastic tubes of glitter and buttons and bugle beads and fat quarters for quilting.

The two of them always had a project – they made up their minds what it would be on the first day, poring over

Iris's crafting magazines, and then spent the whole summer trip working at it. One year they made a farmyard of animals – a cow, a pig, a chicken and a sheep – layering newspapers on to balloons to make the papier-mâché shapes and then, once they'd dried, painting on the details. Another year they learnt how to make mosaics out of coloured glass and shells, sticking them on to wooden boxes and mirror frames. There was the summer of knitting and crochet – long, colourful scarves and baby blankets. And one year Iris had bought an old doll's house before Tess got there and they had done it up – wallpapering the bedrooms, and tiling the roof with tiny terracotta tiles they'd sent off for in the post.

It had seemed, to a young Tess, that Iris knew everything, could remember everything. She knew the answer to every question Tess had ever asked her, at least until GCSE maths and science homework, and she'd been able to explain so many things. Tess had thought of her as the smartest, wisest, most interesting person she had ever known, not just the most loving.

Iris had a small greenhouse in her back garden with a thrillingly exotic grapevine in it, which produced a small but delicious crop of grapes, and they also grew tomatoes and lettuce for their salad lunches. Iris would send Tess out with a glass bowl to pick what they needed.

If she was ever tired, or bored, Iris never showed it. She seemed, then, to have boundless energy, and limitless enthusiasm for whatever they were doing. In the playground she could sit on the seesaw and keep going until Tess was tired of bouncing. She never said no to a game of Operation or Mousetrap after supper.

And always there was chatter. They talked all day.

Laughing at nothing much. 'Look at us! We'd laugh to see a pudding crawl,' she'd say, so they'd giggle all over again, because that was so ridiculous. Tess had grown up thinking everyone said that. Somewhere across the years of their friendship, Holly had started repeating it.

Played now, in this room, they were a reel of pure, golden memories – vivid and powerful and the absolute happiest of Tess's life.

This silent, still person whose hand she held now was reduced, in every conceivable way, to a husk of that person whom she had loved so much. But she loved her still, and the pain of missing someone who was alive and breathing next to you was so sharp it caught in Tess's chest, just below her throat, and when her mother came noisily back into the room with a tray of tea, muttering about something inconsequential, it was a sheer relief to have her there to distract her from the ache.

There was a gentle knock on the open door.

'Come in.'

It was Gigi, the woman from the day room, that first day. 'I thought it was you. I'm the nosiest of the nosy. I saw your grandmother's name on the board – they always put a new resident's name up there – and I remembered you'd said she was Iris. I'm so glad.'

Tess smiled. 'Mum, this is –'

'I'm Gigi. Gigi Gilbert. I met Tess when she was looking around.'

'Donna. Pleased to meet you.' They must be about the same age, Tess thought. But there the similarities between them seemed to end. Gigi was round and soft; Donna angular and sharp. Gigi emanated an open warmth; Donna seemed guarded and careful beside her.

'And this is Iris?'

Gigi took Iris's hand in her own. 'Hello, Iris.' Her soft voice was kind and patient, but not patronizing. 'Welcome.'

'Gigi visits her father-in-law,' Tess offered by way of explanation. 'James, was it?'

'That's right. Four doors down, on the left. I won't stay any longer. I just wanted to say hello. And that I'm here if you need anything. At all . . .'

'That's so kind.'

'I'll see you again. You too, Donna.'

Iris had dozed off in the chair, her head back against the headrest, her mouth slightly open. Tess wondered about moving her, but she didn't look uncomfortable. Donna was leaning on the windowsill, looking out at the gardens.

'It's nice here, really, isn't it? You could just imagine it, how it must have been once . . . beautiful. The gardens are lovely. That's a pond over there, isn't it? More of a lake, really.'

'Mum?'

'Yeah?'

'Do you know who Tom is?'

Donna thought for a moment, her forehead furrowed. 'Nope. Can't think of one. Why?'

'The nurse said Iris had been talking about a Tom. I think she must have been talking about Grandad. But she said she wasn't.'

'She doesn't really know, though, right?'

'She seemed adamant.'

Donna shrugged. 'I don't know . . .'

Tess thought for a moment. 'Is there stuff you wish you'd asked her, or told her . . . you know, before?'

'Like what?'

Tess laughed. 'I don't know. Nothing specific. But all kinds of things. I keep thinking of things I don't know about her. I had all those years, and I never asked. Not big important stuff. Not just that. Little things. I think it's just that you know you can't now . . .'

Donna came over and squeezed her shoulder, her voice soft and gentle. 'You loved her. She loved you.'

'She loved you too.'

Donna sighed, and took a moment to answer. 'I know she did. You've gotta let it go, sweetheart.'

'I know that.'

'You've had too much time to think, sat by this bed.'

'That's probably true. But it's where I want to be.'

Week 15. Apple sized. And now your head is just a head, and not all prehistoric and Garpy any more. There's a proper neck, and a chin. You look just like a baby now. Two arms, two legs, bendy knees and elbows, ten fingers and toes, ears and a nose. You're still soft around the edges – but you're all there. Inside your eyelids – still shut – it's all about your eyes this week. Apparently, you can make facial expressions now – you know, scowl, smile, gurn. I wish I had a scan machine at home. I'd like to see you every day.

Tess

'Shit.'

Tess had reversed out of her space in the Clearview car park without looking, distracted. Distracted by having stayed with Iris longer than she should have done, by being likely to be late for work, by feeling stressed about that, and then more stressed because she knew she wasn't supposed to be letting herself feel stressed. It was incredibly bad for the baby. All the websites said so. She was making a conscious effort to channel a bit of Donna and be a bit more zen. It wasn't coming naturally.

And now she'd gone and hit another car, one that had evidently pulled in front of her as part of a reverse-parking manoeuvre into a space in the row behind. Neither of them had been going fast, thank God, but the sound of the impact, corner to corner, was sickening nonetheless. 'Bugger.' This didn't help the lateness or the stress.

Tess gripped the steering wheel tightly with both hands while the unpleasant shot of adrenalin made its way around her body, taking deep breaths and muttering to herself.

She heard the door of what she presumed was the car she'd hit open and close, and braced herself to look up at the driver as he approached. To her shame and embarrassment, as if hitting him wasn't enough, now she was going to cry. Tears came so much quicker and more easily these days, damn them.

She heard him before she saw him.

'You okay in there?'

She put one hand out of the open window and waved in a way that said she was, while the other hand rubbed at her face, willing the tears to stop.

Of course the voice came to the window anyway. Stooped and leant in towards her.

'Hey. All right?'

She looked up at him, powerless to stop crying.

'Oh God. You're not all right. What's wrong? Are you hurt?'

'No. I'm fine. Just . . . humiliated. And stupid. I'm so, so sorry.'

'Hey, it's okay. It was just a bump, that's all. Just a bump.'

'It was completely my fault. I'm insured –'

'Don't worry about that now.'

'No, but I am . . . I know you're never supposed to admit it was your fault, but that totally, totally was. I'm so sorry.'

'I'm sure you are. Just take a moment.' He produced a handkerchief from his pocket and handed it to her through the window. 'Here.'

She looked at him now. He looked to be about her age. Short, wavy hair. Smart. Kind eyes.

'Are you a visitor or do you work here?'

'Visitor. I've just been to see my gran.'

'I'm Olly. Just on my way to see my granddad.' He smiled. That was kind too.

'I'm Tess.'

Recognition passed across his face. 'I know you.'

'You do?'

'My mum's talked to me about you. That sounds weird. She's mentioned you, not talked about you. You're new, right?'

She nodded. Remembered. 'You're Olly?'

He smiled at her again. It was, she realized, rather like the sun coming out and warming your skin on a spring day. Unexpected, welcome, nice. God, that was corny. She'd rather die than describe that to someone. But that was exactly how it felt. 'That's me.'

'God. That makes it worse, I think . . .' She might cry again, which horrified her. 'Your mum is so lovely. She's been so kind. Sorry. I'm so sorry.'

'You said.' Now the smile was a grin. He seemed as relaxed as she was wired. 'Enough with the apologies. And it should make it better, not worse.'

'Is it bad?'

Olly stood upright and walked around to the back of Tess's car, bending over to assess the damage.

'Well, I won. Put it that way.'

Tess undid her seatbelt and went to join him. He was right. She'd broken the red glass on the rear light on her car and stoved in a small part of the panel beside it. But she'd caught his on the bumper, and it looked like that was all.

Her heart was thumping.

'See. No real damage done.'

'But your bumper –'

'And the clue is in the name. That's what they're for. Bumps.'

She looked anxiously at her own light.

'Listen. I'm no expert, but I think you're all right to drive. There is still plenty of red glass. The bulb behind looks fine. It'll need repairing of course, but it's not urgent if you can still see a red light. You need some tape – bet they've got some in the office. That'll hold the cracked glass in place until you get to a garage. Long as you do it in the next week or so I don't think you'll get in any trouble.'

'D'you think?'

'I do. Can I help you? Go get some tape?'

Tess knew she should refuse – at least pretend to be a competent, independent woman. Ordinarily she would have done. She wasn't quite herself, for a myriad of reasons.

He wasn't waiting for a reply. 'Let me just park up. You go forward into the space. Unless you want me to –'

'No, no, I can.'

And he was in his car and reversing. She got into her own and edged it the six or seven feet forward back into the space she'd been coming out of.

'I'll go get the tape . . . wait here for me, or come inside and have a cup of tea or something.'

'I'll wait. Thank you.'

So Tess waited, wondering whether what she felt was just gratitude. Telling herself it had to be, because raging, disobedient hormones aside, there was no other rational explanation.

And inside, while Olly waited for the girl on reception to find some duck tape with which he could repair the broken rear light, he tried hard not to wonder why helping this girl with the luminous, wide blue eyes full of tears had suddenly become the only important thing he had to do with his day.

Gigi

Richard wasn't coming to see James today. He was playing golf with friends, and having dinner, and going to some award ceremony or other afterwards – she neither knew nor cared about the details – so the day stretched long and free. Chris and Emily had been invited to a colleague's wedding – childfree. Gigi had jumped at the chance to have Ava and had even persuaded them (persuaded Christopher – in truth Emily hadn't needed convincing) that they should stretch the day into a well-deserved Ava-free weekend. The travel cot had duly been dropped off, with various other bits of baby paraphernalia; Christopher had handed her a list of numbers, emails, addresses and GP information; and, with much fond eye-rolling from his wife, he'd finally handed over the baby and driven off. Now Gigi was delighting in having her beloved granddaughter to herself for two whole sleeps, and days. Ava was more and more interactive each time she saw her, and it was an unalloyed, albeit exhausting, joy. As much as she loved Emily, there was an undeniable pleasure in autonomous grandparenting.

Ava's appearance at Clearview was greeted with much the same enthusiasm with which crowds greeted visiting popes. From the girl on reception, who'd leapt up from her seat and gone round the desk to cluck over her, to the nurses and custodial staff and the caterers in the canteen, every-one fussed. Ava took to the fanfare like a duck to water, beaming prettily at a parade of strangers as though this was her destiny, grabbing badges and hair where she could, and making those enchanting baby-talk noises for all the world as though she was having an in-depth discussion.

She even sat on James's lap, though it made him more anxious to hold her than she was to be held, and he begged Gigi to take the 'beautiful, precious girl' he didn't know off his lap after a minute or two, afraid, he said, that he'd drop her. Gigi remembered him, completely comfortable, with Meg – how he'd hold her, facing him, and bounce her on his knee, her fat little legs kicking with delight, her chortle echoing. That James had never been afraid of hurting his grandchildren, and he never once had. Lucky them. She'd taken a few fast photographs on her iPhone and then rescued Ava.

She noticed Iris sitting across the room. She was staring at them and smiling fondly. Gigi rested Ava comfortably on her hip and went over to her.

'Hello, Iris.'

'Hello.' There was no sign that she knew who Gigi was, but her voice was calm and friendly. 'And who is this little lady?'

'This is Ava.'

'Hello, Ava. Aren't you beautiful?'

Gigi leant towards her, Ava gurgling and chattering. 'Would you like to hold her?'

Iris looked touched. 'Could I?'

'Of course. Here you go, Ava . . . you have a cuddle with Iris.'

Iris held her with the competence and confidence of a mother, uncertainty falling away from her the instant the baby was on her lap. She put one arm around Ava's waist, and, with the other hand, gently stroked her baby curls. All the while she murmured softly to her. Ava relaxed and sprawled happily against Iris's chest, leaning her head back and staring, enthralled, at where the voice was coming from. For a few minutes, Iris was just lost in Ava. The two of them stared at each other, Ava mimicking Iris's exaggerated facial movements – mouth opening wide on an intake of breath, a nod, wide eyes.

They were lovely to look at, and it was a few moments before Gigi noticed that Tess had come in. She'd been half expecting her – Iris wasn't usually in the day room unless they expected visitors, and Tess was far and away the most frequent of those – the only one for Iris, apart from her mother, Donna. But Gigi had been riveted by Iris. She'd only known this lady confused and old. But watching her now, with Ava, you could see so very clearly who she had once been.

When she caught sight of Tess out of the corner of her eye she could see at once that the sight was doubly poignant for Tess – who *had* known her otherwise.

She went over to her, and hugged her briefly. 'Look at your gran.'

'I know. Is that your granddaughter?'

'Ava.' Gigi nodded. 'I'm sole-charge granny this weekend – Chris and Emily have gone off to a wedding in Dorset . . . I'm in heaven!'

'She's adorable.'

'And look at Iris. She's had her for ages. They're old friends at this point.'

'She looks so comfortable with her.'

'Doesn't she?!'

'It's gorgeous.' Tess kissed her grandmother's head. 'Hi, Gran. Who've you got here?'

Iris thought for a moment. 'Ava. Like Ava Gardner. The film star. Except she wasn't as lovely as this little one is, was she? No, she wasn't . . .' And it was more like she was talking only to Ava, in that melodic tone.

Tess laughed. 'She's so happy with you.'

'Ah, she's a happy girl, aren't you, Ava? You were like that. You'd sit on my lap for ages. You'd go to anyone, for a cuddle. Just like this. Friendly, and easy.'

'Was I?' It was clear from Tess's expression that it had been a long time since Iris had offered up a memory.

She smiled at Gigi and the two women held each other's glance for a moment, sharing the sentiment, both made happy by this brief recapturing of something.

'You have a hold, Tess.' Iris was looking right at her.

Tess looked at Gigi. 'Go ahead.'

Iris went to lift Ava, but she was too heavy. Tess scooted to take her before she lurched forward, and held her at some distance from her body, under both arms, staring at her for a moment. She smelt of powder and milk and fabric softener: delicious and quintessentially baby. Tess instinctively rested Ava against her shoulder, one hand under her well-padded bottom, the other on the back of her neck, although Ava had hers under full control. She bobbed slightly at the knees too.

'See, you're a natural.' This was Iris too, looking on approvingly.

Tess looked at Gigi, who was looking at her in a way she couldn't quite interpret. When she caught her eye, Gigi nodded. 'A natural . . .'

Gigi

Oliver had rung earlier in the week to check if Gigi was working on Wednesday – he had a client call to make near the coast, he said, and he'd come by on his way back to town if his mother was going to be home. Take them both to the pub for supper, if they'd wanted. Gigi said she was on an early, but she'd rather cook at home for them. And, because she couldn't help herself, might Caitlin be persuaded to join them?

Oliver didn't think so. She was at a conference, he said quickly, so it wouldn't work. Gigi didn't entirely believe him – the excuse rolled too quickly off his tongue. If they'd been face to face, she'd have called him out on it, but on the phone she had no choice but to accept it.

She loved having him at home. And she was glad, in truth, he was on his own. She loved him filling the kitchen, like he always used to, with his big laugh, peering under saucepan lids, pouring them big glasses of wine from the bottle he'd bought. He'd given her early daffodils too – a big bunch. They sat in a vase on the kitchen table, a bright visual of how he had the power to change her mood. He livened up a Wednesday night in the best possible way.

'Mmmm. Smells delicious.'

Gigi dried her wet hands on a tea towel and took a swig of wine. 'It's just a casserole.'

'It's never just a casserole when you've made it, Mum.'

He did his best Dervla Kirwan M&S accent, deep and Irish. 'It's not just a casserole, it's a Gigi Gilbert beef and Guinness casserole . . .'

She joined in, her accent not so good. 'With buttery mashed potatoes and honey-glazed carrots.'

Oliver sat back and tapped his stomach in anticipation. 'Delish . . . Cheers.' He raised his glass in her direction. 'Dad.'

'Hmm.' Richard was here, but not. As per usual. 'Cheers.' But he didn't actually drink anything. Gigi rolled her eyes, and Oliver winked at her.

'I met your friend the other day.'

'What friend is that?'

'Your new Clearview buddy . . . Tess?'

'Oh. Yes. Lovely Tess. How come?'

'She reversed into me in the car park there.'

'You're joking?'

'It's okay. It wasn't bad. Just a touch, really.'

'God.'

'And a new back light for her.'

'The poor girl.'

'What's her story?' Oliver was keeping his tone casual and conversational.

'It's her grandmother – Iris, she's called. She's older than your granddad. I think Tess said she's ninety-six or something.'

'She just moved in?'

'Yes, just.'

'She seemed upset.'

'I think she's got a lot on her plate.'

'Yeah?'

Gigi narrowed her eyes, mock-suspicious. 'Why the interest?'

'What do you mean?'

'Well, I've got a few mates at Clearview. You end up making conversation, you know, while you're visiting the people with whom you can't really make conversation . . . there's a sort of a Dunkirk-spirit vibe. Would you like to know *their* stories?'

'Would you like to tell me?' Oliver winked at her.

Gigi deliberately didn't answer. No return of service. Were Oliver's cheeks just a little bit pink?

'Are any of them as good-looking as Tess?'

'Oh, you noticed, did you?' She opened her eyes wide.

'Good-looking as who?' Richard was reading the newspaper. She hadn't even known he was listening. Now he'd lowered the broadsheet and was peering at them over the top of it.

'Tess.' They spoke together. Richard raised an eyebrow quizzically.

'The newbie, at Clearview . . . I introduced you.'

'Oh, her. She *is* good-looking.' God, Gigi thought she must be, if even stuffy old Richard had noticed.

'She's a poppet too. A sweetie,' she couldn't help adding. She doubted anyone had ever called Caitlin a poppet. Oliver didn't answer. If he caught her heavy-handedness, he didn't let on. He pursed his lips and nodded, then picked up the '2' section of *The Times* and hid his face behind it.

Gigi turned back to the casserole. It had been on the tip of her tongue to mention that she suspected Tess had even more on her plate than she'd owned up to yet. But something had stopped her.

It wasn't unheard of for Oliver to show an interest in her friends. He liked people, and he'd never been particularly hung up on age, like some children were. He'd talk to anyone. But it was just a bit unusual – this interest in Tess.

Not that she'd do anything to encourage him. She was pretty sure Tess was pregnant. That was actual baggage. And she was doing her very best to be respectful and accepting of Caitlin. Wasn't she? But he was the one who had asked . . .

Gigi

In the end, Gigi didn't choose the moment she told Richard she was leaving him. The moment chose itself, and in some ways it surprised her almost as much as it shocked him. A regular weekday evening. Between a supper she'd cooked a thousand times, eaten with minimal conversation, with the *News at Ten* in prospect before another night falling asleep back to back after a chaste kiss and five pages of a novel. If she'd thought about it at all, ahead of time, she'd have thought it would be more explosive, that there'd need to be a trigger – something infuriating that caused an eruption which made it possible for her to say what she knew was going to cause so much hurt and disruption and change. Surely that was what it would take, for her to cause so much drama – a dramatic beginning. As if Richard might be capable of doing something that made it okay – understandable even – for her to implode their lives. She hadn't even had a drink for Dutch courage, for God's sake.

But it turned out that it wasn't a moment of high drama. It was the opposite. It was the crushing mundanity of the moment that brought the words into her head and out of her mouth before she'd even really decided what order in which to say them.

'I can't do this any more, Richard.'

The remark hung between them. Richard, who'd been reading the newspaper while she loaded the dishwasher, looked up. She met his questioning gaze.

He took off his reading glasses, genuinely puzzled. 'Do what?'

She spread her arms desperately. 'This. All of this. Any of this.'

She almost backed down. His confused expression physically hurt her.

'I don't understand, G. What's got into you?'

She knew he didn't. That was exactly the problem.

She sat down close to him. *Please*, she thought. *Please let me make him understand this. Please let him feel it too.* That would help us both. That would help me.

'We're not happy, Richard. You know we're not.'

'I'm fine.' His tone was defensive.

'Oh God. You're not. I'm sure as hell not. But, even if we were, Richard, what kind of a word is that to describe your life? "Fine".'

Richard shrugged. 'I'm sorry you don't like the word. Let me use another one. I'm happy, okay. Is that a better word?'

'Except that isn't true.'

'How do you know how I feel?' Indignant.

She took a very deep, slow breath. 'Okay. You're right. I'm sorry. I don't know how you feel. You never really tell me, not any more. So how could I? I know how you seem, but I don't know how you feel. So. Let me tell you how *I* feel. I am not happy.'

'You're unhappy . . . with me?'

Another deep breath. It felt like the most important thing in the world to make him understand.

'With you, with me, with my life, with our life . . . Yes. With all of it.'

Richard wouldn't meet her gaze. He was staring at the

table now, running the edge of his thumb up and down a deep scratch on the surface.

Gigi resisted the urge to speak into the silence. He had to be the next one to talk, and she made herself stay quiet while he absorbed her words. She knew each one had fallen on him like a physical blow. She felt a horrid pain too. These were the worst, the hardest things she'd ever said. But she could go only forward now. There was no taking them back.

When he did speak, there was fear, and a trembling in his voice, and he still couldn't meet her eye.

'Are you . . . have you . . . Is there someone else?'

'Of course not.' She registered surprise that he thought she might do that. And irritation. It was men who couldn't leave unless they had someone to leave for. Not women.

'It's not about that.' She put her hand on his. 'I would never, *never* do that to you.' He pulled his hand from under hers.

'It's about you and me, and this half-life we're living . . .'

She felt like she was clubbing a baby seal. His eyes were wide, and frightened. His expression was bewildered. It seemed like he'd instantly physically diminished – he was smaller, somehow, in the chair beside her.

But she knew she couldn't stop now.

Richard took a deep breath. 'What does it mean, Gigi?'

'It means I have to go, Richard.'

'Go where?'

'I don't know. I haven't been planning this, I promise. I'm making it up as I go along.'

'Well, stop, then.'

'I can't stop.'

'But this is madness. This is our home. Yours and mine.'

'I know.' She wanted to cry, but she clamped her jaw shut on the tears. Not now. Not in front of him.

'I don't want you to go.'

'I know that too. But I have to.'

'Is this forever?'

That, she didn't know. How could she know? When she'd been boiling the water for rice, she hadn't known any of this would be happening tonight. All she knew was that it was necessary. For now.

'Anyway. That's not how it goes, is it? Women stay. You mean you want me to go, don't you?'

She put her hands up. 'No. I mean the opposite. I need to get away from everything.'

This lovely house is like a prison to me now, she thought. Its walls and its fabric and its routines are a part of the problem, and I can't solve any of it – I can't fix me – if I stay here.

'I need something for me. For a while, at least.'

'How long?'

'How can I know that, Richard?'

They sat for minutes – five, ten – Gigi wasn't sure. A fog of misery hung about them.

There was fresh despair in Richard's voice when he spoke again. 'What about the children?'

The children. They weren't children, of course, any more – none of them. Except that they always would be, to them. 'We can tell them together.'

Something like a sob broke from him.

'Or I can tell them. This is my decision. They're not children, Richard. They're adults.'

'They're our children. What will they think of all this? Really, G?'

That was the part she almost couldn't bear.

'I don't know. I hope they'll understand?'

'How can they, when I can't?'

'Please, Richard. I need you to try.'

'I want to, Gigi. But I don't. I mean, what is it? Is it menopause? Mid-life crisis? Is it the cancer?' The tremor on that last one made her wonder if he knew how he'd let her down . . .

He couldn't look at her, and she was glad. He stared down at his big, familiar hands. 'Or is it me . . . something I've done . . . or just me . . .'

Gigi made herself look at him. 'It's a part of all of those things. I'm not denying it. We change. You've changed.'

'I haven't.'

'You have. And I have. And you don't even see me.'

'I see you, Gigi.' He looked right at her. He looked old.

She shook her head. It felt hopeless.

She longed for him to say something that made it easier for her, although she wasn't sure, right now, that she deserved that.

'Is there anything I can say, G? To stop you going?'

'I don't think there is.' She shook her head more de-cisively than she felt. 'I need to do this.'

He nodded a form of acceptance. She could see he was trying not to cry. He looked like a boy, fighting against showing weakness.

'I'll always love you, Richard.'

'Then you must see that this makes no sense at all.'

'You'll see . . . at some point, I believe you'll see that

it does. The two things aren't mutually exclusive. I *will* always love you. We will always have had these years, these decades together. We will always have those three beautiful children, and their children . . .'

He was still staring at his hands.

'But we are not old. We are not dying. *I am not dying.*' I thought I might be, she remembered. I thought I might die. That's what this is all about, and maybe he can't, maybe no one can understand if they haven't had that moment, in a doctor's office, when the world stops and they tell you something that makes you realize you could die. That it all might be over. A phrase from an O-level English class a hundred years ago kept rolling around her brain. *Memento mori. Memento mori.* Remember you will die.

'And *this* is not enough. Not for me, and – I truly, truly believe this – not for you either.'

He shrugged in a gesture of resignation. He looked utterly broken.

She didn't know what to do now. The weight of what she'd done was just dawning on her. It was nine o'clock at night. She had no idea where to go.

'I'm sorry.' It sounded inadequate, even to her.

He stood up, pushing the chair neatly back under the table. 'I'll sleep in one of the boys' rooms.'

Then he nodded curtly, and left.

Gigi sat there for a lot longer, knitting and unknitting her fingers, hoping that her heartbeat would slow down, and listening for sounds from Richard, although she heard none. She thought she'd cry, now that he'd gone, but strangely the tears would not come. The enormity of what she had done was just sharpening into focus. It was another hour before she climbed the stairs herself, hesitating outside the door to Christopher's room, shut firmly now. She almost turned the knob, but she knew there was nothing she could do now to help him, because she had inflicted the pain. It wasn't fair to look to him for comfort, or to try to offer it herself.

Alone in their bed, one arm across his cool, unoccupied pillow, she wondered if she would ever sleep soundly again.

Tess

Holly's name lit up on the screen of Tess's phone around 4 p.m. She'd be on her way home from school. Tess answered.

'You're coming to ours for supper. Bring your toothbrush. You can sleep over.'

'I'm not. I've got a ready meal for one with my name on it.'

'Ew. You cannot eat processed food. You are growing a person. That settles it.'

'Really, Hols, you are a darling, but there's no need.'

'There is every need. It's waifs-and-strays night at ours. There are non-alcoholic beverages and everything.'

'I was going to go home and put my feet up.'

'No arguments . . . We have pouffes.'

Tess laughed. 'I give in.'

'Good. I was always going to win.'

'When have you not won?'

'Last time was 2002, I believe. A game of *Trivial Pursuit*. But only because I can't possibly justify remembering sporting achievements. I'll give Ben a call, let him know to throw another handful of rice into the pot. Dulcie will be thrilled to see you.'

'And Ben won't?'

'He adores you, you know that. Besides, if you're there, he'll be able to skulk off and watch golf . . . If he didn't love you for you, and he does, he'd love you for that alone.'

She'd been a regular third wheel to the almost irritatingly happy Ben-and-Holly show over the years. Festivals, holidays, Sunday lunches. Holly said he secretly loved it – it made him feel like he had a harem. Theirs was a friendship that had never had to exist outside of their mutual adoration of Holly, thank goodness, but Tess guessed it probably could, so long as he didn't dare hurt her friend. Then, she'd have to kill him. He sometimes joked that Tess filled the gaps Holly couldn't – she would watch a game of rugby with him and understand the rules, she'd have a good row about politics . . . But Tess knew there weren't really any gaps. To Ben, Holly was perfect. Tess couldn't fancy Ben – he was nice-looking but not her type, and besides, he'd always been Holly's so she never thought of him that way – but on some level every boyfriend Tess had had since Holly had found Ben had been compared with him, if only on the adoration front, and found wanting. Ben and Sean had given it a good try, but they'd never gelled.

When Tess arrived at around 7 p.m., Ben answered the door. He'd obviously been home long enough to change into his off-duty uniform of sweats and bare feet, and to open and half consume a bottle of beer. He adopted a formal tone, like a 1950s telephonist. 'Surrey Home for Unmarried Mothers. Welcome.' Folded her into one of his enormous bear-hugs. She let herself be held, grateful to feel as slight as he always made her feel.

Behind him, Dulcie had run down the stairs in time to hear his greeting crack, and she slapped his back. 'Dad. Not funny. We've been learning about that shit in PSHE. Unmarried mothers had the most ghastly time, in the olden days.' Tess loved her god-daughter's earnestness and her incredulity. She didn't quite speak her father's adult language.

'Darling, I'm kidding.' He smiled at Holly as she came

down the stairs. 'Besides, I know all about that . . . Your mother could have been one, you know, if I hadn't done the decent thing.'

Now it was Holly's turn to play-punch his arm. 'Took two to tango, you cheeky bastard.' She'd had a shower, and her hair was still wrapped in a towel.

'It wasn't the tango that did it, as I recall, my sweet.' He took Holly's freshly scrubbed face in his hands and kissed her mouth.

Dulcie squealed in disgust and put her hands over her face.

'My eyes. My eyes. Gross. Totally gross. I'm going to puke if you two don't stop that immediately.'

'Less of the two of us. I'm not the PDA perp. I'm just the woman in the turban.'

'You sexy beast . . . Okay. Okay.' Ben held up his hands in surrender. 'Can I help it if your mother is still utterly irresistible to me, after all these years, even in a turban? You should be glad, Dulc.'

'I'm with you, Dulcie. I really don't need my nose rubbed in this nauseating togetherness either. Not in the state I'm in.' Tess smiled ruefully.

'Ah, yes. No man will ever want you again.'

Dulcie put her arm through Tess's and pulled her in the direction of the kitchen. 'Take absolutely no notice of my idiot father.'

'I never have, lovely, I never have.'

Ben cooked a chilli and drank another beer, while 'his harem' sat around the table and waited to be fed. Dulcie was making a decent pretence of doing some French homework. Holly drank a glass of wine she said was big enough for both of them and told anecdotes for *Surrey: A*

Novel, while Tess nursed a fizzy water. No one asked anything of her or from her. About Sean or the baby, or even work or Iris. There were many questions they could have asked, she knew. She was being an absolute ostrich about Sean, for a start. There were things to be resolved. A ball to be rolled. She hadn't found the energy yet, for that. There was time for lawyers, if they were needed, and for agreements, if they could manage without. But not yet. And they understood. They let her be. She let the banter wash over and around her, like warm water. This was a family that loved each other dearly, unconditionally, rudely. They would tell her she was a part of it, but she wasn't – not really. They belonged to each other and themselves, and she was just a lucky bystander, the little match girl in the night staring through the window at the family gathered around the roaring fire.

This baby, this baby and Donna and Iris – that was the family she had been given. She'd just have to do the best she could with what she had.

Tess

Iris's house was almost empty by the middle of March. What had seemed insurmountable in January had been methodically dealt with. Tess had given most of Iris's furniture away on Freecycle, taking pleasure in good things going to good homes. Iris would have liked that. She had sold most of the pictures and rugs through a local auction house, although she kept a picture she'd always loved – a watercolour of Salisbury Cathedral from the meadows. They'd walked that way home through Harnham so often when Tess was a child, dawdling because they had nothing to hurry for. Tess spent a whole day doing Oxfam runs with Holly, emptying the kitchen cupboards of china, glass and pans. What wasn't saleable went into the big recycling boxes at the local tip. Tess had gone to the sideboard half expecting to find it full of the crafting equipment she had always seen there as a girl, but there was just a pile of old *Radio Times*, kept for reasons beyond Tess's understanding, and some postcards tied with a piece of string, all of London landmarks: St Paul's Cathedral, the Houses of Parliament, the Tower of London.

The house looked sadder and shabbier without Iris's things in it, but the agent felt optimistic about a quick sale. It was near a well-regarded primary school, and an easy walk from the station, with three double bedrooms. He felt confident that if they priced it right, it would sell quickly. Tess was relieved he didn't suggest any redecoration or cleaning up, bar a good vacuum – she hadn't the time, much less the energy. Let someone else do that, their own way.

Her mother had come with her a couple of times, but Holly had been far more helpful. Donna had moped in a way Tess found quite irritating and unproductive. Donna's sadness – and she knew now that was what it was – felt crushing to her at this point. It was new, so new, to her, and right now it was too much. What she needed, on these days, was just completely practical, pragmatic help. It wasn't hard to persuade Donna not to come. Holly, on the other hand, got completely stuck in, chattering inconsequentially, and didn't keep trying to bring the topic of conversation around to Iris. She brought biscuits and sachets of hot chocolate. And every time Holly told her off for lifting something heavy, Tess wanted to hug her.

Iris's clothes and jewellery had been the hardest part. The wardrobe just smelt of her. A powdery, floral scent Tess associated utterly with her grandmother. She hadn't taken a great many clothes with her into Clearview. There hadn't seemed much point. Most of those still hanging at home wouldn't fit her any more anyway. Tess had bought her a new dressing gown and slippers when she moved in, and her ancient candlewick robe, full length and cyclamen pink, hung on the back of the bedroom door.

Tess sat down on the stool at Iris's dressing table. The drawer held a Max Factor Crème Puff Powder and a Rimmel lipstick. The end of the lipstick was flattened off from where Iris had applied it. For the first time that day, she thought she might cry.

There was a small photograph of Iris and Wilfred, taken on their wedding day, in an enamelled frame. Just the two of them, outside a church. If Tess had ever known where it was taken, she didn't remember. Iris's dress was ballerina length and lace and tulle, with an impossibly small waist. Tess stroked her own stomach ruefully. She'd never had a waist like that, and now she had no waist at all. Tess wondered what had happened to the dress – she'd never seen it. There were a hundred questions she hadn't asked when she'd had the chance . . . She couldn't honestly remember whether she'd ever tried. Children didn't always have a real sense of the lives adults had lived before them. Like they'd been cryogenically frozen, waiting for them. Perhaps she had. Perhaps she'd been told things, and she'd forgotten them. More likely, she thought, she hadn't considered it. They'd been such a unit of two. She'd had a clear picture of her grandfather, Wilf, from stories and anecdotes and photographs, though. Had it all been a diversion? A hundred things she'd never know now. Iris's hair was bouffant, a veil clipped on to the top of her head, and her tiny bouquet was lily of the valley, her favourite flower. Tess remembered that the wedding was in April, when they were in season. Even so, they must have been expensive. She smiled at Iris's wedding extravagance. Good for her. Wilfred was wearing a dark suit, with a buttonhole that matched. The cane he held in lots of photographs – the one with the carved duck's-head handle – wasn't in evidence. He stood proud and erect without it. They looked glamorous, like film stars, posed formally like people who weren't photographed often did. And so happy.

Holly stood in the doorframe. 'What you found?'

Tess held the lipstick out. Holly came over and took the

tube from her hand, reading the label on its bottom. 'Heather Shimmer. Go, Iris. God, do you remember that? I swear I had one. Sun In, Rimmel Heather Shimmer and Body Shop White Musk . . .'

Tess laughed. 'We must have all looked exactly the same.'

'And smelt exactly the same!'

Holly examined the drawer. 'That's it? That's *all* her makeup? I need three shelves in the bathroom cabinet. Dulcie needs a bloomin' sack. Contouring. Highlighting. Discuss.'

'That's it. Half the time she didn't even wear that. Soap, water and a flannel. I remember her saying that's why her skin was so soft. That and Pond's Cold Cream.'

'Don't get soppy.' Holly stood behind her and looked at her face in the dressing-table mirror. She squeezed Tess's shoulders.

'Trying not to . . . Someone's coming for this and the sideboard at four. No sense keeping these.'

She sniffed hard.

'How is it downstairs?'

'Pretty much done. Just that suitcase we found before, with all the papers. You can take that home with the jewellery box, and go through it in your own time. It can't be anything all that important. You've got the key stuff already at the solicitor's, haven't you?'

'I think so.'

'Might have some things you'd like to keep. It's locked, so you'll have to force it. There's no key that I can see. Mind you, she was operating an eclectic organizational system, bless her . . . I found three tins of peas in with the laundry stuff. And there are about two years' worth of weird and wonderful catalogues behind the curtain in the downstairs loo.'

Tess tipped the powder and the lipstick into a black sack in the doorway and slipped the photograph into her cardigan pocket.

'It's so strange and sad, packing away someone's life like this.'

Holly stroked her shoulder gently. 'It's just stuff, Tess. It's not them.'

'When it's gone, though, they start to fade, you know, the memory of them gets less vivid because you can't see the things that remind you any more . . .'

'I suppose that's right . . . like how you think you remember some things better than others, but it's because you've seen them in a photograph.'

'Exactly. I've been coming here for so long. All my life, really. I won't always remember it like I do now.' Tess wanted to cry.

'You'll remember what matters. The rest really is just stuff.'

'You're wise, you know that, Hols?'

Holly nudged her towards the door. 'Wise enough to know I'm getting you out of here before the pity party gets into full swing.'

Tess laughed sadly. 'Wise and harsh . . .'

Gigi

Richard had abdicated all decision-making since Gigi's declaration.

In the days since that dreadful conversation at the kitchen table, Gigi had made momentous decisions. Alone. It was an underused muscle, and she ached all over. They'd always decided things together. Where to holiday? What colour to paint the hall and landing? How much allowance to give the kids when they went off to university? A million everyday decisions. But she couldn't involve him in these choices. This was all her.

She'd told her friend from the hospital, Kate, that she needed some space from Richard, and Kate, alone in her family home for some years since her own husband, Owen, had left, had immediately offered her spare room for as long as Gigi wanted it, without asking for details, for which Gigi was enormously grateful. She'd be glad of the company, she'd said at once, and Gigi had tried to ignore the shiver of fear that passed through her when she heard that. Loneliness and the possibility and the strange unfamiliarity of it hovered at the back of her mind all of the time.

She'd said she'd take the room, but it had to be short term. She knew she couldn't be a lodger in someone else's home, however lovely the person or the home. That was so far from the point. And it would encourage Richard in the belief that this was a phase, a mad moment, and that she'd be home once she got it out of her system. She was sure that was what he was telling himself. It needed formalizing. She wasn't ready to go to lawyers and sign documents – it was too soon for that. But she needed to do this properly – rent a place of her own. Along with the fear there was excitement. A sense of what she recognized to be freedom and adventure. Light at the end of this tunnel she had been in for so, so long.

Packing a suitcase to take to Kate's had been so strange. This was very different from a holiday. In some ways she was still utterly horrified that it was happening. It still felt shocking. But it still felt necessary too.

Richard had been at work when she'd done it. She'd wandered from room to room, looking at all of their things – all the stuff a family had accumulated across decades of a life together. The stuff you stopped really looking at, just resented dusting. She took a framed photograph from the mantelpiece in the sitting room – a shot from Christmas, all of them in their finery, baby Ava star of the show, front and centre. But when she'd laid it in the suitcase, on top of her uniforms and pyjamas and shoes, she decided it wasn't fair to take it. She'd have to get copies of things like that, if she wanted to have them. It was ridiculous. She felt at liberty to deconstruct their entire lives, but not the fabric of their home.

The suitcase had been by the front door when he'd come home. It felt wrong just to go, so she'd waited for him. He'd looked at it, hard.

'Don't do this, Gigi. Please.' He was crying. She'd seen him cry maybe once or twice in their whole lives together – when Christopher was born, when his own mother had died. For her to be the reason he was crying now was almost surreal. It turned everything on its head.

'I have to, Richard.'

'I love you.'

'Don't.'

'Why not? Isn't that what you want?'

'It's too late.'

'It can't be.'

'It is. I have to go.'

'Where?'

'To Kate's. For the time being.'

For a horrible moment she thought he was going to bar her way. He was still stood in the hallway, between her and the door. She could see him think of it too. But after a moment he stood aside. Again, she had to push against the muscle memory of their life together – it wasn't her job, now, to fix him. This, she could not make better.

She didn't look back, and the door closed gently behind her. As she got into the car, suitcase stowed in the boot, she could see the great shadow of him pressed against the glass panes. She drove off before he moved away from the door.

That had been ten days ago. She'd tried not to communicate with him, believing it was best. She desperately wanted to know that he was okay. That he was eating. That he'd figured out the washing machine. That he was sleeping. But she knew that it wouldn't help to ask. There'd been an awkward email exchange about money. They'd always had a joint account: both their salaries were paid into it, both drawing on it as they needed to. Megan told her she was hopelessly old-fashioned. Richard was a good earner, so they hadn't had to worry for a few years now. They were lucky – both boys had been financially independent for years, and Meg was the only one still 'on the books', as Richard put it. The mortgage on the house, which had seemed insurmountably huge at the beginning, had been paid down considerably over the years. If they had to sell it – and Gigi couldn't think about that now, not yet – they would both have to compromise quite a lot. It might buy two much smaller homes, but they'd be able to live. They'd be okay.

Money had never been the flashpoint for them that Gigi knew it was for some couples. As his salary had grown, hers had too, in proportion, although she had always earned less. Richard was as generous now as he had always been, and she was never extravagant. Well, not often. Now, he said he didn't want her to worry. She could have what she needed. There was no need, he said, to make hasty decisions. Gigi knew that would mean he could see what she was spending, and where, and that this could no more be a permanent arrangement than her bunking up with Kate was. But that didn't seem to matter as much right now as keeping things on an even and civilized keel. Those things were aftershocks, and they were still reeling from the first explosion. They could all wait. For now she was grateful. She was luckier than a lot of women, she knew, forced to stay where they were unhappy.

The one thing she had had to insist on was that they needed to talk to the children. They needed to know, and soon. She felt strongly that the least damaging way in which they could hear was if they were all together. But she knew she didn't have the right to insist. This was her mess. He'd be entitled to make her do it alone. But Richard didn't refuse. He was strangely passive and it was infuriating. Gigi knew she'd feel better if he raged and shouted, but she also knew that it wasn't his job to make her feel better. It was how he was.

It was Gigi who called the three children and asked them to come to the house on a weekday evening. Olly had agreed easily, not asking any questions, and requested lasagne. Christopher, of course, had been instantly suspicious.

'What's it about?'

She'd lied, more easily than she'd thought she could, determined not to give anything away over the telephone. Some papers, she'd said, that needed explaining. Nothing to do with the C word, she promised.

'God. Morbid.' But Christopher had agreed to come. She hadn't invited Emily, although she sensed she'd find an ally in her daughter-in-law. Inviting Emily would mean including Caitlin, and she didn't think she could do it – not properly, not the way she wanted to do it – if Caitlin was in the room.

It was Meg who made her feel most wretched. For the first year or so after her all-clear, Meg had asked if the cancer was back almost every time Gigi had looked serious. She'd texted, always the most reliable way to communicate with her youngest child, keeping it light and easy-breezy, and Megan had replied that she could – she had a big paper due the week after, and wouldn't be able to stay long, probably just the night, but she'd come and bring washing, and could she put the train fare on her dad's credit card?

Meg was the only one of their children who technically still lived with them, in the holidays at least – the only one not fully 'launched'. The one for whom she might have waited, if she possibly could have done. The mantle of guilt settled familiarly on her shoulders in the days leading up to the meeting, making her doubt herself horribly.

She let herself in with her key, carrying two big bags of Sainsbury's shopping, feeling like she hadn't the right to turn it in the lock. Not any more. She half expected Richard to be there, called his name when she was in the hall, but he didn't answer. His car hadn't been in the driveway. The kitchen was clean and tidy, more like normal than she had expected, but the fridge wasn't full. The leftovers in it weren't wrapped properly – the edge of a block of cheddar was dry and pale. She didn't go upstairs. Gigi busied herself, the radio on too loud for company. She made a lasagne and salad, laid the table, tidied the sitting room, just like any other day when she was expecting company. What was missing was the delicious frisson of excitement she always felt when her nest was to fill up with her chicks, replaced instead by a heavy dread in the pit of her stomach. She worked quietly, rehearsing lines as she went through the domestic routines so familiar and well practised and now so strange. She was determined not to cry in front of them, even as she knew she'd cry her heart empty once she was back at Kate's. She wondered if they'd even eat the damn lasagne.

Richard didn't appear until five minutes before the children were due. He went straight upstairs, calling through to her in the kitchen that he was going to change, and she felt sure he hovered up there until the doorbell rang, heralding their arrival. They all came together – Chris had picked up his brother and sister at the train station on his way past. They burst in through the door as they had a thousand times before – loudly joking with each other about Meg's duffel of laundry and Chris's old-man driving and Olly's customary dishevelled appearance. Meg was the spoilt baby, Chris was more uptight than the rest of them put together, Olly was hopeless . . . those were their default family roles – safe territory for humour – how they had always spoken about each other.

Gigi didn't want to break the spell of having them all home. But she didn't want to wait either. The lasagne would feel like sawdust in her mouth. The meal would be a lie. Richard wasn't playing, anyway. He wore the hollow, morose expression he'd had since she told him. He was grey around the gills, and dark-eyed with sleeplessness. He looked ill, Gigi realized, seeing him through her children's eyes, and she knew they would think that they'd gathered to hear the grave news of his health. That they'd castigate themselves at having worried about their mother, while he got ill instead. She didn't want to put them through that fear, so she started her speech as soon as they all sat down with a glass of wine. The three kids were on the sofa – she and Richard in armchairs, separated by a side table, facing their children. It was like an interview.

'Kids. You'll be wondering why we've got you here.'

'Yes. The mysterious invitation . . .' Meg made a face of mock mystification.

'Ssh, Meg. This is difficult. If you let me talk without interrupting, we'll answer as many questions as you have afterwards. Just, please, let me explain.' She wasn't sure 'we' would be answering anything. Richard wasn't going to make this any easier.

She hated seeing their faces change, become serious. Meg looked instantly tearful.

'Your dad and I . . .' That wasn't right. How had she said it, in her own head? Gigi clamoured for words. She'd found a better way. She just couldn't remember it now.

'That is to say. Me. Me. I'm not happy, kids. I haven't been for a while now. I've decided . . . I think the best thing . . . I've decided to leave your dad, and be on my own.'

There was a tiny flood of relief at having said it, but for a moment she couldn't look at them, or at Richard.

The five of them sat in stunned silence. When she did look at them, Chris and Meg were focused on Richard. Olly was looking at her, the light of understanding in his eyes. His smile was small, but it was kind.

'Fuck.' Megan. Then 'Sorry.' She stood up, and went to sit on the arm of her father's chair, her arm around his shoulders protectively. Richard let her.

Now, with her maternal urge to emolliate, Gigi found some more words. 'I'm sorry. I'm so, so sorry. I want to say that it isn't anyone's fault. It certainly isn't your dad's. There is no one else involved. Not for me or for your dad either. That's true, okay?' She leant forward to emphasize her point. 'It's just that I don't feel that the marriage is working any more. I'm sorry. But I don't. I need to find something for me. I need to try to feel happy again. I don't expect you to understand it, necessarily. You don't see us that way, I suppose. As people, adults. I don't expect you not to be horribly upset. Of course I know you will be.'

It was Oliver's face she focused on. He was looking right at her, the least crushed, the kindest. He nodded almost imperceptibly, encouraging.

'But I want you to remember that your father and I love you all as dearly as we ever have, that you will all always be the most important and most wonderful facts of our life. That doesn't change.'

She looked at Richard now, but he wouldn't meet her gaze.

'Since when, Mum?' Meg's voice was accusatory. 'Since when have you been so unhappy?'

She shrugged. 'Since . . . for a long time now, Megan.'

'But everything's been fine.'

'Everything has *seemed* fine, darling. That doesn't necessarily mean it has been.'

'This is stupid, Mum. It's just some mid-life crisis bullshit.' Gigi felt herself wince. Looked at Olly. He was frowning at his sister. He looked like he was about to speak. She raised her hand to stop him. Let Megan's words rain like blows. It might even feel better. 'It's so . . . it's so selfish.' Megan's pitch was getting higher. 'How could you? Seriously? I can't believe you can do this to us. To me.' Megan was reassuringly self-absorbed.

Gigi waited for Richard to say something to his daughter, but it was Olly who did, in the end. He stood up and put a hand on Megan's shoulder. 'Meg. Ssh.'

Megan shrugged it off angrily. 'Typical Olly. On Mum's side, are you? What a shocker . . .'

'I'm not on anyone's side.'

Megan snorted derisively. 'Right!'

Christopher rubbed his face, an anxious boy again. 'Can we all just calm down? Meg — Oliver's right. That's not going to help.'

'It's all right for you two.'

'It isn't all right for any of us. It's horrid, okay. But this is between Mum and Dad. Not us. And you going off on one isn't going to help.'

'Well, excuse me for caring.'

'That's just daft, Meg. And you know it. We all care.'

Megan burst into angry, wounded tears. Gigi reached out, but Megan brushed her away. 'I can't, Mum. I can't fucking believe this . . .' Richard flinched and Gigi knew it was the swearing. Poor Richard.

She left the room. Gigi started to stand up. 'Let her go, Mum. She'll be okay. She needs a minute.' This was Olly, his expression concerned, and his tone almost tender.

'I think we all need a minute,' Chris laughed, a small hollow sound. 'Are you going to say anything at all, Dad?'

Richard looked directly at Gigi. 'This is your mum's decision, boys. Not mine. It's not what I want.'

She'd asked for that, even if the disloyalty, in the moment, was almost breathtaking.

Christopher looked at her for a response, but Gigi didn't know what to say.

'So what's happening? In a practical sense, I mean,' Olly asked, his voice calm and gentle.

'I'm staying with my friend Kate for now.' He nodded.

'Are you going to get divorced?' Christopher was processing too fast. He always had. Oliver threw him a warning glance.

'I don't know, Chris.'

'So you might get back together?'

Gigi rubbed her forehead wearily. She felt exhausted. 'I don't know that either. I'm sorry I haven't got definitive answers for you.'

Chris's expression said that she should be.

'You don't owe us definitive answers, Mum.' Oliver put his arm around her shoulders and kissed the top of her head, and she let herself lean back into her boy.

'She owes them to Dad, though, doesn't she?'

'Back off, Chris. This really isn't our business.'

'They're our parents, for God's sake. This is our home.'

'This was our home, Chris. Emily and Ava. They're your home now. They're your family.'

'This is still our family, Olly.'

Oliver couldn't argue with that. 'I know, mate. I know. Look – they've got us together, they've told us together. They didn't need to do that. That was brave.' He squeezed Gigi's shoulder. 'We all need to just back off now, and let Mum and Dad sort it out.' Gigi smiled a tight, sad smile at her younger son, more grateful than she could ever remember being.

No one ate the lasagne, in the end. It overcooked, black edged, in the oven, and Richard burned his hand taking it out. It sat, dried out and singed, on the worktop. Gigi filled a deep bowl with cold water and made him sit at the table with his hand in it.

Christopher left first, hugging both his parents awkwardly. Gigi wondered what he'd say to Emily, and what Emily would think of her. The thought of Ava was another wave of sadness.

Olly took Megan with him, along with her duffel of laundry. Megan wouldn't look at her mother when she left, kissing her perfunctorily, and refusing her customary bear-hug, but she'd clung, snivelling, to Richard. Olly held Gigi for a long moment. 'I'll keep her with me tonight. She can stay a couple of days if she needs it. She'll calm down. Don't worry. I'll call you tomorrow. It'll be all right. I love you.'

And it was just her and Richard again. They stayed in the hallway – both knowing she was leaving too.

'I almost hated you, just then, for what you did to us all.'

'I hated myself.'

'I wanted to. But I couldn't.'

'I'm sorry.'

Richard nodded. 'You said.'

Tess

Tess and Donna were sat on the sofa in Donna's sitting room. They'd finished dinner — Donna had made a Thai stir fry with noodles. She turned out to be quite a good cook. Tess wondered when that had happened: she remembered a lot of jacket potatoes with baked beans and fish fingers.

She turned out to be quite good company too. They'd just finished watching *Masterchef.* Donna had made her laugh with her running commentary. Tess reached for the remote control and pressed the 'off' button.

It was comfortable, between the two of them. Which surprised her. Iris — and their different approaches to her, and her home, and her care — was where the irritation came, still. Here, things were okay. They were better than okay. Tess had imagined she'd be desperate to get out, but she found herself pushing that raft of decisions to the back of her mind now. She looked at her mother, and Donna smiled back at her.

'You asked me, a while back, if there were things I wish I'd talked to my mum about.'

'I remember.'

'I've been thinking about it.'

'And?'

'You're right. There are things I wish I knew. About her life, before me. About her marriage. How she felt being alone after my dad died. We never talked about it.'

'I would like to have asked her more about my granddad.'

'He was a good man, my dad. A man of infinite patience, and real kindness. Calm, you know? He always had time to fix things, broken things. We once found a bird, a tiny thing. It had fallen out of its nest. Dad said it didn't have a chance, but I couldn't bear to leave it. I still remember him talking to me about it. About why it couldn't survive. Making me understand, you know, be okay with it. He always had that kind of time. To think about things. You always knew he was . . . right . . . about stuff. Wise. That's what I remember most about him. He used to listen to Gregorian chants. All the time.'

'Monk music?'

Donna laughed. 'Monk music. I suppose it is. I'm convinced that's where he got his calm from. We should try it . . .'

'Maybe we should.'

'He'd have loved you. And, God, he loved my mum. To absolute pieces. He was devoted. Her to him too. I don't think I've ever known a happier married couple, to be honest.'

'He was quite a bit older than her, wasn't he?'

'About fifteen years, yeah.'

'So, he was quite old when they got married. I mean, Iris was too, for that era.'

Donna nodded. 'She was thirty-five, I think. I suppose it was old for then. She used to say he brought her to life. It was something they used to say to each other. I never really considered it. To me it was just, you know, sweet nothings. But that was what she said. He brought her to life. It's odd, now that you think about it.'

Tess contemplated the idea. 'I wonder what she meant? What was she before him?'

'I don't know . . .' The two women were thoughtful for a moment.

'She was an elderly primigravida too.'

'What?'

'That's what they call me, in my hospital notes. Pregnant for the first time at thirty-five.'

'Charming.'

'But neither of them had been married before?'

'Not as far as I know.'

'I wonder . . . do you know how they met?'

Donna thought for a moment, a nostalgic smile breaking across her face. 'On the bus, commuting to work.'

'Really? Are you serious?'

'Yep. I think so. Yes. I remember.'

'So you *do* know this stuff. How come?'

'I did have a life with her before you came along, you know.' But her voice was kind, not sarcastic.

'The bus!'

'Different times, I suppose.'

'I wish I knew what happened to her wedding dress. It was so beautiful . . .'

Donna laughed her throaty laugh, but it died in her mouth. 'I can help you there.'

'Really?'

She looked at her mother, saw her mouth contort a little, trying to control itself. Donna brought her hand up to cover it and inhaled sharply.

'Mum? What?'

She took a deep breath. 'She kept it. I mean really looked after it. Acid-free tissue paper, a sealed box – all of that – on top of the wardrobe. All my childhood. I remember begging her to get it out sometimes, when I was little. It was a palaver – getting the box down, unpacking it all, putting it away again – but I don't remember her ever saying no to me. I loved it.'

'It was stunning. All that tulle.'

'It was. I always used to say I was going to wear it to my wedding . . .'

'You didn't though, did you?'

'No. It was 1981 when I married your father. The fashion was completely different: that dress was classic late-fifties. The eighties were something different. It was all Lady Di. Crumpled silk and taffeta and lace. Not that I was into that either, particularly. Looked like it needed a good iron.' Tess smiled. She'd heard Iris say exactly that about Diana's crumpled Emanuel dress. Donna sounded just like her.

'Anyway, I didn't want to wear it. It just wasn't what I wanted. Even if it had fitted.' That last was an aside almost to herself.

'That waist.'

'Indeed. I was built more like my dad's side, I think. Never had a waist like that.'

'Was she upset?'

'She was amazing. She said I shouldn't wear it, if I didn't want to. That she understood completely. But she offered to take it apart, let me have the silk from underneath. It was really good-quality stuff. We took it to the dress-maker's, they took it apart, lost the froth from all the tulle petticoats underneath, and just used the silk. There were metres of it – her dress had a big circle skirt, you know, just gathered on to a waistband. Completely preserved for all those years in that acid-free tissue paper. So it was like new. Made my whole dress.'

'Wow. I can't believe I didn't know that.'

Donna smiled. 'It pleased her, I remember. That I was wearing it, albeit reincarnated into something that looked completely different. She liked the fact some of it walked down the aisle on me, she said. Not that there was an actual aisle. But figuratively.'

'What happened to it? Have you still got it?'

'That's the rotten bit. I threw it away, when your dad left. Couldn't bear to look at it.'

'Oh God.'

'I didn't even tell her.'

'Did she know?'

'She never asked.'

'You were upset. She'd have understood.'

'That's no excuse. It was mean. I always felt lousy about it. One of many things . . .'

'You've never really talked about when you and my dad broke up. About why.' Tess waited for Donna to stiffen, give her the brush-off. But she didn't. She looked down at her legs and picked imaginary bits of fluff off her trousers.

'You were so young.'

'I'm not now. Got my own epic break-up story now, and everything. If you wanted to tell me yours?' They hadn't talked much about her and Sean. Like Holly, Donna seemed to understand, without being told, that she didn't want to talk about it. She knew Holly understood her. It surprised her that Donna did too.

Donna smiled. 'Hey, what's this? Filling in the blanks before I get like my mum? I'm not losing my marbles yet, you know.'

'I know. But I'd . . . I'd like to know.'

'Going to need a glass of wine, if we're going there.'

'Make mine a peppermint tea, will you!'

Donna stood up and went to the kitchen. Tess lay her head back against the sofa and closed her eyes, her hands across her belly. When Donna came back, with a large glass of red and a mug of tea, she sat cross-legged on the floor opposite Tess.

'Okay. I'm going to tell you. Iris is the only other person who knows this story, and she obviously never told you. Sometimes I wondered if she would – you two were so close.'

'She never said anything at all.' Donna raised her eyebrow.

'I was only twenty-one when I met your dad. We were both at someone's birthday party, in the back room of a pub. I can't remember whose. He was a friend of a friend, I think . . . anyway, we got together that night. Started going out a couple of times a week. He was the first proper boyfriend I'd had. I mean, there'd been fellas, but nothing that had lasted very long. This was different, right from the start. He was a couple of years older. Had a job, so that ticked my dad's box. Was polite to Iris, when he came for Sunday lunch, all of that.

'Everyone assumed we'd get married. I think I did too. It was what you did. It was not so much that he asked me, just that we were sort of on that path and we all knew it.

'I think, when I look back, it's one of the reasons I didn't build much of a career, before you were born. I hadn't set the academic world alight, as you no doubt remember, but I think I'd been more ambitious for myself before I met Harry. That part sort of fizzled away afterwards. It sounds mad now, but, then, it was like I was waiting for marriage, babies . . . all of that. Harry earned enough to get a mortgage. I was just messing about at working, really. Nannying. I liked the kids, it paid well –'

'I never knew that about you.'

'No. Well, I wasn't your classic Mary Poppins type. I was always a bit scatty. I think I was just being a big kid myself – it was good fun, and not too onerous. I worked for this family – the Rossis. He was Italian, she was English. They had these four gorgeous kids. Three boys and a girl. All big brown eyes and curly hair, they were. Almost totally feral. I think that's why they liked me.

'So, anyway . . . I'd been working for them for a few months. Then Giovanni, the father of the family I worked for, lost his father unexpectedly. His family owned a vineyard in Umbria. Nothing massive, but a family business, you know. His brothers had stayed there, but only one of them knew the business . . . Giovanni worked in the wine trade in London. But he had to spend some time at home, after his dad died. Sort his mother out. Help his family with the business. It was the beginning of the summer holidays, so they were all going to go . . . they asked me to go with them. I said no, at first. Harry definitely didn't want me to go. But they begged. And they offered me a fortune – or at least it seemed like a fortune at the time.'

'So you went?'

Donna nodded. 'For six weeks.'

She got up and went over to the desk in the corner of the sitting room. It was one of those that had a lid that closed and locked. Opening it down, she bent over and rustled around in some shelves at the very back. After a few moments, she stood up, exclaiming, 'Ah, I knew it was here.'

She handed Tess a small photograph with a white border. It was unmistakably her mother, as a much younger woman. Slimmer, and slighter somehow, but with the same familiar stance, and the same smile. She was standing against a mellow-coloured brick wall, behind which an astonishing valley stretched out to the horizon in every direction.

'It's a place called Gualdo Cattaneo. It's a medieval hill town about forty-five minutes from Perugia. That's where the vineyard was. Still is.'

'It's beautiful.'

'It was the most beautiful place I'd ever been. We flew to Rome. I'd only been as far as France, really – my parents liked a *gîte* holiday. Warm milk from cows. All that.'

Tess nodded enthusiastically. 'Iris is mad about milk warm from cows.'

'I know. She always was. She grew up on a farm. I suppose that's how she remembered it. Disgusting.' They laughed.

'Rome . . . Rome was something different. We hired a car at the airport, and they drove us through the centre, so I could see the Coliseum and the Pantheon. It was amazing. I loved it. Then out into the country. Higher and higher . . . and eventually, a couple of hours later, we got to this town.'

'And that's where you stayed?'

'We stayed at the vineyard with Giovanni's family, a bit outside. You could walk there, uphill, slow 'cos it was so hot, and have a gelato in the square.'

Tess nodded.

'And that square is where I met the person I thought was the love of my life.' Donna was lost in a reverie now.

Not so much telling Tess a story as reminding herself of something long buried away. Tess daren't interrupt, just waited for her mother to start speaking again.

'He was Italian. He was my age. He worked locally, on a farm, where he'd grown up. He was a big noise in the town. You know the type – easy laugh, broad smile, twinkle in his eye, gorgeous. Everyone loved him. He was always in the centre of it all. Well, I fell hard. I didn't expect him to be in the slightest bit interested in me. Why would he? I'm not exaggerating, honestly, when I say he could have had any of the girls in the village. I didn't even speak Italian – just some I'd picked up working for the family – really basic stuff. The kids had to translate for us when he started talking to me.

'He was learning English. He said he was glad I'd come – he could practise on me. That's how it started. Conversational English. I'd take the kids up to the square in the late afternoon, when he'd finished work. We'd buy them ice cream. As much as they wanted. As much as they could eat. And we'd try to talk.

'I can't explain it. But for me, he was it. People talk about the thunderbolt, all that . . . and it sort of was . . . d'you know?'

Tess didn't. There hadn't been a thunderbolt with Sean. Or with anyone. There'd been love, she knew. But no thunderbolt.

'There is no way to explain it without sounding hokey. Thunderbolt. Whatever. Like you've met before, or like you've always known you were going to – like you sort of recognize something in each other . . .' She shrugged. 'Hard to explain. You sort of have to feel it. Then you know the difference between that and everything else.'

'For him too?' Tess was suddenly afraid she knew how this was going to end.

'For him too. He was the first one to say the L word. The A word.'

'*Amore.*'

'*Amore.* I expect it all sounds very Mills and Boon to you. Very holiday romance –'

Tess put her hand up to protest.

'I know it does. I can't explain it. It was instantaneous. I know people say love at first sight is a myth, but I know it isn't. They say it's lust, but it wasn't. He was from a good old-fashioned Catholic family. He was completely respectful. Far too bloody respectful, for my liking, but I couldn't persuade him to be otherwise. I just loved him.'

'What happened?'

'You happened.'

'What!' The shock on Tess's face broke Donna's nostalgic spell.

'No. No. That's come out wrong –'

'Is Harry not my father?' She was sitting bolt upright now.

Donna raised her hands and shook her head. 'Yes. Yes. Of course Harry is your father. That's the whole point.'

'I don't understand.'

'I loved Marco. As far as I was concerned, that was it. I wanted to give up everything I'd left behind at home. Not just Harry – everything. It seemed very clear to me, all of a sudden, that what I felt for Harry wasn't real love. It was affection, but it was . . . well, it was nothing compared with this. You can't be in love with one person and fall in love with another one. That, I do not believe to be possible. I knew I would hurt him. I felt sad about that. But I also felt – it's hard to explain – like I couldn't help it. I saw my life lived in Umbria, with Marco. A home of our own. Kids of our own. There was something simple and easy about it. I was so, so sure.'

'And that's what he wanted too?'

Donna nodded. 'He'd asked me to stay.'

'So what happened?' Tess's heart was beating fast.

'I found out I was pregnant already. I'd never slept with Marco. It was too fast, anyway. I must have been pregnant when I left England. I was a couple of weeks late, I suppose, but I wasn't all that regular anyway. I didn't think about it. Then weeks went by . . . nothing. It took me a stupidly long time to get it. I wasn't really thinking about anything except how happy I was. I didn't have symptoms or anything. I just realized one day, when another girl was talking about getting her period and not wanting to go swimming. I'd been swimming every day, *Wham*. It was like being hit by a truck. I don't know how it was for you . . .'

'Definitely like being hit by a truck. I was on the pill.'

'I wasn't. But we'd been careful. I thought so anyway.'

'What did you do?'

'What could I do? I was trapped. I thought about not having the baby' – she looked at Tess – 'you . . . but it didn't feel like an option for me. I would have had to tell so many lies. And I'm many things, a lot of them not great, but I'm not a liar.' Tess realized the remark would have stung her a great deal more a few months earlier. The new empathy between them was almost startling to her.

'So you came home.'

'We were coming home anyway, by then. The summer was over.'

'What did you tell Marco?'

Donna rubbed her hand across her face.

'There's a thing they call a *festa*, a big hooley – the whole town gets together night after night for a week right at the end of the summer. There are games, and races, and it's all a big competition. Lots of drumming. Tables all over the town, everyone eating together. Fireworks. They do this extraordinary run from the valley floor to the town square. It's the grand finale, sort of. They train all summer – all the young men. And they won. Marco's team. He was ecstatic. Bragging rights for a whole year, you know.'

Tess nodded.

'Then it was the fireworks, and he was so happy, and proud. We were leaving the next morning.'

'You didn't tell him, did you?'

'No.' Donna's voice was very quiet. 'I couldn't find a way, and I couldn't find a moment to tell him.'

'So you just left.'

'It broke my heart. I mean, almost like it literally did. It physically hurt.'

'And then?'

She shrugged. 'I came home. Gave up work. Married Harry. Had you.'

'Without telling anyone.'

'Just Iris. She could see I was unhappy. She more or less guessed.'

'You told her about me?'

Donna shook her head. 'No, not at first. I told her about Marco.'

'What did she say?'

'She said I should go back. Be with him. I've never forgotten. She said love should be the simplest thing in the world, and that it was always the most precious thing. She was amazingly adamant about it.'

'But you didn't?'

Donna shook her head. 'I did the right thing. Harry proposed very quickly after I got back, as soon as I told him I was pregnant. We were married before I was really showing.'

'Did she understand, then, when she found out?'

'She knew I was pregnant by the time we got married. I sometimes think that's why she gave me her wedding dress.'

'And that was that? You never talked about it.'

'We were never all that good at talking about things. You see that now.'

'Do you think she thought you were doing the right thing?' Tess asked.

'I think she was utterly certain I was doing the wrong thing. It was between us then, and it was probably always between us after that. But I did the right thing,' she said again, emphatically. Then, just a whisper, 'I just always blamed Harry.'

'And me?'

Donna put her hand on Tess's cheek and rested her forehead against hers. 'Sometimes. I'm sorry.'

Tess thought it was the most searingly honest thing her mother had ever said to her. She didn't feel angry or hurt. She felt the weight of a decades-old sorrow, and she felt pity. And something else – a chink of understanding.

'It was never going to work, starting that way. Poor man. We were very, very unhappy. I'm amazed it lasted as long as it even did, to be honest. I think it was pride that kept him with me. I was awful.'

'What about Marco?'

Tess saw tears in her mother's eyes. 'Oh, there's no fool like a lovesick fool.' Donna laughed bitterly. 'I went back to look for him. When Harry and I had split. Before Martin.'

'Did you find him?'

'Oh, yes, he'd never left. He was married. He'd married a local girl a few years younger than himself. I hadn't known her. They had a baby. An olive-skinned dark-eyed chubby baby who looked just like him. He was nice to me, you know. But there was nothing there, not for him. Maybe he hadn't felt it in the first place. Maybe I'd hurt him so badly I'd really killed it off. Maybe time had just passed. He was so patently completely in love with his wife, with his beautiful baby. I was just a nice memory. And, for me, he'd been this . . . this huge love of my life. He introduced me to her. She knew all about me. I wasn't even a dark secret for him. He'd been the cause and the reason for so much of who I was and what had happened to me. And I was his summer romance. I felt so bloody ridiculous.'

She sat and stared down at her hands in her lap.

'I married Martin on a massive rebound. It wasn't fair. He deserved better. I drove him away too.'

She was crying now, gently and quietly. 'Sometimes I feel like I've just been looking for something ever since, and I'm not even sure what I'm looking for. What my mum and dad had, I suppose. What I thought I'd had with Marco. What we read about. That simple easy thing. I resented not having it. Sometimes I believe myself unworthy of it; sometimes I'm just mad at the world for not giving it to me. Sometimes I'm just in blind, chaotic pursuit of it, whatever the cost to the people around me.' She shrugged. 'It's made my life selfish. And all that time, it's made me a pretty lousy daughter, and an even worse mother.'

Tess took her hand. 'I'm glad you've told me, Mum.'

'Are you?' Donna looked up and into her eyes. 'Why?'

'You're my mum. You weren't a lousy mother. That's not

true. You took care of me. It's just . . . you were remote. You were restless and still, somehow, exhausted all the time. This . . . what you've told me . . . it sort of makes sense of it, somehow.'

Tess wondered if Donna was going to say it. 'Forgive me.' But this time she didn't. Understanding had to come before absolution. If absolution were hers to give. For the moment, though, Tess felt grateful for this moment. She felt closer to her mother now than she could ever remember feeling. That closeness went some way, unexpectedly, towards filling just a part of the yawning hole Iris was leaving. It was a relief.

'I never tell you what I think . . . I suppose I don't ever really feel I have the right to. But, for what it's worth, Tess, I think you've done the right thing with Sean. I think, maybe, he was your Harry. You know?'

Tess nodded slowly.

'This baby' – and Donna put her hand flat, fingers splayed, across Tess's stomach – 'you love this baby.' Tess put her own hand on top of her mother's, and the two of them sat that way for quite a while. 'Let that be your simple, easy love.'

'This would have made Gran so happy.' Tess looked at her mother, who smiled, and nodded.

Later, in Donna's guest bed, Tess lay with her hands behind her head and thought about everything she'd learnt this evening from her mother. So many secrets. Iris had never really known Sean – they'd met, but Tess hadn't got together with him until the dementia had started to take hold of her grandmother, and so she'd never really known what Iris thought of him. She'd treated him politely and kindly but much like he was the postman or the man who'd come to read the meter. Tess had so wanted to ask. Maybe that was part of what had stopped her from completely committing to Sean. It was an unsettling thought. Was she really saying she needed Iris's blessing or approval for any relationship she ever had? What did that say about her dependence? Would it always be that way? Iris's words kept reverberating around her brain. She'd told Donna to go back to Marco. She'd told her love should be the simplest thing in the world. Tess had heard her say it too. For whatever reason, one she'd never know, Iris had kept Donna's secret. For all Tess knew, she'd kept ones of her own too. But the message had always been the same. Tess knew now what Iris would have said to her, about Sean, and about the baby: it was suddenly clear.

Gigi

Gigi had always seen Emily – with or without Christopher – regularly. Since her daughter-in-law had gone on maternity leave last year, a few weeks before Ava's birth, it had pretty much been weekly. With Emily's own mother several hours' drive away, Gigi had fallen easily into the role of adviser (never unsolicited) and comforter. They'd shopped together for Ava, and Gigi had answered a million questions about pregnancy and birth. It had made them even closer. After Ava was born, the bond strengthened. Sometimes, Gigi had simply gone round on her day off, and sent an exhausted Emily upstairs to bed while she cared for Ava downstairs, like her own mother had done for her when Christopher and Oliver had been young.

Since Gigi had left Richard, they'd met up a couple of times most weeks, usually for walks with the baby, sometimes for lunch or a potter about the shops. No heavy interrogations or questions. Just their normal relationship, ramped up a bit. And Emily texted her most days, checking in. Gigi was incredibly touched by the concern, and profoundly appreciated the kindness, as well as the fact that Emily didn't cross-examine her.

She knew Emily and Christopher hadn't taken sides – they both saw Richard, she knew, and she was glad of it. If Oliver was probably on hers, and Megan – at this point – very firmly on her father's, Emily and Christopher were definitely Switzerland. She knew too that Emily would have advocated on her behalf with Christopher, if needed. Her tacit support was hugely important to Gigi. Emily had asked her once, very early on, whether she wanted to know about Richard – how he was doing . . . She'd said no. How could it help? Then added, because she couldn't help herself, and because old habits died hard, that if Emily thought there was something she *should* know about his state of mind, or just his state in general, that she'd like to be told. So far, there hadn't been anything. Sometimes she was curious – but she didn't let herself ask. She told herself it wasn't her business or her concern.

Emily just seemed to know what she needed.

She remembered when Ava had been a new-born. Christopher had called at breakfast time one Saturday morning, when the baby was barely an hour old, and Gigi and Richard had gone straight to the hospital. They were closer geographically than Emily's parents, and so they were the first visitors. The delivery had been straightforward, but Ava had had a touch of jaundice, so they were keeping them both in for the first night. Emily had been in bed, holding Ava, when they got there. She'd immediately held her out for Gigi. Not a second of hesitation or new-mother possessiveness. She was a generous and empathetic girl then and still. The restorative powers of a good cuddle with delicious Ava were undiminished, and Emily always offered her daughter easily, like the human medicine she was.

Oliver was being brilliant, as she could have guessed he would be. He had made it easy, from the start. She supposed he was probably the least shocked of all of them. Maybe even less than she'd been herself. He'd called her at Kate's, the wretched morning after the big revelation, let her know that he'd put Megan – roughly still in one piece,

he said, and at least okay enough to eat a bacon sandwich –
on the train back to university, and he'd asked to see her on
his own.

'Come to mine. Next night off. I'll cook us something.'

Gigi was grateful to her boy – she knew she was almost
certainly going to cry and she didn't want to do it in public.

'Will Caitlin be there?'

'No. Of course not. Just you and me.'

Over a whisky, then a bottle of red, sometimes in floods
of tears, she'd talked and talked, and it had been such a
relief to be able to. Oliver had listened, and held her hand,
and pulled her into his arms to stroke her hair and tell her
it was all right.

At some point in the evening she'd tried hard to pull
herself together.

'This isn't right. I shouldn't be talking to you this way.'

'Why not?'

'Because he's your dad. I'm your mum, for Christ's sake.'

Oliver had smiled. 'And you're both just people. And
I'm not a kid.'

'I know.' She'd cupped his beloved face in her hands. 'I
know, my love. But still –'

'So don't worry about it. You've listened to me enough
over the years. It's fine. I'm not writing it down, and I won't
quote it back to you anytime. I'm not holding you to anything you've said. As far as I'm concerned, for the record,
you're being brave. You're saying something isn't right, and
that you're not happy, and you're trying to do something
about it.'

'And making everyone else miserable in the process . . .'

'I'm not miserable, Mum. Chris is fine – he's got a family of his own. Dad – he's miserable. Can't sugar-coat that

one. None of this is what he wanted. But that's part of the problem, isn't it – at least how I've understood it. Adherence to the bleeding status quo . . . He's part of the problem. He might see it differently once you've been gone a while. That might be exactly what's needed. And Meg . . . Meg'll be all right . . .'

And it was Megan who kept her awake at night. Hurting Richard wasn't nice, but it didn't torture her. She and Richard had been willing participants in their own marriage. Meg was an innocent bystander: the only victim, so far as she could see. How much longer could Gigi have waited? Graduation didn't mean adulthood – God knows she'd seen that with the boys. Until Megan had her own home? Her own family? How much more of her half-life would she have had to live, waiting until Megan was ready? She couldn't have. She'd been diligently working at letting her go since she'd first left for university – before, even – but this was too much, too sudden. Knowing that Meg was angry, too angry to want to have anything to do with her – it stung. If she was perfectly honest, it felt slightly like a betrayal too. Did she really deserve it, from her own daughter? Is that still all she was to Meg – a wife and mother? When might a daughter be expected to see her mother as a woman?

'Go and see her.' Oliver was loading the dishwasher. The flat was pretty tidy, for Olly. There was no evidence of Caitlin here – it looked as it had for the last couple of years. Slightly in need of a woman's touch. Comfortable, with proper furniture now, not the flat pack of earlier years, but stopping just short of stylish. If Caitlin was spending much time here, she was doing it on Oliver's terms . . .

He'd made a cup of coffee for them both, and now he sat down across from her again, his hands cupping the mug. 'I'm serious. Just show up. Don't give her the option. What's she going to do then?'

Gigi shrugged. 'Walk right past me?'

'She won't do that.'

'Are you sure?'

Oliver rubbed his forehead. 'No. I suppose I'm not sure. She's a kid. She's mad and stupid. She knows nothing. But what have you got to lose? I bet she won't be able to keep up the cold shoulder if she's looking right at you.'

'Maybe . . .'

'I could come with you. If you wanted.'

Gigi shook her head. 'I think it's up to me, love.'

'She's taken the position that you're the baddie, Dad's the innocent party. You're a home-wrecker. Her home, by the way, not Dad's. She's selfish . . . What a baby. I blame you, by the way. You have spoilt that girl sinful.' He was smiling, but Gigi knew he wasn't wrong about that. 'It won't even necessarily be what she still thinks. But she's proud and she's stubborn, and she *hates* to be wrong, and she'll find it really difficult to back down, even if she wants to. Trust me. She'll come round. And if she doesn't, you'll have to go up there and call her bloody bluff.'

Tess

Iris's suitcase sat in the corner of the Donna's spare room for a few weeks before Tess could face opening it. She didn't know what she'd find inside, but she was afraid of any more sadness. She'd had enough. Eventually, though, curiosity overcame fear, and she pulled it up on to the bed one evening when Donna was away: she'd taken a job doing reportage wedding photography at one of those OTT three-day affairs. Donna hadn't been looking forward to it, but she'd used what she called 'yoga maths' and reasoned it was worth the hefty fee. She'd left the day before, and now Tess almost missed her. But she wanted to be alone when she opened the case. Alone with Iris.

It was one of those old-fashioned ones – not leather, but very thick card, black, with metal rivets on the corners, a bit beaten up, but still intact. She didn't remember seeing it when she was little. Iris had used a white case that lived on top of her 1930s wardrobe; it had a little mirror in the lid, and a satin pocket. That was long gone. Tess tried to pick the lock, which would once have had a tiny metal key – lost, she assumed, in the mists of time, rather than hidden – with a paperclip, and, when that failed, she used a pair of pliers Donna kept in a kitchen drawer to pull it open. It came away easily enough.

On top of some papers was her wedding album. This, at least, Tess did remember from her youth, though she had forgotten it until she saw it now. It was covered with silk, watermarked ivory, discoloured yellow in parts. The photographs – all black and white – were slipped into photo corners, layered with tissuey, waxy paper pages. There weren't many – they filled only the first ten pages or so. They were variations of the framed shot she'd taken from Iris's dressing table, which sat now on her bedside chest. There was a brochure from a bakery, slipped between the pages, with several wedding cakes pictured, one circled, its price handwritten in Iris's curly, old-fashioned script beside it. And a picture of Iris and Wilfred cutting into the same cake. One of Tess's own drawings fell out of the pages into her lap – she recognized a design for an elaborate many-tiered wedding cake of her own imagination, done when she was nine years old. Iris had kept it and written her name in the corner. *Tess's cake. 1990.*

There was an envelope in the back, with some older photographs she'd never seen, so far as she could recall. She knew, from Iris's handwriting on the back of each one, that they were pictures of her parents and their farm. Her great-grandfather, standing proud, chest out, by a five-bar gate. One with her great-grandmother, in a wedding dress of her own, sepia-tinted. She looked like a picture Tess had seen once of the Queen Mother at her wedding. It was dated May 1919. Another one of a baby, with a little boy. The baby was on a stool, the little boy, not much more than a toddler himself, stood with his chubby arm protectively around her, his hair wet and brushed to the side. She turned it over curiously. *Me and Tom. 1921.* And one more. A very small, very old picture of a young man in uniform. Tess stared at it. It wasn't her grandfather. She knew Wilfred had served in the army: he'd been conscripted quite late in the war because he'd been older, and been injured in

France in the months after the D-Day landings. But this wasn't him. This man was in an Air Force uniform. This man, she realized, was too young to have been Wilfred, who was closer to forty when he was called up. This man looked just like the little boy holding Iris, only grown up. Barely. This man was Tom.

Iris had been talking about a Tom. About how they'd loved each other. Tess had thought she was just confused. But he was her brother.

How extraordinary. Tess tried hard to remember Iris talking about her childhood. She knew Iris had grown up on a smallholding in Wiltshire that she'd left to nurse with the VAD in London at some point in the war. VADs weren't trained nurses – they supported them. They'd washed sheets and sluiced bedpans and boiled bandages and taken temperatures. She had talked about the farm, about lambing in the springtime, and about missing school to help with the harvest. She'd talked about crying when her father butchered a pig she'd reared from a piglet.

But she'd never wanted to talk about the war, never been drawn, even when Tess had been studying it in history and had really tried to make her speak of it, though she *had* spoken about feeling hemmed in by the city, how it had seemed so dirty and noisy after the country and how she'd missed the smell of fresh air, and the sounds of the farm, and her mother's drop scones. She knew Iris had been homesick, when she went to London. She'd been a fool, she said. A young fool. She should have stayed. She'd have been useful, on the farm. She frightened everyone, going headlong towards the bombs and the city. But she wanted an adventure. It seemed that everyone else was having one, and she wanted one too. Doing her bit on the farm may have been a valid, necessary contribution, but it was hardly the stuff of the films and the BBC broadcasts. VADs were being posted all over the world, to help the trained nurses, on the front lines in France, and Africa, and all over. Iris had never got out of London in the end. London had been enough, she said, to show her she didn't want to go one mile further. The war wasn't an adventure, she said. And that was all she'd say.

Tess had a small, peculiar memory – stark and precise, where others were vague and fuzzy – of asking her if she'd seen a dead body. Of feeling she'd made her cross with the question, which went unanswered. It was a child's memory – of an afternoon that hadn't been quite right, of trying to fix it with bright talk.

Iris had never once mentioned a brother. In fact, she'd definitely talked about how small their family was. How it was just her and Wilfred, Donna and Tess. She'd never asked, because why on earth would she?

Tess wasn't finished with the case yet. She wanted to find more about Tom. There were old passports next, stiff black ones with their bottom corners cut off to show they'd expired, and the details written in a cursive style with fountain-pen ink. Three were Wilfred's, three Iris's. They had all begun and expired on the same day, posted together. The photographs were a history in themselves, in black and white: Iris with a beehive in the sixties, and Wilfred with thick-rimmed glasses and greased-back hair, longer sideburns in the seventies, thinning on top by the eighties. Both of them older. Greyer. She flicked through the pages and read the stamps, mostly European, imagining the two of them travelling.

And, in the bottom, as she had begun to hope there

might be, there were letters. Because people wrote letters once. Tess's heart leapt with excitement. Only a thin sheaf of them, wrapped carefully in brown paper, thin and soft and torn in places with age. She tipped them out on to the bed. There were perhaps fifteen or twenty, and they were in several different hands. Some were in envelopes, and some just loose. They were old but well preserved, as though hands had smoothed them carefully back into their original folds.

She split them, gently, into different handwritings, and then into date order. A few were signed by her mother. And some by Tom.

She stroked them reverently. Twenty minutes ago she hadn't known Iris had had a brother. Now she'd seen a picture of him. And she had letters he'd written in her hand. It was a lot to take in.

The first letters, the ones written in the early years of the war, she read with fascination. They told of Tom's conscription, late in 1940, of his basic training on Salisbury Plain, and then of his deployment. Details got sketchier after he left England, and his writing more lyrical. He obviously shared a lot with his sister that he didn't want his parents to know. He asked questions about the farm, and their mother and father, but often said he wasn't going to tell them things in his letters home, that he thought it was better, especially for their mother, to protect them.

The letters from Iris's mother started from when she left the farm and went to London. They had obviously not wanted her to go. At first her mother entreated her to come home, her tone hurt and anxious. Then she must have given up. None of Iris's own letters were there. But Tess could deduce details of what must have been in them from her mother's responses – she must have been writing about some of the men she nursed, about what had happened to them. The writing was old-fashioned. There was just one letter from Iris's father, stiff and formal, containing only farm news. Tess read them quickly, riveted.

It was the later letters that twisted her heart. She read those twice over, more slowly the second time, struggling to take in what they contained, her heart beating fast, her sternum aching.

Donna read the letters in one sitting, on her return a few days later, curled up in the corner of the sofa. She'd lit a fire in the log burner before supper, and it burned brightly. Tess had been living with the characters and their story every hour since she'd discovered them. But she didn't want to paraphrase. Tess had handed them to her with a brief explanation, and then stayed quiet while her mother read, adding another log to the fire from the wicker basket in the corner. She silently opened a bottle of wine and poured Donna a glass, which she accepted with a small smile and sipped while she read. Tess sat opposite her, and watched her mother read, watched a few silent tears escape and slip down her cheeks on to her sweatshirt. For ages, just her sniffs punctuated the serenity.

When she'd finished, Donna spent ages smoothing down the paper of the letters as reverently as Tess had done, ordering them and neatening the pile, the way Iris must have done so many times, before she put it down gently beside her and looked at Tess.

'Wow.' She rubbed at her nose with the sleeve of her sweater, pulled down over her hand, and Tess thought that her mother looked like a girl. 'I didn't know any of that.'

'Nor did I.'

'You can't conceive of it, can you, keeping something like that to yourself for so many, many years.'

'Do you think she did?'

Donna looked at her quizzically. 'I mean, she didn't tell you and she didn't tell me. Do you think my granddad knew?'

'I don't know that either.'

'I hope she did. It's too much for a person to keep to themselves.'

For a while, they both looked into the fire.

'What was he like?'

'Wilfred?'

Tess nodded.

'He was . . . dignified. You know. Old school. A gentleman. Upright. Proper. He never came downstairs in his PJs, that kind of a man. A sports jacket and an open-necked shirt were his idea of slobbing out.' She laughed. 'We had a few words about that stuff, when I was younger. He pretty much hated the way I dressed. He always shaved . . . don't think I can remember seeing him with stubble or even a five-o'clock shadow. But he had one, in the hospital, the last time I saw him – a day or two's growth. It was grey. It made him look . . . uncared for. I hated that. He'd have hated that.'

'But was he . . . affectionate?'

'Oh God, yes. He absolutely worshipped the ground she walked on. Iris. Me too. He wasn't necessarily the most physically demonstrative, you know. There wasn't all that much hugging and kissing. He didn't say it all the time, not like we do now. "I love you." It wasn't like that. He was older than most of the dads. A bit out of his time . . . But I knew.'

'How?'

Donna shrugged. 'The look on his face. The way he held her when they danced. Which they did, in the kitchen, all through my childhood. The way he spoke to her. About her.'

Tess nodded.

'It was like . . . this might sound weird . . . but there was this gratefulness about him. You always had the feeling he couldn't believe his luck that he had us, you know? Maybe it was because he was that bit older. Maybe it was just how he was.'

Donna hadn't looked at her much while she spoke, but she did now, her eyes still full of tears.

'What was it like when he died? How did Iris react?' Tess had never asked. It seemed important, now, to know things.

Donna took a deep breath. 'Well, it was quick. Unexpected, at least as far as I knew. Heart attack. He never really woke up. We weren't with him when it happened – Iris got the call, went to the hospital. I hadn't lived with them for quite a long time, but I came, quick as I could. I think she knew, when she called me, that he was going. She wanted me to have the chance to see him, before it happened. But it was too late to talk to him. At least, for him to talk to us. Iris talked. She was sat by his bed, holding his hand and talking to him when I got there.'

'What about? Do you remember?'

She knitted her brow together, thinking. 'Stuff about their life together. About how happy he'd made her, how grateful she was to have had him. Things like that.'

Donna's tears were falling fast now, her voice full of sobs at the memory, dredged up from long ago and far away.

'I remember that she didn't cry until afterwards. She held it all together at the hospital. She did at his funeral, though. She said that was what he'd want her to do.'

Tess smiled. 'Dignified, right?'

Donna nodded. 'That's it. But that first night, after we had to leave him at the hospital, you know, for the under-takers to come and get the body . . . I went back with her. Insisted. Stayed in my old room. And I could hear her. She cried all night . . .'

Tess got up and went to her mother, who let herself be held. The two of them sat staring into the fire, each lost in their own memories of Iris, tessellated now by the frag-mented story told by the letters.

'I want to ask her about her brother.'

'Are you sure that's a good idea?'

Tess shrugged. 'I'd go careful. This must have hurt her so much. There's a reason she didn't talk about it all these years.'

'She might not remember it at all.'

'And she might not want to.'

5 July 1944

Dear Iris,

I am well. Please tell Mum and Dad that I am all right. You know I can't talk about where I am or what I'm doing. Normally it's hard to write these letters. Short of saying you're alive and you're well, what else can you put? But today I can write about the existence of angels because today I know that they are real. I've just read that back and it sounds like I'm drunk and perhaps I am, Iris eyes, but trust me when I say there is precious little booze around here.

I'm in love. Iris, I know, I know, I've said it before. You've probably got a list. But you know, like Romeo at the beginning of that play, I thought it was true before but now I know it never was. Because this is real and absolute. And I feel happy for the first time since I left you all. I feel bloody ecstatic.

I have to tell you, because my mates would rib me something rotten.

I haven't long to write, and I know how you and Mum long for news of me, so that is the news. I'll write more later . . .

I hope all is well with all of you. When I close my eyes, I can smell the farm at this time of year, and I can picture everyone there. Mum, Dad, you and me. As we were.

I wish you had stayed. They'll be missing you. It would be easier for me to think of you there with them. I know you want to make a difference, be a part of the war effort, but you could do that there with them, and be safe, and I worry for you in London.

I just want all of this to be over. They think it will be, soon enough. We're definitely on top – got them on the run, everyone says. Perhaps we'll be home for Christmas.
Stay safe, Iris. Stay safe.

Tom

18 July 1944

Dear Iris,

You can tell Mum and Dad that I am well and that things are not too bad where I am. I got two letters from you at once this week and I am glad to hear all the news from home and from London.

I confirm that I'm still in love. With the same girl. I told you this was the real thing. Now I have a bit more time I can tell you more about her. Her name is Manon. So, yes, she's French. But she speaks excellent English. Just as well. I have just about mastered Bonjour, s'il vous plaît *and* Merci beaucoup. *You were always the brains in our family. So we speak English.*

We were billeted near her farm, a while back. Can't say where, but one day I'll be able to show you on the map. See, she's a farmer's daughter like you. She and her brother brought us eggs. I hadn't had an egg for so long. Just the powdered stuff we get here. I thought I might cry, from the taste of it. The yellow yolk.

She's short and slim, blonde, with freckles which she hates, of course, because no one with freckles ever understands how lovely they are, and the bluest, bluest eyes. She looks much younger than she is, because she's small. I don't see her often but, when I do, it's always like clouds have parted and I swear sometimes I hear celestial choirs. I sound mad, I know. I don't care. Maybe I've been here too long, surrounded by the sounds of war. Guns. Screams. Bombs. Men who cry for their mothers. Her voice is like a salve.

One day you'll meet her, Iris. I know you will. I want to bring her back, and she says she'll come. We've made a bloody awful mess of this place. There's almost nothing left. I thank God, whatever else, for an England that no German army ever set foot on. I thank God for an England where there is still green grass, and fields of wheat, and buildings that stand, with their glass windows unsmashed.

Love to everyone at home. Stay safe.

Tom

15 August 1944

Dear Iris,

Thank you for your letter. Your stories about the porters at the hospital getting things on the black market are good to hear. It's like a bit of normality. I read some of them out to the boys, and we all have a laugh. It makes us feel normal. I'm sure there are very grim times too, and I'm grateful you only share the funny silly details of your life with me, although I hope we will talk, properly talk, when I am home. When I am home. I love to write that. It makes it real. I hope you are well. I hope you are happy.

I wanted you to be the first to know. I have asked Manon to marry me, and she has said yes, so we are engaged. Her father has given us his blessing. I rather think her mother had to convince him that I was all right, being an Englishman. Once this is all over, I *will marry her. I want to bring her home and live with her on the farm, with Mum and Dad, while they are still alive. And you, Iris. It will always be your home too. This place is such a mess, and we want to be somewhere peaceful, where the landscape isn't scarred and the people aren't haunted. We dream of it. I don't describe things as well as you do but I do try. I have told her about the animals, and the village, and my mates from school. I wonder how many of us are left. How many more might die before this is finished, even though we feel we are closer to the end than we have been?*

Maybe to you it seems fast, reckless. You might think I am a fool. War makes me hurry. Life is precious. The future still seems far away but it got a little closer when I asked her and she agreed. It seems like an idea, the life we can have, but it became more real when she said she would marry me. I know you'll love her. And when Mum and Dad get to know her they will too. I say that but I'm not sure, of course. She is different. But she is good, I know that for sure. You'll help, I know.

I never thought I would be so happy in the middle of all this. I'm the luckiest bloke in France. It's been so hot here, and the sun is so strong. When it's quiet, and you lie back and close your eyes and feel it on your face, you can almost forget it all.
My love to everyone,

Tom

23 September 1945

Dear Iris,

So I am home. They tell me I am one of the lucky ones — the war in Europe ended only a few months ago, and here I am, back on the farm. There are just so many people to move. An enormous puzzle of humanity. It makes your head spin just to think of it. But I am home for the harvest.

I was gone for nearly three years. 1,032 days. I counted every one of them, and I dreamt of it for 1,032 nights. Everything looks more or less the same as it did before I left, except that you are not here, and I am sorry for that. I have missed you, my Iris. Mum and Dad are older. They temper their joy and their relief at my return when we are in the village. It seems so many of their friends have not had their sons come home to them. Or not whole, at least.

I've been gone a long time, Iris. You're all grown up. Have you fallen in love? I don't think so — I flatter myself that you'd have told me about him, whoever he was. I hope I am in time to save you from it.

Mum says twenty-nine men from the villages around here have died. Dozens more are not back yet. Some of the boys have been fighting the Japanese and Dad says they are in a far worse way. I am one of the lucky ones. I keep hearing it.

I try to believe it. But I can't. Dad's told Mum not to ask me anything. He understands, he says. And maybe he does, some of it. Maybe you would, if you were here. But I don't want you to think it's your fault — because you're not here. I want to try to explain.

Manon is dead. She died with her mother and her aunt in Royan. They were killed in the bombing there, in January, but I didn't know. I hadn't had a letter for so long, but that didn't mean anything. There was so much chaos. I didn't hear until May, from her cousin. She'd already been gone for five months. It's strange — you'd think you'd know. She wasn't supposed to be in Royan. But she was, and I'll never know why, and she died there.

And the thing is, Iris, the awful thing is, that her love is what kept me alive. Loving her kept me alive. Sometimes I think it was the only thing that did. People say we instinctively fight for life, but, in war, there are moments — at least for me there were — when I didn't think I wanted to. That it seemed easier to let death win. That the world seemed so wicked that it didn't seem worth fighting to stay in it. That it might be a relief for it to be over. There's a lot said about duty and about courage and comradeship. I knew men — I served alongside some — who fought with those principles, lived by them and sometimes died by them, but I wasn't one of them, Iris. I'm sorry. I wasn't. I wish I could have been. I never felt brave. And sometimes I didn't want to live. But not after her. Never once after her.

I never believed in God. Did you know that? Every Sunday we sat there, you and me, squashed between Mum and Dad, and sang and prayed and listened to the vicar. And I never believed, because He never showed me a reason to. Until her. I started to believe He'd sent her to keep me alive. To show me that the world wasn't hopeless. To make me fight to stay in it. Every night, no matter how scared, or how uncomfortable or how wretched I was, I closed my eyes when I lay down and pictured her face. Told myself a dream of us — of a future, and a life once the war was over. So when I woke up the next day, she was the reason to keep going. And it was selfish, perhaps, but it was better than duty and fear and courage, because it wasn't just an ideal. It was real. We'd had so little time together. Moments, really. But I knew. And when we were apart, I know that her love kept me alive.

But mine couldn't do that for her. It wasn't enough.

And now I can't live without her, you see. I won't. I feel like I died when she did. This is just my body and I have no use for it.

I know what you'd say. What Mum and Dad would say, if they knew. Give it time. You'll heal. I won't.

Don't let yourself love someone as I did. It's too dangerous. Promise me that, sister.

I'm sorry for the hurt this will cause you, and our mother and father. Explain to them, or don't — whichever you think will help them more. You are the only one who knows about Manon. I never told them. I wanted to bring her home.

Your brother Tom

28 September 1945

Dear Iris,

This is the hardest letter I have ever had to write, my darling daughter. I'm a coward. I cannot bear to telephone you, and I cannot come to where you are, and so I am sending you news I know you will hear alone, and that thought would break my heart if it wasn't already broken.

Tom is dead. I won't try to find a gentler way to give you the news. It wouldn't help. Your brother has died.

For so, so long, during the war, we waited for this news. I know you worried as much as me and your father: I know how close you were. You used to be such a gang of two. But I was his mother. His survival and his comfort were my first and last thought every day he was gone. When we crowded around the radio to hear the news, it was always him I was thinking of. We tried not to mind the censored letters so long out of date. We kept the faith. In the villages and towns, people we knew lost their sons and their brothers and their husbands, and each time we held our breath, and our sorrow was tinged with a relief that felt shameful. And we bargained with God. Let it not be Tom. Let it never be Tom. My only boy.

Do you remember VE Day? The single most glorious day. When I think of it I remember church bells, a thousand of them, ringing. It was over, and our boy had survived.

It wasn't until he came home that I realized not all of him had. I fed him as much as he would let me. We cleaned him up, and he dressed in his old clothes. He was thinner and paler, but he looked like Tom again. Each day I told myself he was coming back to us.

He was haunted. Of that I am certain. He never said a single word to us about the things that had happened to him.

Give him time, your dad said. He'd been to war. I listened to him. I wish I hadn't.

Tom couldn't give himself time.

I know you will want to know how. Your father was out in the fields, I was hanging out the washing. He said he was going for a walk, and I didn't kiss him goodbye because I had an armful of sheets, and I didn't see which direction he headed in for the same reason.

By lunchtime he hadn't come home. Your father went out to look for him late in the afternoon. He'd hanged himself in the wood. Your father managed to cut him down but it was too late. He carried him home. He'd never have been able to do that before, but Tom was so thin. And your father said he couldn't have borne to leave him in the wood while he went off back for help.

I looked everywhere for a note, Iris. But there is nothing. His bed was made. He'd packed his clothes into a case.

We won't see his name on a memorial, but the war killed him just the same. We have lost, as so many people around us have, but I find there is precious little comfort in that.

Come home, my darling girl, for the funeral. We must all be together on that dreadful day.

Your mum

Tess

Iris was bathed in the watery winter sunshine, sat by the window, when Tess arrived. There was a brightly coloured crochet rug tucked over her knees; her hands were folded neatly in her lap. Tess smiled. Of all the things her grandmother had been able to teach her, of all the projects the two of them had worked on over the summers, she'd never managed to get her crocheting. Tess remembered watching the two hooks working furiously in Iris's hands, blankets growing by the hour, while she grew frustrated by her own piece, the size of a beermat, more knot than anything else.

Iris didn't move her head as Tess approached, her attention seemingly held by the garden, where a robin was at the bird feeder. There'd been a hard frost – the weak sun hadn't made it across the whole lawn yet, so some of the grass was shimmery white, and there was still a deadly slick on the paving stones by the wall.

Tess would have come to visit her grandmother today, anyway. She came every weekend, and often during the week as well. But she'd felt adrenalin, this morning. This morning was not the normal Groundhog Day of these trips. Reading the letters had unlocked something magical for Tess, had transformed Iris again. Not back to the grandmother she remembered, the one she'd been mourning the loss of for so many months now. But to the girl Tess had never known. It wasn't so much the secrets she wanted, intrigued though she was. She already knew the unbelievable sadness of it, and she ached with it – both that Iris had lived through it, and that she couldn't share it with her. It was that glimpse of Iris that she really craved.

She knew that dementia patients often did better in the distant past than the recent past. She'd seen YouTube clips of people seemingly completely lost in the jumble of their own brains, brought back by a song, or a story. Not forever, not even for long, but for a moment . . . and she wanted that moment with Iris. It seemed important to try to get it.

'Iris?'

Now her head turned, her eyes milky-pale. 'Hello, Iris. It's me, Tess.' She kissed her powdery cheek.

'Hello.'

Somewhere down the corridor, people were singing Vera Lynne songs in warbly voices. On the television in the corner, an old repeat of *Saturday Kitchen* was playing to a tiny audience of people who would never cook again, or worry much about what they ate. Rick Stein's warm voice enthusiastically extolled the virtues of red-mullet soup in vain.

For a while, Tess just sat there with her grandmother. She'd brought the letters with her in a canvas bag, but she probably needn't have bothered – she hadn't seen Iris read anything in a long time.

They both watched the robin, until a grey squirrel swung on to the feeder, sending a scattering of seeds across the lawn, and the robin to the shelter of a nearby tree. Iris gave a little tut, her head bobbing almost imperceptibly.

'You love the winter, hey?' It was true. Autumn had always been Iris's favourite season. But winter was almost as good.

Iris nodded, but didn't answer.

'I bet winters were hard, though, on the farm. You know, when you were young?'

Again, a non-committal nod. It was clumsy, and obvious. But Tess didn't know any other way to do it. To try to take Iris back. And she so wanted her to go back.

'With Tom . . .'

Iris turned her head sharply now, her eyes narrowed.

'Tom.' It wasn't a question. She said his name slowly, as though she was testing it out.

Tess nodded eagerly. 'Yes. Tom. Your brother.' She searched Iris's face for recognition, but Iris turned back to the garden.

'The water in the troughs froze sometimes . . .'

A door had opened. Just a crack. Tess held her breath, and resisted the urge to push it harder.

'We had to break the ice with a spade. For the animals.' She lifted her hands, just for a moment, faintly aping a movement, a weak mime.

'You and Tom?'

'Mostly Tom.' She smiled now. 'I helped him. He hated the cold mornings.'

For maybe three or four minutes, Iris didn't speak, and she held her face so that Tess couldn't see her, staring out. The squirrel swung alarmingly on the feeder, but didn't fall. It seemed like the door had closed again. Tess was about to give up. She told herself she could try another day, because hoping for a day when Iris might be more lucid was better than nothing.

Then, suddenly, Iris's head dropped towards her chest, her face crumpling horribly. She visibly sank in the chair, like a deflating balloon, her neck at an unnatural angle, pushed into her shoulder. It was a violent gesture. For a second, Tess imagined a massive stroke was killing her. But it wasn't that. Infinitely more frightening was the keening noise that came from her now. The sound of grief. It was as fresh, and as shocked and new, as if she'd just been confronted with it. Her voice was louder than it had been for as long as Tess could remember.

Loud enough to bring a nurse over, her face concerned. 'Is everything okay?'

Tess was embarrassed. 'I'm sorry . . . I was just talking to her.' She sounded, to herself, like a child caught in a bad deed they didn't want to confess to.

'It's okay,' the nurse tried to reassure her. 'It happens, sometimes.'

It hadn't happened to Iris. Not as far as Tess knew. Not in front of her.

'Some of our residents can get quite upset.' The nurse bent over, a hand on Iris's arm.

'Ssh. Ssh now, Iris. Don't go upsetting yourself. You're all right. It's me, Debbie. This is your granddaughter.' She looked at Tess. 'You're Tess, right?' Tess nodded helplessly. 'Yes, see, it's Tess. She's come to see you . . . Don't cry . . .'

It didn't mollify her grandmother. If anything the sound was getting louder, and it cut brutally through Tess.

Everyone in the room was staring. A male nurse was coming over – two more had come to the door. Iris had pushed Debbie's hand away, and she was holding herself, hands clamped tight on her upper arms. Tess touched her shoulder, horrified, but Iris shrugged that off too. Through the crying, Tess could make out one word: 'Tom.'

The nurses were talking in low voices to each other. One left, and came back with a wheelchair.

'We'll take her to her room.'

Distress was evidently contagious. A couple of the other residents – the ones who had been calmly staring through Rick Stein a few minutes ago – were looking agitated at the noise Iris was making.

'Is she going to be okay?'

The male nurse smiled kindly at her. 'She will be. She'll calm down. It's just that in here –'

Tess put a hand up. 'I know. I get it.'

Iris didn't stop wailing while they picked her up – so easily – and put her in the wheelchair.

'Should I come?' She stood up and grabbed her bag.

'Up to you. You might want to give us a minute . . . Have a cup of tea while we try to settle her. One of us can come and get you.'

She felt like a coward, staying behind. Debbie touched her arm. 'I'll stay with her.' Tess nodded, gratefully.

She wanted to put her hands over her ears to block out the sound, but it gradually got quieter as they took Iris down the corridor towards her room. Tess felt shaken, shocked. And horribly guilty. Did they have to do this often? She was gripped by the sudden fear that this happened regularly and that she was never here. The thought of all the pain made her want to cry.

She stared determinedly at the bird feeder in the garden, trying to focus, trying to control her breathing, which had become ragged. But taking deep breaths did nothing to stop the tears that ran down her cheeks.

She felt a gentle hand on her shoulder. She rubbed under her eyes with two fingers, pushing the tears away, and turned, expecting to see a nurse with an update. But it was Gigi's son, Oliver. She sniffed hard.

'Bad day?'

'Not good.' It was all she could manage. She heard the sob in her voice.

He walked around and sat in the chair Iris had been in.

'I'm just going to sit here for a minute next to you . . .'

It might have seemed odd, but somehow it didn't. It felt kind. He reminded her so much of Gigi. There was just . . . something about them. She nodded and smiled weakly. His not asking had the perverse effect of making her want to tell him everything.

Once Tess realized he wasn't expecting her to speak, was just sitting beside her, she started to calm down. The sobs subsided, her breathing slowed. Her nose was still running, though.

Eventually she turned to him, and he smiled the big smile she remembered from the car park.

'We've got to stop meeting like this.' There was something like laughter in his voice, but it was gentle.

'It's not funny. You're always finding me in a mess.' She sniffed again.

'I'm not laughing. Here, take this.' He lifted one hip off the chair, pulled a blue handkerchief out of his pocket and handed it to her.

'You're pretty old-fashioned, aren't you?'

'What can I say? Just like my dad.'

'Thank you.' She took it, shook it out and blew.

'Okay?'

'Better. My gran, she just had a . . . a turn, I suppose you'd call it.'

He nodded. 'I was here. I saw.'

'I'm sorry.'

'That's an odd thing to say . . . What on earth would you have to be sorry for?'

It was my fault, Tess thought. You wouldn't be so kind to me if you knew it was my fault.

'I've seen it happen before. To other poor devils in here. It's like . . . something suddenly haunts them, you know?'

'Exactly.' He'd got it completely right, without knowing a thing about the specifics.

'It makes sense to me, in a way.' She looked at him quizzically. 'I mean, think of what your brain – your healthy, young brain – does to you at, say, 3 a.m., when you can't sleep: you know how it magnifies stuff that you wouldn't give a damn about in the day. Like it thinks – *Oh, you can't sleep – let me flood you with worries about everything you ever did, or didn't do, or said . . .*'

Tess laughed in spite of herself.

Oliver laughed too. 'Self-sabotage. It makes damn sure you're wide awake.'

She nodded.

'So this is kind of the same thing . . . Do you see?'

'I think so.'

'I suppose none of us lives a life without regret, or without buggering something up.'

The sound Tess made was almost a snort. Oliver opened his eyes wide and smiled knowingly.

'Those will be the things that come and mess with our

minds, when we're sat in places like this, in fifty years' time.'

'Wow. Way to cheer a girl up.' But, somehow, he was . . .

He laughed again. 'Yeah. Sorry. I suppose we must just resolve to live without regrets.'

He was looking at her closely.

'Well . . . I already regret that you keep catching me in such a state. I'm not always like this, I promise.'

'I can see that. It's this place . . . it's hard on all of us. If we –'

But then Debbie was back, with her kind face and her professional manner. 'She's calmed down a lot. You can come now, if you want.' She saw Oliver then, and Tess swore her eyes lit up. 'Oh, hello . . .' She watched Oliver smile at her. It was the same warm, winning smile. The one that made you feel everything would be okay. The one that felt like it was just for you – like the beam of a bright torch. You daft cow, she thought. For a second, just then, she'd almost thought he was going to suggest seeing her away from this place. His 'If we' had been full of something . . . Delusional fool. Have you seen you? A weeping, foolish woman who can't drive, with an ever-increasing muffin top. He's just a kind, sweet man who feels sorry for you. Like his mum. Stop being pathetic. As if . . .

She looked ruefully at the balled-up handkerchief in her hand, as she stood up.

'I'll wash this and give it back to your mum.'

'Or me.'

'Thank you for being kind.'

She heard her tone. Dismissive.

If it confused him, he didn't let on. 'I'll see you again.'

She nodded, backing away now.

'I hope your gran is okay.'

'Thank you, Oliver. Thank you . . .'

She didn't see that he watched her until she turned the corner.

Gigi

Later that day, Gigi sat in a sandwich shop with Olly. They hadn't planned to see each other. He'd reckoned on a quick run to Clearview, then back to town. But Gigi had agreed, happily, to meet him. The lunchtime rush was over, and there were only two or three other tables occupied. They ordered at the counter, and chatted about nothing much until the flustered young boy working there brought over a tray with their food and drinks on it. He was obviously new, and he made quite a performance of putting the right plate in the right place, and slopped coffee into Oliver's saucer, apologized, and fussed around with paper napkins. Eventually, he retreated to behind the counter and left them to it.

Gigi reorganized the chaos he'd delivered, then looked at her boy.

'You're spoiling me with visits.'

'And you should be spoilt.'

'I can't argue with that. This is lovely . . .' She gestured towards her panini. 'Melted cheese, hot chocolate and my boy. Three of my favourite things. Not necessarily in that order. But I only saw you a while back and here you are again. To what do I owe this honour?'

Oliver tried to smile, but didn't quite carry it off.

'Love?' She knew her face was full of concern.

'No fooling you, hey?'

'Plenty of fooling me. But not from you. What's up?'

He took a deep breath. 'I think I've made a bit of a mess.'

'Caitlin.'

'You assume.'

'Am I wrong?'

He smiled sadly at her. 'Hardly ever . . .'

Gigi wanted to say a lot of things. How she'd known something was off. How worried she'd been. How she suddenly felt giddy with relief . . . But she didn't say any of them. She slowly and deliberately cut her panini into squares, and stirred her hot chocolate, and left him the space to try to explain.

'She's a great girl.'

Gigi wasn't convinced that was true, but it seemed inflammatory to say so. Either way, the sentence was damning on its own. You hung out with a great girl. You didn't marry her. You married a wonderful, one-off girl.

'I am really, really fond of her . . .'

There was such a 'but'.

'I mean, I love her.' And a question in his voice, on the word. 'She's bright. She's sexy. She thinks I'm the dog's bollocks.'

'Bee's knees.' She raised an eyebrow, mock-mother.

'Bee's knees. Sorry . . .'

'And frankly, Golden Balls, she's not alone in that sentiment. There's always been something of an orderly queue.'

Oliver brushed off the maternal compliment. 'We think the same about lots of things.'

Do you, do you really? Gigi thought. *Do you feel the same about family? God – never underestimate the colossal importance of a shared vision of your future . . .*

She said the 'but' for him. 'But?'

'But I think I'm supposed to be feeling some things that I'm not sure that I am.' He looked embarrassed.

'Like what?'

'Well, I'm supposed to be walking on air. Right? Obsessed. I'm supposed to want to be with her every minute. I'm supposed to not be avoiding any conversation about a date for a damn wedding. I'm supposed to be thinking that I couldn't or I wouldn't want to live without her. She's supposed to be' – and here he put out both his arms expansively – 'everything.'

'Yeah.'

'That's how you felt about Dad, right?'

'When I married him?' She thought about it. 'Yes. It was.' Her stomach twisted. She wasn't sure whether it was for Oliver, or for herself. For them both, maybe.

'And I'm not saying I'll never feel like that . . . it's just . . .' He stopped, and thought. 'It's gone so fast. And she asked me.' He shrugged. 'She's been let down, once too often. Mostly by men. Her dad, for a start.'

'And you'd have been letting her down if you said no.'

'Well, I would.'

'Love. You can't marry someone to be polite.'

'I know.'

'Or because you are kind, or because you are hoping for or expecting that the right feelings will follow afterwards. It's hard, marriage. Hard work. If the right feelings aren't there before you start, they won't come.'

'So how do you know?'

Gigi shrugged. 'I think you just do. I think you said it already. I think you know what you're meant to be feeling, and I think you've just told me you don't.'

'Maybe . . .'

'Can you slow things down?'

'That's just cowardly, isn't it?'

'I can't tell you what to do, Oliver.'

'I know that.' He sat forward, tapping his feet nervously against the floor, so that his knees shook. 'Fuck. Fuck . . .' He buried his face in his hands.

Gigi laid a hand on his shoulder.

Something was missing. Gigi sensed there was something he wasn't telling her. Her mother's instinct told her that this wasn't just an accumulation of feeling. There was some kind of catalyst. She knew it. She just didn't know what it was. And she didn't want to push.

She couldn't pretend she'd been excited about Caitlin becoming part of the family, but she knew she'd have done her best, her very best, if she was the person Oliver had chosen. It sounded like Caitlin had chosen him. Like her beautiful boy had done what he thought he should – what he thought was right. She only hoped he had the sense not to compound the original mistake by carrying on. It couldn't work, if it started like this.

And he hadn't asked about Richard, about how she was feeling and how she was doing, and she was glad. It was a relief that Oliver was thinking about himself, and not about her and his father. It made her feel less guilty.

For his part, Oliver felt a sense of simple relief at saying out loud some of what had been in his head these last few weeks. He was grateful for his mum's quiet ear, even though he knew, really, she hadn't liked Caitlin. Or at least the idea of her. Or at least the shadow she cast over the family.

If he was absolutely honest with himself, seeing her against the backdrop of his family had been the beginning

273

of the real doubt. It hadn't worked. Not like Emily worked. Gelled. Not even like other girlfriends he'd taken home had worked. Before Christmas, he'd told himself some of what was missing was just myth, the schmaltz of the smug. That there wasn't some prescribed list of feelings, of boxes everyone had to tick. After Christmas, that had got harder to believe.

There were bits of him not given over to Caitlin, and he was suddenly, without fully understanding why and how, aware that they might be vulnerable, those bits, to someone else.

Tess

Tess was signing in at Clearview when Gigi came up behind her, and held her briefly in a light embrace that might have seemed overfamiliar if it wasn't Gigi making it, but, since it was, it just felt nice.

'Hello, lovely.'

'Hello yourself. Coming or going?'

'I was going, actually. You?'

'I just got here. Traffic's rotten.' She'd meant to come earlier, in truth, but, for the first time, after last time, she'd almost dreaded it. She'd procrastinated at home – Donna wasn't there – and so she'd put on a wash, unloaded the dishwasher and dawdled for too long. That, and then the traffic, had put her back.

'Really? I might hang around a bit longer, then – let it clear a bit.'

'Good idea.'

'Don't fancy a coffee, do you? I don't want to keep you away from your gran . . .'

'Actually, I didn't have breakfast. I'd love to grab something.'

'Deal. Come on, then.' Gigi linked arms with Tess companionably and pointed them in the direction of the cafeteria.

'They might still have some croissants or something. Too early for lunch.'

The cooking smells hit Tess sideways, once she was in

the room, and she settled for a cup of mint tea, which could usually head off a wave of nausea.

Gigi noted the change of heart, and raised an eyebrow as they sat down.

'I thought you were hungry?'

'I am. And not . . .'

Gigi looked at her, a small smile forming.

Tess laughed. 'I'm pregnant, Gigi.'

The small smile broke into a beam. 'Oh, Tess – that is happy, happy news. Congratulations!'

Tess smiled shyly back. 'I thought you might have guessed already. You being a midwife . . .'

Gigi put her hands up in a gesture of surrender. 'Occupational hazard.'

'It's okay. I'm glad to say, actually.'

'How far along are you?'

'Around five months. The baby is due at the beginning of August.'

'Wow. That's brilliant. Summer babies are a joy. Twenty weeks or so?' Tess nodded. 'And still sick?' Professional curiosity had obviously kicked in.

'Mostly fine now – it was never too bad, actually. But every now and then something just . . . gets me . . . and then I don't fancy anything. Believe me, highly out of character – normally no pastry is safe in my vicinity, but I'd honestly heave if that pain au chocolat came anywhere near me right now.'

Gigi laughed conspiratorially. 'I was the same with raw meat. Couldn't stand it.'

Tess blew out her cheeks and smiled ruefully. 'Yup. I get that.'

'You need something, though, to go with that tea. If you

haven't eaten all day. Forgive the bossiness. Mother, grand-mother and midwife, so you're buggered. Think you could manage a ginger nut?'

Tess smirked, knowing resistance was probably futile. 'I could try . . .'

Gigi took out her purse and stood up. 'I'll grab some.'

She ate two small packets, in fact, while Gigi made small talk, and was amazed to find that they did help.

'Better?'

She nodded gratefully. 'Better.'

'It's rotten.'

'It's not so bad. I'd been dreading being one of those women who are really ill all the time – like poor old Kate Middleton.'

'That's grim. Particularly, one imagines, if one is so much in the public eye.' She said it in a faux posh voice. 'But hyperemesis is quite rare. With most women it passes in the first few months, and it isn't even every day.'

Tess nodded again. 'In time for stretch marks, swollen ankles, haemorrhoids, breasts the size of zeppelins . . .'

'Sometimes! But don't forget the glow, the thicker hair . . . the baby you get at the end of it . . .'

'God, I sound negative, don't I? Sorry.'

'Nothing to be sorry for. Some women love being preg-nant. Some women don't. It's all okay.'

Tess smiled gratefully at Gigi. 'You're very kind.'

'Just telling it like it is . . . It's a lot – a lot of changes – not just the physical ones, although they can be over-whelming on their own. It's other stuff too.'

'And that's if you've got your life sorted.'

'And you haven't?'

Tess ran her fingers nervously around the edge of her

empty teacup. 'Not really.' And then, she didn't quite know why, except that Gigi was so lovely, she said, 'Not at all, actually . . .'

'Oh, love.' Gigi stroked her shoulder.

'It's a bit of a mess. I'm not with the dad. I mean, I was, when I got pregnant. I'm just not now. And I'm not going to be. I don't really know how he's going to fit into the baby's life. I'm being a total coward about sorting it all out, to be honest, but we're not going to be together . . .'

'Are you sure about that? Babies can change things.'

Tess's face was very serious. 'I'm sure.' Her tone brooked no argument, and Gigi nodded, no doubt wondering what on earth had gone on between them to make her so sure.

'And he's moving to New York anyway. Which isn't the why, by the way.'

'Okay.'

'So breaking up with Sean – that was his name, Sean – meant I was homeless. We'd been living together, but it was his place. I'd given up my flat to move in with him. Idiot. So I'm back at my mum's house. In my damn thirties . . .'

'And how is that?'

Tess shrugged. 'It's okay. Better than I thought it would be. I mean – it's good of her to have me. We haven't exactly been close these last years. Ever. Iris has been more like my mum. But Donna did want me to stay, and it's been okay. Still, it's not where you're supposed to be, is it, when you're having your first child? You're supposed to be married to someone you adore, in your own place, painting a damn nursery and hanging mobiles, aren't you? Not kipping in your mum's spare room while you try to figure out what kind of flat you can afford.'

'You're still working?'

'Yes. And I'll get the full maternity, and all that. I mean, I can afford something . . . but I'll be alone there, with the baby, and, frankly, the thought scares me to death.'

Tess looked tearful. Gigi squeezed her hand.

'You know, unsolicited advice can be the worst thing in the world, but –'

'I'm soliciting it, I think.' Tess half laughed.

'Well, then, I'd say this, Tess. One thing at a time. One thing at a time. It's too much, if you try to sort everything all at once. You've got to prioritize. Right now, what matters is you and the baby. Staying well and healthy, rested. You've got your mum, you've got your job, you've got somewhere to stay . . .'

'I must seem such a flake to you.'

'Not at all.'

'You're sweet, but I don't believe you. You're so sorted.'

Gigi laughed more bitterly than she had expected to. 'Appearances can be deceptive, lovely.'

Tess snorted. 'You're lovely. Lovely husband. Lovely kids. Lovely home, I bet. Lovely job, which I know you must be brilliant at . . .'

Gigi looked into her eyes. 'I left that lovely husband.'

'What?'

'I left him.'

'Oh God. I'm sorry! Wow. Big mouth. Sorry . . . sorry.'

'Why should you be?'

'I've been going on –'

'And that's fine,' Gigi interrupted. 'I asked. I just wanted you to know my life wasn't exactly all squared away either. I don't think anyone's is, truthfully. We're all just faking it, aren't we, to some degree?'

Tess smiled gratefully. 'Are you okay?'

Gigi took a deep breath and exhaled slowly. 'Not yet. But I will be. So will you.' She squeezed Tess's hand.

'Do you want to talk about it?' Tess felt awkward suddenly. She remembered how little she knew Gigi. And for how short a time. It just fast-tracked things, being in here, having this common bond. All of them a bit vulnerable and upset, a bit of soft under-belly facing upwards. And she was grateful. Gigi had been so kind. And maybe she was even a little desperate – for the connection.

'Not really. Not to anyone. You're sweet to offer. I've got to organize my own thoughts before they can be words. I've done something so extraordinarily out of character, I think I'm still in shock. Can't say what I mean about it, because I'm not even sure what I mean. If that makes sense?'

'Such sense you cannot imagine!'

They looked into each other's faces and understood each other, without facts or explanation, and both were surprised by how much comfort there was in that.

Gigi

Richard hadn't called her mobile phone in a long time. Even before she left. He didn't like the phone. It had been ages since he'd checked in with her during the working day, for no particular reason, but 'just because', and those days of not hearing from him had been a part of her loneliness. Other people's partners rang or texted – sent messages about their day, or the idiot in the car next to them, or what to have for dinner . . . And now here he was, calling while she was in the condiments aisle in Tesco, realizing that she could buy crunchy peanut butter instead of smooth. She held the phone in her hand, staring at his number, and didn't answer – he'd caught her off guard. After five rings, the words MISSED CALL flashed up on the screen. She stuffed the phone into her handbag and tried to concentrate on jams. Another minute after that, it trilled again with a voicemail. Maybe it was something about the kids? Gigi took a deep breath, and listened to Richard's message, curtly telling her that he was at Clearview, that James had been taken ill. That he thought she should know. That she could come, if she wanted to. She couldn't tell from his voice whether or not he wanted her to.

That didn't matter. She left her trolley where it was in the aisle, got into her car and set off for Clearview. She wasn't thinking about Richard now, but about James. She'd seen him a few days ago, and he'd been well. Confused, like always, but well. They'd done the crossword, which usually meant she did the crossword out loud and he listened, or not, and this time he'd got a word, which happened less and less these days. He'd known that 'e.g. an anteater, 13 letters, 5 across' was insectivorous, which was more than she did, and that bit of dredging up of memory had made them both smile. But there'd been nothing specifically wrong with him. Richard hadn't given her any details in his message – any sense of how bad this was. She drove a bit too fast.

Richard was in the corridor outside James's room when she arrived, looking at his phone. She put her hand on his arm and he looked up, surprised. She wanted to hug him – maybe even expected to, but he pulled away and took a step back from her.

'Is he okay?'

He nodded briefly. 'Stomach flu, they think. Just a bug. He's been pretty sick. Both ends.' He managed to look and sound like he was actually standing in a puddle of it. 'But he's okay . . .'

Gigi felt relief, then surprise at the relief. She knew James would have been happy to be carried away by an innocuous stomach flu. It shouldn't be a relief. But it was.

'Is he in there?'

Richard nodded. 'They're getting him comfortable.' He grimaced.

He'd always been hopeless when the kids were ill – no good at dealing with the mess of it, however sorry he was, and he always was, that they felt rotten. She had a sudden memory of him standing with an infant Oliver, covered in vomit, holding him out at arm's length; but she was the one who had to grapple with a sick-soaked duvet cover and organize a warm bath. Worried about his boy, but unable to do what was necessary to comfort him. Poor Richard. He always let her do it, then made her a cup of tea and told her she was wonderful. She'd always known he meant it.

'How? I don't understand.' It wasn't a rational question, not really. Especially not for someone who worked in the NHS. But she wasn't feeling rational.

'One of those things, I suppose . . . They're not immune in here.'

'Was this overnight?'

He nodded. 'They called this morning. Once the worst was over.'

'But they didn't take him to hospital?'

'No one said anything about that being necessary.'

'Is he on a drip? For fluids?'

'I don't know, Gigi.' He sounded exhausted. 'I haven't asked. I haven't seen him yet.'

'We need to talk to the doctor.'

'He's with someone else. The nurse said he'd come round shortly.'

An uneasy silence descended. There were things other than James that they could talk about – the kids, the flat she was going to see, work, the weather . . . But it was odd – standing here with him, and all their past; the sudden, brutal absence of their future had unbalanced everything, shifted everything. She wondered if they'd ever have a normal conversation again. She knew she badly wanted to try.

'Do you want to go and get a cup of tea? Wait until he's ready?'

Richard shifted from foot to foot. 'I don't think I can. Probably shouldn't have rung you.'

'Come on, Richard. Don't be daft. It's still me.'

'But it isn't, G. Everything has changed . . .' He felt it too – that sickening lurching away from normal.

'This hasn't.' She gestured around her.

'What do you think he'd say about it? If he knew?' he almost snapped.

It was a low blow, and it hit its target, almost taking her breath away. She supposed she couldn't blame him. She stared at the carpet, her eyes smarting.

But cruelty wasn't Richard's métier. That was too unkind for him. He spoke first, and his voice was completely different. 'Just as well he doesn't, I suppose . . . Sorry.' When she looked up he couldn't meet her gaze.

'Richard –'

'I think I'll go, actually. No sense both of us waiting.'

'He's your dad, Richard. I can go.'

'He'd probably rather see you. You're better at all this. You always were.'

His voice was so sad, and small.

She was going to argue, maybe even going to ask him to stay with her, but, as she started to speak, the door to James's room opened and two nurses with yellow plastic aprons and gloves came out, one pulling backwards a wheelie bin with a metal lid. The other smiled at them both, and said, 'He's all yours . . .' and, because the door was open and Gigi could see James, pale and asleep in the wide bed, she moved instinctively towards him. When she turned back to bring Richard with her, he was already gone.

Tess

'It's like a film . . .'

'I know. I can't stop thinking about how incredibly sad it is.'

Tess and Holly were in one of the new nail bars that had proliferated on the high street. The prettiest one. Holly had decreed that they couldn't give up their regular outings, but that they should probably give up the pubs and wine bars that were their habit – and so they were having their toes 'done'. On a school night. 'While you can still see yours, that is,' she'd joked to Tess, when she'd rung to confirm the booking she'd made.

Tess had told Holly about the letters.

'And how extraordinary for Iris never to have said anything. I mean, she's got to have told your granddad, right?'

Tess shrugged. 'How would I know?'

'And there's no one to ask?'

'No one.' Tess thought about Iris's face, when she'd asked her.

Holly was watching her. 'Do you wish you hadn't found them, in a way?'

Tess considered. 'I don't know. It's frustrating. No. I mean –'

'That's clear, then,' Holly smiled fondly. 'And Donna? What does she say?'

'She's like me. Except I suppose it's even weirder for her, not having known before.'

'You and she . . . you're getting on, aren't you?'

'Best we have in . . . can't remember. Best ever, maybe.'

'I'm jealous.' Holly was ninety per cent joking. Her bottom lip was jutted out for comedic effect. 'I'm still your favourite person, right?'

The girl crouched at Holly's feet held up the bottle of dark-red polish for confirmation. Holly nodded. Tess's girl was still bent studiously over her cuticles. It wasn't an entirely comfortable sensation. Not nearly as comfortable, truthfully, as sitting in a deep, upholstered booth at the pub with a small bowl of ready-salted crisps in front of you, but Tess didn't want to be churlish.

'My favourite ex utero person, absolutely. Indubitably, in fact.'

Holly narrowed one eye. 'Never really knew what that word meant, to be honest.'

'And you a teacher! The shame . . .'

'Piss off. I mean, I'd just about got rid of that Sean character. The pesky kid is still months away . . . I was in, man. Right in.'

'You've always been right in, Hols. Despite my best efforts to get rid of Ben and Dulcie.' The two of them laughed at their own banter.

'And now Donna is doing a passable impression of being your mother.' Holly was allowed: she'd been around for years. Tess laughed. 'Muscling in on my person action. I mean, I was going to suggest myself as your doula,' Holly told her.

'You what? What's one of them?'

'Like a midwife, but not. A birthing companion.' Tess nodded, and considered the proposition.

Holly's face was suddenly more serious. 'I mean, if you were worrying about being by yourself . . .'

'I wasn't, until now.' Not quite true. Being alone and in labour was one of the late-at-night thoughts Tess had.

'I mean, strictly at the head end. I've gone this long without seeing your bits, despite some memorable nights out and Turkish baths, and I can go longer. But I'm serious, Tess. If you wanted someone with you . . .'

Tess squeezed Holly's hand where it lay on the armrest between them. 'Thank you.'

'I can peel grapes, count gaps between contractions, put flannels on your head. I've watched an awful lot of *One Born Every Minute*. I'm practically qualified, I think.'

'Thank you.' She was still holding Holly's hand. When she looked at her friend's face, Tess was surprised to see tears in Holly's eyes.

'Oy. I'm supposed to be the one with hormones all over the place. What's wrong?'

'Nothing's wrong. I just . . . I just love you. I don't want you worrying about stuff like that.' Holly rubbed a tear away roughly with her free hand. 'Sorry.'

'I love you too. Can we stop this now, please?' She moved her hand away. 'I have a far more pressing issue . . .'

Holly looked at her quizzically.

'Dark red. Or bright pink? For my toes. While I can still see them?'

Gigi

Gigi had been to a Pilates class. She liked how that sounded when she said it in her head, so she said it out loud, in the Geordie accent the guy from *Big Brother* had. 'Gigi has been to Pilates.' She felt Amazonian. She hadn't been to an exercise class for years . . . since leotards went right up your bum, and Olivia Newton-John might well have provided the soundtrack. But she'd gone once, several years ago after Megan had nagged her into submission, to a Zumba class at the local sports centre. Megan had been developing the Victorian pallor of the GCSE student, and she'd gone only to ensure Megan went, afraid she'd lose the use of her lower limbs and develop rickets if she sat in the study one hour more. Nothing other than the love of mother for child could have persuaded her to don sweat clothes and enter the terrifying cacophony of 'Zoe's Zumba . . .' The less said about that display of mal-coordination the better. But suffice to say Megan had laughed for some hours afterwards.

But she'd gone to Pilates this morning entirely voluntarily. It was much better than Zumba. Alone, unprompted and with no one nagging her. Okay, so she'd chosen a pitch right at the back of the hall, and okay, so she'd lied through clenched teeth to the willowy instructor and said she could 'feel it' in her 'inner corset', which meant she was doing it properly. She was more of an outer-corset Spanx girl, and hadn't felt all that much except stiff, and slightly anxious about the possibility of public farting. But it was a start, and she was sure she *would* feel it soon enough, if she kept going. Correction, *when* she kept going, for was she not Gigi of the Fresh Start? She felt, sitting in the car, drinking from a bottle like a toddler's sippy cup that she'd bought at the same time as her new, brightly striped 'athleisure wear', rather modern, and rather pleased with herself. This might be just the beginning. Maybe she'd get Kate, or Emily, or both – a gang – to sign up and do the Moonwalk with her. Or even one of those Tough Mudders that looked so much dirty fun if you could do them without hyperventilating or actually dying. Maybe there was a slim, sporty woman trapped inside her after all, who might have endorphins, and she'd just been keeping her anaesthetized with gin and cake for all these years . . .

Her mobile phone rang from the dark recesses of her new hobo handbag. She rifled and failed to find it, eventually upturning the bag impatiently, spilling its contents across the passenger seat in the car, and grabbing for the green button just before the call went to voicemail.

Gigi had answered the phone to her boy a thousand times over the years, and she had a mother's sixth sense, gleaned from the simple tone of his voice, or just a pause, about when Oliver was in trouble. There'd been a few heart-stopping calls in his younger, adventuring years – he'd crashed a car, run out of money, fallen off a motorbike in Thailand, decided he'd had enough of uni . . . Mostly he'd needed practical help, or sensible advice, admonishment, even, just to prove the universe was as it should be, but sometimes, she knew, just to hear her voice, when something was wrong . . .

And today, something was. Her self-deprecating Pilates humour would have to wait.

She hadn't bugged him since the conversation in the coffee shop a few weeks ago. She hoped she'd planted a seed, and she'd left it to germinate. She couldn't control what happened. She'd spoken her truth, quietly and calmly, and let him speak his. She'd thought about it every day, but she knew she couldn't push. Her son was fighting a battle between what he knew to be true and what he thought to be right. He was the man she'd raised. She couldn't join the fray. But maybe this was it . . .

'What's up?'

Oliver laughed wryly at being so well understood. 'I wasn't sure how I was going to tell you.'

'Just talk to me.'

The laugh again, a bit forced. 'You think it is that easy, huh?'

'Not easy. Spent decades trying to get your father to do it. But you've called me. So shoot.'

She waited, and heard him take a deep breath. 'Caitlin has left me. Broken up with me. Broken it off . . . the whole thing.' There was quiet surprise in his voice, but no break or wobble in its timbre.

'Darling!' Gigi was genuinely shocked in the first instance. Her own feelings about the development, surging in the back of her mind, were rightfully filed behind an immediate concern for her son. This was unexpected. Caitlin had a demeanour – that time at lunch, before that at Christmas – which suggested she'd made up her mind and was not for turning. What had changed?

'I'm okay. Surprisingly okay. Unsurprisingly surprisingly okay. One of those anyway.'

'Why?'

The deep breath was now a deep, slow exhalation . . .

'Big question for the phone, Mum.'

'Sorry . . . Where are you now?'

'I'm at work.'

'Shall I come?'

A brief pause. 'No need for that.'

The pause was her permission to push. 'I'm coming. Meet me for lunch.'

'For you or for me?'

'For me of course. I need to see you.'

She heard the smile in his voice. 'Then let me come to you. I've got the car; it'll be quicker.'

She knew her boy. She knew he wouldn't ask. But he wanted to see her, and she was glad to be that lucky.

She thought quickly. They both had a car. 'Meet me at Wisley?'

'It's not a nice day.'

'It'll be quiet, then . . . Bring a hat.'

They'd spent years walking the acreage of the RHS's gardens at Wisley together, Gigi and her brood. James had given them an annual family membership for Christmas every year since the boys were small, and, although they'd visited other gardens over the years, on holiday in Devon and Cornwall and the Lake District, it was Wisley, with its orchards and its rock garden, that they knew and loved the best. As boys, Christopher and Oliver had been fascinated by the tropical foliage and the unseasonal warmth in the enormous greenhouses, and Megan had learnt to run on its lawns one hoary, frosty autumn morning. As a six-year-old, Oliver had once been saved by a passing man who grabbed his ankle just as he almost tipped himself into the large lily pond one hot summer's day: his sun hat had floated into the middle, out of reach, all of them laughing, helpless with gratitude and relief. It was one of the golden memories they all shared. Not Richard – he'd been at work, of course. But her and the children. It was their space, and it had been their time. Its orchards and rose gardens were full of happy ordinary family memories.

Oliver had been right about the weather, and Gigi about the visitor numbers. It was cold in the dampest, greyest way it could be. Drizzle threatened. The gardens were almost deserted, save a few hardy types who strolled through the grounds determinedly. Gigi bought tickets – their membership having lapsed years back – and was waiting by the entrance with two hot cups of tea when Oliver arrived. She held the cups away from her body while he gave her a bear-hug, and then took one from her gratefully. The collar on his Crombie coat was turned up, and he hunched his shoulders inside it against the chill wind.

'No hat.'

'No hat. I'll see if there's one in the pond . . .' It was a family joke.

She linked her arm through his, and they started walking.

'When shall we discuss the sports kit?' She hadn't gone home to change, just pulled on her coat over the leggings and hoodie.

Still the old sparkle in his eyes.

She mock-punched his arm. 'How about never?'

'You look good, Mum. You look great.'

Now she rested her head against the same arm, for a brief moment, grateful for the compliment and the affirmation.

'So what happened?'

'She found me out.'

'Oliver. You didn't . . .' Now she was really shocked.

'No, no. Sorry. I didn't mean it like that. I'd never –'

'You haven't messed her around?'

'Not like that. Not with someone else . . . of course not. You know that.'

She had, deep down. 'Then?'

'But I have, haven't I? Messed her around.'

'You're talking in riddles, my boy.'

'I mustn't have been hiding it. Those doubts and stuff we were talking about. Not that I should have been hiding it. I should have been fucking honest about it.'

'And you weren't?'

'I think I was trying to find the way to say it . . . or being a massive coward. Bit of both.'

'You're being quite hard on yourself.'

'I'm being as hard as I should be. It wasn't fair, I knew all along. I'm not some naive kid. I know how it works. I said yes. I went along with all of it.'

'So if you didn't say anything, what happened?'

'She said it for me.'

'Said what?'

'She said . . . well, she said a lot of stuff.'

Gigi refrained from saying that she couldn't imagine Caitlin saying 'a lot of stuff' all at once, and patiently listened.

'She knew I wasn't all in. She said she'd known for a while, and thought she could change it. But she'd realized.'

'Not all in?'

'That it wasn't right. She said she knew I'd go through with it, because I was a good guy, and she knew a good guy when she saw one, because she'd met enough bad ones. And she said she was tempted to go along. She said she thought she could try enough for both of us.'

Gigi felt a wave of sympathy lapping at the edge of her feelings for Caitlin.

'But she'd woken up . . . that's what she called it – waking up – and she'd seen it wouldn't work. That she was setting me free to find a person I really loved. That she wanted to wait for someone who really loved her. That we both deserved better.'

Thank God. Gigi couldn't help thinking it, although she could and would stop herself from expressing it now. She sent a silent prayer of thanks for whatever gave Caitlin the revelation. Hadn't she loved Richard more than life itself when she married him? Hadn't he been her sun, moon and stars? And look – even that wasn't necessarily enough. Starting out in a marriage without that . . . it must mean you were doomed to broken lives and smashed hopes.

It was that, predominantly, that had made her so uneasy about the engagement. The other stuff – the jarring effect she feared Caitlin would have on their family – was secondary. And hadn't she jarred the hell out of it all on her own? It was the fear of the unhappiness Caitlin and Oliver would be storing up for themselves that had kept her awake.

'Do you know what happened? To make her change her mind?'

'No. She blamed herself. Not me. There was no ranting and raving. No big fight. No tears. I got home and she had packed what little gear she had at mine. She was sitting waiting for me on the sofa. I kissed her hello. Then it all came out. And she left.'

He pointed at a bench, and they sat down side by side. Gigi felt the cold wood through her Lycra and shivered. Oliver put an arm around her.

'So that's that?'

She felt him shrug. 'That's that, I think.'

'Poor girl.' Gigi didn't know what else to say.

'I know.'

They sat in silence for a while. She wanted to tell him it would all be okay, but it seemed better, for now, to stay quiet. For Caitlin, for him. There'd been times in her children's lives – all three of them – when she'd wanted a fast-forward button to press, to whizz them safely and quickly through something difficult, knowing with her mother's wisdom that it *would* be okay on the other side, knowing that they didn't necessarily believe her when she said it was true. Attacks of croup, exams, heartbreak, spots and braces . . . You couldn't. All you could do was be there.

He needed to let himself off the hook, was all. His heart had probably always been safe, in this relationship. It was his conscience that was the problem.

She stood up eventually and offered him her arm. He allowed her to pull him up, never actually letting her take his weight. 'So . . . I've started Pilates.'

'Okay . . .'

'First class this morning. Hence the attire.'

He smiled and nodded.

'Gotta be good for a slice of carrot cake in the café, I'd have thought?'

He kissed the top of her head. 'Definitely, you mad old bag . . . most definitely.'

Tess

April

It was a while until Tess saw Oliver again, and when she did it was at the train station, not Clearview. It was early one Wednesday morning. She was coming, he was going.

It was always bizarre, in somewhere like Waterloo Station, teeming with thousands of people, to bump into someone you knew. Stranger still to see someone in such an unfamiliar context. Sometimes you'd spot a face and spend a few moments processing whose it was, where you knew them from. Not now. Not with him.

Tess had just gone through the ticket barrier. Oliver was standing about twenty-five yards in front of her, arms folded, looking up at the information screen, wearing a deep-blue suit, a brown leather messenger bag across his body and holding a Pret à Manger coffee cup. Tall and good-looking.

Tess realized she'd stopped walking when she heard the tut of a commuter to her left. That was the trick, really, in the city, wasn't it? Keep moving at the same pace as everyone else. Don't get in anyone's way. But she had.

Hoping he'd notice her.

Sad.

And he did. His eyes left the board, scanned the surroundings and then alighted on her. His face was neutral at first – then showed recognition. His eyebrows went up and he smiled broadly.

And Tess felt warm.

She smiled back, and then took two, three steps towards him. He did the same. Then they were in front of each other.

'Tess. Hi.'

'Morning. Where are you off to?'

'Andover. Got a meeting. You?'

'Work. Holborn.'

He nodded.

It was the same sensation she'd had with him before. Hard to describe. She wanted to talk. Wanted to stay in his radius. Maybe that was what people meant when they talked about other people having magnetic personalities. She'd never really known. But maybe it was this. She was disproportionately pleased to have bumped into him. She hardly knew him at all. But she wanted to stay like this.

'What time's your train?' Why was she asking that? What was she going to suggest? Breakfast at the café on the concourse, for God's sake?

Oliver looked at his watch. 'About seven minutes.' She heard regret in his voice, and felt it. Not long enough for breakfast. Not even long enough for coffee.

Neither of them moved. They looked at each other. Dozens of people milled about them, but it felt to her like they were very still, in the eye of the storm.

'How's your granddad?'

'Good, I think. The same. Your grandmother? She's . . . better?'

Tess nodded. 'I think so.'

'Good.' It was the smallest of small talk, but it felt big. She wouldn't have been able to explain it. Even to Holly. Who'd probably make *Brief Encounter* references anyway.

He spoke first this time. 'I wish I had a bit more time. I'd love to grab a coffee . . .'

She looked pointedly at his cup, smiling.

'Another coffee.' He grinned. 'Maybe even a croissant.'

It was flirting. She remembered flirting, though it had certainly been a very long time since she'd done any herself. But maybe Oliver was one of those people who flirted with everybody.

'It's good to see you anyway, Tess.'

'You too.'

He looked up at the board. Bit his lip. 'Gotta go.'

Tess nodded. 'Have a good day. I hear Andover's lovely, at this time of year.' Was that flirting back? God, who'd know? She was more than rusty . . .

Oliver took a step back. Then a step forward. He put one arm very briefly, very lightly, around her shoulder and kissed her cheek. She smelt his aftershave and the faint tang of coffee, felt his cheek, slightly stubbly against hers.

And then he was gone, walking backwards for two or three steps, smiling at her, then turning, his arm raised in a wave.

But the sensation of him lingered.

Gigi

Gigi had lived at home with her parents, in the same house where she'd quite literally been born – a semi with swirling patterned carpets and prints of *The Hay Wain* and *Sunflowers* – until she'd left, at seventeen, to go to nursing school in London. The student accommodation the hospital provided – although initially wildly exciting for its proximity to everything the city had to offer – had been pretty grim then: narrow rooms in draughty Victorian buildings, cheaply partitioned, with vertiginous ceilings, their proportions all wrong and somehow claustrophobic, their bathroom facilities vaguely workhousey. The girls had all kept their doors propped open with textbooks and shouted to each other, so they'd felt less like they were in cells. She'd gone from that to the first home she and Richard had shared, after they married of course – starting in a rented flat and painstakingly climbing their way over the years up the property ladder and further away from the city, to the last, lovely home they'd shared. Graduating from hand-me-down mismatched furniture to wobbly flat-packed stuff and finally to new things, even the odd antique. From framed posters and blank walls to pictures people had actually painted, bought at the Affordable Art Fair, and, once or twice, after a bonus or a windfall, from a gallery.

But she'd never lived alone. Not in her entire life.

Gigi wanted to laugh. It seemed so absurd. And so strange,

to be standing here now, agent's details in her hand, staring up at this house, where she might come to live. Alone. The thought made her almost breathless with excitement and fear, and it was the first thing to come close to blotting out the guilt and the misery her departure had caused. Forward motion, Gigi, she told herself.

A five-bar gate that looked like it was never closed marked the start of a wide gravel drive, patchy and bald in places, which ran up to the front of the house. The flower-beds on either side were deep and wild-looking, with all sorts of fronds and suckers spilling on to the driveway. They would have Richard tutting and reaching for the secateurs, but Gigi rather liked the unkempt look of it. It was messy, but not unattractive. The house itself was higgledy-piggledy. That was the only word. It was Arts and Crafts, she thought, with black beams randomly dissecting a whitewashed render. The windows were all of different sizes. Richard always called them 'fenestrations' when they were house-hunting. It was a word he reserved only for conversations with estate agents – a response to their own 'mainly laid to lawn' and 'commanding position' way of speaking. Meant to make him sound knowledgeable and experienced. The sort of man you couldn't fool. It had always made him sound the exact opposite. He wouldn't like this fenestration much. It was neither symmetrical nor smart. It was all a touch neglected. Gigi wasn't going to hold that against the house. She was a bit neglected herself. She liked the big bay windows and the leaded panes. To her the house looked a bit smiley, like houses and cars could, and she smiled back in response.

Just then the agent, Sam, he of the slicked back hair and spivvy suits, drove a bit too fast into the driveway (she had parked respectfully on the street outside), scrunching the gravel and stopping abruptly beside her. Sam was about Olly's age, but not half so appealing, as far as Gigi was concerned, anyway. Richard would dislike him on the grounds that his hands were always in his pockets, and his shoes – the pointy-toed kind – were never apparently polished. He'd be 'fenestrating' all over the place. If he was here.

'Sorry, Mrs Gilbert. Running late.'

He was always at least five minutes late. She'd tried – the first couple of times they'd met – to persuade him to call her Gigi, but he didn't seem to want to, so she'd given up, and now she accepted both his apology and his smarmy formality with a nod and a smile. What she really wanted was to get inside and see this flat. She had a good feeling about this one.

Sam held up a key. 'Flat's empty. Owner's away. So we've got this one all to ourselves. The flat's got its own entrance – round the side – this way . . .'

He turned the key in the lock of an unprepossessing black door and stood aside to let her in. There was a small pile of post – flyers and pizza menus – on the floor. She stepped over them.

'Straight up, Mrs Gilbert. The office did say this one was a maisonette, right?' They hadn't. No one in there ever seemed to know what they were doing.

Sam went on, defining 'maisonette', in case Gigi didn't know what it meant. Even she was tempted to 'fenestrate' him, see if he knew what *that* meant.

'That means it's on two floors. In this case, this side of the house. Large reception room, kitchen and so forth on the first floor, and two beds and a shared bath above . . .'

'How many other flats in the house?'

'None. Just the owner's.' Sam spoke slowly, fact checking on the file he carried with him. 'The whole of the ground floor, the other half of the first floor and the top floor belong to the owner. Nice chap.'

The stairway was woodchip and whitewashed, with wooden treads. There was another door at the top of the flight. Gigi turned the handle and went in.

On this level, there was clearly just one room – a room in which to cook, eat, live. Resolute open-plan living. But what a room. Gigi felt a broad smile break across her face. The bay window she'd seen from the front was just one of them. Opposite it was a huge, square window, right to the ceiling, with a deep window seat in front, and a view across the back garden to the hills beyond. The light flooding in through it showed all the dust motes in the air, the odd spider web and the wear on the original herringbone wood floor. The kitchen part was new, and plain enough, but small. There wouldn't be room in the oven for much of a Christmas turkey. But it was glorious.

Sam, in a rare moment of good sense, wasn't waffling now. He must have seen the grin, watched the room sell itself to Gigi, of whom he was, frankly, a little wary. But when she went to the only other door in the room, he spoke up again.

'That leads to the staircase, which goes up to . . .'

Gigi was already there.

A big master bedroom, with windows on two sides and a small cast-iron fireplace; and one more, with a smaller sash window and a sloping ceiling. Both were magnolia, with horrible office-style venetian blinds and a regulation oatmeal carpet, but they were clean enough. The bathroom between the two had a shower over the tub, which had claw feet, and one of those faux-Victorian loos with the really high cistern. She liked the black-and-white-tiled floor. Here too was evidence that someone had cleaned recently.

Gigi wandered between the three rooms, trying to think practically about wardrobe space and where Ava's cot might go if Chris and Em visited, but the truth was she felt almost breathlessly excited about the possibility of this place being her home. It had beautiful bones, and it was a blank canvas. She could see herself here.

Back downstairs, Sam stood expectantly.

'When can I move in?'

He almost spluttered. He hadn't expected this client to be that easy. He'd had several more lined up to view. He hadn't even mentioned rent.

Gigi waved the unspoken subject away airily. 'I know how much it is. The office told me. That's fine. When is it available?'

Gigi wasn't sure whether she was acting this way because she'd fallen for the flat, or because she and Richard had never house-hunted this way, not even in the early days when everything had been new and exciting. He'd have looked at everything Sam had to show him. Considered, pondered. Worked out the cost per square foot and measured to see if the bed fitted. Certainly slept on it before making a decision, even if he risked losing it. But this was only a rental. She wanted to commit with less consideration than she might give to a new pair of shoes, or to ordering from a restaurant menu. She wanted to be impulsive.

And this wasn't his decision. She didn't want to do that. She wanted to live here, by herself. And she wanted to say so now. Right now.

She and Sam parted in the driveway, with his promise to confirm later in the day when he'd had a chance to speak to the owner. Gigi lingered just a while after he'd backed out and sped off, knowing she was alone: she stared at the house, taking in all the details, imagining herself there. Then she turned and walked back to her car, out on the street.

An estate car had just pulled into the driveway of the house opposite. A young mother had released two small children on the gravel, and was currently leant over, evidently releasing the seatbelt on a car seat. The two children waited impatiently, one plucking at her mother's raincoat, the other kicking gravel with his wellington-booted feet. Both were chattering incessantly in their high-pitched little voices. The mother was answering patiently when she found a gap in their questioning. She turned towards Gigi as she pulled the car seat, a fairly new baby nestled within, through the car door. Their eyes met for a moment, and the woman smiled broadly at Gigi, rolled her eyes in a very familiar, happy, exhausted gesture, before she gathered her brood and headed for the front door, chatting all the while. Gigi slid into her own driving seat, but she couldn't help watching the mother usher the children inside, her free hand stroking each of their heads as they passed her. It made her tearful, watching them. She'd been her, once upon a time. She'd had that.

'What's all this?' Kate looked tired. Gigi passed her a glass of wine as she slumped in a kitchen chair and kicked off her shoes.

'I'm cooking you dinner. Tagliatelle with sausage, rosemary and porcini mushrooms.'

'Delish. You're a doll.'

'Least I can do, in lieu of the rent you refuse to accept. And, besides, we're celebrating.'

'You've found somewhere already?' Kate looked momentarily crestfallen. Gigi nodded.

'You didn't have to move so quickly, G. You know you can stay here as long as you like.'

'I know, and I love you for that. And for having me these last couple of weeks. I honestly don't know what I'd have done without you . . .'

'Premier Inn and takeout food?'

'Exactly. But I do. I need to.'

Gigi was draining a large pan of pasta into a colander in Kate's sink. 'I need to get on with this fresh start.' Before I lose my nerve, she added, silently, to herself.

Kate took a deep drink from her wine glass and refilled it, emptying the bottle.

'Bugger. I'll have to go back to the wine boxes, once you've gone. It's been so much more civilized having you here.'

Gigi clinked her own glass against Kate's. 'I'm not off quite yet, if that's okay. I get the keys tomorrow. But the landlord is apparently quite happy for me to paint, tart it up a bit, before I move in, as long as I don't go mad. Just another week or ten days – I've taken the time off.'

'Of course. I can help, if you like.'

'You're on. I've got a paint chart that I grabbed on my way home in my bag. We can have a look after dinner.'

'What's the vision?'

'The lady in the shop says grey is the new cream. Not crazy about grey. Something different for the bedroom. I've always wanted a really girly bedroom. Boudoir. You know . . .'

'Not Richard's thing.'

'Exactly.' Gigi smiled. She'd have to tell him. And the kids.

'I can really see the point of doing it your own way, you know.'

'What do you mean?'

'Well, just look around you. This was our house. Mine and Owen's. Just like it was when he was here. He got the fresh start, when we broke up. I got all the old crap. And all the old memories.'

'I see no crap.' Gigi gestured around. 'This is lovely. And memories go with you.'

'That's true to a point, G. Places hold memories. They don't let you forget them. You know that. We sat here when . . . we painted this . . . we fought over this wallpaper . . . all that stuff.'

Was that what Richard thought, wandering around their home? The now familiar little bubble of sadness rose in her throat, and she stared intently at the paring knife on the chopping board until it passed. Kate didn't see the moment, and Gigi didn't want her to.

'I'm going to miss you, G.' Kate's voice almost broke. 'I hope you're doing the right thing. I hope you're sure. I hope you're ready to be lonely.'

Gigi came to the table with the two plates of pasta. 'But I *was* lonely, Kate. I've *been* lonely. For a long time.'

Kate put her hand across Gigi's. 'I know.'

'And you don't think there's a chance you can actually be *more* lonely with someone than when you're actually physically alone? I might be by myself, but I won't be being ignored. I'll stop being part of the fixtures and fittings.'

'He won't be ignoring you. But maybe everyone else

will, once that front door is closed behind you.' Kate grimaced at her own harshness. Made her voice softer. 'At least, sometimes it can feel that way. Like life is happening everywhere else.'

'Oh, bollocks. It's a side door anyway. And that's pity and Pinot talking, Kate.'

'Ah, my constant companions. Pity and Pinot. Boxed.' Kate took a big swig from her glass, but she was smiling now. 'Okay, then, my brave-new-world friend. The Norma Rae of middle-age marriage. I'm not going to press the point that I'm about ten years further into this game than you are. I'm not going to be the one to crush all this enthusiasm for the future.'

'Good. Admit you're still alone because you want to be.'

Kate harrumphed. 'Like I'm batting them away with a stick? Who can be bothered with all that? And have you any idea who is out there? Seriously. I'll check in with you after a few internet dates and singles nights.'

Gigi laughed. 'That is *so far* from what I'm thinking about now.'

'Planning on being single for the rest of your life?'

'I wouldn't call it planning. There's no plan. I'm winging it. Just bloody determined to be happy for the rest of my life. That's as far as I've got.'

'Okay, Pollyanna. If you say so.'

'Can we eat now, please?' Gigi twirled a strand of tagliatelle around her fork and winked at her friend. 'All this cynicism and bitterness is making me hungry.'

Tess

Tess had ignored the advice on the leaflet. 'Ultrasound scans can sometimes find problems with the baby. You may like someone to come with you to the scan appointment.' Well, tough. She hadn't bloody well brought someone. Alone at twenty-four weeks. Alone for the next eighteen years. Might as well get used to it. Holly would be furious if she knew she was here alone. She'd call her a martyr, an idiot. Thinking of Holly threatened a wobble. Holly would chat and jolly her along and whisper pithy observations about the other people in the waiting room, and then, once they were in the screening unit, she'd hold her hand, like she had the last time, for the first scan. Which she hadn't realized until now was just what she'd wanted. Donna might wonder too why she hadn't asked her. Might be hurt, even, to be excluded. It was just how she felt right now. It might be wallowing, just a bit, disguised as independence. Now that she was sitting here, it didn't seem like a brilliant idea. Too late now. Holly was in the classroom, reading Emily Dickinson to teenagers. Donna was in West Sussex, taking engagement photographs at a minor stately home. She was here. Alone.

She hated hospitals. This one was nicer than some she'd been to – it looked clean and it felt more modern – there was a Costa coffee shop in reception, and a Marks & Spencer food store – but still, hospitals were hospitals, however nice the snacks available. She could practically feel her blood pressure rising walking through the doors – chronic white-coat syndrome. She'd broken her collarbone falling in the playground when she was ten, and had a horrible chest infection as a teenager. That was it. Once to the casualty department, and a few out-patient appointments. Before Iris had started to get ill. Far too many times since. But she'd hated the idea of them before that. Behind every curtain and closed door lurked terrors.

This was supposed to be a happy place, this particular bit of the hospital. Obstetrics. Not like geriatrics. Mostly good stuff happened here. But it was still all . . . medical. Holly would have been right to say it – she *was* an idiot. Almost anyone would be a better distraction than herself and a stack of out-of-date parenting magazines.

And it *was* worse than sitting alone in a restaurant on Valentine's Day, with a higher loving-couple ratio. Even the girl with the bump who didn't look old enough had her mum with her.

And, although she was technically very late for the scan, which really ought to have happened two or three weeks sooner, she was congenitally early on the day, even though she'd been called in slightly-to-incredibly late to every doctor's appointment she could ever remember having, so she'd been sitting here contemplating her aloneness for what felt like forever. Couples had actually arrived after her, been called in and left again, with their fuzzy black-and-white photographs. And still she sat here, pretending to be calm.

This was called the anomaly scan, the books said. If ever a scan had had bad PR, this was it. It had been twelve weeks since the last one. The books told you a vast array of things had been happening. You couldn't know they were happening as they were supposed to. Now she was going to find out, and she felt gripped by a fear and sense of foreboding she imagined was within normal limits for this sort of occasion, but which felt overwhelming.

Then, across the waiting room, she saw Gigi, not recognizing her at first because of the uniform. It took her a second to register who it was. Gigi always looked good, when she saw her at Clearview. She was a stylish woman. With big wavy hair. The navy tabard with white piping and straight navy trousers seemed alien on her – definitely not her best look, and the generous curls were tucked into a well-controlled bun at the nape of her neck. She was handing a manila folder to the receptionist, exchanging a few words. Gigi laughed her throaty laugh at something the receptionist said. The sight of her inexplicably made Tess want to cry, and she bit on her lower lip to control the urge. She picked up an ancient dog-eared copy of *Parenting* magazine and stared at an article on cots, but sudden tears made the words and pictures swim. She wiped her eyes and sniffed, hoping Gigi wouldn't see her like this.

'Hello, love.'

Gigi's voice was tentative and gentle, her smile as warm as usual.

Tess smiled and hoped her voice wouldn't give her away. 'Gigi! Of course! This is your hospital.'

'You've switched your care to here?'

Tess nodded. 'While I'm staying with my mother, this is the place.'

Gigi didn't let the moment be awkward and Tess was grateful to her. Gigi must think she was such a flake, but she didn't let it show. 'Of course. Do you think you'll deliver here?'

'I hadn't really thought that far ahead. Maybe . . .'

'Well, you'll be in good hands if you do. This is a great team.'

'That's good to know.'

'You can take a tour, check it all out . . .'

Tess nodded. She didn't know what to say.

'Are you on your own, Tess?'

Tess had to look at her to give a quick nod in answer. A single tear betrayed her, spilling down her cheek. Gigi's eyes filled with concern. She slid into the seat next to Tess.

'Are you okay, sweetheart? Is everything all right?'

She nodded again, taking a moment to trust her voice.

'It's my second scan. I'm fine. It's just a routine appointment.'

She wondered whether she needed to explain the tears. Gigi put her hand – cool and dry – across her own for the briefest moment.

'I get it. Even the routine stuff can feel a bit overwhelming. All gets a bit much, doesn't it?'

Tess smiled, grateful for the understanding.

'What time is your appointment?' Gigi wore one of those upside-down watches, old school, pinned to her tabard. She tipped it up expertly.

Tess looked up at the clock. 'Ten minutes ago.'

Gigi rolled her eyes. 'I said they were great. I didn't say they were always punctual! Want me to go and see what's happening?'

She shook her head quickly. 'No, no. No need. I don't want to be difficult.'

Gigi smiled kindly. 'Okay. I'm sure they'll call you in a minute or two.'

They looked at each other for a long moment.

Ask me, Tess was thinking. *I don't want to do this by myself. Ask me.* She half wondered if Gigi was willing her to say those words out loud.

But the moment passed before she was brave enough, and as it did a sonographer stepped out of a door and called her name. She stood up, raising her hand in acknowledgement.

'That's me. You summoned her up!'

Gigi gave her a quick hug. 'Good luck, darling.'

'Thanks, Gigi.'

'See you at the weekend, maybe?'

'I expect so.'

And Gigi was gone.

The room was dimly lit, and the sonographer briskly efficient.

'If you'd pull your skirt down to low hip, and your top up to under your bra for me, please. You know the drill. Just like the first scan.'

She pulled three or four sheets of blue paper from a dispenser and tucked them into Tess's skirt without speaking any more.

Lying back, Tess's belly rose like the small Teletubbies hill, moon-white in the light from the monitor. How was it possible that some women didn't even show at this point, or for another six weeks or so either? She stroked her tummy gently. She was so definitely, absolutely pregnant.

The jelly was cold – it made you breathe in, and Tess knew she was holding that breath, waiting for the rushing whoosh of the heartbeat. The probe rolled backwards, forwards. The sonographer dug it in so that it was almost uncomfortable, and rocked it. *I wonder if you can feel it, baby?*

It felt like ages.

'There we go. Good, strong heartbeat.' And Tess exhaled.

More probing. Measurements and checklists. It was unnaturally quiet in the room, but Tess couldn't think of anything to say.

'All looking good for dates. Right on track size-wise. Good. Good.'

Well done, baby.

Without looking up, the sonographer asked, 'And are you wanting to know the sex today?'

'I wasn't sure you were allowed to tell me.'

The sonographer smiled. 'We never guarantee it. It's not one hundred per cent. But yes, I can tell.'

She hadn't been sure she wanted to know, but now it was unbearable that this person might know and Tess not. 'Yes, please. I'd like to know.'

'It's a girl.'

'Oh. Oh my God. A girl.' This time Tess didn't even attempt to check her tears. They welled out of her eyes and ran down into her hair. She hadn't known until that exact moment that's what she'd wanted. 'I'm having a little girl.'

And then there were a few moments of silence, more probing, and the sonographer pushed her stool back and stowed her wand in its holster.

'I've seen something I'd like to show a doctor.' She put a hand up. 'The baby is absolutely fine, Tess, so try not to worry, okay. I will be back as quickly as I can.'

It was the first time she'd used her name.

Alone in the room, she felt an absurd urge to run away. They couldn't tell her anything bad if she wasn't there, could they? 'You are absolutely fine, baby. That's what she said. Absolutely fine.'

She spread both palms across her stomach and concentrated on breathing in and out.

The door opened, letting bright light from the corridor in, and the sonographer was back, with another woman in blue scrubs and Adidas trainers. She looked too young to know anything much.

'I'm Dr McCullough, the obstetric consultant. I'd like to have a look at you, if that's all right.'

'What's wrong?'

The doctor smiled kindly. 'Give me just a moment.'

Tess forced herself to stay quiet while she was examined again, for long minutes. She dug the nail of her forefinger into the soft pad of flesh on her thumb to stop from crying, and longed for Holly, who didn't know she was here, or Iris, who might not know who she was, or even Gigi, who'd been a stranger to her just a few months ago. She did not feel brave. She felt terror. She tried to think of all the clichéd things – the palm trees on the beach, the breathing in and out – but her mind played the early weeks of the pregnancy back at her on a high-speed loop. The days when she didn't know she wanted to keep the baby. When she'd contemplated not keeping it. Keeping her.

Eventually Dr McCullough nodded decisively at the sonographer, handed Tess some more paper towels and sat on the sonographer's stool as she stood behind.

'Okay. You can clean yourself up, Tess. The first thing to say is that everything is perfectly normal with the development and health of your baby. She is right where we want her to be at this point, all right?' Tess nodded.

'What is causing us concern is you – your cervix, to be specific. What's happening is what we call funnelling. If you imagine your cervix, what we want it to do, once you are full term, is to open from the bottom up.' She made a shape with her hands. Tess forced herself to concentrate on the words, supressing the panic. 'Yours is opening already, and it's opening from the top down.'

'What does that mean?'

'It carries a risk for your baby. You're only' – she looked back at the screen – 'twenty-four weeks or so.'

'That's far too early. Am I in labour, then? I haven't had any pain, or any show or anything . . .' Tess felt self-conscious using the language of the books and the websites – her new lexicon. Holly had laughed at her, and said she was probably a qualified midwife by now, but the laughter had been fond and understanding.

Dr McCullough shook her head. 'No, no. You're not. But your cervix is what we call – rather unkindly, I always think – incompetent. Left alone, it will shorten and open with the increased size and weight of your baby, and that's not safe for baby.'

'So I'll go into labour early?'

'Not if we have anything to do with it. But, yes, left alone, that is the risk. Tess – this is not an uncommon problem. And we've no reason at this point to be unduly worried. It's one of the things we look for in this anomaly scan and that's because we stand a very good chance of fixing it. What we need to do is a simple procedure – it's called a cerclage. We pop a small stitch in your cervix and that stays in place for the rest of the pregnancy. Keeps everything tight and closed. You'll stay here one night. We can chat about anaesthetic – whether we use a spinal or a general. Rest at home for a week or so. Take it relatively easy for the rest of the pregnancy. But basically, Plan A is that you'll be able to live your normal life. No vigorous exercise. At thirty-six or thirty-seven weeks, when medically we consider you to be near enough to full term, we take it out again, so your body can do its thing and it won't matter. This is your first pregnancy, am I correct?' She looked at her notes. Tess knew she was reading 'elderly primigravida'.

Tess nodded.

'Any questions?'

'Would I need it again . . . with another baby?' She had no idea of why she was asking that.

'Most likely. Incompetent cervixes don't usually correct themselves, I'm afraid. Any history of miscarriage in your family?'

'I don't think so. Is there a risk of that?'

The doctor smiled gently. 'There's no such thing as a risk-free pregnancy, Tess. But this is a safe, common procedure, with an eighty to ninety per cent success rate if it's elective, which this will be. We have every reason to believe that, once the cerclage is in place, you'll go on to have a completely normal pregnancy, a safe delivery and a healthy baby.'

Tess clung to those three things, trying to make them promises.

'I know it sounds ridiculous, but do try not to worry. Book yourself in at the desk. Any pain or bleeding, any at all, before the appointment, you come back stat. Right?' She'd told her not to worry and then she said things like that. The doctor was looking at her file now. 'Did you come alone today?'

'I did.'

She frowned for the first time. 'Bring someone with you, won't you, when you come in? It's not a big deal, it only takes about ten minutes, but anaesthesia can make you feel a bit shaky, and we do understand it's worrying for you.' Her face softened. 'You'll need someone to take you home. They may as well stay and keep you company, okay?'

'I will.'

'And have a cup of tea today, before you go. Take a moment. Don't get straight into your car, or go straight back to work. It's a shock.' She squeezed Tess's arm reassuringly.

She was as kind as she needed to be. Tess was grateful she wasn't kinder. It helped her to keep herself together.

The doctor left, and the sonographer busied herself replacing the giant paper roll on the bed while Tess finished tidying herself up. 'Weren't you talking to a midwife when I called you in?'

'Gigi.' Tess nodded, realizing she didn't know her last name.

'Gigi Gilbert. She's fab. Friend of yours?'

Tess smiled. She hoped so.

'Do you want me to see if I can find her?'

'No, no. I don't want to be a bother . . . she's working.'

'I'm sure she'd love to come and see you, if she's free.'

'Really . . . I'm fine. Thank you.'

But somehow she was there anyway. Tess wondered whether she'd hovered on purpose, but she didn't care. She was beyond glad to see her. As Gigi walked towards her, her open, smiling face asking for affirmation, Tess felt her shoulders drop, and her face crumple, close to dissolving. Without a word, Gigi folded her into a warm, maternal embrace.

She held her for ages. Then, as Tess pulled away, recovered enough to become self-conscious, Gigi pulled a packet of tissues from her trouser pocket and gave one to Tess.

'Come and sit here a minute, and tell me what happened, if you like?'

She nodded understanding while Tess explained what she could from her conversation with the obstetrician.

Gigi squeezed her hand.

'Well, then, you're going to be fine. This is not uncommon, Tess.'

'That's what she said.'

'Because it's true. They don't lie here, not even a bit. They can't. They give it to you straight, and that's what she's done, and you're not to worry. I've delivered so many healthy babies whose mums had this done earlier in the pregnancy.'

'You have?'

'Dozens.' She smiled reassuringly, and then dried a tear on Tess's face with her thumb. The gesture was intimate and tender, and it made Tess want to cry again.

'Why on earth didn't you bring someone with you?'

Tess shrugged. 'I'm an idiot?'

'I know things aren't . . . things are up in the air with the father, but what about your mum?'

'I don't know.'

'I'm not in the business of giving unsolicited advice . . .' Gigi paused, then laughed. 'Actually, if any of my kids were here, they'd be hysterical if they heard me saying that. I probably am. I definitely am.' Tess giggled. 'So forgive the overstep, but . . . love, I'm a mum. She'd have wanted to come with you. I bet she would . . .'

'You're right. I'm being stubborn.'

'You're trying to be independent. Nothing wrong with that, nothing at all. But you might be trying a bit too hard. No one can do it all on their own. No one should have to.

You're going to need support. And there is nothing wrong with that.'

'You're so kind.'

'And I'm right too. Believe me.' She winked at her. 'I'm going to get you a cup of tea from Costa. What comes out of that machine doesn't really count as tea. I'll be a minute . . . You stay here. Call your mum while I'm gone. You have your phone with you?'

Tess nodded.

'So use it. Midwife's orders.'

Donna made her wish she'd taken her with her. She'd got her act together for the journey home – Gigi had sat with her and made lovely small talk while she drank her tea – and she'd made it back through the traffic dry-eyed and calm, Radio 4 distracting her. She'd cried again the minute she'd seen her mum, though, and let herself be held again. Donna asked gentle, careful questions, and Tess relayed as much of what the obstetrician had told her as she could remember.

'So it sounds like this is going to be fine, love. Fine. She told you – it's not uncommon.'

'I know . . . it's just that . . . I'm just a bit shocked.'

'You're bound to be. It's difficult enough, without complications.'

'That's it . . .' Tess was grateful that Donna understood. 'I had spotting, with you.'

'You did?'

'Well – they called it spotting. It was more than that . . . it was bleeding, and I was terrified even to move. I was afraid that if I did, it would get worse . . . that I'd lose you.'

'I didn't know that.'

Donna smiled. 'Because I didn't. You were tougher than that. And so is this one.'

319

'Did you ever find out why?'

'There's no why, Tess . . . I mean, there are medical reasons, and I'm sure, at the time, I looked them up or the doctor told me . . . but it just was. That's how my body did it. This is how yours does it.'

'Incompetently.'

'Well . . . what can you expect from an elderly primigravida?'

'Shut up.'

But now they were laughing, the kind of laughing that is very close to crying, and that happens when all your emotions are right at the surface, and the fear is slowly but surely subsiding. Donna pulled her back into an embrace, stroking her back and starting to talk about what she was going to cook for supper, and what they might watch on the television later, and Tess had the strange thought that what Donna had said was pretty much what she might have expected Iris to say, and the thought was incredibly comforting.

She called Holly too, later, while Donna cooked. It took a village, right? She rang on the pretext of asking about Dulcie, still a bit uncomfortable at the idea of putting herself front and centre, but Holly, of course, asked, as she had known she would.

'Don't you dare even think about going to that appointment on your own, you daft mare.'

'I won't.'

'Doesn't have to be me, although I think it should be.'

'You do?'

'Absolutely. I am great in hospitals.' Tess loved her boastfulness. 'You have people, you know. Don't be stubborn. Take someone. Any-bloody-one. Except Sean. Not Sean.

Did not mean Sean. Me or Donna . . .' She drew out the syllables of Donna's name slowly, still just a tiny bit incredulous about her mate's mother's renaissance.

'Promise.'

'I promise.'

'I'd bring snacks.'

'Snacks are good.'

'Just saying. I'm excellent in hospitals.'

Week 25. Very nearly Week 26, even. I'm sorry, baby mine. I've let you down. It was bad enough that I saddled you with an elderly primigravida for a mother. Got you a bum of a father. Okay – he's not a bum. But he's not what you deserved. Nowhere near. I haven't got us a place to live. Now I've got a crappy womb. Cervix. Whatever. I'm buggering everything up. Nothing is like I would have wanted it to be. God knows I've judged people like me . . . I'm so scared. You have to be all right. You just have to. I realize there's nothing more important, nothing I wouldn't do, to get you here, with me, safely. But you've got to bear with me, little one. I'm going to be better, I promise. I'm going to get it right, from now on.

Gigi

Oliver was right about Megan, in the end. With gargantuan effort, Gigi gave her the weeks of space that Olly thought she needed, preoccupying herself with work and settling into the flat and trying not to torture herself with all the insignificant and enormous episodes of Meg's life she was missing. She wished it was Megan every single time her phone rang – grabbing her mobile and pulling her glasses off her head on to her nose to read the caller ID frantically – but Megan didn't call.

So she took the train one Wednesday when she wasn't working, not wanting to drive home wobbly and tearful, if things didn't go well. She resisted the urge to collect up treats – Megan's favourite biscuits, posh shower gel – stuff she would normally have done before a visit. She wasn't trying to buy back Megan's goodwill. And she didn't want to reward her unkindness. She wanted to fix things between them, but she badly didn't want to be pathetic either. She gazed out of the window and wondered what she would say, face to face, as the train sped through the countryside.

Gigi had arrived before she realized she didn't have a concrete plan. Of course she knew where Megan's house was, but it seemed invasive to just knock on the door. She and Richard had once dropped in unexpectedly on Oliver, years ago, and found him hungover and sound asleep, in a room that looked like it had been ransacked, at three in the

afternoon. She almost smiled at the memory of he
crazy-haired and pale-green, answering the door wrap
in a grubby duvet. God knows what Megan might
doing. She had no idea of her schedule. The idea of comin
here unannounced and uninvited, let alone unwelcome
suddenly seemed stupid and desperate to her. Kids milled
around, a hoodie army, but she didn't recognize anyone,
and they all ignored her. She bought a coffee in a polystyr-
ene cup from the café in the middle of the large atrium
space that seemed to be at the centre of everything, and sat
down on one of the uncomfortable, trendy sofas to ponder
her next move, which might very well be to go straight
home.

She'd finished the coffee, and was watching a young
couple smooch over a laptop, oblivious to everything but
each other, when she heard Megan's voice, laughing and
chattering. A quick flood of relief – both that she'd found
her and that she sounded so . . . so normal – was almost
instantaneously replaced by a rush of adrenalin, and her
heart raced. When she turned away from the young lovers,
Megan had already seen her. She'd peeled away from a
small group of boys and girls she'd been walking with, and
was coming towards her, files clutched against her chest,
omnipresent headphones around her neck, wide-eyed with
panic.

'Mum?'

Gigi stood up. 'I had to come . . .'

'What's wrong? Is Dad all right? Is everything okay?'
She should have realized her appearance might frighten
Meg. Gigi put up both hands, as if they could stop the
anxiety.

'Everyone is fine.'

gan visibly exhaled. And Gigi inhaled deeply. 'But not okay, Meg.'

They stood about three feet apart, staring each other wn. Gigi knew Megan so well that she could almost ear the debate going on in her lovely daughter's head – stubborn, posturing, angry adult versus girl, a girl probably very much in need of a cuddle, and a truce.

She watched the girl win. Megan's eyes filled with tears, and she just stepped forward into Gigi's arms, not caring who was watching.

They went to a pub and sat outside. It wasn't quite warm enough, but it was quiet. Megan pulled her sleeves down over her hands, and Gigi didn't tell her not to, like she normally would have done.

'I'm sorry you've been so upset, my darling.'

'What about Dad?' She was persisting with the anger, though it was hardly convincing either of them now.

'Of course I'm sorry he's upset too. I don't expect you to understand, Meg.'

'Well, I don't –'

'But I did expect, I think, that you'd at least try.'

Megan looked shocked. Even Gigi hadn't known this was the tack she would take.

'We've babied you all your life, Meg. Not your fault. Ours, I know. But you are not a child.'

'I know that.' Gigi wished the tone wasn't so petulant.

'You are old enough to understand that your dad and I are just people. I am just a person.'

'That's what Oliver says.'

'He's right.'

Megan's lip trembled. 'I know he is. I just . . . I hate this. I hate Dad being so unhappy. I hate not knowing you're both at home. I know it's selfish. But I can't help it. It's not how it's supposed to be.' Gigi's heart twisted. 'I know so many people, from school, here . . . so many people who have divorced or separated parents. I just never thought it would happen to me, you know? I mean, I know it's happened to you too, but you sort of made it happen. It's so . . . weird . . . you not being together. It's weird and I hate it.'

Gigi latched on to something she'd said. 'Those people you know . . . do they have relationships with both parents?'

Megan shrugged. 'I suppose. Mostly.'

'Do they still go home at the end of term? Still go on holiday?'

She shrugged again.

Gigi put her hand on Megan's, gripped it tightly through the material of her sweatshirt. 'It's like I said, love: we're your mum and dad. We love you to bits. We'll both be here, while we've breath in our bodies.'

'Fighting . . . being miserable . . .'

'Fighting – no – not when it comes to our kids. Never. Being miserable . . . That's an entirely more complicated question. But I hope not. Together or apart . . . I wouldn't be doing any of this – I wouldn't have dreamt of making any of this mess, Meg, if I wasn't trying to make things . . . better.'

'But you mean for you, Mum, not Dad.'

'I mean for both of us.'

'That's not true. That's not what Dad wanted.'

'I'm not sure your dad has been any happier than me, Megan. Honestly I'm not.'

'Are you sure you aren't just telling yourself that?'

Gigi couldn't answer that.

'Are you sure this is permanent?'

'I'm not sure of anything, except that something needed to change.'

'So you might get back together?'

'I don't want you to fixate on that.'

'But you might –'

'Megan . . . listen to me. This is what is important right now. I want you to stop being in a sulk with me. I want you to let me back into your life. You need me. I need you. We both know it. So you need to stop shutting me out. See me, speak to me. See your dad, speak to your dad. Let us both do what we've always done. Get on with your life, secure in the knowledge that your family is still your family, even if it's been shaken up. Even if your dad and I are not together. Grow up a bit, lovely girl. Forgive me.'

'Okay. Okay. You've made your point.'

But there was a small sob in Megan's voice, and her face was softer now – her angry jaw unclenched.

Gigi held her awkwardly across the table, her head on her shoulder. Megan was nestled in, so her voice was muffled when she said, 'But you might get back together again . . .'

When they pulled apart, they laughed for the first time, and for the first time since the night she'd lined them up on the sofa and shattered at least Megan, Gigi felt okay about her daughter, and the relief was extraordinary.

'So . . . are we going shopping or what?'

Tess

Gigi had told her, a week or so ago, that Oliver had split up with his girlfriend. No real details, just the facts. Tess had expressed what she hoped was an appropriate concern that he was okay, wondering why her heart had leapt in a distinctly teen-magazine sort of leap, and blaming hormones. She told herself it was beyond pathetic to develop a crush on a man simply on the grounds of his being kind, and reminding herself harshly that she was hardly the sort of prospect that would excite attention from most men, let alone one so appealing as Gigi's son. She slapped herself down for wondering why Gigi was so keen to tell her, and why she'd looked at her the way she had when she'd said the words, her eyes narrowed and appraising.

Still, when she'd bumped into him a few days later, all the stern talking to in the world didn't stop the Sixth-Form feelings.

He was so bloody easy to talk to. Not small-talk talk. Not conversational elevator music. You sort of got down to it right away with him – said proper, real things. It was incredibly refreshing. If it was his schtick, he was very, very good at it. But she didn't believe that. You could just tell he was interested in things.

So she told him things, despite herself. She told him about Sean. She told him about Donna. And she told him about Iris's letters. Just like that. Confessions about the relationships dearest, and most confusing, to her, secrets her grandmother had kept for decades disseminated like blowing seeds off a dandelion. She'd let him read them too, when he'd expressed an interest. Maybe she'd done that so she could watch his face while he read. He never spoke about the girlfriend, but he told her things too. About Gigi and Richard, about his brother and sister, about what he hoped might happen at work. Small bright building blocks of something. Colouring in each other's outlines. Inching in from the edge of each other's lives, slowly and surely . . . whatever they might say to themselves, and never to each other, about why it was impossible . . .

Gigi

It was one of those spring days that awakens both the memory and the possibility of summer. The chill had gone off the breeze, the sun had enough strength, at last, to warm your skin where it hit it and the winter only lingered in the shadows.

Gigi had the whole day off. She could do whatever she wanted. The freedom was intoxicating. There was no laundry to do because, for the first time in forever, she washed only for her, and the bin filled up much more slowly. There was no food either, but the only person she needed to feed was her and she didn't care. The almost empty fridge rather delighted her after years of catering for a family, and, latterly, the memory of a family – a compulsion to have supplies to feed a small rugby team at a moment's notice, when there were only two of them. She was free to lie in bed until noon, flicking through the interiors magazines for which she had developed a new fondness, or watching rubbish on the television. To bathe and dress at her leisure, or to stay dirty if she preferred. But none of that was what she had in mind.

What Gigi had in mind was nesting. This empty nest didn't hold the same sadness as the one she had left behind. The kids had never been here – their laughter and their shouting didn't lurk in the corners. This nest was being feathered just for her, and for now that was enough.

She'd taken down the ugly venetian blinds in the two bedrooms and hidden them away in the back of the wardrobe. She'd ordered ready-made curtains – diaphanous white things, too long, so they pooled on the floor in a nice, trendy way that would have driven Richard mad, all flowy and girly – and Olly had helped her hang curtain poles. He'd been her first visitor bar Kate, who'd helped her move in. He'd driven down, taken her out for brunch and then spent a few hours doing DIY for her, the pair of them listening to the radio and not talking too much about what was happening in either of their lives, which evidently suited them both just now. She loved him for not making her talk about Richard, and repaid the kindness by staying off the subject of Caitlin. He'd made it seem perfectly normal, this setting up his parent in a flat, and she was grateful for it.

Megan was no longer ignoring her, and she felt like things were almost, if not quite, back to normal between them. In the early days, Gigi sent her a WhatsApp most days, keeping her tone light and breezy, using more emoticons than was judicious for a woman of her age. Most went unanswered; some received cursory replies. Megan wouldn't be drawn. When she'd sent something longer and more emotional, her daughter had snapped back that she needed time, and wanted Gigi to leave her alone while she concentrated on her exams. After that, Gigi forced herself to send a message only every few days, always telling her she loved her. She knew Emily was checking in with her, knew Oliver messaged her too. She knew she was safe and well – at least as much as you ever knew your child was when they weren't with you – but that was all she knew. It hurt, and it still felt odd, those negative emotions sitting uncomfortably with her contentment at being here. Distracting her from the self-belief that had made this happen. But she knew she had to give her time. Accepted that things might never be exactly the same between them. She knew she'd pulled a rug out from under her daughter. She might understand it one day, better than she did now. But she would still always have done it to her, and she had no choice but to own that.

So not talking about any of it was best just now. And not thinking about it too much either . . .

The curtains had made both rooms much nicer, and she didn't mind that they didn't keep much light out. It was nice to be woken up by the early sun, even if you put a pillow over your head and went back to sleep again. They might lose their appeal in the winter, but it was spring, and winter was a long way off. Gigi had given up thinking in the long term. For now, they were just what she wanted.

And now, today, she was going to transform her sitting room. She'd seen it in a magazine and confirmed with the agent that she was allowed to do it. She'd hired a floor sander online the night before and collected it early this morning. A nice young man had carried it from the counter to her boot and shown her how to use it.

Sadly, he wasn't here now. And the sander was surprisingly heavy and unwieldy, and already messing with her mojo. She'd wrestled it out of the boot, which she'd left open, and managed to lurch to her front door with it, but now she had to hump it up the stairs, which suddenly looked Himalayan. Kate was coming to help (or more probably to laugh at her attempts), but she wasn't due for another couple of hours, and Gigi was eager to get started.

As she stood contemplating the task, she heard the door to the main part of the house open and close, and felt an immediate flush of embarrassment. She hadn't met her landlord yet. Being caught in the act of DIY seemed a rude beginning. It implied criticism.

'Do you need a hand?'

He didn't seem cross, if this was indeed him. Maybe a bit perplexed. Gigi pushed her unruly curls back from her face and offered her free hand, aware that her cheeks were pink and that she was far from presentable.

'Hi. I'm Gigi.'

'Good to meet you, Gigi. I'm Adam. Welcome.'

'Yes. Thank you.'

'Settling in okay?'

'Yes, thank you. It's a lovely flat.'

'I'm glad you like it.'

'I'm just trying to get this bloomin' thing inside . . .'

'Shall I close your boot for you, firstly? Then help you get that contraption upstairs.'

'That's kind. I'm okay, really.'

'It's fine. I'm happy to help.'

'You're on your way out –'

'To nowhere important, not in a hurry.' His voice was slow and kind.

'Thank you.' There didn't seem to be anything else for it. He seemed to have made up his mind to help her. She might avoid a prolapse if she let him.

She watched him walk over to the car. He was tall enough to have that slight natural stoop, and thin, with an enviably thick head of silvery-grey hair. Scruffy, but in a vaguely intentional and trendy way, rather like his house, she thought. Good bones. As he walked back towards her, she saw thick, wild eyebrows, and kind eyes to match the voice.

'Right. Let's get this upstairs . . . blimey. It's heavy. It's got to be a hundred pounds.'

But he lifted it easily enough.

'You go first . . .'

She skirted around him and went up the stairs, wondering why she felt self-conscious.

Inside the flat, he put the sander down gently. 'That's very kind of you. Thanks.'

He didn't seem in any hurry to leave. He looked around. Then leant against the doorframe.

'So you're settling in okay?'

She nodded enthusiastically. 'I love the flat.'

He nodded. 'Good. Good.' He was looking at her now, for a second longer than convention demanded. His gaze was hard to interpret and just a tiny bit unsettling.

Then he gestured at the sander. 'Have you done this before, then?'

She wondered whether to lie, decided against it.

'Nope. I watched a tutorial online, though, last night, on YouTube. It looks easy enough.'

'Well, then . . .' His eyes were laughing at her, but not in an unkind way. His mouth twitched. She didn't feel demeaned, though. Not the way he did it.

'Looks like hoovering. Just way, way more fun. And it comes with all the instructions . . .'

He'd missed several cues to leave now.

'I have some time, if you'd like a bit of help. I *have* done this before. Not that I'm suggesting you're not perfectly capable.' Again, the slightly mocking tone. Gigi wondered what it was about the way he said it that meant it wasn't offensive, but she couldn't put her finger on it. She hoped it wasn't because he was handsome: that would be just too pathetic of her. But she definitely felt – well, a tiny bit girlish were the only words for it. And Gigi couldn't remember the last time anyone had made her feel that way. The thought that Kate would be rolling her eyes furiously now ran through her mind.

'Well it's your house . . .' Was she flirting? It had been so damn long, she didn't actually know if she was or not.

He interpreted her hesitation exactly as he seemed to want to, taking his jacket off and laying it across a chair.

'So . . . where are these instructions?'

Which is how, two hours later, Kate, walking through the still open front door and up the stairs unnoticed, found them both, hot and tired, sitting close together on the partially sanded floor with their backs against the wall, drinking mugs of coffee and admiring their work, which had rendered the floor stylishly matt and pale.

Gigi felt strangely as though she'd been caught at something. She scrambled to her feet.

'Kate – this is Adam. He owns the rest of the house.'

Adam stood up and shook Kate's hand. 'Good to meet you, Kate.'

And now, suddenly, he took the cue to leave.

'Your friend has this completely under control, so I'll leave you two to it . . . I'll see you, Gigi.'

After he left, Kate raised an eyebrow.

'What?'

'What indeed . . .'

'Oh, for goodness' sake. He was just helping me. He found me trying to wrestle it up the stairs. Stayed to help. That's all.'

'Okay.' Kate was grinning at her.

'Kate! Seriously. It's his house. He probably just thought I looked completely incompetent and wanted to save his floors.'

'If you say so.' She bumped her hip against Gigi's, who shoved her playfully in return.

'You're being ridiculous.'

'You're being disingenuous. He's gorgeous.'

'He's all right.' She wouldn't have said gorgeous. Nice-looking, definitely. Very nice-looking.

'I hate you.'

'Why?'

'I've been alone for years. Not so much as a sniff. You've been alone for all of five minutes, and you've got silver foxes showing up to sand your floors . . . which is, I'm sure, merely a euphemism. Can't remember the last time my floors had a good sanding . . .'

Gigi laughed. It was so stupid. 'Don't be daft.'

The eyebrow had a mind of its own and refused to lie flat. Gigi ignored it and poured another mug of coffee.

'What does he do, then, your "landlord"?'

Gigi realized she had no idea.

'We didn't really talk. Other than about this machine. We *were* in fact actually sanding the floor. As you can see.'

She gestured theatrically.

'Hmmm. If you say so . . .'

Gigi punched her friend's arm. 'I say so. Now shut up, drink this and give me a hand. I've got to get the machine back by 4 p.m.'

Tess

Sean's text came on the day after the scan. She wanted to see him before her hospital appointment. She hadn't decided what to tell him. It depended on what he was going to tell her, she supposed.

> I don't know where you're staying. I'm back from NY. I thought we should meet up. Is there a time that's good for you?

He wasn't giving anything away.

Tess had asked Sean if he'd meet her in a small Italian restaurant near his flat. They'd eaten there, but it hadn't been 'their place'. She wasn't ready to go to the flat. And she didn't think it would work with Donna, having him at the house. Neutral ground seemed best. Sitting at a table in the corner, facing the door, she looked down and realized this would be the first time he'd seen her actually looking pregnant. She smoothed her top over her tummy. She was still wearing her own tops, the baggiest ones at least, but she'd abandoned all her trousers and skirts a couple of weeks ago, swapping buttons and zippers for the relief of large elastic panels and forgiving waistbands. Holly had gone with her to a maternity-wear shop, passing things into the changing room.

'You're going to wear that baby like a football, damn you. Remember what a zeppelin I was with Dulcie?'

'I just remember you glowing.'

'Liar.' Holly snorted. 'I was a whale.'

Tess laughed. 'No. Not a whale. Maybe . . . a seal . . .'

'Elephant seal.' Now they were both giggling. It was true. Holly had been vast, but, to Ben, and to Tess, still beautiful. The glowing bit was true. Even the waddle had been endearing.

'I've still got quite a long way to go. I could blow up.'

'Nah. I can tell. You're gonna be one of those deeply aggravating women who looks perfectly normal from behind and can still button up her winter coat right at the end.'

'That's not how it feels.'

'Well, it's how it blooming well looks.'

'Anyway, she's due in August.'

'Okay, then you'll waft around in linen things, without girding underneath. Please console me by telling me you've got at least one stretchmark.'

'You are *not* a good friend.'

'I am the best friend you've got. Now show me . . .'

'No. Get off . . .'

That was before the anomaly scan. She hadn't been anxious then, just, finally, starting to be excited. Gigi had been brilliantly reassuring and Tess wanted to believe what she said, like she wanted to believe what the consultant had said.

The appointment was made for three days from now. She knew she was holding herself taut. Being careful. Jumping at every twinge. She could only hope most of the feeling would pass after the procedure. Although she knew, really, that the news at the scan had robbed her of a carefree pregnancy.

But, anxious as she was, she was feeling less bleak than when Sean had left. Less alone. He'd left a furious, weeping wreck of a woman who didn't know what she was going to do. A mother bear, roused to rage. He hadn't known that woman – God knows she hadn't either. She hadn't quite existed before. The fact that he'd left when she was in that mess was almost as damning as what he'd done. And neither was an act of love. Time and distance had told her that. Listening to the women in her life – even Iris, and passing through Donna in a way she would never have imagined – had shown her that. Whatever he thought love was, that wasn't it.

And somehow love was all around. Maybe it was pregnancy hormones. She felt . . . supported. Holly was brilliant – but she was the given. Donna was a revelation. Even Gigi – wonderful, warm Gigi – was a blessing. Donna's house might be temporary, but it might be temporary for longer than she'd ever guessed. Donna had asked her to think of staying at least until the baby was born and she'd had time to recover. And she just might.

Iris was somewhere warm and comfortable and safe. Not having to worry so much had an incalculable effect: she hadn't realized how perpetually preoccupied she had been.

Work knew about the baby. She knew maternity-employment rules back to front, of course. How many pregnant women had crossed her desk in the time she'd been working in HR? How strange to be one. There'd been the odd raised eyebrow, and half-asked question. But, manners or laws, or more likely both, had prevented either going any further. She had a plan, and there was huge comfort in that. She was going to take the full year of

maternity leave. A whole year with the baby. A whole ;
to make the next plan.

And she'd done it all without Sean. If she was total.
honest, she'd done it all without even thinking that much
about Sean. She didn't know if he'd broken the spell with
what he'd said that night in the flat, or whether, if she was
honest, she'd never been under the spell in the first place . . .

On the way over to meet Sean, she wondered how she
wanted him to react to her. Would his face cloud over with
concern? His hand reach instinctively for her new belly?
His voice promise she wouldn't have to go through it
alone?

How much would he want to be involved? Would he
want to contribute? Participate? Co-parent from the front
row of nativity plays and recorder recitals?

She already knew it was too late for all of that. She just
didn't know whether he did.

She stood up when he came in, so he could see her in
profile, her hands clasped under the bump, like starlets on
red carpets did it. Whatever she'd said in the changing
room with Holly, she was quite proud of this belly.

He didn't reach, but he stared, his eyes wide, for a
moment before his gaze travelled to her face. 'Wow. Hi.'

He kissed her, an awkward dry peck on the cheek, his
hand on her arm. Sat down opposite her. That funny thing
happened – she looked at him and couldn't remember feeling desperate about him. Then a funnier thing happened.
Oliver Gilbert's face superimposed itself over Sean's, just
for a second, smiling that warm, broad smile, where Sean
was so earnest and thin-lipped. Tess blinked, and he was
gone, leaving her wondering what the hell that had been.

he waiter came over, and Sean ordered a Martini. She
.ed for another glass of sparkling water.

'How are you?'

'I'm well.'

'And . . .' He gestured at her stomach, but couldn't form
a sensible sentence. And she knew then that she wouldn't
tell him, if he couldn't ask. She wouldn't tell him the baby
was a girl, or that she had to have the stitch.

'We're fine.' She put her hands protectively across herself.

'Good. Good.' He gave a small, curt nod.

'How was New York?'

He looked so nervous. There were beads of sweat in his
hairline. He rubbed at them fiercely. 'It's brilliant. Amazing.'

'Everything you'd hoped?'

He nodded again. 'Yes.'

'I'm glad.'

'Are you?' He looked at her sharply.

'Don't, Sean.'

'I'm sorry. I'm incredibly nervous. This is . . . odd.'

'Look, Sean. It's okay. It's okay. You're off the hook.'

The waiter came with their drinks. Once upon a time,
they'd have clinked glasses and toasted something.

'What if I don't want to be off the hook?' She didn't like
the petulance in his voice.

'Well, don't you?'

There was a long pause.

'It's my baby, Tess.' Which wasn't exactly an answer.

'But I'm saying you don't have to be involved.'

'It's my baby. It will always be my baby. There is always
going to be this child walking around, and it's going to be
mine.' Tess almost flinched at the 'it'. She realized he might
not know that she even knew at this point. She hadn't

known about the timings, had she, before she'd studied the internet and the baby book. 'Are you saying I can't be involved?'

'No. Of course not. I'm saying you're not under any obligation.'

'Bloody hell, Tess.'

'To me. I'm saying I'm not looking to you for anything. Not for money. Not for weekend parenting. I can do this on my own. That's what I'm going to do. You're off the hook.'

Another long pause. Tess stared down at her hands on the table. Sean middle-distanced.

'Don't you want my help? My involvement?'

She didn't answer right away.

'It sounds like you don't . . .'

'I don't need it.'

He recognized the subtle difference.

'And you don't want it?'

Before he spoke again, he sat forward on his haunches and put his face in his hands, rubbing it in exasperation. 'I'd think I was an asshole.'

'What do you mean?'

'If I heard about someone like me just walking away from something like this, from someone like you, then I'd think he was an asshole.'

She didn't answer.

'See?'

Tess shook her head. 'I did think so, at the beginning. I can admit that. You can admit it too, if you're honest with yourself. What you said was a shitty thing to say. I don't think I'll ever properly forgive you for what you suggested.'

'I'm sorry. I was –'

She waved away his apology. There was nothing he could say that would *un*say that. He couldn't know how it had felt to hear it. Or how it felt to be her now. He couldn't know, because if he had the slightest inkling of how it felt to be her, to be carrying this baby, he could never have thought it, let alone have said it.

'But I've had time to think about it. Really think. Separate out the feelings and stick to the facts. I got pregnant, Sean. It was an accident. Neither of us was planning on it. I wanted the baby. You didn't. That's the bottom line, isn't it? You can't help how you feel.

'And the real truth, the real reason it has to be this way, is that if you'd wanted me enough, if you'd loved me enough, the timing would have been something you'd have got past. It would have been a story we'd tell our baby on its eighteenth birthday. It would have been the future you'd wanted, deep down, and it would have been okay that it was all topsy-turvy and not in the plan.'

'Tess –'

She put her hand up to stop him. 'And the other inexorable truth, Sean, is that if I'd wanted you enough, if I'd loved you enough, I could have forgiven what you said in shock. I could have.'

'What are you saying?'

She took a deep breath and thought of Donna, and Harry, and then said what she'd barely even rolled around in her head, let alone said in a sentence. Quietly at first. Almost to herself. 'You're not the one. You're the father of this baby, but you're not the one. Not the one I'm supposed to be with. You're not the love of my life and I'm not the love of yours.'

'How do you know that?'

She smiled sadly at him. 'I just know. If we were, this would be so much simpler. This would be easy . . . I just know, and you'll know too.'

Later, she sat on the bus heading home, her arms crossed protectively.over her bump. They'd parted more in sadness than anything else. They'd left the door open, said that they could iron out details later. She wondered what he'd want. She wondered how they'd make it work. She whispered an apology and a promise to the baby that, whatever it was, however he wanted to fit into her life, and the baby's life, that she'd make it work better than Donna and Harry had made it work for her. Because she'd worked it out sooner.

She was calm and collected by the time she got home. She hadn't realized how much she'd been dreading seeing him, and, now that it was done, now that she'd been more honest than she had even thought she knew how to be, things seemed clearer and simpler. Until she got into bed and curled up, a pillow wedged under her side so she could get comfortable, and remembered imagining Oliver's face when she looked at Sean.

Tess

It was Holly who came with her to the hospital. She'd almost, almost asked Donna to take her instead. Felt a moment of shyness, a flicker of fear at risking the fragile new closeness between them. If a shadow of disappointment had briefly crossed Donna's face when she'd left, she'd disguised it quickly, given her a brief hug, said she'd wait to hear. Then pulled her back into her arms and kissed her cheek.

'Talk to me about you. It's all about me just now. I'm the worst friend. What's going on with you?' Tess asked.

'You're not. Don't be daft.'

'Still. Distract me. I'm starving hungry and nervous as all hell.'

The procedure was going to be done under a local, spinal anaesthetic. She'd been told not to eat after midnight, and it was 10.30 a.m. now. She was in a ward, in a backless gown, hooked up to an IV. They'd performed an ultrasound, so she'd heard the baby's heartbeat, strong and steady, but her own felt fluttery and too fast. Nerves. Holly's eyes had filled with tears when she'd heard the baby. She'd grasped Tess's hand tightly and kissed her forehead. 'That's amazing. That's your baby.' Tess realized how much she'd missed having her there for the last scan.

The obstetrician had stopped by to explain the process again and to ask if Tess had any questions.

But now they'd all gone away, except Holly, and she was

waiting to be wheeled down for the stitch itself. They'd put the spinal in there, but she still had to go on a gurney, they had told her. Just as well, with her arse hanging out, Holly had said. God, how Tess loved her.

'So distract me with your life. How's Dulcie? I haven't seen her in ages.'

Holly grimaced. 'Ask me about anyone but Dulcie.'

'Why?'

'Because you're having a girl, and I don't want to scare you.'

'You already are. A bit. What's going on with Dulcie?'

'Oh, Christ, Tess – girls are horrid.'

'What's happened?'

'I almost can't bear to talk about it. It's so stupid –'

'So tell me.'

'You don't want to hear about this now.'

'Now is exactly when I want to hear about this. Please . . .'

'Okay. So there's this boy who really likes her. Jake. She liked him back, I knew she did. But this friend – this frenemy, more like – of hers, some queen bee, you know the kind, she liked him too. Nothing has ever happened between the two of them, by the way. She warned Dulcie off. So for weeks and weeks – months even, Dulcie's been giving this boy the brush off so she doesn't upset this girl, and he doesn't get it, right, because he knows, really, that she likes him too.'

'Okay . . .'

'So eventually the guy confronts her about it, wanting to know why she won't give him a chance, you know, and she tells him this other girl likes him, and that's why she won't go out with him. And because he's a boy and boys aren't so . . . so bloody ridiculous, he goes to this other girl and tells her he isn't interested in her, that he's interested in Dulcie.'

'Good for him. I like the sound of him.'

'Except now this other girl is waging a total war on Dulcie. She's telling everyone Dulcie's gone behind her back and got with this guy even though she knows *she* really likes him – you know, like it's some major betrayal or breaking the girl code, or whatever. Making out they've been friends for years, and that Dulcie has no loyalty.'

'What a witch.'

'I know. She's totally out to get her. She's made all the other girls choose a side. Like it's bloody teams. They've all chosen hers, of course. Probably terrified of incurring her wrath. God. It's fucking foul. It makes me so mad, just talking to you about it.'

'I see that.' Holly's face was red and her neck blotchy.

'Sorry. I told you not to ask about Dulcie.'

'Don't be daft. I want to know. What are you doing about it?'

'What can I do? Dulcie would die if I went into school. Besides, what would I say to them, if I did? They're not babies. They're fifteen, most of them.'

'Will it pass, do you think?'

Holly shook her head. 'I suppose so. They've got exams . . . Someone else will transgress, eventually – draw the fire.'

'Is Dulcie upset?'

'Of course she's bloody upset. She's being ostracized. Not invited to stuff. Left out. They've got these stupid groups – you know – Snapchat. Stuff like that. She's been told there's been a vote, and she's not allowed to join the chat, so she misses all the gossip.'

'How horrid.'

'Oh, Tess, you've no idea. They can be so cruel. So casually, horribly cruel. And I have to go to coffee mornings and parents' evenings with their mothers, who think butter wouldn't melt in their mouths . . .'

'You should tell 'em what their little darlings are up to.'

'Which would make me feel better for exactly two minutes. And would only make it worse for Dulcie.'

'I know. I'm not serious.'

Holly laughed. 'Nope. We have to swallow it. I fantasize about telling these girls which way is up. Seriously. But I keep telling her revenge is a dish best served cold.'

'Please, please tell me she's going out with the boy . . . Jake, did you say it was?'

Holly rolled her eyes. 'Hell to the yes she's going out with Jake. She's my daughter!'

'Good for her.'

'Oh, it'll pass. I can't even believe I'm talking about it . . . Though it helps.'

'And I was asking for it.'

'Yes. You were. And this little darling' – Holly reached out and stroked Tess's tummy – 'she'll have to deal with it too.'

'Forewarned is forearmed, I suppose.'

Holly smiled. 'You've got a few years to go yet.'

'Something to look forward to.'

'You know, you think the first bit is the hardest. Getting them to sleep through the night, teaching them to latch on. The first time they run a fever of a hundred and one in the middle of the night and you have to decide what to do about it. The endless puking and poo . . .'

'Wow. Really talking it up now, Hols.'

'I'm serious.' But she was laughing. 'You think all that crap is the hard stuff . . . But it's the easiest. Teenagers . . . that's when it gets almost impossible.'

'Nurse . . .' Tess raised a hand.

'Mostly, when they're little, you can fix things for them. When they got older, you can't fix it any more . . .' Holly's voice trailed off. Tess patted her friend's hand where it lay on the edge of the bed.

'I'll tell you one thing – you are *so* the godmother of this baby. I clearly need all the expertise I can call on.'

'Seriously?'

'Who else would I ask?'

'Oh, Tess. I'd love it.'

'Good. Will you shut up now? Because you are frankly scaring the bejesus out of me.'

Holly nodded and made the zip gesture across her lips.

She reached into her tote bag and pulled out *OK* magazine.

'Let's do celebs instead . . . That Kate Middleton . . . she really *is* too thin . . .'

Gigi

It was after nine o'clock when Gigi heard the knock at the door. Her heart sank a little. She'd worked a long shift, most of it in the post-natal ward, checking endless stitches, and she was exhausted. A shift with an active labour always went faster, and, though she still loved the work she did with the newly delivered mothers, tonight her feet throbbed. She'd come home, wondered about cooking, been momentarily very glad that there was no one else who needed feeding, and decided that hot buttered toast and a big glass of wine were far easier. She'd peeled off her uniform and pulled on her fluffy dressing gown while she waited for the bathtub to fill with gloriously hot water and bubbles, having poured at least a quarter of the posh bubble bath from Emily under the tap.

There couldn't possibly be good news at the door. A misdelivered food order, a misguided salesman ... or worse. She thought about ignoring it and hoping whoever it was would go away. But maybe something was wrong. Gigi sighed, turned off the tap and went to answer it, putting the chain across first.

She could see – in the three inches of space the chain allowed – Adam. He leapt back when she opened the door, as though he'd knocked by accident.

'I'm sorry. Is it a bad time?'

'No. It's fine. Hold on a minute, let me take the chain off . . .'

She closed the door, and found herself checking her reflection in the hall mirror. She pulled the robe tighter around her and pushed her messy hair behind her ears. The steam from the bathroom had made her pink and shiny. She rubbed her face against her sleeve quickly and opened the door.

'Adam. Hi.'

'Hi. I'm sorry. I saw the car pull in . . . I didn't realize . . .'

'I'm always in a bit of a hurry to wash the hospital off me after a long shift.'

'Of course. Sorry. Again.'

She smiled, wondering what he wanted. Perhaps she was parking in the wrong place. Making too much noise. Using too much hot water . . .

She'd seen him three or four times since the day he'd helped with the floor. Just for chats – one of them always coming or going. He seemed more antsy now than he had done on any of those occasions. Less cool.

'I'll get to the point, then. Then you can get back to your –'

'Bath.'

'Yes. Your bath.' He seemed positively embarrassed.

'I wanted to ask if you'd have dinner with me.'

'Tonight?'

'No, no. Not tonight. When you're free. Say, Friday. Saturday?'

'You want to have dinner with me?'

He smiled now, and the smile restored his demeanour. That slight laugh behind his voice. 'That's the general idea, yes. I'd like to take you to dinner. If you'd like to go . . .'

Gigi pulled the robe tighter still around herself. She had a horrible feeling she was breaking out in hives. If this was a date, and it rather sounded like it was, then her brain was whirling – counting – and telling her that it was, well, more than thirty-seven years since anyone had asked her out.

She hadn't the vaguest notion how to be cool about it. She was flattered, petrified and, mostly, bemused.

Adam shifted slightly from foot to foot, looking at her, his eyes shining, his hands buried now in his jeans pockets.

A tiny voice inside her head spoke for her.

'I'd love to.' What was she playing at?

The tiny voice was still talking.

'Friday is good for me.'

Adam looked delighted, confidence restored almost to swagger level.

'That's great. Do you like Thai?'

Apparently, the tiny voice was very enthusiastic about Asian cuisine. And 7.30 worked for her. She made the arrangement, thanked Adam for asking and wished him goodnight, all while Gigi stood and wondered why in the hell Adam would want to have dinner with her. And why she'd agreed to go.

After he left, she closed the door and leant back against it, catching the breath she was suddenly short of.

She changed, unchanged and rechanged her mind about a dozen times between Tuesday and Friday afternoon. She wanted to tell Kate, but something stopped her. Probably the thought of Richard. She couldn't shake the feeling of disloyalty – the feeling that she was betraying him.

But at 7.25 on Friday night, she was sitting in an armchair, drinking a very large gin and tonic faster than was prudent. She'd done her hair and her face, and the ten discarded outfits strewn across her bed were testament to the care she'd taken over what to wear. She'd settled on a black wrap dress and heels. She almost never wore heels, but she'd felt dumpy in the dress until she'd put them on. They'd stretched her silhouette out into something vaguely acceptable, and Spanx had squeezed it in. The wrap's neckline was low, so she'd taken the dress off and added a silky vest to cover the three or four inches of cleavage she thought would be overdoing it.

She'd even thought about painting her nails, after inspecting her workaday hands with some dismay, but her wedding ring had stopped her in her tracks. She'd never taken it off her hand, not since the day Richard had put it on. She couldn't get it off if she wanted to. She knew because she'd tried. With cold water, and hand lotion, and even a lump of butter . . . it hadn't budged. Her finger had grown around it. A jeweller would have to cut it off, and that seemed so . . . final, and so violent, somehow.

Now, although she didn't want to, she was thinking about her first dates with Richard, in the late 1970s. A lifetime ago. She'd thought he was the best-looking bloke she'd ever seen. She'd never believed in butterflies in the stomach and delicious palpitations. The stuff of Georgette Heyer, not of real life. But he had given them to her. They were all courting – her fellow nursing students. The atmosphere was redolent with lust and love and daydreams. She remembered the excitement of Saturday nights then, getting ready in her flat – Fleetwood Mac's *Rumours* on the record player – all of them fighting for hot water and mirror space. Farrah Fawcett flicks and blue eyeshadow, an intoxicating cloud of perfume. Smoky pubs and loud discos. Steaming up the windows in his car, thinking about going all the way, and wondering if she might, right there in the car . . . But Richard had been old-fashioned, even then, and he hadn't wanted that. He told her he had too much respect for her, and she felt like a lady. They'd gone to a hotel by the sea for the weekend, when neither of them could wait any longer. She'd already known by then that she'd marry him if he asked her, and he wouldn't have taken her, he told her, if he hadn't been planning to. So serious, down on one knee, a ring in his pocket. She remembered being so very, very sure that it was right. Like she'd discovered the secret, at twenty-one. And she was invincible. The two of them would be indestructible. Had she ever been so sure of anything since? Nothing was indestructible. Life showed you that.

She drained her glass and stood up, to shatter the veil of melancholy that had settled. Gin really was mother's ruin. She wandered over to the window, to see if his car was there. It was odd to think he was just below her, getting dressed for the same date. She wondered what he was thinking. Across the road, the young family she'd seen the first day she'd come to the house was just arriving home. Dad was with them. He was pushing the stroller, with the younger toddler standing on one of those clever skateboard things they had on the back these days, which she'd have loved when Christopher and Oliver were little. Mum was holding hands with the eldest, while fishing the key out of her pocket with the other hand. Tea now, and bathtime. Maybe a glass of wine and a television show for the parents once all was quiet upstairs. How many Saturday nights had she and Richard spent that way, not minding at all that they weren't getting dressed up to go out to dinner? Happy to be at home, a family.

Get it together, Gigi, for God's sake. On impulse, she

scrolled through the songs on her iPhone and clicked it into the dock. 'The Chain'. Still good. She pushed the volume up and up, so that the room reverberated with the sound of Stevie Nick's incredible voice, and started to move. Catching sight of herself in the mirror, she smiled. She might be three stone heavier, forty years older and a bloody load wiser, but she could still dance. As if no one was watching. If no one was watching. And at least the blue eyeshadow was gone.

Adam called for her exactly on time. He was a gentleman too. All the holding-the-door-open stuff. Walking on the outside of the pavement. Asking her what she would like to drink and ordering it with the waitress for her. Once that was done, he smiled broadly at her.

'I'm glad you said yes. I've been looking forward to it.'

'Me too.' Not strictly true. 'Thanks for asking me.'

He nodded acknowledgement. 'You look really nice.'

It had been a while since Richard had said that. He wasn't critical, like some people's husbands were. Never put her down. He just didn't really notice any more.

'Thank you. So do you.' God, Gigi. You're a sodding parrot. He did, though. He was wearing one of those white shirts with a vivid pattern inside the collar and the cuffs, and a fashionably cut jacket. Richard might have said he looked spivvy. But she thought it looked good. Like he hadn't given up entirely.

She blinked hard, trying to banish Richard from the date, and react on her own. Be whole, not just half of a whole that no longer was whole.

'Are you all settled in?' This was his stock first question. Every time. But he always looked genuinely interested in the answer.

'I think so . . .'

'Where were you before?' Okay. Straight in there. She didn't know why she'd have expected anything else. People their age simply didn't come without baggage. Best to see what other people were carrying around with them early on, she supposed.

'I've actually just separated from my husband. Richard.' She didn't know why she'd said his name.

'I'm sorry.'

'That's okay. It's not a secret.'

'I didn't mean to pry.' Which of course he had.

'You weren't prying. It was a simple enough question. It's fine.' She straightened her chopsticks on the placemat and tried to smile brightly. 'What about you? How long have you had the house?'

'I bought it in 2000. We did. I was married too –'

'So are you divorced as well?'

A slight shake of the head. 'Widowed.'

'Now I'm sorry.' God.

'Don't be.' Adam shrugged and smiled. 'It was a long time ago. My wife – Stella – she died in 2005.'

'Was she . . . ill?'

He nodded. 'For a while.' Gigi gave him room to say more but he didn't.

'That's really hard.'

'It was. It gets easier . . .'

'Did you have children?'

'No. No children. Stella never wanted them. I didn't think I wanted them enough to push her . . . What about you?'

'Three. Two boys and a girl. Quite grown up now . . . Christopher, Oliver and Megan. She's my youngest. She's at university. The boys have flown the nest completely.'

'Ah . . . They say that's a dangerous time.'

'I suppose so.' Was she that much of a cliché? 'I'm a grandmother too.'

'No! You can't be.'

'Flatterer. I absolutely can be, and I absolutely am. Ava. Christopher's daughter. She's almost one now.'

'Well, you look very well on it.'

She nodded acknowledgement. 'Thank you.' He was still looking at her in that way she couldn't quite interpret, like he had in the flat, that first time they'd met.

Five more minutes, waiting for their food to arrive and distract them, for careers. Hers as a midwife in a beleaguered NHS, his in pharmaceutical sales. Gigi trying not to gush about a job she loved, and Adam clearly trying not to bore about a job he merely tolerated because it paid for his life.

The starters arrived, and provided some respite. Gigi knew hobbies were probably next. Or politics . . .

She felt strangely exhausted. She didn't know anything about him and he didn't know anything about her. There was a conversational mountain – an information Everest – for them to climb before they could be anything like comfortable together. All this stuff – this superficial stuff – it was supposed to be exhilarating, but it made her feel so tired. This trying to piece together a picture of who the other was without straying into territory that was too sad, or too complicated, or that revealed too much. If she was watching, from another table, she'd say she could see two middle-aged people – a bit trampled by life, trying too hard to find common ground. Walking gingerly across new ground booby-trapped with mines.

She had always dreaded being – with Richard – just

another one of those eating-not-talking couples you saw in restaurants, with nothing to say to each other. Megan could be particularly damning about that type of diner. Gigi had tested Richard, in those last weeks and months before she'd left, by saying nothing when they'd taken their seats. Almost counting how long it took him to start a conversation. Scoring him – no points if it was about the weather, two points for something to do with the kids – they were too easy. Conversational cannon fodder. Ten points if he made her think, or laugh, or said anything that made her want to take him home before dessert and jump his bones. And he hadn't scored many tens. For a moment, looking back, it seemed comfortable and familiar. There was just such a couple in the corner behind Adam now. Gigi was fascinated by them. They'd come in immediately after them, and ordered their food with their drinks, as if they came here often and knew without looking what they wanted. The wife wasn't dressed up at all. She certainly gave no indication of being afraid that if she exhaled too fast, or coughed, her Spanx might roll down. Her glasses were pushed back on her head; her makeup hadn't been touched up since this morning. He was wearing a pullover. They spoke very little and ate quite fast. At one point she showed him something on her mobile phone. He leant over with a prawn on a fork and popped it in her mouth in a totally unsexy way. The strange thing was that they didn't look dreadful to her now. They looked incredibly safe, and relaxed. Easy like Sunday morning.

Adam had turned around to look at the couple, so Gigi must have been staring.

'Do you know them?'

'No. Sorry. I'm a bit . . .' She had no end for her sentence.

'I understand.'

'Do you?'

'It's weird. When you're first back out there. I've got a ten-year head start on you, but I do remember.'

'Have you had girlfriends, then, since your wife?'

'A few. For a while, once I first got up off the carpet, and that took about a year, I was obsessed with finding someone else. Obsessed. I thought I would only work if I was part of a couple. That's all I'd been, for so long.'

'How long were you married?'

'Nearly twenty years. You?'

'Closer to forty. We were married in 1979.'

Adam nodded. '1986. Being widowed is a bit different to being divorced. That's a conscious decision. Albeit a complicated one: I know that. Being widowed isn't a choice. It just happens to you.'

She smiled ruefully. 'I get that.'

'It had just been so long since I'd been anything else but half of a couple. Probably not even the better half. I tried everything. God knows what kind of desperate vibe I was giving off . . . Eau de horribly lonely . . .'

'What did you try?'

'You name it. Blind dates. No single woman friend-of-friends was safe. Speed dating. Online stuff.'

'Blimey. That sounds comprehensive. Did it work?'

'Well, it worked in the sense that I had somewhere to be. Dates. Hook-ups. Some stories I could tell . . .'

'I bet.'

'There are a hell of a lot of lonely people out there.'

Gigi tried not to shudder.

'It took me a year or two to realize that wasn't what I

wanted. There's someone and there's anyone, if you know what I mean.'

'I think I do. Lonely alone and lonely in a crowd.' Lonely at home with your husband.

'Exactly. Exactly!' He seemed so pleased she understood. He banged a fist down on the table. 'Your wife dies, she becomes this perfect person. The best wife, the best woman. You measure everyone against her. But it isn't fair. Of course no one seems to measure up to this perfect ghost. And she wasn't really, not any of those things. I loved her. I think we'd still be married, if she hadn't died. But who can say that for sure? She wasn't perfect. I'm not either. Nobody is perfect.'

It was different, Gigi realized. The widower and the divorcee. Not that she was that yet. Different kinds of loneliness. For a second she imagined her life if Richard had died five, ten, fifteen years ago. Imagined how that would have felt. A small, sudden streak of pain tore through her chest. She made herself concentrate on Adam again.

'So you stopped speed dating.'

'I did.' He shivered melodramatically. 'Never again.'

Gigi laughed and risked a joke, because it felt okay. 'And just started preying on your female tenants.'

'You're the fourth,' he deadpanned.

They both laughed now, and it was real, and even quite easy.

'That's better. You laughed.'

And the rest *was* better, easier. They stayed off the subject of their respective pasts, by mutual agreement, and spoke about less serious things, and drank too much nice wine. The quiet couple paid their bill and left, and they stayed later.

Eventually Adam called a cab to take them home. When the fresh air hit Gigi on the pavement outside the restaurant, she realized she was drunk – actually drunk – for the first time in a very, very long time, since she couldn't remember when. Happy, woozy drunk. In the cab, when the driver took a corner quite sharply, she slid a little in the seat, and their thighs touched briefly. She put her hand out to steady herself, and it touched his, and there was something like a shock in the touch.

In the driveway, she leant against her own car while Adam paid the driver. She tipped her head back and looked at the stars, making herself dizzy, but good dizzy. She was herself, but a lighter self. All the lights were off in the house of happy family.

The cab drove off, and Adam walked towards her. When he was standing in front of her, close, he reached out and put his hands on her waist. The gesture felt intimate but not invasive. She worried for a moment about how chubby she might feel to him, and just as quickly decided she really didn't care. He hadn't known her any other way, had never felt a slimmer, younger version of her between his hands, like Richard had. And he still wanted to put his hands there.

No man but Richard had kissed her since the glorious summer of 1977. It was an absurd thought. And now she knew Adam was going to. He was taller than her husband, and she had to tilt her head back to meet his gaze. They were lit only by a sliver of moon, and the movement-sensitive security light on the corner of the house. They stayed still like that long enough for it to go off, and then it was just the moonlight, so she couldn't see his expression. Just the glint in his eyes.

He didn't move his hands from her waist. He made. make it happen, in the end. She put her hands on his fa and pulled his mouth down on hers. The kiss was dee, and passionate. He tilted her hips into his and pushed himself against her. She was breathless, and her stomach dropped. Drunken desire: there was nothing better. She remembered now. She felt liquid with wanting.

It was Adam who pulled back.

'God.' His voice was raspy with desire. She felt fantastically powerful and wanton.

She ran the back of her hand across her mouth and tried to catch her breath.

'I want —'

'Ssh. I want too.' His hips moved towards her, and she felt him hard against her thigh. 'But . . . and I cannot believe I'm saying this. We're drunk, Gigi.'

'Not that drunk.'

'Drunk enough.' He dropped his forehead to rest on hers, his hips off hers now, and held her face for a moment.

'It'd be the easiest thing in the world to take you upstairs. But we're not going to.'

'We're not?' She nipped at his lips with her mouth. She wanted to see if she could change his mind.

He shook his head. 'Not tonight.'

Gigi straightened up and smoothed down her dress, feeling suddenly slightly foolish.

Adam dropped his hands down on to her shoulders. 'Look, I'm not going anywhere, Gigi. I live here. I had a great night. Best night I've had for ages. I really like you.'

'I like you too —'

'So there's no hurry. This is all new to you. I would rather you were sure, if you want this to go further.'

That is infuriatingly chivalrous of you.'

'Believe me, once I close my door, I'll kick myself.' He
miled. 'But I do know I'm right about this.'

'Thank you.' She kissed him once, gently, on the lips.

'You're welcome.'

He took her keys and opened the side door wide for her.

'I'm going to watch you go up, if that's all right with
you.' He winked.

'That's all right with me.' She took her keys.

'Easier to do when I'm not carrying that damn sander!'

At the top of the stairs she turned and gave him the
smallest wave.

'Goodnight, Adam.'

'Goodnight, Gigi.'

When the doorbell rang the next morning, it woke Gigi
up from a deep and restless sleep. The drunkenness that
had felt so delightful and liberating at 11 p.m. the night
before had manifested itself as palpitations, dry mouth and
a very discomforting dizziness at around 3 a.m. She'd
always been a lousy drinker.

Gigi had sat on the toilet seat willing the room to stay
still and gulping tap water from her tooth mug for a few
minutes; sat bolt upright, horribly wide awake in bed, flicking around television channels for another hour; and
finally swallowed two paracetamol with a piece of dry toast
and fallen back into a fitful sleep at around 5 a.m. The bell
at ten brought her unwillingly back from far, far away.

The mirror by the door made unpleasant reading. Her
hair was wild, and her mascara was smudged under her
eyes. Megan would have said 'Rough' and that would have
been kind. She frantically smoothed down her curls and
rubbed furiously at her eyes with a licked finger. The bell

rang again, whoever was pushing it leaning on it impatiently.

'All right, all right. I'm coming.'

Please let it not be Adam. Please. Actually, please let it not be anyone I know.

It was a delivery. A dozen red roses. Not the meagre, garage-forecourt type of roses. Full, deep-red, long-stemmed, expensive, fragrant roses, not a stem of gypsophilia in sight. They were beautiful.

She mumbled her thanks to the delivery person and closed the door. No one had sent her flowers for years. Grateful new mothers and fathers dropped off bouquets and boxes of chocolates at the hospital from time to time, but not like this. These were serious romance flowers in all their clichéd and effective glory, and she couldn't remember the last time she'd had some.

Who knew they were also a hangover cure?

Gigi put down the bouquet carefully on the table. They were in a cellophane vase, already filled with water, which was just as well – she didn't think she had anything that they would fit in – and very thoughtful of the sender. There was a small white card in an envelope pinned to the arrangement. She pulled it out gently.

I miss you. And I love you. R.

Tess

Week 26. You're a head of lettuce, and you're supposed to be kicking me now. You're also busy practising your grip. I wish I hadn't read that – now I'm waiting, and sometimes I can feel panic bubbling up in me because I haven't felt it. I have to speak sharply to myself. It's called a quickening. I like that – it sounds like what happens to your heart when you fall in love. Please kick me as much as you like so I know you're all right in there. I'm not sure how the procedure felt from your end, but it was okay from mine. On sitcoms sometimes they make men go weird about sex while their wives and girlfriends are pregnant – worrying they'll hurt the baby – I've always thought those jokes are particularly stupid. I kind of know what they mean now. Not that there is anyone to go weird about having sex with me. Pause for self-pity, baby. But not that much. It's the last thing I'd fancy. Cannot get my head around women who get really randy while they're pregnant. Sorry. Too much information, inappropriate for babies. But still . . . you feel . . . vulnerable. And I feel protective. So I'm looking after you, doing exactly what the doctor said, although I go almost out of my mind with boredom staying so still and quiet. The office is helping – someone rings me with a question at least ten times a day, or at least they did until my mum took the phone off me and told someone in no uncertain terms that I was supposed to be resting. Then they resorted to email. But still – turns out I am not the couch-potato type. I'd rather be doing . . . And while I'm looking after you, Donna and Holly are looking after me. I haven't seen Iris, though, and I miss her. Holly has promised to take me in at the weekend.

She didn't hear from Sean while she was convalescing. She didn't expect to, and he didn't know she was convalescing, to be fair. She hadn't told him any of that. She'd stayed with Donna for the first part, thinking herself a fraud as she lay on the sofa feeling quite fine. Donna totally over-did the nursing, becoming suddenly, and disconcertingly, quite evangelical about care-giving. Tess found it touching. Three days of Donna's attention was quite enough, and Tess decamped to Holly's for the second three days the hospital had prescribed. There, Holly was reassuringly neglectful. She let Tess fold laundry and load the dish-washer. Ben was away, as he often was with work, Holly and Dulcie were at their respective schools during the day, letting her rest, and in the evenings, the three of them went uber-girly, painting each other's finger- and toenails, wearing face masks in front of Richard Curtis films with boxes of Lindor chocolates.

Dulcie was deep in revision, with her exams looming. Holly worried that she was quieter than usual; worry about Dulcie was Holly's new default emotion, and it didn't suit her. Being so up close to the vulnerability of motherhood – watching her laid-back, laissez-faire best mate being anxious – was a bit disconcerting.

One late afternoon, Holly left them alone on the pretext of nipping to Sainsbury's, wanting to see what Dulcie might tell her godmother. At first, Dulcie stayed at the kitchen table, surrounded by lever-arch files and index cards. After a few minutes, she sighed deeply and pushed her chair back from the table, going to the kettle. She looked dark-eyed and messy-haired, skinny under her dad's old Pink Floyd t-shirt. Tea made, she climbed under the other end of Tess's blanket on the sofa, and quietly, with a tiny prompt from Tess, retold pretty much the story Holly had told her in the hospital. She fiddled with the cuffs of the shirt, pulled down over her hands, while she spoke, twisting and untwisting the jersey.

'She's jealous of you, you know that, right?'

'Mum says the same thing. That's rubbish.'

'Bollocks. It's always jealousy.'

'What's she got to be jealous of?'

'Are you mad?' Tess was incredulous. 'Apart from the fact that this boy – who obviously has great taste, by the way – prefers you to her! Have you seen you? You've got it all, Dulce. You're gorgeous. Clearest skin I've ever seen. I bet she's spotty. Is she spotty?' Dulcie smiled her narrow, sideways smile. 'Ah ha. Told you. You're gorgeous. Clever. Sporty. Funny. Unspotty. Thin. But thin with boobs. And bum.' Dulcie coloured and squirmed, but she was smiling. 'Sorry, but it's true. Of course she's jealous of you. How sad is she, really . . . trying to get other girls on her side. What is it, kindergarten?'

'So why do they go, then?' Dulcie's face was immediately sad again.

'That's the billion-dollar question. I'm bloody buggered if I know. Didn't know then, still don't get it. I think it might just be that they're afraid if they don't, they'll be next.'

'So they're all basically just spineless?'

God, Tess thought. *They're all just terrified, and insecure. Most of what they do comes from the relief that it's not them, and the fear that they'll be next drives every cruel word . . . They won't be bad people, most of them. They're doing what they need to do to survive in that gladiatorial arena. That's all. If you could pick them off from the pack and make them all see the effect of what they were doing, most of them would be sorry. They're just thoughtless, frightened girls. And I'd like to punch them all in the face.*

'Something like that.'

'So why would I want to be friends with them in the first place?'

'Bloody right. You can add principled to the list of qualities we were just making.'

'And lonely.'

Tess pulled Dulcie towards her in a tight embrace. 'Bless you.' Dulcie lay very still against her, until there was just one, big heave of her shoulders, and Tess knew she was crying. Tess's heart ached for her.

Dulcie tried to pull back, sniffing hard. 'I don't want to hurt the baby.'

'You won't. She's a toughie. *You're* a toughie. You stick with it, kid, you hear? I promise you the worst of this will be over by the time you get to uni. Most people have grown up enough by then not to be total sheep.'

Dulcie let herself be held. 'Promise?'

'Mostly.' It was the best she could do.

'I don't need a bunch of mates. One really good one would do. Like you and mum.'

'I was way older than you when I met your mum.'

'So she's out there, my best friend?'

Tess nodded emphatically. 'She is. Meanwhile, I've put you down for babysitting for the next five years, so that'll keep you so busy you'll hardly realize what a Dougie No Mates you are.'

Dulcie laughed.

'Me and your mum can be your Girl Squad.'

'Okay, Tess. Getting weird . . .' But she was laughing now, even though she was still crying.

Tess ran her thumbs gently under Dulcie's eyes. 'Don't you cry for them, my lovely girl. They are not worth it. They're really not.'

Dulcie rubbed the back of her hand under her nose, and then put the other one gently on Tess's tummy. 'You're going to be a good mum, Tess. She's a very lucky baby.'

Gigi

With Adam, like so much in Gigi's life lately, it wasn't so much planned as it just happened, and it wasn't at all how she thought it would be.

Adam had texted her, asking if he could cook for her. She had texted back saying she'd already shopped for dinner, and that he'd be welcome to join her. He'd sent back one line: 'I'll bring wine. See you at 8.30.'

She'd had time for a quick shower before he arrived. It was a warm night, and she'd pulled on a cotton dress and just combed back her hair from her face to dry naturally. She hadn't put any on makeup. Or shoes.

The windows of the flat were wide open. The sounds of early summer drifted in. Someone was mowing their lawn. A few doors down, there was a barbeque, with laughter and clinking glasses. It would take until ten for it to get dark, the pink sun setting lazily. She lit a few candles.

Dinner had been a simple salad with new potatoes and cold salmon. There were raspberries and cream afterwards. They'd drunk the wine he'd brought and listened to music – taking turns to choose a song on the iPhone – her on the sofa, her legs tucked up under her, him on the floor, his back against the armchair. It was easy and comfortable, but it was charged too, with something new, and undeniably exciting.

And then, when it was very late, but she still felt very wide awake, she'd stood up, taken his hand and led him into the bedroom without any words at all. To the wide, white bed, where no one but she had slept. Where she had never made love to Richard, or fought with him, or ignored him to finish a really good novel. Where she had never given early-morning cuddles to their children, or opened their stockings with them, or taken their temperatures, sheets thrown back because their fever had made them so hot. Where she was just her.

She had pulled the cotton dress over her head, and, on the other side, he'd unbuttoned his shirt slowly. There was only candlelight from the open door, but, amazingly, it wasn't because she was afraid to let him see her.

It could only be this way, she realized. She couldn't decide to do it. She couldn't think about it too much, or she'd never do it. And she wanted to do it. She'd only ever made love with Richard in her life. It seemed absurdly old-fashioned – Meg would splutter with incredulity if she knew – but it was the truth. Richard had been a little older than her, a little more experienced, although only a little, and she had never asked him for details, but she had been a virgin when they met.

Adam only asked her once, when they lay down on the clean, warm sheets. 'Are you sure?'

'Very.' She kissed him, her hand on his face, remembering what he'd said to her that first night, by the car. 'I'm very sure.'

And Adam was different. He felt different beneath her hands, more slender and more hairy than her husband, his chest wiry and tickling against her. And he touched her differently. He was less gentle and less sure at the same time. Richard knew her; Adam was learning.

He watched her carefully. She closed her eyes and let it

all happen, momentarily amazed at how relaxed she felt. She thought she'd be terrified, to the point of finding it almost impossible to enjoy it, but it wasn't like that.

When she came, she wanted to cry. He held her close and still, stroking her hair, and planting tiny, soft kisses on the side of her neck. He eased her around to lie spooned inside his embrace, and they stayed that way for the longest time, without speaking at all. His breath slowed and calmed and she thought he might have fallen asleep.

She was wide awake.

Eventually, he asked her, sleepily, if she wanted him to go, or whether he should stay. Telling him it was okay to stay was the first lie she had told him.

Tess

Sleep had become Tess's favourite second and third trimester hobby. Her maternity leave was only a week or two away now, and when she slept she dreamt of sleeping longer. Getting out of bed to get to work for 9 a.m. had become a Herculean task. A meeting that required her there earlier made her tearful. Never her favourite thing, her alarm had become loathsome to her. And the journey home seemed to take forever. All she wanted to do was to curl up, on the train, on the sofa, on the bed, and sleep . . . She couldn't get through an episode of *Coronation Street*. She could barely even get through the headlines on the news. The weekends loomed large – forty-eight hours of sleep opportunity. Two epic lie-ins. The nesting urge was some way off, she imagined. Nesting sounded far too active.

So she could hardly blame herself when her first reaction to Oliver's text, landing in her inbox on Friday morning as she sat on the 8.15 a.m. train, thinking of the bed she had so unwillingly climbed out of, was a 'Hell no, I'm sleeping.' Followed immediately by an undeniable frisson of pleasure, which might almost have been excitement. It could be so lovely, to see him. Followed by the slightly sinking realization she already had sleep-busting plans on Saturday, the day he'd mentioned.

Saturday was Dulcie's sixteenth birthday. The family-party bit – parents, grandparents, godparents, boyfriend . . . Drinks and dinner at Holly's. 6 p.m. God, what was she going to wear? Decades of friendship with Holly hadn' made her any less scared of Holly's mother and her old fashioned, judgemental attitudes, much less her willingness to share them. Holly had heard Tess groan, when she'd called a couple of weeks ago to book her in for the occasion.

'I heard that. I'll be your human shield. I'll even have a word with her ahead of time . . . for all the good that'll do.' She laughed gleefully.

'I mean it – one mention of the wrong side of the sheets and I'm out.'

'I swear. I'll rein her in. You have to come – Dulc would be devastated if you didn't.'

'Of course I'll come for Dulc.'

'You know you're her favourite godparent.'

'Tough competition.' Dulcie's other godparents were a chinless colleague of Ben's and a chinless cousin of Holly's, both older than them, chosen to placate her husband and her mother. Their mutual chinlessness had first been noticed by Holly and Tess font-side at Dulcie's christening, causing an almost-collapse in giggles. Afterwards, Holly blamed sleep deprivation for her loss of control at her own, unkind observation. In all the posed photographs from that day, Dulcie, wild-haired and angry in the restrictive family heirloom of a gown, wailed open-mouthed, while Holly and Tess tried, not very successfully, to control their mirth, and Holly's mum glared on crossly. Tess knew she thought Tess was a bad influence on Holly, oblivious to the glorious reality that the truth was the absolute opposite.

'Nevertheless –'

'I wouldn't miss it. What time shall I waddle by?'

Holly outlined the plan. 'No raw eggs, no blue cheese.

hat soft drink shall I get in for you, since you won't be
rinking?'

'Oh, Christ. I won't. How profoundly depressing.'

'Shut up.'

'Nice. Ginger beer.'

'Isn't that alcoholic?'

'I don't know. Is it? Ginger ale, then.'

'Done.'

'Was this Dulcie's idea? Grown-up party?'

Holly sighed. 'Mine. I think . . . I mean . . . normally, I
suppose she'd want to do something with her friends.
Things are a bit better, on that front, but they're not exactly
forming an orderly queue.'

'Oh, love her . . .'

'She's okay. She's got her head in the game. GCSEs.
New start at Sixth Form. There's the boyf –'

'Going strong?'

'Seems to be. He's a sweet boy.'

'That's good.'

'That's a lifesaver.'

'Well, I'll be there, with bells on. I'll bring an extravagant present.'

She reread Olly's text.

Hello! It's meant to be lovely Saturday. Fancy doing something?

He didn't specify any time or suggest any particular
activity. It was easy-breezy. She wondered, for just a
moment, whether he deliberated as much over the words
as he wrote them as she did when she read them.

She called Holly from the office for advice, but got the
voicemail. Holly called her back once she was home from
school.

374

'Sorry, sweetheart. I just picked up the message. I ha
frees this afternoon, but I'm stuck into cooking for tomorrow. You okay? Everything good?'

'I'm fine.'

'Phew . . . I've got you on speaker phone, propped up
against the fruit bowl. I'm up to my arse in meringue,
which I'm trying, as I speak, to pipe into kisses on this
baking parchment.'

'Get you . . .'

'Half pink, half white. To be sandwiched with butter-
cream.'

'Yum.'

'Except the nozzle keeps popping out of this damn piping bag . . . oh shit . . . there it goes again.'

'Can't you buy some?'

'Ssh. I already have some. In the cupboard. If all else
fails, I'll whip them out, make sure I put some of this mix
in my eyebrow, to look authentic, pass them off as my
own . . . What's up? You better not be backing out.'

Tess explained.

'Go. Go . . . Go. Why are we even having this conversation? Chew his arm off! When did this message
come?'

'This morning. While I was on the train.'

'And you haven't answered it?' Holly's tone was incredulous. 'It's, like three thirty . . .'

Tess laughed. 'Calm down. Why so keen?'

'Why not? Bit of fun. You know his mother, for God's
sake . . . You know his pedigree.'

'He's not a dog, Hols.'

'No, he's a nice guy, by the sound of it. A nice guy who
likes you. Wants to take you out.'

'I haven't been on a date in forever.'

'So you think it's a date?' Holly's tone was teasing.

'Of course not.'

Holly didn't respond.

'Do you?'

'I think it might be, Tess. Not that I'm the expert. The last date Ben and I went on was to Homebase. To buy mousetraps.'

'Shit. I've never been on a date pregnant . . .'

'It's not like he doesn't know about it.'

'I know, but –'

'But what?'

'So why would he want –'

'Oh, stop it. You're pregnant. Not terminally ill. You do know you're not always going to be pregnant, right?'

'But I am now. With someone else's baby.'

'Someone else who isn't around.'

'Still . . .'

'What?'

'I'm nervous.'

Holly was uncharacteristically quiet for a moment. Tess wondered whether there was a meringue crisis.

'Bring him.'

'What? Are you mad?'

'Bring him. Dulcie . . . come here . . .' She heard Dulcie shout from another room, then appear close to the phone.

'What?'

'You okay if Tess brings a date?'

'Oooh. Yes. Absolutely. Who is it?'

'Get off that meringue. He's called Oliver. He's nice.'

'Bring him, Tess.'

'You're both mad.'

'I'm laying a place. That's that. If you don't bring him you'll have to explain that to my mother.'

'That's mean.'

'Gotta go. Meringue massacre. It's everywhere . . . Hanging up . . . See you at six. Love you.'

Dulcie chimed in: 'Love you, Tessie.'

She had never quite been able to walk away from a gauntlet Holly had thrown down. That had been one of the hallmarks of their relationship in the early years – Holly made her braver, ballsier. She borrowed a bit of Holly's 'bugger it' attitude, and typed a reply to Oliver.

Does the offer still stand?

The screen, with its impatient three dots, told her he was typing a reply a minute or so later.

Yes. Thought you might be ignoring me.
Sorry. Busy day.

She typed in the emoticon that looked like a Munch screaming man. Deleted it again on the grounds that emoticons were for kids and their middle-aged mothers. Pressed 'send'.

No worries. What do you fancy doing?
Are you brave enough to come with me to my god-daughter's birthday party?

A brief pause. Then typing . . .

Sounds good. How old?
Sixteen. Yes, I'm that old. Although my friend Holly was a child bride, of course.
Sounds fun.

They exchanged details, and agreed that he'd pick her up at Donna's. She gave him the address. The texts got a bit 'See you tomorrow', 'Looking forward to it', 'Me too' . . . the modern equivalent of not being the first one to hang up. Eventually, Tess put her phone on the counter in the kitchen and wandered through to the sitting room, where Donna was curled up with a book.

'That's a Mona Lisa smile.'

Tess hadn't even realized she *was* smiling.

'Something good?'

She shrugged, lost for an answer.

He was as good as she had suspected he would be. Charming to Holly's mother, pally with Dulcie's boyfriend, complimentary to Dulcie, helpful with Ben, attentive to her. All of which without being the tiniest bit obsequious or creepy. He had that easy knack with people: you'd have thought, if you were watching from outside, that he knew everyone already.

Holly dragged her to the kitchen, on the pretext of checking on something in the oven. She pulled her into the utility room, pushed the door closed behind them. She hissed, rather than spoke. 'How is he still single?'

'What do you mean?'

'I mean – he's handsome, lovely, fit, solvent. What's wrong with him?'

Tess laughed. 'Nothing.'

'Did you say he just broke up with someone?'

'His mum said so.'

'Details?'

'No. Just that she didn't think the girl was right for him. And that she didn't think he'd been heartbroken . . .'

'Living together?'

'I have no idea.'

'I like him.'

'I like him too.'

Holly hunched her shoulders with glee.

'Go for it.'

'Go for what?' Tess put her hands on her bump. 'Have you forgotten?'

'You seem a lot more hung up on this whole baby issue than anyone else is, Tess, including him.'

'You're being ridiculous. This is vicarious titillation.'

'Too bloody right. I've been married . . . oh . . . forever . . . Look, I'm not telling you to marry the guy. Just have a bit of fun.'

'Yeah, right. I feel *so* sexy right now . . .'

'I wasn't talking about sex. Although it is possible, you know. For another couple of months or so.' She thought for a moment. 'It all got a bit *National Geographic* after seven months with me and Ben.' Tess grimaced. 'But I'm not even talking about that. I just meant fun.'

'You're assuming he likes me like that.'

'Tess.' Holly looked at her like she was an idiot, hands on hips. 'He's at the Sweet Sixteen of a total stranger. He's talking to my mother. *My mother.* Even Ben doesn't talk to her if he can possibly help it, and he's under some kind of contractual obligation. He's helping Ben with a Costco fireworks "display", and Ben is just dangerous with that stuff. He'll be lucky to leave with all his fingers and thumbs. He likes you. Hell, even if he's on the rebound and you're just a sorbet . . .'

'Where do you get these expressions?' Tess rolled her eyes.

'The interweb.'

Tess watched him from the kitchen window. It was dusk now. Ben had given him a pair of protective goggles and the two of them were at the end of the garden, huddled over, chatting and laughing. He stood up, rubbed his back and looked for her with his eyes. When they alighted on her, he waved, and her stomach flipped.

Much later, fingers intact, he and Ben lit the fuses, and the rest of them exclaimed at the colourful display. The last one, Ben had proudly announced, was a single ignition barrage, with more than three hundred shots in it, and the two of them came back to the house once it was lit to survey the finale of their handiwork. In the darkness, with the tumbling, whistling stars and bursting fans, Tess felt Oliver's arm around her, and it was the easiest thing in the world to drop her head on to his shoulder. His thumb stroked the bare skin of her upper arm gently, and it was all she could think about.

It was after midnight by the time they pulled up outside Donna's house. Olly turned off the ignition and they sat in the still silence for a moment.

'I had a really good time.'

'So did I. Thank you for coming with me.'

'Thank you for inviting me. They're all lovely.'

'Even Holly's mum?'

'I've cracked tougher nuts than her.'

Tess laughed. 'I bet you have . . .'

They smiled at each other.

'Does everyone fall for you, Oliver Gilbert?'

He looked down and didn't answer for a minute. When he did, it was with a question of his own.

'Have you, then?'

She exhaled deeply. 'Oh. It's complicated.'

He nodded.

'Agreed?' she asked.

'No. Not agreed. Disagreed.'

She looked at him.

'It's simple.'

He unbuckled his seatbelt, leant forward, across the gear stick, and kissed her, very gently, right on the corner of her mouth, letting his lips linger for a moment.

Then he pulled back and got out of the car. Coming around to her side, he opened her door and offered her his hand.

'I'm going to leave you with that one thought: That it might just be simple, you know. I'll see you soon, Tess.'

Gigi

There was a terrible, vulgar expression – one she knew but never used. Gigi couldn't get it out of her head. She didn't even know where she'd last heard it, and she certainly didn't know anyone who regularly said it, but it kept saying itself aloud in her brain. *Don't shit where you live.*

She knew exactly what her subconscious meant, though, with its mantra. What it was really trying to say was 'Don't have sex where you sleep.' Or maybe 'Don't sleep with your landlord.' Either of those would apply: they both worked.

The thing was – he knew where she was. When she left for work. When she got home. Whether she'd taken the car or the bus . . . who visited her . . . Adam didn't have to snoop to know it – no stalking required. She was right there. He was right there . . .

Like she watched the family across the road without meaning to, he watched her. She hadn't thought it through. There was no opportunity for things to grow organically – this embryonic relationship was on a faster track than she could probably cope with, simply by dint of topography. He was omnipresent.

And she knew he was trying so hard not to be – to be cool, and easy-breezy. No pressure. Hadn't he been that way from the start?

He just wasn't as good at it as she had thought he might be, back at the very beginning. It didn't matter – he couldn't help being there – it was his house.

She hadn't told anyone what had happened between them. Not even impartial, non-judging Kate. So far as her friend knew, nothing beyond flirting had gone on. She could have told Oliver but something stopped her. She wasn't so much ashamed as completely unable to frame the facts with her own opinion. She didn't know how she felt. About Adam. About it. About anything. Not even Richard. There were things that she missed . . . there were lots of things that she missed.

And she really liked Adam. The sex had been good. It had been great. Thank God for the wine, because, sober, she almost couldn't remember or comprehend how unselfconscious and relaxed she'd been about it. The getting naked, and the rest . . . He'd felt wonderful under her hands, against her body. It had been a long, long time, since she'd felt some of the sensations he'd made her feel. Desirable, attractive, appreciated.

But there was no plan, and she didn't know the rules of this game because it had been decades since she'd played it. Let's face it – when she'd last played it the rules were completely different anyway. She knew it wasn't that she'd used him. She liked him. Cared about him, even. When had that happened? Wine or no wine, she'd gone into it knowing exactly what she was doing, wanted what had happened to happen . . . It was the feelings that swelled, afterwards, that she didn't know what to do with.

He must have sensed her distress. Which, of course, was one of the things she liked about him. The next thing he suggested they do together was brunch, and not at all in a 'How do you like your eggs in the morning' kind of way. An unthreatening, easy-going meal on a day when he knew she was most likely working in the afternoon. She went because she couldn't think of how or why to say no, and she went because she wanted to go. In equal measure. He'd made a full English, and been out to get all the Sunday papers. There was even freshly squeezed orange juice.

'Trying too hard?' He smiled when she commented on it.

'It's delicious . . .'

She liked his space. It was maximalist, whereas hers was decidedly minimalist. Bookshelves ran all along one wall, filled with novels and large-format art books. There were interesting pictures on the walls – 'Ah, my Affordable Art Fair retail problem' – vivid still lifes and modern land-scapes. Deep, worn, leather armchairs and bare floorboards. It was male, but comfortable. Lived in. Like Adam. The radio was on in the background, and she'd ended up sitting on an old kilim cushion on the floor, her back against the sofa, him in the tan armchair across the room, reading the paper. Reading little snippets out loud to each other when something was interesting or funny, and it was almost like they'd been doing this for years.

He made an easy listener. He had that knack of letting you know he was listening and interested without speak-ing back to you much. She talked to him about Meg, how nervous she got before exams. And about Oliver, and how glad she was Caitlin had let him go. And it felt natural. He didn't offer solutions to any of the issues, as Richard would have done, and she liked that. Then again, Richard was invested in the kids, and Adam had no need to be. But it was nice. And there was no sex, because she was going to work. Which, in the end, she sort of wished she wasn't. But there was a kiss, before she left, that could easily have led to it if there was time, and left her feeling on edge in the sexiest possible way for the rest of her shift, remembering his hands on her face, and his mouth on hers.

Which was why she agreed to a cinema date a few days later, heavy though it felt with the expectation of sex at the end of it. (Did it, though? Maybe she was putting that there . . .) He put his hand on her knee in the film, which created a small tremor of — was it? — desire, but they were too old for snogging in the back row. They both needed glasses to see the screen clearly. And it was a good film, a complicated, well-crafted political thriller, so they concentrated. His glasses made him look intellectual. Afterwards they had coffee and cake in a place near the cinema, and talked, about the film and other stuff, close together on a sofa.

It was easy, and natural, to go into one home, when they got back, into one bed. She opened her eyes more this time, watching him loving her, and it was because it made it sexier, and not at all because she was trying to keep an image of Richard out of her head. It wasn't until they'd finished that the fear of what feelings would come next encroached. But, almost as if he knew she had lied the first time about being okay with him staying, after he had held her for a time, he said he had an early start and didn't want to wake her when he knew she had a day off and surely deserved a lie-in. He left to go back to his place. She was incredibly grateful. And even a little bereft, after he'd gone.

If he was biding his time, he was doing it very well, and maybe it was even starting to work. And maybe it could have . . .

Until he asked her to go with him to the garden centre.

And she went, because she had nothing else to do, aware that Megan would laugh and call it an old people's outing, and because she liked being with him, even though Megan was probably right.

And it was okay until he asked her whether she would prefer a clematis or a wisteria in the front bed of the house.

He wasn't watching her, when he asked. He was unself-consciously reading the labels attached to the plants in the climber section. A wisteria could take three or four years to flower, whereas a clematis would flower in its first year. Both liked a sunny aspect, the tags said. Both could be purple or white, although he thought perhaps the white wisteria was a bit yellowy. And both would suit the soil and be suitable for planting now, although it was a bit late for both. It was more a question of which flower one preferred. She preferred. And there it was.

Maybe it was because he read out 'sunny aspect' and conjured up Richard, laughing at estate-agent speak. Maybe it reminded her of the wisteria they'd planted when Megan was a baby, which had grown lush and green but never flowered, and become a comforting, infuriating conversation she and Richard had on a loop every year afterwards. Was it too close to the wall? Could a wisteria be blind?

Maybe he meant nothing by it. But, because he wanted her to choose, that made her very afraid, suddenly, as she stood amongst the plants and the tools and the weird books no one wanted to buy, that he was planning a future with her. That if she chose the wisteria, she'd still be there in three or four years when it flowered.

He looked up at her face for a verdict and read there instead the fear of hurting him, and she was too late to rearrange her features into something less honest. And it was too late for him not to have asked her. And they both regretted it.

In the car on the way home, he tried chatting, but she knew her answers were rubbish. He turned on the radio. The mood had changed. Not quite clouds coming over the sun, or the heavens opening with hard rain. But a shift in the quality of the light. Bruce Springsteen was singing about hungry hearts. Of course everyone had one. She did. Adam did. Richard did. Every one of them could be hurt. She didn't want to be hurt any more, but she also very badly didn't want to do any more hurting.

Tess

Work was winding down. She almost needn't bother to go in. She felt excluded from the long-term plans being made – her closest colleagues were mostly female, and their attitude towards her differed depending on their own position in relation to hers. The ones above and to either side were sympathetic – many mothers themselves. The ones below struggled to hide their eagerness to shine in her absence. But for all of them, in the short term at least, she was a dead woman walking, and the combination of their load-bearing kindness and unwillingness to involve her meant her in-tray was neither full nor particularly interesting. It wasn't like work was a passion anyway. Living with Donna and watching her enthusiasm for what she did – hearing Gigi talk about her work, even . . . And Oliver . . . Maybe she needed a change. Maybe her career was like her relationship with Sean: she'd been going through the motions. She had almost fallen into HR – a placement at university had led to a job offer with one company that she'd parleyed into a job with another. Two, three, four rungs of the corporate ladder. More money, a bigger space in the open-plan office, and then an office of her own, once she was having the difficult conversations. Nothing to love. She thought of Donna and her passion for photography. Maybe she had a passion and she just hadn't discovered it yet. Florist? Ceramicist? Baker? Wedding-invitation calligrapher? Lifestyle blogger, getting paid in stuff, to plug stuff online? Now that was a career. There were a million things to do, and she might love one of them. Not that it mattered now. Beggars couldn't be choosers, and, although she was hardly a beggar, she'd have no choice but to go back to work once the baby was born. Single parents didn't necessarily have the option of pursuing a passion. Self-pity threatened, and Tess resented work for not crowding her mind enough to shut it out. Perhaps if she stopped a bit sooner, let them buy the obligatory balloons and cake to see her off a week or two earlier than her planned leaving date, the nesting she kept reading about in the darn books would become her passion and her distraction . . .

Tess hadn't heard anything from Sean in ages. When his name popped up in her email inbox, she realized she hadn't even really thought about him for a while. Seeing his name triggered a rush of adrenalin, and she clicked quickly on to the note, her eyes scanning its contents. He wondered if they should see a solicitor – or a mediator – and formalize something about the baby. He felt he needed to do the right thing, and that he wasn't sure what that was. That maybe they should find out . . . His tone was conciliatory. He didn't say anything about her – about him and her – just that he hoped she and the baby were well. That he was in New York for the foreseeable future. It was going really well. He also said he hoped that she would let him know if she needed anything. At the bottom, almost like an afterthought, there was one more line. He'd met someone, he said, an American girl at work. It was early days, and it was far from serious, yet, but that he thought it might be, and he wanted Tess to know.

Of course he had. And so he should. She almost smiled.

Sean needed a girl with big hair and white teeth and a perfect manicure, a girl who wanted to jump out of bed at 5.30 a.m. with him and work out. A girl who wouldn't fall pregnant until such a thing was agreed and scheduled, and would no doubt go back to work minutes later in her size-zero pencil skirt, chasing the partnership or the deal or whatever it was she and Sean would be chasing. Of course he had. Not the slightest twinge. How amazing was that?

But the stuff about the baby did cause a flutter of anxiety. He'd made it sound all about him doing the right thing. Not like he wanted to be involved. Not like he wanted anything. Like he was trying to do the right thing. She fervently hoped he meant it that way. Holly had asked her a litany of questions. What would she tell the baby, down the line, about him . . . whose name would she put on the birth certificate . . . would she let him, or ask him, to contribute maintenance? It was okay that Holly asked: their friendship had always been straightforward that way. Iris might have asked, if she could. Donna probably not – and she might not have earned the right, yet. Holly could. But still, Tess had minded the question, but only because she didn't have an answer. She only knew that Sean didn't feature at all in any of her imaginings.

And, yes, she saw the irony in reaching for her phone and summoning Oliver's name in the contacts list. For perhaps a full minute her finger hovered over the call button before she put the phone down and watched the screen until it went blank.

She'd once said to him, in a moment of vulnerability, that she must seem pathetic, that she knew it was wrong of her to talk to him about the baby, that he wasn't responsible. He had looked at her with an almost frightening intensity. Like he'd wanted to say something. His mouth opened, closed again. 'I don't mind. You're maybe the least pathetic person I know.' It hadn't been what he was going to say, she was sure, and she wished she knew what he'd actually thought.

Gigi

It was always going to be a dam that burst, and if Gigi had had to guess, she'd have guessed that it would be with Emily that it happened. And so it was.

She'd given Ava a bath while Emily made them some supper. Christopher was away at a conference. Ava was sitting up now, her little Buddha belly holding her centre of gravity low in the bubbly water. They had a sort of rubbery, plasticky ring thing with suckers on the bottom that held her safe so she could play. They had so many new things these days, for babies. Ava loved the bath; and any efforts Gigi made – pouring small cups of water over her head or sending little tidal waves towards her – were rewarded with peals of delighted laughter, and fists splashing furiously against her kicking thighs, encouraging more, more, more. You could lose yourself in Ava and bathtime, and Gigi had luxuriated in doing just that, kneeling against the side of the bath, her sleeves rolled up, but wet anyway.

Afterwards, she let Ava kick, naked, on her towel for a while. She rolled over now and tried to pull herself up. It was a wrestling match to get a nappy on her, a contortion trick to button up her Babygro. All the while they chatted to each other – Ava without words, but nonetheless effusive and communicative for it. Gigi loved that she knew her. Loved that she trusted her. Loved that someone else was cooking supper so there was all the time in the world for this, not like when she'd been Mum and cook. She just loved her.

Then it was time to calm down and let the lavender of the bubble bath and the warmth of the milk make her sleepy. Ava looked up at Gigi while she sucked on the bottle, eyes wide open, then lids slowly drooping. Exhausted by her day, Ava relaxed and grew heavy in Gigi's arms. From the next room, Gigi heard the *Archers* theme tune. Emily was flitting about in the kitchen: cutlery and glass clinked against the table, something on the stove sizzled, and she smelt garlic and herbs. The phone rang, and she heard her daughter-in-law answer, heard her voice soften and slow when she realized it was Christopher. She couldn't hear the conversation, but they talked for a while, and laughed a little at something. At one point, Emily came into the sitting room, smiled at her – 'Your mum's here doing bedtime, the absolute angel. I'll tell her . . . Sending you his love' – and checked a detail on a letter on the desk. 'Yep. Says the 15th. Ten fifteen.' *My day. Your day. Our life.* Plans. Normal married stuff. A dull ache started pulsing in Gigi's chest.

Off the phone now, Emily came back in with a glass of white wine for her. She leant against the doorframe for a moment, smiling at the tableau of her sleeping child in the arms of her grandmother. Then she saw Gigi's face crumple. Without a word, she put the wine down, picked up the baby, limp now with sleep, and took her up to bed. 'Drink the wine, G. I'll be down in a minute.'

Gigi was crying too hard to drink anything when Emily came back down a few moments later. She sat on the footstool beside the sofa and hugged Gigi's knees.

'What is it?'

For a moment, Gigi couldn't form any words that made sense. Eventually, she spluttered, 'I'm such a fool.'

'You're not. Ssh. Please don't cry. You're not . . .'

Gigi sniffed. 'I've made such a bloody mess of everything.'

'Hey. Ssh.'

'You don't know . . .'

'Don't know what?'

Taking a deep breath, Gigi blurted out what she hadn't told anyone. 'I've left a good man. A man who loves me. The father of my children. The man I've spent more than half of my life with. I've broken his heart, Em. Broken all of him, actually. Just broken him. Destroyed my family. Or at least the togetherness of my family. The wholeness. And I've slept with Adam.'

That was the stinger. That last bit. Emily sat up like a meercat.

'Adam your landlord Adam?'

'Adam my landlord Adam.'

'Christ.'

'Exactly.'

'When? Sorry. None of my business . . .'

Except Gigi was making it her business.

Emily rephrased her curiosity. 'I mean . . . like a one-off? Or are you a thing?'

She said 'thing' with incredulity, despite herself.

'I don't know.'

'Okay.' Emily was buying herself thinking time, clearly entirely unsure about how to react to this news.

'You must promise not to tell Christopher.'

'Of course. Does Richard know?'

Gigi shook her head vigorously.

Emily took the glass of wine she'd poured for Gigi off the coffee table and swallowed a big glug. 'I was giving up alcohol mid-week. Sod that . . .'

She laughed. Gigi laughed too, although the sound of it was very close to tears.

'Do you want to be with this guy?'

'No . . . I don't know . . . maybe.'

'And Richard?'

'I don't know. I miss him.'

'Lawd.'

'See . . . told you . . . a bloody mess . . .'

'And totally inappropriate behaviour for a grandmother.'

'I know,' Gigi wailed, and Emily hugged her.

'I'm sure this is an overshare, but I never slept with anyone except Christopher's father before.'

'No?'

'No.'

'Brave.' It was an unexpected word. Gigi was grateful to this loving, lovely girl. Not only for not judging her, but for seeming to understand.

'I totally one hundred per cent completely have no idea what to do. I feel like an idiot.'

Emily shook herself, and looked straight at her.

'Right. Stop that. You're not an idiot. And you're not a mess either, by the way. Stop. Look – you're an adult, Gigi. Working through some stuff. Trying to be happy. Trying to be happy without making other people unhappy, which is laudable, even if it isn't always possible. Maybe sleeping with Adam was a mistake. But it's just sex. Or it's more than that, I don't know. Maybe leaving Richard was a mistake. Maybe both were, maybe neither. You've committed no crime. And, more to the point, you've closed no door.

Sleeping with Adam doesn't mean you owe him anything. Doesn't mean you've ruined things with Richard either. Whether he finds out or not. Your life, your body, your decisions, your right to take a bit of bloody time out of a life lived so much for other people to decide what *you* need.'

It was quite a speech. Emily had a hand on either hip now. She nodded her head decisively.

'So no more of this mess talk. And no more tears, please. I can hardly bear those.'

'Sorry.'

'And no more sorry, dammit.' The rage was faux. 'I saw you unhappy with Richard. And your marriage was never any of my business, any more than anyone's. But I confess I always thought it needed tweaking. Not obliterating. There has always been love. You can see when that is there and when it isn't. And Richard loves you. Maybe he just needed shaking up a bit. But your going seems like the right thing to me. Space. Time. I'm not necessarily right. Only you know that, Gigi. You two. If I'm wrong, and you're happier on your own or happier with Adam, or some other guy you haven't even met yet . . . that's all right too. You haven't wrecked things for us. Your kids still have two healthy parents. Their own lives – even Princess Megan . . . Even Richard would survive. You've got to do what is right for you.'

'It feels so selfish.'

'It's what everyone else is doing all the time. You've just not flexed the muscle for a long, long time.'

Gigi smiled. 'You make it sound okay, you know.'

'Because it is. Or it will be . . .'

Gigi almost believed her.

Tess

'Hello.' Tess hadn't seen Olly. She'd forgotten for a moment where she had parked, and was cursing her pregnancy brain, holding up the keys and clicking the fob in the hopes she was close enough to trigger the lights. He appeared from her left and made her jump. But in a nice way, she realized.

'Olly! Hi.'

'How are you?'

Her car flashed, identifying itself in the next row.

'You leaving already?'

She nodded. 'Early shift. This' – she indicated the bump – 'is waking me up pretty much at dawn. I've given up trying to sleep longer. How about you? What's your excuse?'

Maybe he was looking for me, she thought. *God. So sad. Have you seen yourself?*

Olly shrugged. 'I was awake too. I love this time of year – when the mornings are so light so early and the days feel so long.'

They stood for a moment, Olly shifting from foot to foot, beaming at her.

'How is your granddad?'

'Good, I think. Good. How's Iris?'

'She's good.'

'Good. Good.'

Tess smiled. 'So we've established we're all good.'

397

'Yep. Good.' They both laughed. 'So where are you off to?'

She sighed. 'I was going to tackle Mothercare. Can't put it off a minute longer; according to the book I was supposed to have done it all by now.'

'There's a book that nags you?'

'There sure is. Got a list as long as my arm. One tiny person needs an unbelievable amount of kit. Really . . .'

Olly laughed. 'I am familiar. My brother's baby, Ava, pretty much needs her own trailer when she goes anywhere.'

'Apparently that's normal. The baby bible says I should have it all by now, so I'm off to shop.'

'On your own?'

She shrugged. 'Yep. My friend Holly was going to come with me, but something's come up her end, and I've sort of got the bit between my teeth now, so yes.'

'Do you have to go right now?'

She didn't immediately understand his meaning. 'Iris is asleep.'

'I mean, can you wait, say, ten, fifteen minutes?'

'Why?'

'If you give me a few minutes to see my granddad, just to say hi. I'd like to come with you.'

Tess was taken aback. 'Why on earth would you want to do that?'

Oliver shrugged. 'Because it sounds fun.'

'Really?' She was incredulous. 'I find that incredibly hard to believe.'

'Because I'm big and strong?'

Tess giggled. 'Did your mother put you up to this?'

'No, she did not!' He sounded indignant. 'And you might buy me lunch for helping you . . . and I've a free day and nothing much planned . . . We could go in one car, come back here later.'

'Are you serious?'

He smiled. 'Why not?'

'And it's not a pity invite?'

'You didn't invite me. I invited myself.'

'You know what I mean. You're not feeling sorry for me. Poor single mother . . .'

'Not a chance. Not one ounce of sympathy. On my life.' He held his hands up in a gesture of surrender. 'Swear.' He put one hand reverently across his heart.

Tess laughed, and decided.

'You're mad.'

'I'm helpful. Face it, you need the help. That's not pity, that's just fact. That *was* you not remembering where your car was just now, wasn't it?'

'I thought I'd got away with that.'

'Nope. I see all.'

Tess clicked her car locked and put her keys back in her handbag.

'Okay. I'm going to give in graciously. It would be lovely if you came with me. And helpful. And more fun. Thank you.'

Olly gave a mock-bow and ushered her towards the door.

The Mothercare superstore was on an industrial estate on the outskirts of town. It took about fifteen minutes for them to drive there in Oliver's car. He left the radio on, so they didn't talk much except when she gave him directions, but it was companionable sitting next to him while he drove. A couple of times, when he was stopped at traffic lights, they looked over at each other and smiled, a look that lasted just a tiny bit longer than social convention dictated. Olly parked up and collected a trolley while Tess unfolded the sheet of paper she took from her handbag. She read out loud from the list:

'Moses basket, baby monitor, sleeping bag. Receiving blankets. Are they different from other blankets?'

Olly shrugged. 'Search me.'

'Scratch mitts. Hats, socks, sleepsuits. A changing mat.'

'You've got to get this thing my brother has. It's like a white plastic Dalek. You feed it stinky nappies and it exterminates them. Neutralizes them. Something like that. Completely essential.'

'It's not on the list.'

'Trust me. When did you last change a baby's nappy?'

'God. Not forever. Dulcie. So that's years ago.'

'Well, once smelt, never forgotten. Ava can make my eyes water, I swear. Put it on the list.'

Tess laughed. 'Nappy Dalek. You change your niece's nappies?'

'Okay, I did it once. Under duress.'

'Baby sling.'

'They're brilliant. Ava loves it. Pushchair? You've got to get one that you can collapse without a manual. When Ava was born, my sister-in-law Emily once had to leave her car in the multistorey and walk all the way home because she couldn't put hers down.'

'God. Okay. Simple pushchair. I suppose so. Car seat, definitely. I don't think they even let you out of the hospital without one of those. Baby bath. Bath thermometer.'

'Don't you just use your elbow?'

'I feel like you know more than I do about babies.'

'It's all spin. But, to be fair, you do appear to know not

a lot.' His twinkling eyes. His big smile. His teasing voice. She wanted to lean into him. Let it all wrap itself around her. He made everything seem fun and doable and light. It was infectious and completely appealing. She had to remember he wasn't hers. He wasn't anything to her. Or this baby. He was just a nice man being kind and sweet to her. That was all.

'That's fair. Although I'm pretty sure you're supposed to be bolstering my confidence, not scaring me to death . . .'

He stopped and looked at her, suddenly serious.

'You're going to be a good mum, Tess.' He said it like Dulcie had. Almost like she ought to believe it.

'Oh, really? How do you know?'

'I haven't known you long, and I don't know you well, but I've seen you with your gran. It's bloody obvious. I think the kid got lucky.'

He held her gaze for a moment. Then broke his own spell.

'Did you know babies can see only black and white until they're about five months old?'

'I did not, Dr Spock.'

'Not sure what that's got to do with *Star Trek*, but okay. So people go mad with all these colours and colourful stuff, and basically their babies would do better with a room decorated like a barcode. Have you decorated yet?'

'Not yet. Long story . . .'

'*Quelle surprise*. Stripes. Black-and-white stripes.'

'Sounds awful.'

'When is your baby coming again?'

'She's due in August.'

Olly stopped, and beamed. 'She's a girl?'

Tess was touched by his reaction.

'Pink, then. Lots of pink. Oooh, and a mural. Fairies, unicorns – all that stuff. She'll see it eventually. Come on. This isn't going to fill itself . . .'

Ninety minutes and a staggering amount of money later, they emerged, blinking at the natural light, with a trolley full of boxes. Inside the store he'd been surprisingly serious and fully engaged – discussing the safety features of car seats with the sales assistant. When she'd referred to the baby as his, he hadn't corrected her. When they'd passed the nappy bins, he'd picked up the top-of-the-range model his brother had and added it to the trolley. 'A gift,' he'd smiled. 'You'll thank me . . .'

He'd watched closely in the clothes section, as she considered the rows of tiny cotton garments. 'Excited?'

And she realized that she was. She smiled at him, her eyes bright and wide. 'Yes.'

He'd squeezed her shoulder gently, his thumb briefly stroking her.

'Did we get everything?'

'Pretty much. God. It's a lot . . .' Tess tried not to think about Donna's guest room, maybe fourteen feet by twelve. There wouldn't be a lot of space, once this lot was all unpacked.

'My first car wasn't much more expensive than that.'

'Mine neither.'

'Is this even going to fit into your car?'

'I hope so.'

She lifted something off the top of the load.

'Oh, no, you don't. Put it down, lady. Do you realize you're pregnant? You're not moving any of this. Back off.'

It wasn't necessarily the way she'd imagined it being expressed, and he certainly wasn't the person she'd expected to say it, but it was the order she'd wanted to hear for so long. From someone other than Holly. She wanted to weep with joy.

He worked fast, oblivious to the effect his words had had on her. 'Where are you taking me for lunch? Come to think of it, I think I'd better buy lunch.'

Tess laughed. 'I think I can stand you lunch. As long as you'll be happy with a Starbucks.'

'Bugger that. I've earned a gastro pub at the very least. Come on. I know a good place not far from here. We can argue over who's paying while we eat.'

At the bar, Olly ordered a tomato juice for Tess, a pint for himself, and two Welsh rarebits, with chips.

Tess watched him order from a table in the corner. He chatted jovially with the young girl behind the bar, like she'd seen him chat comfortably with the nurses and catering staff at Clearview, making them laugh. She envied him his easy way with people. Turning towards her with their drinks, he beamed at her. It made you feel warm, and safe, that smile. Gigi's was the same.

He clinked his glass against hers. 'Here's to being ready.'

'To being ready. Thank you. Really.'

'My pleasure. My absolute pleasure.' He held her gaze for just a moment longer than necessary. Then he looked down at his pint. When he raised his head, his expression had changed.

'It wasn't an accident, you know.'

'What wasn't?'

'Me . . . you . . . the car park . . .'

'What do you mean?'

'I hadn't come to see my grandfather.'

Tess raised an eyebrow, confused.

'I'd come to see you.' For the first time Tess could recall, Olly blushed. It made him look boyish.

'How did you know I'd be there?'

Olly shrugged. 'I took a chance.'

Now Tess felt herself colour.

'Why?'

'Okay. Here goes . . .' Olly took a deep breath. 'Because I like you, Tess. Really, really like you. You still don't know? It's not sinister. I just want to get to know you better. To spend more time with you.'

'You don't know me very well –'

'You're right. And I'd like to change that. I just like everything I've seen so far.'

She nodded several times, buying herself thinking time. 'I don't know what to say.'

'You could say you like me too. If you do, that is.'

'Of course I do.'

'Not just to be polite.'

'I'm not. Of course I do . . .'

Olly winced. 'God. There is such a but in that sentence.'

'But . . .'

'No.' He put both hands up as if to shield himself from a blow. 'No but . . .'

'But Olly . . . look at me . . .'

'I am looking at you.' This Olly was unnerving. At least to Tess.

'Well, I don't get it.'

'What don't you get?'

'Why?'

'Because.' He sounded like a schoolboy.

'That's a daft answer. It's not an answer at all, actually.'

'What's the question?' His eyes were twinkling.

'Why? I'm very pregnant. My ankles have all but disap-
peared. I'm quite homeless. I'm sad, lots of the time. I'm a
bit of a mess, frankly. Most of the time you find me snotty
and weepy . . .'

'Wow. You should definitely not write your own Tinder
profile.'

Tess laughed in spite of herself. 'As if. I'm being serious,
Olly.'

'You're being tremendously negative.'

'I'm being honest.'

'And so am I, Tess. You're . . . there's something about
you, all right?'

'Are you a pregnancy fetishist?'

'See, you're funny. That's one thing. Kind, sweet, gorgeous, funny . . . And the greatest of these is funny, by the
way. And no. I'm not. I haven't got a thing for cankles
either, before you ask.'

'Pity cases?'

'I don't feel sorry for you. Okay, that's not true. I do, a
bit. You're obviously having a shitty time. But that isn't it
either. I know we have something. It's simple.'

'It isn't. You just broke up with somebody. I just broke
up with somebody. The father of this baby.' She gestured
at her stomach.

'Who is clearly stark raving mad, by the way.'

'Says you.'

'Look. I'm not asking you for anything, Tess, except to
let me like you. Let me care about you. From a distance or
from as close as you like. I'm not trying to complicate
your life.'

'Good. I don't think I can take any more complications.
And you don't need mine.'

'Isn't that up to me? You're not exactly hiding anything. I know what I'd be getting into.'

'And I can't be getting into anything at all. Not now.'

'And I understand that. But I'm not going anywhere.' He leant forward and kissed her cheek. Left his face close to hers after the kiss for just a couple of seconds. He smelt of shampoo.

The waitress arrived with their meals.

'Ah. Saved by the rarebit. I'm starving.'

Week 29. You can open your eyes! The web says you are the size of a little pumpkin, and so I weighed one and it's more than a kilogram, and that's you. You are going to triple that weight before you're born, so, basically, I can eat whatever I like from now on! You're all over the shop, turning and kicking, making the most of the room before you get too big and have to keep still, I suppose. In the picture the baby's head has downy hair on it. I feel you every day now. It's weird and fluttery and lovely. It's our secret. I try to figure out whether you're reacting to me and what I'm doing or whether you're just doing your own thing in there. Your in utero cultural education is going pretty well. We're working our way through the classics, music-wise. You've heard a lot of Abba. Rolling Stones. Especially 'Wild Horses' because that's the best song ever in the history of songs. Except maybe 'Let It Be'. But you've heard plenty of the Beatles too. I've not neglected the classic classics either. Lots of Elgar. Bruch. That makes me cry, but apparently it makes you dance. 'Dancing Queen', nothing. Bruch's violin concerto and you're doing the dance of the seven veils in there.

Gigi

A few weeks before the official end of the term, Megan asked both her parents to pick up a load of the stuff that she no longer needed with her at university. She just had exams, then parties, to come, she said, and she could get herself home if they'd leave her the basics. The house had to be deep-cleaned if they had any chance of getting their deposit back, and that would be easier 'with less crap in it'. She asked them separately, and afterwards none of them – except Meg – knew whether it was self-absorbed student ditziness on her part that she'd asked them both, or a daughter's calculated move to force them to spend the day together. Perhaps it didn't matter which it was.

Megan was in a rented house. Rented hovel, Richard called it. She was sharing with two guys and three girls. She'd lost the room ballot and got the attic room – slightly bigger than the three on the next floor down and the cupboard of a room next to the kitchen, which smelt permanently of fried food – but draughty as hell, with rattling windows and peeling wallpaper. And a hatch instead of a door, and something more like a ladder than stairs leading up to it. Potentially fatal after a drunken night out, Richard had said, when she'd first shown it to them. Megan had winked at him and thrown an arm around his shoulder. 'Good job I don't drink, then, isn't it, Dad?'

Three emails and two phone calls after Megan's double booking was first uncovered, they'd agreed to go together, in one car. Gigi had said she'd prefer to drive, but really she wanted to pick up Richard, not have him collect her. She hadn't told Adam they were going together. She hadn't lied, exactly, but she'd definitely said 'I' and not 'we'. He hadn't pushed her, although he'd had to have known she would be dropping Megan off at Richard's. He'd said he'd be home that evening if she fancied a drink after all the exertion of the day. His tone was light, but his face had the shadow of something sad across it. Gigi tried to ignore the guilt, forcing herself to remember Emily's words, but the feeling persisted.

Richard was waiting by the front door when she pulled into their driveway in the early afternoon. He kissed her cheek when he got into the car. She wondered whether to mention his flowers, but decided not to in case it embarrassed him. They made small talk for a few minutes, chatting over the safe territory of the kids, and of Ava, but neither of their hearts were in it, and by the time they got to the M25 Gigi had put the radio on and lost them both in the chatter of Radio 4. Politicians evaded answers and blamed their opposite numbers for everything that was wrong. This was a shared interest – they had both voted the same way for the last forty years, except for 1997, when they'd fought over Tony Blair and his New Labour vision – and for the rest of the journey they were on the familiar ground of hectoring Jonathan Dimbleby and his guests. Gigi fleetingly wondered how Adam voted. They'd never talked politics. Never gone together to vote. Gigi always got emotional when she voted. Richard could repeat the speech she made every time, about the suffragettes and the black South Africans in line for hours in 1994, word for word. How many times had he heard it?

Megan was not as ready as Richard had been. She wasn't ready at all despite the hour. She answered the door in a dressing gown, her hair at its 'hedge backwards' best, her eyes bleary from the end-of-exam celebrations the night before.

'Mum. Dad. Hello . . . you are . . .' She looked at her watch. 'Oh shit. Exactly on time.' Her breath was boozy.

She sent them to the café at the end of the road, promising she'd be entirely ready in the time it took them to order and drink a cappuccino.

Gigi sat at a table in the corner and watched Richard order. Joke with the waitress about something. Search in his pocket for some change for the tip jar. He weaved through the tables with a tray and sat beside her. Two cappuccinos and two cakes. Eccles for him, a piece of carrot cake for her, with a perfectly iced carrot atop the cream-cheese icing. Her favourite.

'I'm glad we're doing this.' He smiled at her.

She smiled back. 'Me too.'

'Are you?'

'Richard . . .'

'You're not just tolerating having to spend this time with me, for Megan's sake?'

'Please.'

'And really hating every moment.'

'Of course not. There's absolutely nothing to hate, Richard.'

He smiled again, relieved. 'We've done a fair bit of this, haven't we? You and me.'

Gigi laughed. 'God. Bags of it. Literally. Bags. Although the boys never had as much stuff as Meg.'

'No, but that bloody drive.' Christopher had studied in

Durham. Hours and hours, on the very best day, and the M1 didn't have many best days.

'And did we ever once get there and it *wasn't* raining?'

'I don't think so.'

'He loved it, though, didn't he?'

She nodded, remembering. 'He did.'

They were quiet for a few moments. They were both, she supposed, playing the cine films of their shared history in their own minds. Listening to the laughter, the map squabbles – the soundtrack of their past. Wondering when it went wrong. Wondering how the hell they'd ended up here.

There was a rack of newspapers on the wall behind the table where they were sitting. The truth is, if they'd been here even a few months earlier, Richard would have taken one out and started to read it, his head and shoulders disappearing behind a broadsheet. Almost as soon as he sat down. He'd have been irritated that Megan wasn't ready. Hell – he might not even have come: he might have been playing golf, asking her if she could manage without him. Which was really telling her that she should be able to. If he had come, he wouldn't have bought her a slice of cake. Not without her asking for one, at least. She didn't even know that he knew it was her favourite. They'd have been sitting at the table together but alone. Now he was watching her. Looking for reactions. Trying to please her. Eking out time together.

Everything she'd said she'd wanted and needed. Only she could decide whether he was too late.

Tess

Week 30. Today you are about 3 lb. Sadly, the book says I only
need 300 calories a day more than normal, even though you're
getting bigger so fast. I'm struggling to visualize you as a vegetable
at this point, since the large cauliflower I picked up in Sainsbury's
as I waddled around (Yes, I waddle now. When I'm not peeing.
Very attractive.) at lunchtime is round, and you are, presumably,
longer than that. And less . . . leafy and florety. I'm not sure all
this fruit and vegetable stuff is helpful. I weighed it, nonetheless, in
the scales they have. Tried to figure out what you might weigh now.

Tess hadn't intended to drop in on Iris – she had had a
midwife appointment that morning, and they almost
always ran really late. This time, though, they'd been amazingly prompt – early even, as one of the mothers ahead of
her hadn't shown up. And, since the office wasn't expecting her until lunchtime, she had decided to nip in for a few
minutes. It was as much for her as for Iris – she felt peaceful, sitting with her grandmother. Good thinking time.
She'd never raised Tom with Iris again, after that horrid
reaction. She never would. It was more important to her
that Iris stayed calm and relatively happy than it was to
keep pressing her for answers to all the questions she had.
She had to accept that she'd never get those answers. Had
to acknowledge that Iris hadn't wanted her to know, to
understand – neither her nor Donna. It was hers alone.
She thought of the bundle of London postcards she'd

found piled with the *Radio Times* in Iris's house. Had she stayed in London after that last letter, from her mother? Had she gone back for the funeral? The questions persisted, but Iris mattered more than the answers. Iris was speaking less and less, and, when she did talk, what she said made less sense than before, like she was seeing through a veil. Tess had almost, but not quite, stopped hoping. You probably never did. Like a gold digger, sifting through pans of grit and rock, hoping for a tiny, shining, valuable nugget of the good stuff . . .

Donna had signed in the book twenty minutes or so ahead of her. She hadn't said she was coming, when she'd seen her last night. She'd been working late, and Tess had made her a cup of tea when she came in exhausted at ten. Since Tess could barely keep awake after that time, they'd chatted only briefly, on the landing.

Iris's door was ajar, and Tess heard Donna before she saw her. She stopped, just out of view, and listened for a moment. Donna was telling Iris about the shoot yesterday – her voice gentle and soft – little stories about the anxious mother, who'd had to be sent out of the room before the children would do anything vaguely worth photographing, and the father, who was stiff and uncomfortable. Tess liked the tenderness and affection that were clear in Donna's voice – both for Iris and for yesterday's subjects.

When she turned to enter the room, she saw that Donna was combing Iris's hair. The sight of the two of them was so poignant. She remembered Donna in the hospital, when Iris was first ill, and this new reality of what she needed was presenting itself – that brittle, tense woman seemed like someone else entirely. It almost flooded her with relief, now, to watch them together, to be a part of this.

Donna smiled at her. 'Morning. Great minds think alike. I was going to sprawl in bed this morning, catch up on some rest . . . but then I just realized I'd rather be here.'

Tess nodded. Words caught in her throat.

'Are you okay? What did the midwife say?' Donna's face crowded with concern.

'I'm fine. Everything is just dandy. It's just nice, seeing you two . . .'

Donna winked. 'You're one walking hormone at this point, aren't you?'

Tess laughed and sobbed at the same time.

Iris smiled beatifically at both of them, vacantly happy.

Tess went to the chair and kissed her grandmother's cheek. 'Sorry about the waterworks, Gran. Occupational hazard.'

Iris seldom, if ever, acknowledged the pregnancy, but now she put one hand on Tess's tummy and gently patted it. Which didn't help.

'I never knew you read to her. In the hospital. The nurse told me, after you left for Goa.'

'Why would I tell you?'

'I thought . . . I mean, I think I gave you a hard time . . . made out like you didn't care as much as I did.'

'It isn't a competition, though, is it?'

'But I'm sorry. You cared all along.'

'Of course. She's my mum.'

'I know.'

'But you don't need to be sorry. I got a lot of stuff wrong. You weren't all wrong about me either. I was the reason that we weren't close . . . me and her . . .'

'Do you know why?'

Donna nodded. 'I think so. I've had a lot of time to

figure it out. It goes back a long way. She knew my truths. I was trying – for so long – to live a lie, and her truths, and her knowing my truths – that would have got in the way, while I was with Harry, at least. I shut her out to keep the honesty away. If that doesn't sound totally half-baked. It was easier that way. And that gets habit-forming. It gets harder and harder to let someone back in.' Tess knew that was true. 'And I didn't let myself think about how that might hurt her, you know. And I'm sorry. So sorry. For that.'

Tess nodded.

'I think I told myself that I was making up for it by letting her be so close to you. It made me jealous, and a bit sad, and that was my penance, I suppose.'

She sniffed hard.

'And then I just left it too bloody late. You were going the same way . . . distant. I worked hard at not letting you need me, and then I was shocked when you didn't . . . And when you get so far down that road, it gets bloody difficult to find a way back. And, once Iris was ill, it felt like muscling back in. I suppose I was afraid you wouldn't want me, wouldn't let me.'

Tess wondered if she would have.

'And so, because I had so bloody much to say, and no clue how to say it, and she couldn't hear me anyway – not properly hear me – I read the damn book. My voice. Not my words.'

'I believe she did hear you.'

Donna smiled and squeezed Tess's hand. 'You want to believe that.'

'No. I do believe it. I believe in the chinks and the moments. I believe the love she had for us is that strong . . . that it comes through cracks.'

'You sound just like Iris. Her sermon on the strength and simplicity of love.'

They both smiled. 'She's not wrong, though, is she?'

'Ah – you're right. There are the moments . . . Can I show you something?'

Tess nodded.

Donna went to her black portfolio. It was propped against the wall, by the door. Tess had seen it when she came in, assumed Donna was on her way to a meeting.

Donna lay it down on the floor and carefully unzipped it, taking out a few pictures, face down. She brought them over to the table where Tess was sitting and turned them right way up.

'I took these. I've been wanting to show them to you.'

They were a series of Iris, close-ups, all in black and white. Some were of her asleep, her face relaxed. In some, she was staring at something unseen, eyes milky, her skin lined. There was an almost haunted quality to them – she looked lost and anxious – bewildered. And, in others, she was smiling, straight to camera, and she looked quite as she always had, to Tess. Like she was about to speak, or she'd heard something that amused her. Like she was waking Tess up in the single bed in Salisbury, about to ask what the plan for that day was. Those last ones were more moving to her than she could say.

'Those are the moments, right?' Donna put her hand on Tess's shoulder. 'There she is . . .'

Week 31, darling. Starting to get squashed in there. I'm sorry. I hope you're okay. I've a new, bad habit of reading about miracle babies on the internet. Babies born early. Babies who spend days, weeks and months in incubators, on sheepskin pads, with wires and tubes and nappies for dolls. Babies whose parents post pictures of them online lying beside iPhones and Coke bottles to show how tiny they are. Who grow up and go to school and are just fine. I try to count weeks, not days. The women who've suffered speak in days. They write on forums about being 23 weeks + 3 days. Like that. Because they know that, that early, days count. How afraid they must be. Once it's happened once. I'm scared. But I'm scared of a loss I can't understand because I haven't experienced it. How much worse – how paralysingly, obsessively, chillingly terrible – it must be if you have. The acute fear I had about you after the stitch has softened over the weeks. You've stayed in. Clever, wonderful, amazing you. I just need you to carry on holding on. I don't miss Sean. But I miss a partner who would know what I'm feeling. Who would lie beside me every night and see me wide awake and anxious and tell me I'm daft and silly and that everything is going to be fine. And make me relax. I miss that. Do you know when I feel most okay? When I'm with Olly. Ssh. I can't say that to anyone else. He's so calm and kind and he's so sure, somehow, that the universe is good. Gigi called him her golden boy to me once. He is. He's golden. I want to wrap his optimism around me like a cloak. But Olly isn't your father. He isn't my boyfriend. He certainly doesn't lie beside me every night. I can't rely on him. It isn't fair and it isn't sensible. You and me. You and me. They've made the appointment – the stitch will come out in a few more weeks. When it's safe. When they know you'll be all right. Hang on until then, baby mine. Hang on.

Gigi

Oliver had phoned the night before and invited himself to lunch after a visit to his grandfather, requesting his favourite salad and offering to bring dessert. The salad was modelled on something they'd ordered almost daily on a holiday to the Amalfi coast, years ago, when Megan had still needed a buggy and the boys had exhausted themselves running up and down the steps in Positano: farro, and tomatoes and basil, with Parmesan.

Gigi had countered that James was also due a visit from her, and that she'd meet Olly there and they'd drive back to hers in tandem. She'd been out early to shop for food; made and refrigerated the salad, and laid the table, stepping back to admire the white linen cloth and two fat peonies in a small Ikea tealight glass. It all looked fresh and modern and pleasing. She loved that about the flat. That magazine look she'd never managed to achieve anywhere else.

Sometimes, when she considered her domestic renaissance, she had the fleeting, worrisome thought that she might have achieved the same relief leaving Richard had given her if she'd just painted the whole of the old house in Farrow and Ball Skylight and smashed all her old, dated china so she could replace it with Sophie Conran. Maybe she was that shallow.

At Clearview, James had been the same. Not worse and not better. Present-ish. Happy enough. Olly had been jumpy. Turned to look every time the door to the day room opened. Only half paying attention to his mother's conversation with his grandfather, interjecting just slightly off topic, a beat too slow.

She'd stuck her head in on Iris, when they were leaving, but she was asleep and Tess wasn't there. Gigi was glad. She should be somewhere else on a Saturday morning, that lovely girl. Not hiding from the world in here.

Adam was in the front garden when their two cars pulled into the drive. Gigi swore softly under her breath. He was wearing gardening gloves, scruffy jeans and a shirt buttoned up just one button out, so the hem hung unevenly and his collar gaped slightly. He was pruning and weeding – the brown wheelie bin was open next to him. He looked up with a smile when Gigi parked, and then looked momentarily confused by Oliver. He wiped his forehead with his shirt sleeve and stepped out of the flower-bed, pulling off his gardening gloves.

'Hello.'

Oliver proffered his hand and Adam took it, shaking it warmly. 'I'm Adam.'

'I thought so. I'm Oliver. Gigi's son.'

'Good to meet you.'

'You too. Hard at it?'

'Not really. Staying on top of it is what I go for, when it comes to gardening. My wife had the green thumb . . .'

It was a stark and odd sentence, presupposing knowledge on Oliver's behalf that he didn't have. Oliver didn't really know how to respond, and Gigi didn't know how to rescue the encounter.

'We've been to see Oliver's grandfather.'

Adam nodded, smiled sympathetically. 'How is he doing?'

Gigi saw Oliver notice that Adam did possess knowledge about Gigi and her life, and cursed quietly again to herself.

'He was okay, today. Thanks.'

'That's good.' The moment when Adam ought to have turned back to his task came and went. Oliver was now regarding him with real curiosity. Of course. She ought to have known that he'd sense something.

'We're just going to go up, then . . .' She started towards her entrance.

'I've been promised lunch.' Oliver smiled. For a ghastly moment, Gigi thought Oliver was going to ask if there was enough for Adam, ask if he'd like to join them, but he didn't.

Adam turned, then, raising an arm in goodbye. 'Good to meet you,' he said again. 'Enjoy your lunch.'

'What's his story?'

Gigi had wittered once they'd got into the flat, attempting, she supposed, to distract him. He'd uncorked a bottle of wine and poured two glasses, admired the peonies and taken off his jacket, making himself comfortable in the armchair while she took things out of the fridge. But then he'd asked.

'He's a really nice man, Ol. He was widowed. A few years ago now. I think.' She felt such a fraud adding the 'I think'.

She badly didn't want to tell Oliver about Adam. And she wasn't quite sure why. She was closest to him of all her children. Apart from Em, he was the most understanding, she knew, the most compassionate about what had gone on between her and Richard.

She wasn't embarrassed. Or ashamed. Was she? He was the least judgemental of her kids, too.

Maybe she already knew it was over. Maybe that was why.

Oliver looked at her speculatively. Like he was deciding which direction to head in. Made his mind up.

'He seemed really nice.' Then, 'Now, where's that salad you promised me? I am starving.'

Tess

The doctor listened to Iris's chest. Two aides helped to lift her from the mattress, and a nurse gently pulled up her nightdress so he could listen to her back. Tess went to the window so she didn't have to see Iris's frailty. When they'd laid her down again, the nurse smoothed her hair, smiling tenderly at her. The doctor turned to Tess.

'I'm afraid I think it's pneumonia.'

Tess took a deep breath and nodded. 'Will she need to go to hospital?'

He shook his head. 'We can keep her comfortable here.'

'Thank God.'

He paused. 'You should be prepared, Tess. In my opinion, it's quite unlikely that Iris is going to recover from this.'

'Whatever we do?'

He nodded, choosing his next words carefully. 'Care would be largely palliative at this time. Keeping her comfortable.'

'That's all she'd want. It's all I want for her.'

'We can keep her comfortable. She can stay here.'

Tess stroked Iris's arm.

'How long?' She didn't look at him. Her eyes stayed focused on Iris.

'It's hard to say specifically. Not very long, I would think. She's quite weak.'

'And will she be . . . is she likely to be responsive at all?'

'Again, that's hard to know at this stage. She'll sleep,

most of the time. We'll be giving her something to help with that. But I can't say for definite that she won't wake. When was she last lucid?' He looked from Tess to the nurse.

Tess wished she could remember.

The nurse shook her head gently. 'She's been very calm. I haven't seen her distressed. She's an angel to look after, aren't you, Iris?' She stroked Iris's other arm.

'This isn't an exact science, Tess.'

'But she won't be in any pain?'

'No. She won't. She'll slip away. I hate that expression, but it's the truth. It is mostly very gradual.'

Tess nodded, wanting to thank him, but suddenly couldn't speak. This was it. It was better, she knew, this way. The residents' lounge was full of people much haler than Iris. Living half-lives. This is what Iris would want, what she would choose if she could.

The doctor and nurse went together into the hall, pulling the door to. She heard him issue instructions, saw the nurse make a note on her chart.

Tess felt peaceful. There was nothing more she could do. This was it. All she needed to do was to be with her. She took her seat next to Iris's bed. She'd need to text Donna. She'd need to do a lot of things. But, right now, she needed to be here.

She whispered, 'It's okay, Iris. You can go. You can go.'

Gigi

Park benches were for covert conversations. They were where spies always met. Spies and lovers. Neutral ground.

It was a beautiful day, mid-morning, and the park was getting full. It was too early for lunch, so the office workers weren't here yet, loosening their ties and taking off their shoes and socks to let their feet luxuriate in the feeling of the grass. But there were mothers with toddlers, parking buggies and laying out blankets, and old ladies with shopping trolleys.

Gigi had suggested they met here. It was a place she'd come to often when their kids were young. Usually without Richard. It was almost on the way home from school, if it was a warm day and you had time for a diversion. A bit further along was a playground with swings and seesaws and those whirligig things – the boys had loved those. There'd always been an ice-cream van parked along the fence on summer days. She remembered them wheedling for Fabs and Feasts. Meg in a buggy with a chocolate beard. The best years.

Not such neutral ground. Infused with recollections.

Gigi chose an empty bench and waited for Richard. She saw him before he saw her – his gait was so familiar to her. She watched as he scanned the benches, alighted on her, and approached. A million years ago, the sight of him might have made her heart jump. Butterflies. The whole thing. It had, right? It must have done. Ah, she was too old now for all that.

She thought of Adam. Was she a fool? An old fool? Megan's voice spoke in her head. 'What are you doing, Mum? For fuck's sake. What are you thinking?' Emily's: 'You haven't shut any doors.' Olly's: 'You have the same right to happiness we all have, Mum. You just have to figure out what is going to make you happy.'

And that was the hard part.

Some cheesy song from the seventies played in her head. 'Torn Between Two Lovers'.

Snap out of it. You're not torn between two lovers. Richard's your husband.

She'd tried to compartmentalize them. Richard as the past; Adam as the future. That didn't work. Richard refused to stay in the past. Adam couldn't deliver a future, not as a concept. She couldn't imagine it. He was very much a present.

And now Richard was here beside her on the bench, very much also in the present.

She looked at him. He looked older. Tired. He was freshly shaven, but he'd nicked himself a couple of times – there was a drop of blood on the collar of his shirt, which was ironed, but not well ironed. He looked a bit thinner too, and it didn't suit him. He looked diminished, somehow. *I've done that*, she thought. *I've diminished him.*

'How are you?'

'Not good, G.'

Silence.

'You know the best time I've had in ages? It was when we picked up Megan. Those few hours . . . when things were most like they used to be . . . that's the happiest I've been since you went.' Richard shook himself a little. 'I'm sure I should try to be less pathetic. I'm sure it doesn't help.

God knows I don't want to bare myself to you. But I'm not good.'

She let him talk. She wanted him to talk. He didn't look at her as he spoke. He sat staring straight ahead.

'There's no shape in my life without you, Gigi. There are all the things I've always done. Work. The kids. The house. Bloody golf. But when you're not there, there's no shape. It's . . . bewildering. I'm not even slightly used to it, and it's been weeks. Months. But we have had decades. My whole life, it feels like. So this is still so new and so bloody awful. I don't want to get used to it. I don't want to re-arrange everything into a new shape if you're not in it. If you need it to be a new shape, so you can come home, then I'll do anything you want.'

'Richard.'

'No.' He turned his head towards her, just briefly. 'I want to say this. Let me.

'I don't know if this is repulsive to you. If I seem like a pathetic old man. I don't care. I'm begging you. I'm begging you.' His voice broke. 'I know it hasn't been good. I've had all this time to think about it. I know I haven't been . . . we haven't been . . . Maybe you think I don't know what makes a good marriage, but I do, and I know ours hasn't been, not for a while. A long time, maybe. And I know it's mostly been my fault. But if I know what's gone wrong, if I understand it, I mean, then I can try to put it right . . . but. You. Have. To. Come. Home. So I can try.'

He stopped. She felt like he had more to say, but that the effort of saying what he just had was exhausting.

'I saw you with him.'

'When?'

'I went to where you're living. One night. I was driving around. I couldn't stand just being at home, you know? Christ, that house without you in it. I wasn't going to come in. I don't think I was. I just . . . I just ended up there. Parked outside. God, that sounds stalkerish. There were no lights on. I figured I'd wait. Just to see you. You know, if you came home. I wasn't thinking particularly straight. I didn't even know if you were coming home.'

Oh God.

Gigi remembered. She remembered Adam paying the taxi. She remembered leaning on the car. She remembered him kissing her. And how sexy the kiss had been. How she would have let him come up – because she was tipsy and relieved that he found her attractive and because she'd felt lust for the first time in a long, long time – and how he'd stopped her.

'Oh, Richard.'

'I saw the two of you together.'

'Nothing happened that night.'

'I know. I watched. You kissed. That's not nothing. It cut me like a knife. But you didn't go in together.'

'No.'

'But since?'

'Have you been spying on me?'

Richard laughed, but it was a small, bitter laugh. 'God, no. You think that didn't almost kill me, just seeing that?'

Gigi felt small, and cruel.

'I didn't do it again, I swear.' She believed him. 'I didn't want to know.'

She remembered something else. 'You sent flowers.'

He nodded.

'After *that*? You sent flowers.'

'It was that or wait for him and punch his fucking lights out.'

The phrase was so absurd, the swear word so out of character, spoken in his small, sad voice, that they both laughed.

'Are you two . . . together?'

There was no more lying now. She didn't immediately know how to answer, but she wanted to be honest. 'We could be. I think.' Another long pause before he answered.

'Is that what you want?'

'I don't know. It's . . .' He sighed, and the sound stopped her.

'Can I tell you something?'

She smiled ruefully. 'I think we're past secrets, don't you?'

'I was unfaithful to you, G. Once. One time.'

Gigi took a deep breath. A few months ago, the very words would have been a body blow. Words signalling a cyclonic reordering of the universe.

But everything was different now.

She'd have had questions. Dozens. She'd have wanted to hear every detail. She'd have shouted, cried, screamed at him. She could almost play the movie of how it would have gone in her own mind. Almost hear herself.

But it happened. Acceptance before understanding wasn't something she'd expected of herself. None of this – none of how these last few months had played out was what she had expected of herself.

She nodded slowly, looking at his profile as he looked down at his hands clasped in his lap. 'Do you want to tell me about it?'

He gave a small, curt nod. 'It was years ago. Before . . . before you were ill.'

'When?'

'The boys were teenagers. Meg was little. Life completely revolved around them. Exams, university applications. Bloody sports teams. Ballet lessons. Endless birthday parties. They were all-consuming. I used to wake up on a Saturday morning and listen to my to-do list. *Drive here. Pick up here. Fix this.* I'm not blaming anyone but myself, by the way. That sounds like an excuse and it isn't. It isn't even a reason. I haven't ever blamed you. But I sometimes think it's an explanation. My life was . . . You didn't see me, G.'

Those last words resonated, reverberated around her head.

She thought about those years. There'd been so much to do. So much to carry.

'I should have tried harder. I know that. You were so busy. So preoccupied. But I should have made you carve out time for us. I should have made the time for us.'

And so should I, Gigi thought.

'We never had sex. Not for months at a time. We barely touched, sometimes. When we did, it sometimes felt like I was on the to-do list.'

He was right – he had been. She remembered.

'Who was it?' She didn't hear anger in her own voice. Her brain wasn't frantically sifting through recollections, trying to figure it out. It almost didn't matter at this point.

Again, Richard's small, sad laugh. 'Well, I'm the biggest cliché in the book. There was a younger woman. Single. We met through work. Drinks.' He shrugged. 'Pathetic. She said there was nothing sexier than a married man. A faithful, devoted, married man . . .'

He stared down at his hands.

'It was once. At her flat. She had a flatmate, for Christ's sake. I didn't stay . . . afterwards. It was tawdry. It was just sex.'

Adam wasn't just sex. She wasn't sure what he was, or had been, or could be. But it hadn't been tawdry. It hadn't been just sex.

'That's what people say, isn't it? How many bloody Sunday night BBC dramas have we watched where people say "It was just sex." What does Megan call it? That revolting expression. "Bumping uglies".' Gigi laughed, despite herself. It was so obscene to hear him say the words. Richard looked at her sideways, and then he laughed too. What else could you do? It was absurd: He stopped laughing first. 'But it was, G. You and me – we weren't having sex. Hardly ever. I missed it, G. You were always so tired. You never initiated it. Sometimes you submitted. That's how it felt. Like you submitted.'

'God.'

'I'm sorry.'

'I'm sorry.'

He waved her apology away. 'It's not an excuse. For what I did. I hated it. It was bad.'

'I never knew.'

'I didn't see her again. I was completely disgusted with myself . . . And then you got ill. And I know I didn't get that right.'

'I don't think there's a wrong and a right way.'

'There is. I was so scared . . .' His voice broke again. 'And you just moved further and further away from me. And I should have tried harder. I should have tried to get you back then. I was a fucking coward . . .'

A young woman was walking towards them with a brand-new pram.

'Gigi?'

Gigi focused on her face, recognized her.

'It's Emma. Emma Flynn. You were my midwife . . .'

Gigi smiled. 'I remember.' Richard sniffed, rubbed his hand under his nose. Then he smiled too.

'And this is Callum.' She wheeled the pram over to them and pulled the sunshade back, so that Gigi was obliged to peer inside.

'He's sleeping. He loves to be wheeled.'

They talked for a few moments. Emma was in the baby-joy bubble, somewhat oblivious to anything else around her. Gigi didn't know how to get her to go. Eventually, Emma looked expectantly at Richard. Constrained by convention, and damned manners, Gigi introduced him.

'This is . . . this is my husband, Richard.'

The woman beamed at him. 'Well, I'm sure you already know, but I have to say that your wife is just brilliant.'

He smiled back, as brightly as Gigi knew he was capable of. 'I know she is.'

'I'm serious. I could not have managed without her.'

Richard nodded, his lips pursed tightly. Gigi knew he couldn't trust his voice.

Emma went eventually, when Callum started to wake up, with a bright wave and a quick, grateful kiss on the cheek.

It wasn't easy to get back to where they'd been before she interrupted. Gigi put her hand on Richard's knee, lightly. For a moment his own hand hovered above hers, but then he changed his mind. 'I'm glad you told me,' she said.

'Why? It doesn't solve anything.'

'Because it's honest. I'm glad I know.' She nodded her head. 'So we're even?'

A wry, half laugh. 'What are you going to do?'

'I need time.'

'Would you tell me, now, if you knew it was hopeless? Would you tell me, if you knew you weren't coming home?'

She turned towards him. 'Of course I would.'

'So there's hope?'

'Richard.' Gigi put her hand up to stop him, but he'd stopped himself already, nodding slowly.

'Don't answer that. I think I'm done with pathetic, for today.'

'You're not pathetic.'

His gaze was sure and still. 'I love you, Gigi. I've loved you all my life.'

'I'm not sure this –'

'Ssh. Listen. I've loved you all my life. I haven't always loved you well enough. Shown you enough. Cherished you. I'm a pompous old fool. A coward. A bastard. But I have loved you. And I will love you for the rest of my life too. Whatever you decide.'

She smiled.

He smiled back.

'Good speech.'

He laughed gently. 'Don't laugh at me.'

'I'm not.'

Richard leant closer to her, until their foreheads touched. He took both her hands in his, and they sat for a moment, foreheads together. Then he stood, still holding her hands, and backed away until their arms were fully extended, only dropping them when he had to.

'Don't choose him. I know it's not just about that, that it's so much more complicated and nuanced than that, G.

I know that's a hopelessly reductive request. But there's a part of me that just wants to lie on the ground and hold your ankles and beg you not to choose him because he's straightforward and there's no history and he hasn't caused you any pain. Don't choose him.'

Tess

It was Oliver's idea, to go to see the village where Iris had grown up, one Saturday. It was strange, she realized, that she'd never wondered why Iris hadn't taken her. Now she knew, of course. She'd sifted through her memories, searching for clues. There were precious few in the encounters she remembered. Her overwhelming impression of her own childhood through the prism of Iris was the joy and the fun. And she was tremendously grateful for that, she really was. But she felt frustrated too that Iris had never shown her any of the cracks in her own well-being. She could barely conjure up a picture of Iris in her mind where she wasn't smiling with happiness.

There'd been day trips to London, when she was younger, when Tess remembered passing references to wartime London – how almost unrecognizable it was. She recalled standing on the middle of a bridge, it must have been Westminster, she supposed, and staring at St Paul's Cathedral while Iris talked about its surviving being bombed. The story of the Queen Mother holding her head up high in the East End in the wake of the bomb damage Buckingham Palace sustained one night. With a child's understanding, she hadn't easily connected her grandmother with that war, but she'd always loved the stories anyway. All the little boats heading to Dunkirk, the woman Iris had known of whose fiancé died in the Battle of Britain, and who'd kept sheep on Clapham Common in the

Blitz and never married. With a child's acceptance, she hadn't asked about the village of Iris's own childhood. She hadn't ever wanted to join up the dots until it was too late to do so, and now she never properly would.

It wasn't, Oliver said, that they were looking for answers. Just as well. There'd be no one left to provide them. But it was the nearest they could get. She didn't even have a name for the farm. Being in the village of Iris's youth would be like sitting next to Iris, as she was now, in Clearview. Not close enough, but as close as you could be . . .

And they both knew that it was in no small part an excuse just to be together. Away from their everyday lives, and the sad pall of Clearview. To take their tender, new, undefined relationship on the road, to neutral ground. Even if they didn't say so, to each other or to anyone else.

It was a beautiful morning, isolated in a week of relentless wet and grey. Warm and sunny. A pale-blue sky. Oliver picked her up at Donna's, parking and knocking on the door so he could say hello to Tess's mother. Old-fashioned and charming. The man who always had a handkerchief. Tess smiled back at her mother, who was beaming at her from the window of the sitting room. She felt weirdly, stupidly proud of him. Castigated herself for the absurd thought straight afterwards – she had no right. He held the car door open for her.

Oliver's car had a soft top, and they drove with it down. It was hard to talk, with the wind, but it was companionable to sit side by side, and it was early enough in the summer for you to still appreciate the sun on your skin. Oliver took the A roads, not the motorway, not, as he said, in any hurry, and suburban sprawl gradually gave way to verdant, peaceful countryside. Tess felt herself relax and unfurl. She almost dozed off, her head back against the headrest, her eyes closed against the sunshine, coming to with a start as she nodded forward. Oliver smiled at her, then looked back at the road.

The village itself was small and pretty, with a tended green in the centre, and a well-maintained Norman church up a gentle hill. There was a pub at one end, a post office in the middle of a row of cottages with names like Mulberry and Primrose Cottage, and a village hall at the other. You forgot, in the cities and the towns, that places like this still actually existed – coming to one was very slightly like going back in time. The pub offered coffee and cake, according to the sign outside, so Oliver parked up and they sat in the garden under a bright umbrella, sharing a wedge of chocolate fudge cake. The spell of silence cast in the noisy car was in no real hurry to break itself, and it was incredibly tranquil.

'I can't remember the last time I felt so relaxed,' Tess said.

'Me neither.'

'I've always thought of myself as a city dweller. Maybe I'm wrong . . .'

He shrugged. 'It's where the work is. That's why I'm there, and it's great. It's been great, at least. Restaurants, theatres . . . all that.'

'How often do you go, though, to the theatre? Truthfully?' She was teasing.

He thought about it for a moment. 'I took my mum to see *The Book of Mormon* last Christmas.'

'And the time before that?'

'Point taken. It's there, is all, if you want it.'

'There are theatres, you know, in the provinces.'

'Yeah, yeah . . . Truth is, my mates, guys from uni, they've moved out gradually. You know, it was all life in the city in your twenties, then get married, get sprogged, get a pair of Hunter wellies and a shed.'

'But you'd hate that?'

He looked at her sharply, his eyes narrowed but still twinkling. 'I never said that.'

'Not ready?'

He tilted his head. 'You mean Caitlin?'

Tess was slightly taken aback that he would mention her. She never would have done.

'I know Mum will have spoken to you about her.'

She didn't know whether to deny it or not. 'Don't worry – I don't mind.'

He held his hands wide. 'I'm an open book . . .'

'She didn't go into details.'

'I'm not sure she had many to give.'

Tess nodded. Gigi had said as much.

'I wasn't ready to do any of that *with her*, that's the truth of it.' He looked hard at her face, and she smiled at him. 'Do you know?'

She looked down pointedly at her belly. 'Do you see this one's father?' She laughed, a small laugh she hoped didn't sound hard. 'At least you figured it out before she was pregnant.'

'Gigi hasn't given me many details either, you know, about you.'

Tess shrugged, wondering how true that was. 'Equally simple. Sean wasn't ready either. Only it was a bit late . . . He didn't want – what was it? Sprogs and Hunter wellies. He didn't want me enough to take them anyway.'

'I'm sorry.'

'I'm not. Did I sound pathetic?'

'No. Not at all. But you're not sorry?'

'No. I was lost, to begin with. I admit that. I thought I was getting it right, you know . . . University, work, boyfriend, cohabitation. It was an accident, getting pregnant, but they do happen. I figured I was getting the order a bit wrong, but not the bigger plan.'

'I know exactly what you mean. Sleepwalking through your life. Ticking the boxes . . .'

'He woke me up. Rude awakening.' She gazed down at the ground. 'Really rude. But I'm not sorry now. If he'd married me, or whatever, if we'd had this baby together . . . I'd only have been storing up the trouble coming. It wouldn't have lasted. It couldn't have. And it might have made a hell of a lot more mess – for him, for me and for her, if I'd waited, and kept going through the motions. He wasn't right for me.'

'And nor was she, right for me.'

Something vast and unspoken and momentous sat only just unsaid between them. Neither of them was ready to say it, because it was just a feeling. It was too small to acknowledge and yet too big to ignore. But they held each other's gaze and let it sit there, neither wanting to be the first to speak, or look away.

Oliver did. 'Come on. Let's us happy, wise singletons walk off that cake.'

It didn't take long – a lap of the village. There were various roads leading off the main drag, some even had signs to farms, but nothing that triggered a distant memory. They strolled for half an hour or so and came to a natural stop at the war memorial. Three wreaths of poppies still lay at its feet. There were probably seventy or eighty names carved into the stone – from both world wars. They walked slowly around it, reading, and wondering. Tom wasn't there, of course. He didn't die in the war, although the war had surely killed him, like their mother had said in the letter Tess had practically memorized from having read it so often. But each name held a story like Tom's. Each name was a son, a brother, a father, a friend. Some families had lost more than one member, or several across both conflicts. Most villages had. How often did people stop and read the names, and realize? Tess hadn't expected to find it so moving, but she found herself tearful. Oliver had been walking in the opposite direction to her, but he came around now and stood next to her, slipping his hand into hers and gently squeezing, without speaking at all. It was almost overwhelmingly comforting, and Tess wanted to lean into him, for his whole side to touch hers, and to stay that way. It was a powerful, unfamiliar yearning, and it was frightening and wonderful at the same time.

Tess

*Week 36. Honeydew melon. I should cocoa, as Iris would say.
You're making me pretty uncomfortable. Not to complain or
anything, but heartburn is my most constant companion at this
point, and so I'm sleeping sitting up, which makes me irrationally
grumpy and tired, because I really only sleep well on my tummy,
one leg hoiked up under my chin. I'm so much more supple asleep
than awake . . . Or at least I was. If I could sleep, I'd dream of
sleeping in this position. I saw this thing on YouTube where a guy
bought a huge block of foam and cut out a bump-sized hole so his
wife could sleep on her tummy but it made me think of Lego, and,
anyway, you'd be bound to want to move the moment you'd been
'docked', so I bet it didn't work. And I've never quite shaken the
idea that lying on you might hurt you . . . It seems ungrateful to
complain, but Christ I miss eight hours of uninterrupted sleep,
baby mine. And I can't moan to anyone else. I know it's not your
fault. I have to pee every ten minutes. Literally. You should be
upside down all the time now, getting ready to lock and load. I
think you are: the feet in my ribs say you are. I can eat only little
meals now, like Scarlett O'Hara at a Tara barbecue, because I
think my stomach is the size of one of the little angry fists you
pummel my bladder with. I suppose you are squashed too. But you
like it. I've just covered swaddling, in the book. Making you into a
human sandwich wrap, all tucked in. Apparently you're going to
like it because it's going to make you feel all squished and warm
and restricted, like you are now in the womb. You'd think you'd
want to wave and kick and feel free . . . I've washed and folded all*

439

*the Babygros and the vest suits and the muslin cloths and the
Lilliputian clothes and put them in the little white chest of drawers
that used to house Donna's stuff — she emptied it for you, and
painted it so it's all fresh and clean. They're waiting for you. I'm
waiting for you. I hold up the suits and imagine you filling them. I
lay them across my shoulder and pat them, pretending you're in
there, needing to be burped or comforted. I sniff them and wonder
how you're going to smell.*

*They took my stitch out today, darling girl. Which wasn't as
scary as the day they put it in. It means a few things: they're okay
with your coming now. You can come now. I feel like I exhaled for
the first time in a long time.*

*I had a letter from Sean. Your father. It's only fair to call him
that, although I don't think he'll ever be your dad, if you see the
distinction. I recognized the handwriting on the envelope and I was
instantly afraid of what he might have written. The mumma bear
again. I shouldn't have been: he's not a pantomime villain. He's
getting married. That was quick. A very quick stab, because he
was in no hurry to marry me and now he's racing down the aisle
with someone else, but that's just ego, I suppose. The point is,
baby, that he knew you were almost due. He remembered. He
wanted to wish me well, and you too. For the day that you come,
and for the time beyond that. And to say that he'd be there. Not
here. But there. If we needed anything. I wonder if she knows
about us. I hope so: I have no reason to want him not to be
happy, and happiness cannot be based on lies and secrets like that.
I hope she gives him lots of healthy American babies. We won't
need him.*

Tess was at her vigil beside Iris's bed. This was the third
morning that week. It was early, and she hadn't seen
any other visitors — there'd been no other cars in the car

park they used. It was more quiet than normal without their presence in the hallways. She could have come at any time – her maternity leave had started now – but she was glad of the quiet.

She'd spoken briefly to Mary, one of Iris's carers, on her way in. There'd been no change in the night. Not that she'd expected one. The doctor had said she was unlikely to be responsive again, and she hadn't been. Not once. No more chinks and no more moments. This was most probably it, and she knew it. Sitting here with Iris, just the two of them, made it easier to accept. Iris's chest was moving up and down – the movement almost imperceptible, unless you concentrated hard on watching it, and that was what Tess did. It was enough, now, to know that she wasn't in any pain. That she wasn't frightened. Her chest would move, and then it would stop and this would be over.

They had visiting vicars, and priests and rabbis and imams, and probably every other kind of faith too, if you needed it – someone had asked her if she wanted one. She didn't. Iris had never spoken of that being important to her and Tess didn't believe it would make a difference. She wasn't sure, now, that her grandmother had ever forgiven God. She didn't want a stranger in the room, however good their intentions.

There was a gentle knock at the door. Sitting with her back to the door, she heard Olly before she saw him. The sound of his voice was wonderful. She hadn't been expecting to see him, and she was suddenly so very glad that he was here. He was probably the person she'd most want to be with her. How strange. She hardly knew him. He hardly knew her. But he seemed to know what she needed.

'The life that I have
Is all that I have
And the life that I have
Is yours'

He spoke almost in a whisper, the sound intimate and peaceful. When she turned around, he was leaning against the doorframe, looking at her.

'That was lovely.'

'Wasn't it?'

'Who wrote it?

'A man called Leo Marks.'

'Who did he write it for?'

'Someone he loved very much.'

'I guessed that much.'

'For his girlfriend. Ruth. She was killed, during the war.'

'Sad.'

Olly nodded, and looked down at the paper in his hand. 'He wrote it on Christmas Eve, 1943.'

'Sadder . . .'

'Long, fascinating, complex story, actually, but that'll keep. I don't want to muddy my own waters.'

'Is there more than one verse?'

'It's here. There are several more. I wrote it out . . .'

He handed her the page. 'He wrote it for her. I'm reading it for you. You get that, right?'

She smiled at him, but didn't answer, just looked at him. Death was in this room. Death and sadness. And now, with him, life too. Life and happiness. She hesitated because she felt herself hovering between the two. Past. Future. It was almost too much. Almost frightening. She couldn't entirely let go of one, and she daren't entirely trust the other.

'I have been researching –'

'What do you mean?'

'More ways to say it. More ways to convey my message. I've made a mess of it so far.'

She hoped she knew what he was saying. Happiness was insistent. Bubbling within.

'Or I could go old-school . . . "I love thee to the depth and breadth and height my soul can reach . . ." Your actual Elizabeth Barrett Browning.'

'Very grand.'

'Indeed. Or there's a bit of Corinthians. "Love is patient, love is kind." Bit of a cliché – think I've heard it at every wedding I've been to in the last few years, and I have been to a lot. My friends are definitely the marrying kind, by the way. I am too.' He left a pause more pregnant than she was. Tess felt herself blush. 'But it still works for me.'

She raised an eyebrow at him.

'Not moving you yet . . . perhaps you're a classics girl. Then how about the Bard? "Love . . . is an ever-fixed mark." I really don't know what all the fuss about Shakespeare is, actually – the man couldn't rhyme. "If this be error and upon me proved . . . no man ever lo-oved" – all that business. But there you go.' Oliver rolled his eyes.

Tess giggled. She couldn't help herself. The sound's inappropriateness made her clamp her hand over her mouth hard. 'What are you doing?'

'Oh, I like that laugh. I like it very much. Don't stop. It's okay. Iris would like to hear it too. I know she would. You know it too. I haven't heard nearly enough of that laugh. That's all the encouragement I need to keep going. You didn't appear to go for it when I just used my own words. I think that is a grave error on your part. I'm not gifted, but

I'm bloody sincere. But you're a hard nut to crack. So I'm borrowing from other people. Iris wouldn't mind. You told me she liked poetry. I *know* she'd have liked me. She'd have been crazy about me. She'd have been telling you you're an idiot to pass on me. You know I'm right. Iris would *so* be on Team Oliver. She wouldn't mind.'

Tess gestured at her grandmother. 'She doesn't seem to . . .'

'Exactly. There's the medium of song, if poetry feels a bit O-level English to you. Think of me as a human mixtape.'

She put her finger to her lips. 'Ssh. You can't sing in here!'

'Oh, watch me. There's no one else around. It's stupidly early. Iris won't mind, I keep telling you . . . you know I'm right. In fact, I have the distinct feeling that Iris would completely approve of my endeavour. But I shall whispersing. Probably best. I realize I have the face of a choirboy, but that's about it.'

She realized she wasn't going to be able to stop him. And she didn't really want to.

'I'm going to call security and have you thrown out of here,' she joked.

'It's not going to stop me. I have a whole section of baby love songs – in honour of bump. Or how about this . . . *You had me at hello*.'

'No, no. Not films now.'

'Oh, yes. Films now. *Here's looking at you, kid. I luff you. Two ff's. Annie Hall.* Have you seen *Annie Hall*, by the way? Where do you stand on Woody Allen?' He waved his own question away. 'Never mind. We can get to that. It's not a deal breaker for me either way, as long as you like Clint Eastwood and Scorsese.'

'Idiot.'

'And the big finish. Richard Curtis. The king of schmaltz. *I'm just a boy, standing here in front of a girl. Asking her to love him.* That was the other way around of course. But still, you get the point.'

'You have to stop. They are going to come in here. And they are going to judge us.'

'Let them. You're smiling, Tess. At one point you were even laughing and the sound was wonderful. Besides, I haven't done fridge magnets yet. Or greeting cards. There are a thousand of those.'

'Olly. Stop . . .'

'I'll stop if you tell me that my point is made.'

'Your point is made.'

'One more thing . . .'

'I don't know if I can take one more thing.'

'You're going to have to. The thing is this . . .'

He came the two or three strides from his side of the room to hers and crouched down in front of her chair. Put both hands on her face and brought his mouth to hers. The kiss was sweet and tender. He was still a little breathless, from the charades, and she was too, although she had hardly moved. When he pulled back eventually he kept his eyes closed a second longer.

'Thank you.'

'You're welcome. I'm going now. I'm going to let you sit with this a while.'

'Thank you.'

'But I'll be back . . .' He walked backwards away from her towards the door. 'That's not Arnie, by the way. *Terminator.* That's me.'

'I know.'

'How is she?' He looked over at Iris.

'No change.'

'Okay. You need anything?'

I did, she thought. *I did. But you just gave it to me.* Out loud, she said, 'Nope. I'm fine.'

'You call me if you do. Promise.'

'Promise.'

'I'll see you soon.'

'I'll see you.'

She thought he'd gone, but, as she turned back to Iris, the door opened again, and he was miming in the doorframe, where anyone could have seen him. A Beyoncé standard. He was shimmying now, doing the right moves, his arms pumping. He looked ridiculous. He didn't even mouth the words but she knew them. And then he was gone.

His going left a vacuum in the room. He was right about one thing: she couldn't remember the last time she'd simply laughed. Except that the last time was probably also with him.

The catering team were rolling trolleys with breakfast trays down the corridor, chatting to each other about last night's *EastEnders*, and this weekend's plans. Someone put their head around the door and offered her some tea. Everyone was waking up. Except Iris.

Tess

Week 38. You're as long as rhubarb. But you're something much more important than that this week. You are FULL TERM. You're cooked. You're ready. Anything that happens now is right and okay and not scary. Well, okay, that is NOT true. It's flipping terrifying. But it isn't wrong. If I go into labour now, you are not a preemie. We made it, baby mine. Me, Donna and Holly painted Donna's box room at the weekend. Well – they painted, I supervised from a bean bag in the corner: they moved me every time they finished a wall. Dulcie was supposed to come too, but she got invited to some family party her boyfriend's lot were having, and she blew us out. And we were happy to be blown out – she was so thrilled. Holly made some crack about chicks before dicks, but she was teasing. I know how relieved she is: exams are done, torturers have fallen away now that school is out, and the boyfriend looks like a keeper – for now, at least. Donna made us buy non-toxic paint – the softest apricot colour – like the edges of a beautiful sunset. She knows we won't stay, but she wanted to do it anyway. She says maybe you'll come back and stay on your own. She talks about you a lot that way – what she wants to do with you – the things she wants to show you and teach you. Sometimes it sounds like the way I was with Iris. A few months ago it might have hurt me – hearing her talk that way. It doesn't now. I think it would be nice, for you and for her. And for me.

Tess wasn't with Iris when she died, in the end. She'd stayed all evening the night before, but Donna, who'd come after work, had sent her home at ten-ish. 'You need sleep, Tess. The baby needs you to sleep. Iris would send you, and I'm sending you for her. Go home, my love. I'll stay.' She'd kissed Iris, and driven home. She'd been too tired to drink the cup of tea she'd made for herself, slipping gratefully between the sheets and into a deep sleep. Maybe she'd thought there'd be a moment – that she'd wake if something changed with Iris. But she didn't.

At 8 a.m., Donna put a fresh mug of hot tea down beside the bed, moving the full mug of cold. The clink of china woke Tess, and she heaved around to sit up. Donna was still wearing yesterday's clothes. She'd been crying.

'She's gone, Tess.'

'When?'

'Around three.'

'Was it . . .' Tess's voice broke.

'Ssh. Love. Don't. It was very peaceful.'

'Promise me?'

'I promise you. She was asleep. Just asleep. Her breathing changed. Got very slow, very shallow. Then it just stopped. It was easy. I promise. I was with her the whole time. Every minute.'

'Oh.'

Tess couldn't stop the tears.

'You should have called me.'

'There was no point, love, and no need. I don't know that there'd have been time anyway. How many goodbyes have you already said?'

'I don't know why I'm crying. I've been ready . . .'

Donna held her. 'We are never really ready, though, are we?'

'No.' She sounded like a child – she could hear it.

'You loved her. She knew. She always knew. Even at the

448

end, I'm sure she knew. You did everything you could for her. No one could have done more. She loved you.'

'I loved her so much.'

'I know. I know. Ssh.' Donna was stroking her hair.

'Can I go and see her?'

'Of course. If you want to.'

Tess sniffed and rubbed her eyes. 'I don't know.'

'You don't have to decide now . . .'

At nine, Gigi stopped in to see James en route to a shift. One of the carers, Chloe, stopped her in the corridor.

'I thought you'd like to know, Gigi. Iris passed away last night.'

Gigi's heart contracted for Tess. 'Oh, bless her. When?'

'Around three. I wasn't on. I found out when I got in this morning.'

'Was Tess here, do you know?'

'I don't think so. I think it was Iris's daughter. Donna.'

'I see.'

'But Tess was here when I left yesterday. She's been here every day. Since Iris got really poorly.'

'I know she has.'

'I just thought you'd like to know. I know you two are friends.'

'Thanks, Chloe. Thanks.' Gigi smiled gratefully and squeezed Chloe's hands.

Gigi walked back out into the car park and took a few deep breaths of the summer air. It was a lovely day. The birds sang. She took out her phone.

Olly. Tess's grandmother died last night. I'm at Clearview on my way to work. She's not here, but I'm sure she'll be here later. I knew you'd want to know. Mum

She leant against her car and stared down at her phone. The screensaver was the five of them. She didn't know how to change it, should she want to – Megan did all that technical stuff. So it had been the same picture for years, as long as she'd had the phone. It was taken at Christopher's graduation, so he was front and centre, proud and draped in ermine. She and Richard were flanking him in their Sunday best. Olly was on her other side, beaming his disarming beam, and Richard's arm was around Meg, doing her photo half-smile. She'd thrust the phone at a friend of Christopher's and he'd hurriedly taken the picture before the crowds had blocked the shot. Richard had been cross because the friend had cut off their feet, but Gigi loved the picture anyway. It captured all her children exactly as she remembered them being at that moment.

She smiled to herself and pushed the contacts button once more.

Richard. I'm on an early today. Would you like to get something to eat tonight, if you're free?

'For a moment, her forefinger hovered above the 'send' key. And then she pressed it.

Tess

Iris – her body, at least – was gone by the time Tess had showered and dressed, and driven back to Clearview. Donna stayed away. She'd been up all night, and she needed to sleep. There was a special room where you could visit a loved one after they had died – she'd been shown it by the manager, Claire, when she first came here – but, while she'd stood under the hot water in her shower, Tess had decided not to. She didn't want that to be the last time she saw Iris. There was no need.

Iris hadn't wanted any fuss. That's what she'd always said. Tess remembered her talking about Wilfred's committal, the memory still vivid so many years after he'd died. Iris had hated his funeral. How it had been raining and cold and how the pallbearers had almost slipped on the edge of the grave, lowering the coffin in, or at least that she had worried that they might. How desperate she'd felt, watching him go into the ground: how there had been no comfort in it for her – not in any of it. How each little thud of earth hitting the coffin, thrown by the mourners, felt like a blow to her. She'd wished there was comfort. She'd wished she'd believed, but she didn't, she said, and that was that. And going through the ritual because it was expected made no sense to her. Do what's simplest, she'd said. Get rid of my body the easiest way you can, she'd said. Incinerator if you could. No church. No service at the crematorium. No urn of ashes to be disposed of on a windless day. Definitely no graveyard. Wait a few months, she'd said, and then go and stand somewhere with a lovely view on a warm, sunny day and say a poem I'd like into the wind. Plant a tree. That's what Iris wished she'd been able to do with Wilf, and that was what she wanted for herself, and for the people who loved her and were left behind.

The bed had been stripped, and then covered with just a counterpane, on top of which Iris's few belongings had been neatly folded by someone kind and careful. There weren't so many. Skirts, sweaters, dresses, a couple of nightdresses. A pair of sturdy shoes she'd hardly needed, and some slippers Tess had bought for her when she'd first come here, barely worn. She remembered the kind nurse saying that they could deal with the items if Tess wanted. Her grandmother's handbag was next to the pile on the bed, and, beside that, her watch and her wedding ring. Tess picked up the ring and looked at it, thin and worn. She'd never seen Iris without it on. She could see now, for the first time, her grandmother's name and her grandfather's, along with the date of their marriage, engraved on the inside of the band, the words still distinct after all this time. Tess slipped it on to her own finger – the pinkie, it was too small for her ring finger – and rubbed it gently. She wondered whether Iris would want to be cremated with it on – she had never said one way or the other. She hoped not: she wanted to keep it. She felt almost unbearably sad.

And then Gigi was there, her arms open wide.

'They told me.'

'I wasn't here, Gigi.'

'Oh, my love. You were here. She knew.'

'Do you think so? Do you honestly think so?'

'I know that you sat there, and told her you loved her, and I believe – I choose to believe – that at some level, somewhere very deep, she will have heard you.

'But I also believe what matters more, much more, is the life you and she had before she was ill, sweetheart. Those are the memories you should focus on. This was such a short time compared to all the time you two had together. You had her your whole life.'

Tess nodded, rubbing tears away.

Gigi brushed her cheek tenderly. 'Come and have a cup of tea with me.'

Tess laughed. 'The magical powers of tea.'

'It's true, you know . . . I have Assam in my veins at this point, not blood.'

'I'm not going to see her body.'

Gigi nodded. 'That's fine.'

'You're not going to try to persuade me it's important?'

'Nope. Saw both my parents. I'm not sure it was. If you don't want to, don't.'

Tess sighed. 'I don't.'

'Then that's fine. Did you know, I mean, did you talk . . . about what kind of funeral?'

'She didn't want one if it was at all possible!'

'Good for Iris. I'd have liked her.'

Tess nodded. 'You would.' More tears.

'Did your mum know? What she wanted?'

'I'm not sure. She'll be okay with no church, though. She'd be more likely to want to scatter her ashes in Goa or have some shaman ritual or something . . .'

Gigi laughed. 'She should never call you as a witness for her defence.'

Tess laughed too. 'She's all right. You know, if you'd told

453

me even a year ago I'd be living with her, and we'd actually be getting along, I'd have laughed in your face.'

'It's a funny old world.'

'You sound like Iris. She used to say that.'

'And we're both right.'

'She's still a nutter, though. Donna. Complete fruit loop. No way is she in charge of what we do with Gran . . . no way!'

After a few moments, Tess said, 'What will you do . . . for James? Does he not want a funeral either?'

'Richard will want the full monty. To be fair, James would too. He's proper, you know. It'll be all Eternal Father, Strong to Save, black clobber and cucumber sand-wiches at the wake.' She grimaced. 'I think Iris's way is better, to be honest.'

'Me too.'

'Might you want a memorial service?'

'Thing is, she wasn't a believer. Not in any of it. She was raised that way – christened, confirmed, all that. She knew the words to everything – not just the Lord's Prayer and 'All Things Bright and Beautiful'. She'd just rejected it. Now I think I know why. So I don't think she'd want us to do anything in a church.' She looked down at Iris's ring on her finger. Thought of Tom's funeral. How wretched it must have been. She realized that was probably the last time Iris had ever been in a church, and maybe why she'd married Wilfred in a register office.

'I know she wouldn't. She'd come back and haunt us, I'm pretty sure. No. I know what she wanted. She wanted me to plant a tree!' She smiled ruefully. 'And say a poem into the wind on a summer day . . . I think that was it.'

'I can't think of anything nicer, Tess.'

'Neither can I.'

She wanted to ask if Gigi knew where Oliver was, but she felt strangely shy suddenly. It wasn't Oliver's job to comfort her now. It wasn't for him to be there for her to lean on. She never wanted Gigi to think she thought he was.

After Gigi left, Tess spoke to Claire in the office about direct cremation. There were some papers to sign. But surprisingly little to do right now. There'd be meetings, she knew, with lawyers. But not now. Now there was just quiet, and peace. She went back to Iris's room. She didn't want to see her grandmother's body, but she wasn't quite ready to say goodbye to her things. She looked at Iris's handbag and wondered if she might keep it. She'd never use it, but it might be nice to have it. She picked it up. It was unfashionable and old, not vintage, shaped like the Queen's handbags. But she might like to keep it anyway. She'd been so good at being ruthless in Iris's house, but now that her grandmother was actually gone, 'things' had instantaneously taken on more significance. The handbag was almost empty, as it had been the whole time Iris had been here. There'd been no need for things, not even reading glasses, latterly. Lots of the ladies in the home still had them, though, like leather comfort blankets. They connected them, somehow, to the lives they'd had. It was old-fashioned – the kind with brass feet and the clasp on the top that snapped closed – brown leather, worn a little now on the corners.

Tess remembered a bigger handbag. One endlessly capacious, like Mary Poppins's carpet bag, and useful, perpetually stocked with sun cream, barley sugars, plasters, a handkerchief (never tissues), and a colouring book and pens. With Iris's fabulously cool winged sunglasses. The Rimmel lipstick that smelt of powdery roses.

She ran her hands across the warm leather, snapped and unsnapped the fastening. She raised the bag to her face, to see if she could smell her grandmother within it.

She picked up the watch and looked for a pocket inside the handbag where she could safely store it until she decided what to do with both things. There was a small one, but when she slid the watch in she met resistance. There was a folded sheet of paper inside it she had never seen before. Tess pulled it out and stared at it, her heart racing. It was old and yellowed. She unfolded it and didn't recognize the handwriting. It wasn't from Tom. Scanning to the bottom, she saw that it was signed by her grandfather. For a moment she thought she shouldn't read it – it must be a love letter, and love letters were private, sacred.

But it was all she had to keep Iris alive for just a while longer. And so she read it.

10 February 1956
My Iris,

I know you've asked me to leave you alone, and I promise you this is my one last attempt to change your mind. You won't hear from me again after this. It's not in my nature to give up, but I think I must. I wanted to write these words, not speak them, so that you can read them slowly and consider them carefully – if you are going to disregard them in the end, then at least I want you to have time to think first.

I am so very glad you told me about your brother when we last met. I feel like my understanding of you has been like a complicated jigsaw puzzle, with big pieces missing, and you have filled them in with your story, and I see you more clearly now than I have ever done. I see you more, and I love you more, although you have always implied that I would only love you less if I knew you better.

But what it shows me is that for the last ten years you've been hiding, living a half-life, where you risk nothing of your heart, but one where you stand to gain nothing either.

What happened to your brother was a tragedy. For him, for your whole family.

I have come to see that I was lucky. It was my body that the war so damaged, and my body healed. I didn't lose my mind. There are things I saw and heard that I have never spoken of, but I have been able to put them away, lock them up in a part of myself where they can't hurt me, or the people around me. I won't forget — I can't and anyway I don't want to. But I didn't lose my mind. Tom did. Whereas the war made me want to live, and made me determined to live well, it ultimately ruined life for him. But it certainly wasn't love that killed him.

I know one thing for sure. Love could not have saved him either. If it could, you had enough for him to do it. When Tom wrote those words to you, he was trying to help you understand why he was going to do what he did, but he was wrong to make you promise what he did. He wasn't issuing an edict for your life, my darling. He did not mean that you should carry his hurt close to your heart and let it stop you having love of your own. He did not want a lonely, loveless life for you. The waste of it, the sheer awful waste of it, must haunt him.

You did not die when he died, Iris, just as he did not die when Manon died. If he had given himself time, who knows. I believe he might have been happy again, have loved again. The world is full of people who have loved, and lost, and still loved, and loved well, again. Perhaps the war hurt him too badly. We'll never know. But Tom's story could have ended so differently.

457

And so could yours. So must yours. You are alive. You are full
of love to give. So full you'll explode – I see it and I feel it in you,
even if you cannot see it in yourself. You can't save your poor Tom,
or his Manon. You can't live in their past and you do not honour
their memory with a life half lived. You can only save yourself.
And me, because my love for you won't be stopped, and it can't be
given to someone else.

If you let the fear of being hurt stop you, you might as well have
died with him on that day.

If it is not to be me, Iris, then please, at least, promise me it will
be someone. I need to believe that it will be someone. I can live with
that if I must. But love, Iris. LOVE. Love with all your heart,
and with all of Tom's and all of Manon's. Love for them too. It's
the simplest thing in the world, my darling girl. The bravest and
yet the very simplest thing.

I won't write to you again. I will hope so very much to hear from
you, but, if I do not, then just know that I will always love you.

Wilf

Tears streamed down her face by the time she'd read it, and
reread it. This was her piece of the puzzle. She was crying
for heartbroken Iris, keeping a terrible promise to Tom,
and for Wilf, the force of whose love screamed from every
word.

She didn't see Oliver come in, didn't sense his presence
until he was next to the bed, and then it was too late to
pretend she wasn't crying. She didn't even want to.

'You poor thing.'

And she was in his arms, heaving with sobs, his hand in
her hair.

'Mum told me. I came as soon as I got her message.'

'She's gone, Olly.'

She pulled away, sniffing hard. 'It's ridiculous. She's been gone for a long, long time, really. But this . . . this is so final . . . I didn't expect to feel this way.'

He pulled her back into his embrace. 'You loved her.'

'I loved her.'

He held her for long minutes while she calmed down, and she let him, calm in his embrace. When she stepped away, back in control of herself, he smoothed her hair, tucking it behind her ear, and gently rubbed a final tear from her cheek with his thumb.

'I'm disgusting. Snotty and blotchy and pathetic.'

'You're beautiful.'

'I found this.' She handed him the crumpled paper. 'It's from my grandfather. It was in her handbag. She must have kept it with her always. For sixty years.'

'I shouldn't read it.'

'I want you to. You've read the others.'

'Okay.' Oliver sat down in the high-backed chair.

She watched him while he read. His mouth moved silently while he read the words.

Then he exhaled and laid the letter on the bed. 'That is quite a letter.'

'Yep.'

'So it's the last one?'

Tess nodded. 'I think so. My mum was born three years after it was written, almost exactly. They'd married that Easter, just after the letter. They were barely ever apart after that. Certainly not long enough for letters. At least, not that she kept.'

'Wow.'

'I know.'

'You think this did it?'

'It must have done. She carried it, for all these years. All these years, Olly.'

'And she never spoke about it?'

'No. I had never even heard of Tom until she started talking about him that time, in here. She kept him a secret all those years. By the time my mum was old enough to ask stuff, Iris's own parents were dead. There was no one else.'

'Why do you suppose that was?'

Tess shook her head. 'I had no idea until I read this. I feel like the letter makes sense of that. Like she finally accepted something about Tom, about his death. Left it behind.'

Olly nodded.

'It explains all sorts of things. Why she would never go to church. Why she never went back to the farm, even though she hated London.'

'Does that make sense to you?'

'It does. She was the most loving person I ever knew. My granddad was right – she was entirely full of love.'

The baby kicked hard then. Tess gasped and put her hands on her stomach.

'Okay?' He was beside her at once.

'Fine. She's making her presence felt. All this talk of love.'

Suddenly Olly was very close. She had taken his hand before she'd even realized it and put it on her belly, where she'd felt the baby's foot.

Olly stared down at his hand and then back up at her, his face full of wonder, and something else.

'He was right, you know, your grandfather.'

'About what?'

'It is the simplest thing in the world.'

And suddenly, after all of it, even because of all it, it just was.

'It's you.'

His lips were almost on hers, so she could feel his breath in her own mouth.

'You're the one.'

They touched hers. The briefest of touches. Not even, really, a kiss. Then he rested his forehead lightly against hers.

'You're my one.'

It was like he was waiting for permission. His hand was still on her bump. His face was very still.

She kissed him back, gently at first, like his kiss had been, their lips just grazing, their breath merging.

But then, and very soon, she was kissing him like it was the only thing in the world she had ever wanted to do.

And, she knew, with all of her heart.

GARROWAY, IRIS. Passed away peacefully on 18th July, aged ninety-six years. Much loved wife of Wilfred (deceased), and adoring sister to Tom (1918–1945), she will be much missed and fondly remembered by her daughter, Donna, her granddaughter, Tess, and her unborn great-granddaughter. She loved us all with all of her huge heart.

Tess

And then, just like that, it all got wonderfully, happily easy. She was going to be with Oliver. Forever. Just. Like. That. Not a scintilla of doubt. Not a shiver of fear about it. It was done. The quiet, calm joy of it smothered most of her sadness about Iris, so that, almost within days, what she felt was a bruise, and not a wound, where the blow of her grandmother's death had landed. The future won out convincingly over the past, and it lay ahead, a clear and wide and sparkling avenue to happiness. Unbelievably simple.

There were details to sort out. Where they'd live, and how. The baby. They didn't matter, the details. She just knew it would all be okay.

If Donna minded that the first she really knew of Oliver was a fait accompli, she was too careful and protective of their new relationship to let it show. He came to the house and she cooked them a cauliflower curry and he enthused about her photography and drank a bottle of wine with her. Tess sat and watched them getting on, sipping a mint tea and vaguely experiencing heartburn alongside the heart swell. She was fantastically proud of him, and that was a new emotion for her. When he looked at her, or touched her hand, she really did feel all those Disney-type butterflies and violins and stomach flips, and if it sometimes felt absurd to her that she felt them all despite the now vast belly and slightly swollen ankles, he never once made her feel like it was. Everything about him screamed that he thought he was the luckiest man alive. He crackled with happiness.

Holly and Ben already loved him, it transpired. 'Thank Christ for that,' Holly exclaimed, when she told her. 'About bloody time . . .' Dulcie, exams and bullies behind her, begged to be a bridesmaid at their wedding, and Tess giggled, because, for the first time in her life, she knew there was going to be a wedding, and it hardly mattered at all.

But she was anxious about Gigi. She couldn't imagine she'd be what Gigi wanted for Oliver. Oliver wanted them to tell her together, but she wouldn't go with him. 'I want her to be able to react the way she really wants to. She won't be able to do that if I'm there.'

'You're being daft. I know what she thinks of you, Tess.'

Tess shook her head and kissed his cheek gently. 'You think you know what she thinks of the girl she met in the nursing home, the one who was visiting her grandmother. That's not the same thing at all.'

Gigi

'I love her, Mum. She's it.' Oliver had swept into the flat and pulled her into a fierce hug. Gigi looked at her son and knew that it was true, then exhaled deeply.

Her voice broke. 'I'm so glad. She loves you too, I presume?'

'She does. She bloody does.' His eyes were shining.

'So, why didn't she come with you?'

'Because she wanted me to tell you on my own. She's afraid you won't be pleased.'

'Why the hell not?' Gigi frowned.

Oliver shrugged. 'She thinks she comes with too much baggage.'

'Where is she now?'

'She's at her mum's.'

'Will you take me there?'

'Now?'

'Yes, please.' She winked at him. 'Now.'

Olly beamed at her and grabbed his car keys.

Tess answered the door, looking sleepy and dishevelled. It was a hot afternoon, and she'd pulled her hair into a high bun to cool her neck and borrowed one of Donna's voluminous cotton kaftans. It was stretched across her bump.

'Gigi!'

'I've come to tell you, my darling, silly, lovely girl, that I could not be more delighted that you and my boy are together.'

'Oh.' Tess's eyes filled with tears.

'You're perfect.'

Tess laughed and cried at the same time. 'I'm far from that.'

'You're perfect for him. It's been obvious to me and to him for a while now . . . we just needed you to see it too.'

Tess looked past her to Oliver, and nodded. 'I see it too.'

But it was Ava who gave the final, absolute seal of approval. Emily had invited Gigi, Tess and Megan to her house, exclaiming that she just really needed to meet the woman who had so bewitched her brother-in-law, and the four women were sat around a teak table in Emily and Chris's back garden, drinking peach iced tea and chattering like old, easy friends. Each reflected in the pauses on how different this was from other similar situations: Sean's competitive sisters-in-law; frosty Caitlin. Ava was in her mother's lap when she suddenly lunged forward towards Tess, her pudgy little arms clinging to either side of Tess's bump, and planted a long series of her wettest kisses on it.

Week 40. We're here. At the end of this beginning. I'm ready. You're a watermelon. I haven't slept all night for months. I pee every six minutes. I have cankles — actual cankles. My ankle is as wide as my knee. This is not a good look on me. Not your fault, but still . . . enough already. Oliver says I'm ridiculous and beautiful. Clearly he's insane. Wait until he sees how I'm supposed to look . . . That sounds vain. But I'm okay in the half-light when I'm not in this state. I await the return of my waist, and the view of my feet, with some anticipation. But, really, I just want to see you. I'm so excited I can't stand it. Don't be late. Please. I've never been great at delayed gratification and I've already waited longer for you than I've ever waited for anything in my life. Except my driving licence. But that was only because I couldn't master the parallel park. My point is . . . don't be late. I want to meet you. It's like we've been conducting our relationship on the internet for nine months and now we've agreed to meet in person, although there's no way you can catfish me. (Dulcie taught me that word: Dulcie is going to be the coolest pretend aunt in the world, by the way. Or btw, as Dulcie would say. She will be your go-to person when I say no, and you hate me. One day you're going to hate me for something . . . Oh God. Catfish is pretending you're something you're not, btw. Who knew?) You've been grey blobs on a screen. Pictures in a book, and on my computer, and diagrams in my midwife's room. You've been fruit, for goodness' sake. You've run the gamut from pomegranate to cherry to satsuma and now you're a watermelon. You've been my dreams and my wishes and my hopes. You've been pretty damn disruptive, truth be told, but my life has arranged itself around you now. I'm ready. And I want to see you, not just feel you, although you won't know how special and amazing and spooky it has been to feel you until you have a baby of your own. Which I hope you will . . . It's one of a million things I want for you, my little girl.

I so wanted Iris to meet you, baby mine. Even if she didn't know you, I wanted to lay you in her arms, and I wanted to keep that image, of the two of you, four generations apart, in my mind forever. But it's okay that it never happened. I have peace. It's all unfolding like it was supposed to. God, I sound like a hippie. I'm more like Donna than I ever thought . . .

It boils down to this — Iris figured it out. I'm sure she tried to teach me.

May you know the trick of it better, or at least sooner, than I have done.

Epilogue

And so here you are. You tightly folded bud. My tightly folded bud. And you're not the size of a honeydew melon, or the length of a stick of rhubarb, or the weight of bags of dried goods. Not any more. You're here, and you're nothing like fruit. You're 7 lbs, 2 oz (I refuse to call it 3.232 kilograms) and you're 49 cm (I know. I'm difficult. This I don't mind in metric) long. Well within the ranges of normal. Your Apgar score was 8 at five minutes and 9 by ten minutes (no one ever gets a 10, your midwife said, but I don't care anyway – I'm not going to be that kind of mum when it comes to test scores, I promise). You needed a bit of jostling before you cried, but not too much, nothing scary like you see on Casualty or Grey's Anatomy, where doctors exchange anxious glances and babies are whisked away. It was all calm and peaceful, just us in the room. The midwife held you, your tiny back in one big, capable hand, and rubbed your chest for a few seconds, very gently, and then we heard it. 'Come on, baby', she said, and almost whispered, 'Let's be having you.' It was nearly imperceptible, that confident gesture to get you to breathe – it happened on your journey up from between my legs to my chest – but I am not going to miss anything. Not now and not ever. And then I had you. And you had me.

You have hair. Not masses of it, but a small whorl of dark-blonde, downy fuzz. You have quite long fingers and, when I check under the cotton towel they've draped over us, toes too. Long fingers and long toes. People will tell me you should be a pianist. But you will be a cellist, like your great-grandfather Wilfred, if you're anything at all, and you needn't be, if you don't want to be. Your nails are going to need cutting, or biting, if the book is to be believed, soon. It's amazing to me – that you have come out of me with these tiny nails already growing. Your skin is dry, a bit peely, like after a sunburn. White with tiny blue veins in some places, and blotchy, but the softest, most velvety thing I have ever felt. Your chest rises and falls with your breath and I can almost see where your heart is beating beneath your ribs.

You're a hedonist I think. The midwife wrapped you in a blanket and washed your hair at the sink in the room, holding you in one hand and making it look so easy. You loved it, craning your neck at the warm water, like a cat moving towards the stroke of a hand. She says you're too young to smile, and I know it's true, but the pleasure on your face was obvious.

You are strong and you are fragile. I am capable and I am terrified. I have read about what comes next – the next hours, the next days, months, years. I have read it, studied it, but I know nothing. It's the most exciting and the most frightening moment of my life, meeting you. And you have no clue about any of it. I'm arms, nipples, a soft voice, a gentle touch. Still, when you open your eyes, your blue, blue eyes (and they're staying blue, I know), I'm sure they lock on to mine. Perhaps you know me already, darling girl.

You missed your great-grandmother by just a couple of weeks. But that's okay. I know how she would have felt about you. I close my eyes and imagine her holding you, but it's not the Iris of the end, it's the Iris of my own childhood holding you, strong and sparkling – and when her eyes meet mine over the top of your precious head, I understand for the first time all the love in her face.

I'm going to teach you what I learnt about love from Iris. I'm going to teach you right from the start – I wasted so much time, so much. I'm going to teach you that it's the simplest thing in the world, and that you must do it with open arms and an open heart and no fear. Because it's all that matters, at the end of the day. All that matters.

We're all alone now, just you and me. For a moment. The midwife has gone to make me the world's most welcome cup of tea. We have this while, just us. There are people who are longing to see you. My mum. Holly, Dulcie. Gigi. Olly is outside phoning her now. He was brilliant. Of course he was. He never left us. He's as excited and proud and emotional as if you were his own girl. I know now that I could have done all of this, and everything to come, without him, but I'm so, so glad I'm not going to be. We're going to have fun. So much fun, my darling. They're all going to love you so much, and that fun and that love are going to be the hallmarks of your whole childhood. I'm going to love you most of all . . .

So here we are. At the very beginning, baby mine. You'll always be baby mine. But now you have a real name. And your name, of course — and what else could it be — is Iris.

Acknowledgements

This book has been a very, very long time coming, and I need to thank everyone at Michael Joseph for their tremendous patience and understanding. In particular, I am grateful to the deeply kind and clever Louise Moore, who refused to give up on me, even when I had absolutely given up on myself. Thank you to Maxine Hitchcock and Tilda McDonald for your sensitive and insightful editing and warm support, and to Donna Poppy for your painstaking work on the manuscript: it is a better novel because you have all been involved. To Nick Lowndes, Jenny Platt, Ellie Hughes and all of the brilliant and talented Penguins – thank you for your efforts.

I am thankful, as always, to Jonathan Lloyd and his team at Curtis Brown for everything that they do.

And finally, to friends and family who have believed in my ability to write again and told me so – you may not quite understand how important you have been. And to you, Dave, Tallulah and Ottilie, for bringing the joy. I am inordinately proud of the three of you, and I love you all more than I can say.

Reading Group Discussion Points

1. Discuss the novel's varying depictions of marriage. What kinds of relationships seem most likely to fail or succeed? Ultimately, do you think marriage is seen as positive or negative in the story?

2. Meg calls Gigi's decision to leave 'selfish'. Do you think this is fair to Gigi?

3. How do the romantic relationships in the novel relate to the ones between women? Do you think Tess and Gigi could have made the decisions they did without the support of their friends and each other?

4. Motherhood is a key theme in the novel. Discuss the complexities of Tess and Donna's relationship, and how it changes over the course of the story.

5. Do you think we are destined to repeat the mistakes of our parents, or not? How do you think Tess's parenting style might be influenced by the role models of Iris, Donna and Gigi?

6. How did your feelings towards Richard change over the course of the story? Did you feel sympathy towards him — and did you think Gigi should go back to him, or not?

7. Secrets are another key theme of the novel. Consider the effect that keeping or sharing these secrets has on the characters.

8. The difficulties of seeing a loved one suffer from dementia are an important part of the story. Do you think the message is ultimately that we should learn more about our loved ones before it's too late – or that no matter what, we'll always feel robbed of time?

9. What parallels can you see between Iris's relationships as a young woman, and Tess's? What roles do Wilf and Olly play in their lives?

10. Do you agree with Wilf's entreaty to Iris – that 'love is the simplest thing in the world'? How do the relationships in the novel support or contradict this statement?

Keep in touch
with Elizabeth Noble...

f @elizabethnoblebooks

◎ @elizabethnoblebooks

Great stories.
Vivid characters.
Unbeatable deals.